PLANTATION CHAINS

Joe McClain Jr.

This is a work of fiction. Names, characters, places and incidents are either the product of the authors imagination or are used fictitiously. Any resemblance to actual events or locales or persons, living or dead is entirely coincidental. From The Mind Of Joe McClain Jr.

ISBN: 0-692917993
ISBN-13:978-0692917992

DEDICATION

NOTE: I WROTE THIS ALL IN CAPS SO YOU CAN FEEL THE PAIN IN WHAT I WRITE. February 11, 2017 was forever a day that I will dread for the rest of my life. I was sitting at home with my wife, watching the Oklahoma City and Golden State game. As we watched the game, we were also working on our computers. She was concentrating on getting a DJ playlist together. Me, I was delving in ideas for my next novel. Across my computer screen a story popped up. Three people had gotten shot in a home in the Skyline area of San Diego. I thought nothing of it. People had always gotten shot in Skyline. It was the hood and that's what happens in the hood. Same as my hometown of East Chicago. I know it sounds kind of harsh, but you become immune to some things the more you get accustomed to them. I read the story and from what was reported, no one had died. I continued on between the game and work, and that's when I seen that my God sister posted a status on social media. It was kind of odd how the shooting story had came up and then a status pertaining to privacy arose from her. I didn't want to piece two and two together, so I just let it be. Thirty seconds later, an inbox message would pop up on my screen. "Bro. Where U at?" At that moment, I knew something was wrong. I simply asked what's going on? The message that I received next made my heart sink to my stomach. I told my wife that we needed to head to the hospital. We quickly got dressed and headed out towards the hospital. In situations of panic, I tend to remain calm. I like to keep my thoughts as positive and chill as I possibly can. Upon arrival, I walked into the ER and saw all of my family. It was hard because none of us knew anything. The doctors wouldn't tell us much. My God brother and nephew had been shot. From what I was informed of, my brother was okay. My nephew, however, there was no word on him and his condition. I passed the time by talking with family, trying to comfort them in any way I can. Hell, even a few laughs were shared in a somber moment. My best friend, Darrell, called me and asked that I check on his son, who was my Godson, the child of my Godsister. I did, ensuring that he was at the crib good, which he was. About two hours after arrival, detectives arrived at the hospital and my God Mom was taken away. When she came back out, the four most haunting words I ever heard in life were said. "Andre didn't make it." There had been low points in my life before, but this by far was one of the worst. Growing up in East Chicago, my family tended to be separated. I'd go to my dad's side family reunion, and no one from my mom side was there. I'd go to my mom's side, and no one from my dad's side was there. It pained me because it felt like I had to choose sides at times. My actual home was always full of tension. So when people said family, I had a hard time contemplating that meaning. When I moved to San Diego in 2003, The Dunaways over time took me in as family. One thing I noticed was a sense of loyalty among them. When the family got together, the family got together. I didn't have that much growing up. I had instances of it, but nothing like what I experienced with the Dunaways. Hell, I hate using the term God mom, brother, sister or any of that. I just call them my brother, sister and mom. It's not a slight at my blood brothers, sisters or even my mom, because I love them dearly. However, family is not always blood related. Continuing on with the story, as I heard the news, I grabbed Dre's mom as she was hysterical as any mother would be. I tried my best in comforting my fam bam at the time. A lot of people always look at me as the strong individual, so I embrace that role very serious. At the same time, I had a very weak moment. In the midst of my sorrow, I called my 14 year old godson and told him the news. I was weak and felt like he needed to know. He is my rock and I tend not to hide anything from him. I would come to almost regret it as his asthma would start to flare up from crying so hard. I would apologize to his mom the next day, but it's something I wish I could take back. Again, I was weak and fragile at the time. Due to his age, I thought he could take it. Then, I had to realize that not every 14 year old was like me at that age. So to my Godson, I'm sorry. The night went on with sorrow and pain. When I got home that night, well after midnight, I lied down on my sectional and simply stared off into space. You see Andre meant the world to me, along with his brothers Q and Dominique. The same goes for his sisters Shamiya and Liyah. It was already hard enough with Dominique being locked up. However, I know Nique would be coming home one day. To know that I would never see Andre again, it's something that I wasn't ready for. Was he my blood nephew? Again, no. Hell, I didn't even call him nephew. I just called him Dre. I loved him as such, though. I didn't go to bed that night until about three in the morning. Sometime during my sleep, I started having images in my head of my God Mom telling me the news of his demise. I instantly woke up and looked at my clock. It was 8:44 a.m. I sat up on my bed and just put my head down. My wife asked was I okay. I told her yea, but the images woke me up. I could go on with this story for days. The reason I told it is because I want the world to know that this is not just a simple dedication. This wasn't one of those times as an author where you decide to write a story and dedicate it to some random person or group of people. This dedication means more than any words that I could ever write. I want the world to remember Andre Mims as a quiet, laid back, young man who overcame a lot of obstacles in his life to become the person that he was. Hell, he beat cancer. Let me say that again. HE BEAT CANCER!!! That's the type of fighter he was. He gave me strength by displaying his. So to Andre, thank you for giving me the strength to write this book. I know when I hit a roadblock or just got tired of writing, you were there whispering to me to continue going and fight for my passion. This book is dedicated to Andre Mims. Also, this is dedicated to his father, my brother from another, Quentin Mims. You raised a good one man. You inspire me more than you will ever know.

"This novel is also dedicated to the memory of Justice Moss."

CONTENTS

ACKNOWLEDGMENTS

I give a major acknowledgement to Mr. Dave Miller, Marshall Faulk, Jerry Rice and Marcus Allen for enhancing my career. I thank all you gentlemen for what you have done not only for me, but your respective communities.

1 RISE UP

"So here's my question bruh. The Bible starts off with this statement. It said in the beginning, God created the Heavens and the Earth. But my question is this. Who created Him?" Ty just gave me a look with that all too common smirk on his face.

"Nigga are you serious?," he replied.

"Like forreal dog. I'm like asking some real shit. Who created God? I don't think He just popped up out of the air like that." He continued to give me that nigga please look.

"Look my dude. Trust me when I tell you. I don't believe in all that shit. Nigga we energy. Energy never dies. It just transfers into something else. Nigga how you gone expect me to believe that I'm gone get a reward when I die for doing good? Shouldn't I get rewarded for doing good down here? That's like you getting good grades as a first grader, but yo' mama tell you that she'll buy you a bike at your funeral. Get the fuck outta here with the bullshit my nigga. I fail to believe in any religion that says you have to wait to be rewarded. Nigga what kinda shit is that?" It was conversations like these with Ty and I that made us who we were. We were two opposite acting niggas from the same side of the tracks. Compton, California, or "The Hub" as we called it. It was more than just an area of California. It was the epitome of greatness. Here, we emphasized the aspect of brotherhood to the core. I mean, where do I really start with my city? For starters, you can say that when people hear that you are from L.A., one of the first questions that may come out of their mouth is "Are you from Compton?" White folks who try to damn hard to fit in and listen to way too much rap music may ask "Are you from Bompton?" That should let you know how much of a culture icon that the city really is. N.W.A., DJ Quik, Kendrick Lamar, Coolio, Game, YG and the list goes on as far as rap artists are concerned. Serena Williams, Venus Williams, Richard Sherman, Larry Allen, James Harden, Demar DeRozan, Tyson Chandler and the list goes on as far as athletes are concerned. This place was not only a talent pool, but a gangster hotbed as well. The latter is what makes everyone here who they are. You are literally born into this shit. Even if you are a nerdy kid who is deep into his or her books, you have family members who are on the other side, and you become affiliated even if you don't want to be. I remember a homeboy that I was in elementary school with name Jarrell. Jarrell was one of the nerdy kids that I am referring to. He wore thick ass glasses that could see well into the future, but his family lines were not to be crossed. We called him "Stub" because he was real short. One day as school was letting out, we ran across the school lawn as usual, excited to hit our parents cars so we could head home and chill for the day. Not even ten steps out of the door, someone who was at least 12 years our senior ran up and hit "Stub" with three head shots before taking off. In that moment, amongst all the commotion, I asked myself one question. What would make a grown ass man kill a fourth grader? Sad to say, but that's just how things were around here. As for "Stub's" killer, and remember, I said his family lines were not to be crossed, that dude ended up being found in six different places. His torso was found in Park Village. His two feet were found in Lynwood. His hands were found on the corner of Palm and Oak. One of his legs was found behind Tibby Elementary. The other leg was found in a dumpster behind Mickey D's, near Roosevelt Middle School. Finally, his head, well those niggas who murked him removed a stop sign and impaled his head on a pole right outside of Ellerman Park. Like I said, shit was ruthless around these parts. Me and Ty, we survived that shit. Everyday for 18 years, there was a new battle that arose that challenged the very essence of our existence. However, the biggest battle came when we escaped the madness and started to transcend the world on our own.

"Naw man. You gotta look beyond the scope of things. Like outside the box you know."

"Man fuck all that," Ty responded. "You on that religious mumbo jumbo shit. Again, I don't play religion bullshit. God, Allah, Buddha, none of that shit. Now look. I understand you in search of this mysterious truth and by all means my nigga, I respect that. But, that truth you searching for ain't adding up you feel me? Where was God when niggas were getting shot? Where was God when we were struggling with Top Ramen and hot dogs all *** damn night? Where in the good fuck was God when a nigga just wanted to eat some name brand cereal and not no fuckin' Malt-O-Meal? Huh? Where was your Almighty then? Hell you even asked who created God not even a minute ago. So nigga you tell me what to believe."

He left me dumbfounded, sitting on the edge of my seat, pondering my thoughts. My nigga had a point, even though I didn't wanna tell myself that.

"Well look," he said. "While you sit here and think about your God, a nigga gotta head to work. Bills ain't gone pay themselves around this muthafucka. I'll holla at you tonight man." We dapped up and I watched fam get up and head out the door, on his way to the barbershop. Truth be told, we still weren't far removed from the Top Ramen days. We were out of Compton, but the struggle still continued here in Carson. I was in school at Cal State Dominguez Hills, majoring in behavioral science, riding the wave of a full ride academic scholarship that I had obtained coming out of Compton High in 2014. The off campus apartment we were in wasn't much of a gem, but it was four walls and a roof, so we weren't doing too much complaining. I began to indulge in one of my many mandatory reads entitled "The Political Economy of the Urban Ghetto" by Timothy Bates and Daniel R. Fusfeld. Studying the behavior of urban children and the economic disparities of the inner city ghettos, the information that I was obtaining was truly mind boggling. Even though this was released in 1984, much of the information still held true to this very day. My mission was to solve the problem by delving deep into the root of the problem. In order to get to the root of the problem, you must first dig up the soil. We often take things only at the value of what lies on the surface. In order to fix what happens inside of the inner city, you have to be inside of the inner city. And being inside of the inner city does not necessarily equate to living in the inner city or knowing what the blocks consist of. Being in the inner city is learning the inner workings of the minds of the individuals who are residing in the inner city. We tend to forget that the people are the most important aspect of anything. Certain environments will cause people to behave in different mannerisms. You can't expect a suburban American person to know inner hood dealings when they have matured around greener pastures their entire lives. Now, someone may be seeing this saying, but you just said it doesn't equate to what the blocks consist of. What I mean is this. Yes, you will behave in different mannerisms depending on your surrounding environment. However, when you really break down how different races operate in certain environments, you'd see what I'm talking about. White people will see liquor store, but see cheap land at the same time. Then, they will buy it up, build it up, raise the property value and push theirs in while others go out. Asians will see liquor stores, and own the joints, making the money off of the black individuals who incorporate the surrounding neighborhoods. Notice that they will make money off the environment, but they won't live in the environment.

"YO KEV MAN!!! OPEN UP!!!" That thundering voice was accompanied by three thunderous knocks.

"WHO THE HELL KNOCKING AT MY DOOR LIKE THEY CRAZY???!!!"

"It's your favorite," they said with a much calmer tone now. I knew exactly who it was. With that said, I grabbed a knife that was lying on the kitchen counter, walked over to the door, snatched it open and attempted to scare the hell out of Ralo.

"Man if you don't put that knife down. You from Compton nigga. Y'all shoot. Y'all don't stab."

"I'll stab yo' lite bright ass." I tossed the knife in the sink and dapped my mans up as he came in jubilant as ever. I thought he had just finished laying the wood to some broad because that's the only time that I ever saw jubilation like this out of him. "So man what you on today?," he asked.

"Well, what I'm on right now is wondering why you just walk into my pad and grab the Frosted Flakes like you live here?"

"Aww man you know how niggas is. Once you family, then everything is fair game."

"Man, don't eat all that shit up. You know how Ty is about his cereal."

"Man that nigga good." I just shook my head as he reached into the cabinet and grabbed the biggest damn bowl he could find. Ralo was from Hartford, Connecticut. When I first met him, I thought he was bullshittin' me. Weren't any black people in Connecticut I thought besides the few that played for UConn. But, he proved me wrong. He was out here to play basketball for the university and we hit it off quick. Not to mention that we also had a sociology class together and stayed playing the same girl for typed up reports, because no one truly cared about sociology.

"A man, so where Ty at anyway?"

"Damn can you chew with yo' mouth closed nigga?"

"Naw nigga I can't. Now answer the question," as he put another big gulp of Frosted Flakes in his mouth, with milk drippin' everywhere.

"He at the shop man. And from the looks of it, you need to get sliced up bad. That shit on top of your head look like a bag of ass."

"Man fuck you."

"Fuck ya mama. You wanna go?"

"Yeah. Let me kill this bowl real quick." I watched this fool finish off the flakes, tilt up that big red bowl and drink the milk like it was nothing.

"Aaahhh," he let out. "Here nigga. Five dollars. You welcome. Let's bounce." All I could do was shake my head once again as I grabbed the five he put on the table and followed him out. It was a nice sunny day for November, as Cali winters were nowhere near as brutal like the East Coast.

"Yo come on man. You moving slower than molasses."

"Damn nigga. Can I lock my door? Sheesh." I knew fam

was fucking with me, but he was a time hound. He always wanted to make it to wherever he was going in the quickest time possible. Hence the reason that I don't get in a vehicle with him when I drive. I met him at the bottom of the stairs and we began walking three blocks down to where Ty cut hair at. See, Ty came with me when I left. He was never a classroom wizard when we were in high school. He was a C student at best. What he did have however was an artistry when it came to a pair of Clippers. I remember coming up, he had a cousin they called "Bonzi" from Fruit Town. Fam used to cut his head on the steps of his crib near where Plum Street and N. Paulsen Ave met. Now what made this weird is that Ty and I grew up in Spooktown, where the Crips held ground at. However, with Bonzi's street cred, Ty was given a pass and protected by other Fruit Town Pirus while over there. Not to mention that he was slicin' their heads up as well.

Now, Ty may have been affiliated by where he grew up, but a good barber is a good barber. He ended up being somewhat of a Compton legend, as he became a regular barber cutting some of the most notorious cats heads from Fruit Town, Spook Town, Nutty Block and even Mona Park. Again, his pass was stamped by different neighborhoods, which was very rare in The Hub. When we graduated, Bonzi gave him 25 stacks and told him to go with me to make his life happen. Bonzi was stuck in the gangbanging lifestyle for eternity. However, he knew that his fam bam was something special, so he wanted him out of Compton for good and to live his dream. Truth be told, Carson wasn't nothing but a hop, skip and a jump up the 91. However, it was far enough from the madness.

"Wassup negroids. And why did you bring this loud mouth dude up in here?"

"Man I know you ain't talkin' Ty," said Ralo.

"Man you never shut up, with that rag mop on top of yo' head," Ty clapped back. The whole shop started rollin' as the roast battle was on.

"Bruh, I know you don't wanna roast no one with those long ass Blackbeard pirate fingers. I hope you never try to finger a bitch. Ain't gone be no playing with her pussy. Them long ass thangs gone be scratching her kidneys."

"Much like I scratched your sister's last night." The shop let out a roar as Ty had retaliated with the comeback of comebacks. "GOT HIM COACH!!!," yelled one of the other barbers over the roar.

"Man fuck you dog. What's up," Ralo said, walking up to Ty to dap him up while laughing.

"I got another head before you man, then I got you."

"Fasho," Ralo said. Ralo came and sat down next to me as the conversation shifted from roasting to reality. "So Ty."

"Sup Spoon?"

"What you think about Obama about to leave office? You think niggas gone stand a chance?"

"FUCK NAW!!!" Not only did Ty yell it out, but a few brothers waiting for their cuts did as well.

"A look," said Brody, another barber who was a heavy set brother with dreads, originally from Sactown. "Nigga ain't shit lined up for us no matter who in there. This nigga Obama didn't do shit for niggas. But ask those LGBT's what he did and them niggas will dance all around for him."

"So what you thought he was supposed to just look out for us in there?," I asked him.

"Hell naw. But niggas need more than some fucking hope. I can hope a kid don't cross the street when it's a bunch of cars coming. I can hope a broad suck my dick when I leave this hoe tonight. I can hope the police don't shoot me down for mistaking these clippers for a gun. I can hope for a lot. But hope ain't nothing but chewed up grass at the end of the day partna."

"So let me ask you something. Matter fact, everyone in here. What's is it gone take for us to ensure someone looks out for our well being?"

"OUR OWN SHIT NIGGA!!!," Ty yelled out. "But when you think about the shit, every time niggas try to establish some shit, or have established something, the government done came in and kicked the door down on us. Mirror my nigga," he said, passing the mirror to his client in the chair. "You good man?"

"Fosho," his client responded. "Aight cool. Now, back to you. We had Black Wallstreet. They bombed that shit. We had The Black Panthers. They destroyed that shit. We got black colleges, and a lot of 'em starting to get more white students on a yearly basis. Check out Bluefield State if you don't believe me. Give it another 30 years and you won't be able to tell that an HBCU even exists my nigga. So you tell me nigga what we supposed to do?" The conversation in here was golden as you saw a variety of emotions come out from everyone in here. These topics were the inner workings of the barbershop in the minority neighborhood. Particularly, the black neighborhood. The barbershop was almost like another institution of higher learning of sorts. Ralo's turn to get his haircut came and went, then he dipped out. Hell, I was the only one left in the shop now, along with another brother who was getting his Rick Ross style beard lined up. I wasn't intending on staying, but the college football on television had me hooked, even if it was Division II ball.

"C'mon Kev. Lemme hook you up."

"I'm good bruh. I just got caught up in this game."

"Man bring yo ass over here in this chair. I'm a surgeon with these clippers and I know when my roommate needs an edge up." I raised up and went over to the chair. Bruh wrapped my neck and threw the barber drape over me. "So what do you want out of life man?," he asked me, as he cut the clippers on.

"What you mean man?"

"I mean just what I said. What do you want out of life?" I paused as he went to work on the back of my neck. The clipper noise kind of played a fiddle for me to collect my thoughts.

"I want the big city life man. The bright lights. The glitz. The glam. I just wanna be around fun people doing fun things you feel me?"

"So why take the major you taking to help inner city kids if you want the bigger, better deal?"

"Man look. My goal is to help someone else man, but I don't wanna do it living in the same environment that we came up in."

"I understand that. But bruh, we been doing this city shit since we started. Yeah, I know what you thinking. Its Compton. But nigga, it's L.A. Nigga we as L.A. as the Dodgers, Lakers and the Kings. Nigga we down at the Staples Center and Rodeo Drive with not too much far of a drive. Nigga we've done the big city life. Don't you think it's time for something else?" "Like what you mean something else?"

"I mean bruh. Something else. I'm talking about going somewhere where won't anyone think about and leaving a mark. Shit to be honest, I got tired of that shit. Not tired of The Hub, but everywhere I went. I'd tell niggas I'm from there. Nigga after that, it's just a bunch of assuming and questions. The assuming was the worst part. You remember that USC camp I went to years ago when we were teens?"

"Yeah man."

"Yeah well there we were on break. I'm chillin' behind the bleachers and I saw some niggas from Lueders Park I recognized kind of gang up on this other brother. I didn't know the other dude, had never seen him a day in my life. I knew he wasn't from Compton. From the looks of it, he wasn't from the hood at all. We came off break and hit another session of practice. On our next break, I went up to the nigga and rapped with him. I can't remember what the nigga said his name was, but I do remember that he was named after one of those Egyptian Kings. I said yo' mama named you after a pharaoh nigga. He laughed and said yeah. Come to find out. This nigga was from Newport Beach. Now, it would've been easy to just blow him off as not a brother because he was from the other side of the tracks. To me though. Just to me. A brother is a brother. He gone go through the same shit I'm gone go through, except in a different setting. Niggas gone hate him cause he ain't from the hood and he privileged. Niggas gone hate me because I'm from a different neighborhood than them. I just wanna go somewhere where it's all one community. No neighborhoods, no sets, none of that shit. Feel me?"

"Yeah man, but I don't think we can avoid that no matter where we go."

"You may be right my nigga. You may be right. But you can also be wrong my nigga. Now, hold yo head still while I give you this crispy with the razor." Ty leaned my chair back and spread shaving cream along my hairline. Then, slapped a hot ass rag over my forehead. I sat there, kicked back, eyes closed, listening to the announcer call a touchdown for whomever had scored. Other conversation was also happening amongst the other barbers. As he dried my forehead and proceeded to make my lining crispier than some Louisiana Fried Chicken, I thought about what we had just rapped about. He had a point about the big city, but I don't think he got the bigger picture. We weren't mobbin L.A. on a regular. Hell, we were both 20 year olds and I was just a student in college. I wanted to take the time to actually indulge in how city folks operate. I wanted the New York, Chicago and Miami scene on a regular. At least a little bit before I delved deep into my career. He wanted simplicity. Now, that was my man fifty grand and my nigga if he didn't get no bigger, which he wasn't seeing that his growth stopped at 5'10 ½. I just couldn't see it and I thought it was a simple phase that he would eventually grow out of. We were gonna ride this shit out and mob together like we had for the previous 19 years.

Ty finished me up and I told him that I would see him at the house later. I left out around 3:30 in the afternoon, hungrier than a hostage. There was a mom and pops store near the crib, so I stopped in there and got me a peanut butter shake. Lord knows I could finish about ten of these a day if I had the chance. As I left and walked the last block to the house, I peeped the normal scene. Carson was a low key city. It had its drama, but nothing like Compton or Long Beach. It was more chill out here and that's just the way I liked it when it came to where I lived. But still, I wanted to party. I got home and just sat on the couch, wishing I had a shorty who could cook me some grits. I had some in the cabinet, but me and the stove got along like Bloods and Crips. It was sad that a 20 year old didn't know how to properly make something as simple as grits. After an hour passed of me watching television, I couldn't take the hunger anymore. I got up and grabbed them joints out of the cabinet. I read the instructions on the back and proceeded to do just like the instructions said. Two cups of water. Half cup of grits. Pinch of salt. Butter. It wasn't rocket science, so I should have been good to go.

"Nigga what you cookin?," Ty said as he stepped through the door.

"Man I'm finishing up these grits man. I got enough for two. Want some?"

"Naw man. I'm straight. I'll just get me a bowl of these Frosted's and call it a wrap." I knew what was coming next, but I didn't wanna say anything until he grabbed the box.

"NIGGA!!! WHAT THE FUCK???!!!"

"Man it wasn't me. Ralo came over here and murdered yo shit. He left five dollars for you to buy some more."

"So you just let the nigga come in here and have a field day with my Frosted's?"

"Naw man, but the nigga was hungry. So I told the nigga just know he gone be mad." Ty sat down at the kitchen table in high disappointment.

"First off, stir them grits man. You ain't supposed to let the shits boil and pop out all over the stove like you doing now. Now, you get mad when you stub yo' toe. You get mad when someone bump into you and make you spill your drink. You get mad when the Lakers lose to the Brooklyn Nets. But nigga. I get furious when a nigga eat my Frosted Flakes. You can eat Trix for kids, Toucan Sam and even The Cap'n. But you do not fuck with my Frosted's man. That's liable for a death sentence." It was only one thing I could say after that.

"So my nigga. You want some of these grits?" Ty looked like he wanted to choke me and bury me in someone's back yard.

"Yeah sure man. Put some on a plate for me."

"Man I ain't yo maid. Better get up and get ya own shit."

"Damn that's the least you could've done was fix my plate seeing how you let another grown ass man come in here and eat my cereal." As I reached up in the opposite cabinet for two of the three good plates that we had, I started to hear the sound of spitting. Ty had taken a spoon and sampled them straight out the pot. "The fuck is this man?"

"They grits."

"Nigga grits don't taste like this. Man I'm throwing this shit out bruh. You ain't even put no salt or nothing in here."

"Man I put a pinch of salt like the box said." He gave me the Russell Westbrook y'all niggas trippin look.

"Man, you do not pay attention to what the box say. Hand me the grits and rinse this pot out. I'm gone show you how to make grits." This was good, 'cause I shole wanted to see how good this nigga cooking was, even though I knew the answer to that. I gave him a clean pot back. "This how you do it. First, we don't need no damn measuring nothing. See here, this amount of water," as he took a cup he filled up and poured it in. "Now, put the heat on low to medium. You wanna cook your grits, not boil em to death." He let the water get to his desired temp and poured a certain amount of grits in. "You see what I'm doing. Constant stirring. You want your grits loose. Not all tacked together. Now, cut me about half of stick of that butter and hand me the salt as well."

"You want some sugar too?" His eyes got big and cut back towards me, looking like he had seen a demon, all while still stirring the grits.

"Don't you ever in your life put sugar and grits in the same sentence. Anyone who puts sugar in their grits works directly for satan and doesn't deserve to breathe the same air as a normal human." I thought that was somewhat harsh, but that's just how he was when it came to grits obviously. "Now, gimme yo plate." I handed him my plate and he put two scoops worth of grits on there. "I would give you more, but I don't think you know what good food is. Try that." I grabbed a spoon and took in a mouthful.

"Damn nigga. This shit fire."

"Nigga I know. Now that's how you make grits. And ain't no piece of sugar near them grits. Boy, I swear you better learn how to cook. You got the brains out of both of us, but I swear to God you can't even boil water. Ain't no woman wanna be aroused with college conversations after a good night of fucking. She wanna wake up and have something else besides dick to put in her belly." He piled the rest of the grits on his plate and headed off to the other chair that was in the living room. I sat back down on the couch as another football game was coming on.

"So what we on tonight. Shop closed tomorrow and I'm sleeping in."

"Shit what you wanna do?"

"Man them hoes at yo' college ain't having no parties? I mean I know I ain't jumping around with no candy canes or barking like a dog, but a nigga can still get in where he fit in."

"Man I'll make some calls, but I ain't heard about nothing

that's poppin' off tonight."

"Man you ain't got no women to call?"

"Nigga who?"

"Nigga you."

"Watch we end up somewhere tonight. I'll pull more in one night than you will in your entire life."

"Same way you pulled Rhonda Davis junior year huh?"

"Man why you bringing up old shit?" Ty started cracking up, damn near dropping his plate of grits.

"Cause nigga. I'll never forget that. You thought you was the Godfather that night or something. Man you sold that bitch a dream and she sold yo' ass to the door. Shit, she wouldn't have got off that easy with me. You don't waste two hours of my time and then tell me you dealin' with another nigga. Her ass would have paid me reparations." This was us. Ty and Kevin. The wild things that came out of our mouths was as common as the Patriots winning a super bowl with Tom Brady. We continued this Saturday watching football and just chillin' like two young brothers do. The time hit a lil bit past seven and the game was now at halftime.

"A man, I'm a get a cat nap in the room. Wake me up in an hour or whenever you find something to get into," he told me.

"Aight." I stayed in the living room, texting everyone that I knew, trying to find something to get into. Finally, after what seemed like forever, I finally got a text from my guy Raheem saying that there was a house party down south hosted by a couple of girls he knew at UC Irvine. I ran into the room.

"YO TY WAKEUP!!!"

"Man why are you yelling?"

"So the homey texted me. Couple of broads he know throwing a party at their house in Irvine."

"Nigga I'm game then." Ty jumped out the bed like he was Vince Carter at a slam dunk competition. "I'm gettin in the shower." Ty strolled off to the bathroom steady repeating I'm getting some booty tonight. It was crazy how when you brought women into the picture, he would get up and be ready to go in an instant. Me, I dug the ladies, but a woman was a woman to me. This was California. I was used to women of different ethnicities, especially being in college. So to me, women were just that. Women. They were nothing special for me.

"Yo gone head man. The shower all yours."

"My nigga," I said to Ty. "Can you put some clothes on? Walking 'round ass naked ain't cool."

"Nigga ain't no fruit in yo' blood and ain't no fruit in my blood except for my family in Fruit Town. I'm going to the room and getting ready for the hoes." All I could do was shake my head as I headed to the shower to get clean for the night. "Yo nigga you ready? I got my clothes on and ready to go."

"NIGGA I'M STILL IN THE SHOWER!!! QUIT BANGIN ON THE *** DAMN DOOR!!!" Ty banged five more times and I heard him laugh as he moved away from the door. I got out and headed to the room, sifting through all my clothes, trying to figure out what I was gonna wear. I finally decided on some black denims, a grey F.L.A.V.A. shirt, a black and grey Dodger fitted and some black Timbs, just incase I had to stomp someone out in the process.

"Yo, you ready man?," Ty asked as he came through the door.

"Hold on bruh. I'm putting my shirt and stuff on right now."

"Aight man hurry up."

"Shut the door man." I swear he was my boy, but acting like a kid on Christmas wasn't a good look in my eyes. I was fully dressed and I threw the fitted on my head. I looked in the mirror, knowing that I was fly. I popped out the room door and saw Ty gulping down some A&W Root Beer, which he had three cases of in the fridge.

"A, we gotta split the gas. I'm damn near on E."

"I got it man. Just fill up with my tips I got today. Nine heads in four hours turned out pretty good for me today. Especially for just four hours. Let's roll." We headed out the door of our apartment and down the stairs to our Black 2011 Chevy Impala. We split our money and purchased it together when we decided to move out here. Seeing how Ty liked to explore everything on foot, he didn't drive it around that much. I was the primary driver, as I used it for school the majority of the time.

"Throw that old E in the boomin system. Get this night poppin," Ty said. I reached up and grabbed Eazy's first CD that was given to me by my now deceased brother "Carl," a.k.a. C.O.L.D. W.O.R.L.D. He said it stood for Crippin' On Loyalty and Domination With Order, Respect, Love and Devotion. He was gunned down back in 2004 when he was beefin' with a cat from Acacia Blocc over a female. It was his favorite CD and it made me think of him everytime that I played it. *"Woke up quick at about noon/just thought that I had to be in Compton soon/I gotta get drunk before the day begins/ before my mother starts bitchin' about my friends."*

The sounds of the original West Coast gangsta had us feeling good. We hadn't even took off from our parking spot, but we already felt like we were in Hollywood. We looked at each other and just bobbed our heads through the first two verses before taking off. The ladies house we were headed to was down in Anaheim off of Ball Road. Anaheim was cool. It had Disneyland out there, so I don't think neither one of us were really worried about anything poppin' off. A few blocks down from the crib, we hit the gas station.

"You want something to drink Ty?"

"Naw man. Just get me a pack of black and milds, and I'm good."

"Cool." I walked in the gas station not thinking of much around me. It was a typical Saturday night scene with people filling up and buying pick me ups before they headed off to their destinations for the night.

"Is this it for you?," the clerk asked me.

"Yeah man, and gimme a pack of blacks while you at it?" The clerk scanned the blacks, my pork skins and the two green teas that I had. He got his money, I got our goods and I dipped out the store. I walked out seeing Ty now in the driver's seat, bobbin his head to N.W.A's "Fuck tha Police." And obviously, everyone else felt the same way, as Ty had the speakers cranked up to an obnoxious level. The shit was so loud that aliens on Mars could hear it. Everyone seemed to be vibin' to it, even the Mexicans directly across from us.

"Yo man you feeling good ain't you?," I said as I got in the car.

"Yo my nigga. I'm just feeling it tonight man. I'll drive.

You kick back school boy. Let ya boy do this tonight." All I could do was laugh as I put a pork skin in my mouth and enjoyed the vibe with my mans as he pulled off into the night. We hit the 405 South and really got to rollin'.

"Yo man. Slow this muthafucka down. The pussy will be there when we get there. Trust me."

"You know what," Ty responded. "For you my nigga. Just for you tonight. I'll keep this bitch at a decent 75 to 80." That was music to my ears, seeing that he had hit 95 as soon as we hit the freeway. Ironically, there weren't any traffic jams at this time of night. That was rare in itself. Any freeway in L.A. County was hell to be on at any given time of the day. However, tonight, our lucky horseshoes must have been counted. Not to mention that not one police officer was in sight. There wasn't much talking going on as we continued on down the 405. The music was doing all the talking for us. We hit the other connecting freeways and got to the 5. I was vibin' out to the music blaring through the speakers while Ty was on his second black, blowing it in the air as if he were the Godfather. Once we hit Anaheim city limits, we were all game.

"Man I ain't gone lie bruh," Ty said. "This OC shit is nice out here."

"I would have to agree with you my nigga," I said. "Orange County is way calmer than where we at."

"Shit that's what I want bruh. Calm, relaxing, no worrying about a *** damn shootout every twenty minutes."

"So would you move out here?"

"Nah man. Shit too close to Compton still. I want away from California. I mean like far away. Halfway around the world type stuff. See niggas don't see shit in they lives but blunts, videos and violence. Like forreal, forreal." Ty took another hit of the black as we were at a stop light. "What street is this we on?"

"Brookhurst," I told him.

"Ok, take Brookhurst for example. Let's say Brookhurst was a street in Compton. And for shits and giggles, we'll just say they gang was called the Crookhurst Crips. Do you know it would be some niggas that would spend their whole lives just in their neighborhood and not venture out? That shit is unreal man. I had one of my cousins from Mississippi that I met a long time ago when he came out here. His name was Darius. Man that nigga was in the Navy for less than a year and went to Spain, Italy, Bahrain, Dubai, Jebel Ali, Singapore and Hawaii. Nigga you know how impressive that is? Most niggas don't get to see even one of those places in their lifetime, let alone seven in one year. That's the shit I'm talkin about. I mean niggas really need to expand their minds. It's so much more outside of Compton my nigga. Niggas just gotta want it that's all."

"I totally feel you my dude and that's why I fucks with you," I told him as we continued on down the street. "I can see now that me and you gone be set forever mane. No matter what we do, we gone always be in this shit together."

"You sure about that bruh?" I just looked at him after he asked me that, as we were stopped at another light. He began to laugh as he went to take another hit of the black.

"I love you my nigga. Like a damn brother I do. But the day gone come where we go our separate ways. Enjoy this shit man. Enjoy it while we got it." I know we had talked about the different ways of how we wanted to go about in life, but I wasn't trying to think about that right now. We pulled up off a side street that came off of Magnolia.

"I thought you said the party was off Ball?," Ty asked me.

"My bad man. Must've misread it on the text. Thank God for this GPS though."

"Oh well. I ain't trippin. Lets roll in here and see what these hoes like." We got lucky again and found a parking spot directly across the street from the house. From the sounds coming from the inside, it sounded like things were booming.

"Damn wait for me man. You don't even know anybody." I was telling that to Ty as he was speed walking to the door. He got to the door, turned around and just looked at me, signaling for me to come on. I moved as fast as I could out of the car. I was just making sure that I had everything.

"Damn man. I swear you act like you ain't never seen ass before," I told him.

"Man the only thing better than ass is new ass." I knocked on the door, but it opened up the minute that I knocked. The sight we saw was not what we expected. It was a bunch of white folks with a sprinkle of blackness. We walked in and around the house. No one came up to us saying hi or anything. It looked like the typical white kids college party with beer pong and drunkenness everywhere.

"Man it's a bunch of hard legs in here."

"I know nigga," I responded.

"Who texted you about this party?"

"My nigga Raheem."

"Well, when you see Raheem, whoop his ass for me."

"OH YEA DUDE!!!" We heard the scream come from the far room and went back to see what was going on.

"That's it. Nigga I'm out. You and these weird college fucks can have this shit." Ty took off, but I was stuck in a look of awe as I saw the nastiest thing in my life. Some white boy was in boxer briefs and he let these fools put a crab on his nuts. Like a real live crab. No bullshit my nigga. That was enough for me as I headed out the house and back to the car, where Ty was waiting for me.

"Nigga I ain't never coming out with you again," he said.

"Man how I know it was gonna be people in there playing crab grab with they testicles?"

"All I know is that it's damn near 11 on a Saturday night, we an hour from the crib and we ain't got a damn thing to do. Man, look something up cause I ain't just wanna come out here for nothing. Find a spot to eat or something." I felt bad. We drove all the way out here. And now, there wasn't a damn thing to do.

"Hold on. I'm gone look up something right now." I turned into a Google warrior, looking for anything to get into this late on a Saturday night. Upon entering Saturday Night in Anaheim, my attention was immediately taken by the first search result. "Man they got a nightclub called Heat."

"Now that's what I'm talking about man. Sound like something that I can get into. Let's roll." With me now driving, I peeled off into the night headed towards Katella Avenue. First, I had to stop at Jack in the Crack so we could put some food in our bellies before we hit the spot. Some Supreme Croissants would definitely get us back to feeling right. Depending on the way we would feel in that joint, we may have gotten us a couple of drinks and this food would definitely absorb all the liquor. As we pulled out of the drive through, that's when it hit me. "A man, we can't go there," I told Ty. "Why not nigga? I'm gone see some women before this night is over."

"Man we only 20 bruh."

"Aww shit man," Ty said in a despondent voice. "Damn. Fuck it. Just head home."

"Man it's too early for all of that."

"Then what you wanna do then? You tell me? It's past 11 on a Saturday night. In Anaheim. L.A. is always the last resort, but I ain't trying to be out there like that tonight man. Just head to the crib yo." Fuck it is what I thought. We just had to chalk this one up as a major loss. I got back on the 5 North and started the drive back to the house. Ty was leaned back in his seat, on his phone, either texting someone or playing a game. Me, I just tried to block out everything that had just happened.

"A my dude," Ty said to me. "What's that school shit like?"

"What you mean?"

"Like, you really want that shit? Cause deep down, I think its a scam."

"What you talking about bruh?" He raised the seat up. "I ain't saying you ain't smart or nothing like that my nigga. Nah. Like, forreal though. That shit is like one big scam." I side eyed him with the what the fuck look, but I figured I could hear him out. "Just hear me out on this one man. Aight, so we get programmed to get this higher education, right?"

"Right."

"Okay, so you got people who break bread for college, to get a piece of paper, just to say they can do a job. Then they graduate, turn around and get a job, just so they can pay back the cost of college. You don't see anything wrong with that?"

"Not really my nigga. Nah. I mean, it's setting you up for something better. I mean really. How far you think that barber shit gone take you in life?"

"Nigga you serious?"

"I ain't mean it like that bruh."

"Naw. Yes the fuck you did. Look, I make men, kids, women, whoever feel good. You feel how you look. If you look good, you feel good. I cut a nigga hair. Let's say a gangsta nigga at that. I get him fresh, crispy, sliced up, whatever you wanna call it. Now, he so damn fresh, he ain't thinkin' about going out and robbing someone. He thinkin' about going out and getting him a broad. I done saved one person's life, including his. Man you my mans, but don't you ever underestimate what the fuck I do because ain't no piece of fucking paper behind it. Fuck wrong with you?"

"Like I said Ty. I didn't mean it."

"But you did mean that shit. College educated don't mean impactful on the world. Just like being impactful on the world don't mean that a nigga gotta go to school. You ever hear muthafuckas talking about they ballin' and all that shit? Man them niggas ain't doing shit. Technically speaking, and hear me again. TECHNICALLY!!! If we wanna be real. You broke if you ain't part of the one percent. And I say that because they have the wealth and the power. Rothschilds, Bush's, Bill Gates, they got power behind their wealth. Anyone else simply got a bunch of money. Yeah its nice. Phat ass cribs in the hills. $500,000 cars. Rolex's, nice clothes, all that other irrelevant shit. But they can't start a world war with the snap of their fingers. They can't shut down the world's computers systems at the press of a button. So don't confuse money with power. Them niggas got real power. Lot of other people just got money."

"And how you come to this conclusion?," I asked him ever so sarcastically.

"Ask Shaq can he have a world leader who ain't a part of the agenda knocked off?" I had to literally think on that one.

"Yeah you right."

"See and that's what I am getting at. Don't let what the world dictates keep you away from facts. Its two types of people in this world my nigga. Those who run it and everyone else. I'm all for you learning. But make sure you learn that other shit too man. The shit that they won't teach you in any school. Remember, they say if you wanna touch the past, you touch a rock. If you wanna touch the present, you touch a flower. If you wanna touch the future, then you touch a life. I do that everyday cutting hair. Start touching lives man. Less touching books. More touching lives. That's all. I didn't need a fucking college education for that." I became silent as he let the seat back once again and went to messing with his phone. His words left me to ponder a lot. I wasn't rethinking my education. I was however rethinking how I looked at this world. The rest of the drive home was a chill one with YG playing in my speakers and Ty eventually passing the hell out. When he went to sleep, I don't know, but homey was out to the world. As we hit the city, fam woke up and made me stop at the 24 hour convenience store.

"Gimme that five that Ralo gave you." I already knew what he was doing.

"I'm gravy now nigga." I just shook my head as he came back with a box of Frosted Flakes. I already knew what time it was when we got home. We got to the house and on cue, he went to the cabinet and grabbed his red bowl. "A, you know why I'm here," he said. Crazy how a grown man could talk to a box of cereal and a bowl like it was gonna respond back to him.

"Well my dude, you know where I'll be. Goodnight." He took off to the room with his cereal and milk in hand, shutting the door. I plopped down on the couch and let some tension ease up off of my body. I sat there chilling for a good ten minutes. Tonight, I was gonna sprawl across the couch, under the blanket and let my dreams send me into sleepyville. Then, I remembered that Ty had some books on the bookshelf to go along with some of my school reads. I hated reading, but I needed to for school. With what he told me, I wanted to see how deep he was, or thought he was. I got up with the light illuminating from over the kitchen stove and got to skimming through the titles. There were only seven books up here and none of them looked as if they had any real value. Then, one caught my eye. "Monster: the Autobiography of a L.A. Gang Member." With all the juju he was talking, I thought to myself, what in the good hell could you learn from a gangsta book? I thought he had been reading some African lit or something by the way he was talking. But, a gangsta book? Naw. There was only street shit that you could learn from that. I cracked it open and flipped through the pages. I was skimming, but nothing caught my eye. I put the book back and proceeded to take my clothes off and get ready to go to sleep. In typical male fashion, I tossed my clothes on the table and threw on some basketball shorts. I cut the light off in the kitchen and sort of felt my way back to the couch. "Fuck," I whispered out, as I stubbed my big toe on the corner of our living room table. That shit hurt. I hopped my ass to the couch, holding my foot. Damn, I was in so much pain. Once that pain subsided, I grabbed my beats on the table, along with my IPOD and started to browse through my artists selection. I needed something smooth and methodic to put me to sleep tonight. Finally, I decided on some of that Section 80 Kendrick and let his music put me at ease for the rest of the night.

"Wake up. Yo Kev wake up."

"What, what," I said, grumbling, not knowing what was going on. "Shhh. Listen," Ty whispered. I was dead still in the dark and started to hear voices coming from outside. It sounded like a heated argument.

"Who that?"

"Nigga I don't know," Ty whispered back.

"Go over to the blinds and peek," I told him.

"Nigga we black. We ain't white folks. They nosey ass get shot." Ty had a point. As we listened from the comforts of our living room, we heard the voices starting to dissipate and a car pulled off soon after. We didn't know what the hell was going on. It was in the wee hours of Sunday morning and it was truly too early for that shit.

"Well, I'm going back to bed man."

"Aight," I told Ty. I hated that two people woke us up well before dawn with their problems, but it was still Sunday, so I could sleep in for hours and not worry about being tired for the rest of the day. I quickly went back to sleep as did Ty. It seemed that no sooner than we fell back asleep that the sound of a continuous car alarm started rattling through the house. I looked at the clock at it was 5:52 a.m. We obviously did sleep some hours because the initial commotion was around two in the morning.

"Man fuck this man. I'm trying to sleep."

"Ty don't go out there."

"Man this *** damn horn keeping me up. Shit keeping me from sleeping."

"Bruh don't go."

"Nigga I got this." Ty reached up to the ventilation and pulled off the cover. Out of it he pulled a 9MM.

"Yo when the fuck was you gone tell me you had a gun in this house?"

"Never. But you know now. Nigga we from Compton. Don't care if we ain't in there no more. Shit pops off anywhere." Ty opened the door and looked around outside. I was up behind him.

"What you see?," I whispered.

"Nothing, but I hear that horn steady going off downstairs. Stay here," he said. I stayed at the top of the stairs as Ty slowly crept down the stairs. He made it to the bottom and went out of my eyesight when he made the round turn towards where we parked our cars. I wasn't gonna leave my nigga by himself, even though I wasn't strapped. I headed down slowly and as I made it to the second to bottom step, that's when I saw him running back.

"Nigga go. Go." Ty damn near ran me over. I wasn't asking any questions as I quickly scurried back into the house and shut the door.

"What happened my dude?" Ty was out of breath, looking shook as ever.

"A man. A," as he rose up, trying to get his second wind. "You know that Mexican broad Ema who stay in the other building?"

"Yeah."

"Nigga I got down there and she was slumped on the steering wheel. I walked up to the car and saw her throat slashed and peeled the fuck off. Man, bruh, that's the last thing I wanted to wake up to this morning." I was stunned to say the least. This was the closest act of violence that had hit us since we left the crib.

"I'm going back to bed man. You enjoy this shit bruh." Ty walked back in the room and I put my headphones on the highest volume I possibly could to blot out all of the noise that would soon be coming. I occasionally took them off listening for the sounds of the police. After about a half an hour, I finally got my wish, as I heard the sirens and began to see the flashing lights ricocheting off the walls in the house. I kept 'em on from that point. If the police would knock on the door, I wasn't trying to hear them, nor talk to them in anyway. I had my views on the police. I knew that all of them weren't bad, but I couldn't say that I necessarily liked them in anyway. Whenever I saw a cop, I immediately gave no fucks. They used to harass us constantly back home. A nigga couldn't walk down the street without those pigs going in on one of us. Undercovers tried to pretend like they were our friends, knowing damn well it was their way of watching us and trying to find a reason to put a bullet in one of our asses. Where I'm from, the laws were worst than the opposing faction. When you saw the laws, nobody was a Blood or a Crip. No one was affiliated with anything except being black. They had been killing us for years out in the open and America pretended like it wasn't a problem. But they damn sure were broadcasting Chicago every five minutes. When it came to police, in my eyes, I saw Klansmen in blue suits instead of white sheets. It was just another ploy to take us out. **BOOM! BOOM! BOOM**! I heard someone knocking over the sounds of my headphones, but I wasn't going to play them any mind. **BOOM! BOOM! BOOM!** There it was again. I figured that if I didn't get up, they would leave. **BOOM! BOOM! BOOM!** There were the knocks again. Finally, Ty came out the room and flung the door open. "Waddup."

"Well, well, well. If it isn't Wayne "Ty" Russell. Your cousin still running shit in Fruit Town?"

"Man I don't know shit bout that man. I'm living out here. Cutting hair."

"Who's that in the back?"

"That's my roommate Kevin. A college student. Why you fucking with us man?"

"**HEY!!!,**" yelled the other cop. "We'll ask the questions here." I saw Ty getting pissed off, but he had to keep his cool.

"Naw Rog, I got this one. Step outside with us will you. You," as he pointed to me. "You keep your ass right there college boy." They pulled Ty outside and the next ten minutes were tension filled. I didn't know what was going on, but from how that conversation went down, I could only imagine. Ty came back in with angry and upset written all over his face.

"What happened out there bruh?" Ty walked over to the

couch and sat down. "Man that's that pussy ass Detective Slauson who used to fuck with my cousin and 'em over in Fruit Town. I told the nigga straight out. I heard the horn for a long time. I went outside and seen the bitch slumped over the wheel. Told the muthafucka dust for my prints if he ain't believe me, cause I ain't touch the bitch. I'm a barber. **FUCK THEM LAWS!!!**"

"You cool man? You good?"

"Naw I'm not good man. A nigga doing something right with his life but they still end up trying to fuck with a nigga. Swear for God I hope someone fuck his wife and nut in the bitch face. Nigga been fucking with folks since I can remember. The fuck he doing out here in Carson anyway?"

"I don't know man. Look, all I do know is that we still have a whole Sunday to just chill and relax. So just go back to sleep."

"Man fuck it. I'm up now. And since it's too early to call a bitch, I'm bout to open my laptop up. Me and pornhub bout to be at it for the next hour. If I can't beat a chick right now, then the next best thing is to beat my dick. I gotta de-stress. I'll holla at you." He walked in the room and I stood there, looking between the room door and the front door. I was trying to make sense of everything. I was still tired, but I really couldn't go back to sleep either, seeing that something else might happen and I'd have to wake up again. I scanned the house for whatever reason and my eyes locked in on the Monster book again. I went to the bookshelf, picked it up and headed back to the couch. For the next four hours, I sat in that spot and entrenched myself into that book, learning about someone else's struggles. The descriptive actions of the trials that this brother went through were jaw dropping to say the least.

I couldn't believe that I hadn't read this book sooner. As I neared the end of the book, I read about how he was pulled over in the Inland Empire area with his wife and children. This was well after the Monster had died and brother Sanyika Shakur was born. I was amazed at the overall impact that this book had on me. When I looked up, I saw that it was damn near 12 in the afternoon. For some odd reason, I started to think about my brother COLD WORLD and how he was no longer with us. The image of everything played out in my head as the day started to replay in my head.

July 4, 2004

"COME IN HERE SCOOBY!!!" I was nine years old playing video games on the Station when my big bro called me in the room. I paused my Madden game and went in to see what he wanted. "Yeah bro." "Come over here man and sit down." I went over to the couch and sat next to him. He just stared at me. My brother was an intimidating presence. 6'4, around 300 pounds, with a letter "C" tattooed under his left eye. His arms, chest and back were littered with ink of all sorts, with his bread and butter being the huge "SPOOKTOWN" going across the top of his back.

"What you doing in there playing those video games for?"

"I'm just passing time by. Its nothing to do."

"Why you ain't go to church with mama?"

"I didn't want to."

"What I tell you though? Huh? What I tell you?" I let out a sigh.

"To stay in church, stay in school and stay being a good kid to mom."

"Alright then. So let this be the last Sunday I see you in the house like this."

"Okay. But Carl. Why don't you go to church?"

"Don't worry about me youngin. Remember. I been yo' age, but you ain't been mine. Just remember something. I don't want you to make the same mistakes that I did coming up. Mama tried to show me a lot, but a woman job isn't to raise a man. Our daddy long gone, so the only fathers I knew were in the streets. You got me watching over you so you know damn well you ain't got no room for error. You feel me?" I shook my head and obliged. "Alright. Here's ten dollars. I saw your report card. You doing good. Keep it up okay. I love you."

"Love you too bro." He rubbed my head and bounced out the door. I didn't know that would be the last time I saw him. It was the Fourth of July, so mama kept me in the house. It was known to get ugly in Compton on this day as everyone would be out and about shooting their guns. It sucked because as bad as I wanted to light off some firecrackers, I couldn't. You couldn't tell the difference between a M80 and a shotgun blast. The time reached 7:03 p.m., and the sun was getting sleepy, preparing to make its descent below the clouds. My mama was in the kitchen frying some chicken when the phone rang.

"Hello," I heard her say. Then, I heard the most God awful scream in my life. I ran from the living room to see that my mama had literally passed out on the kitchen floor. She was crying hysterically.

"Mama, mama," I kept repeating, shaking her, hoping that she would get up.

"My son is gone. Lord why'd you take him?" That's all I needed to hear as I slowly stood up and realized the power in the words she had just said. I couldn't tell myself that it wasn't true because by this point in my life, I had gotten used to at least a murder per day in Compton.

"C'mon baby, let's go." She grabbed me, snatching me by the shirt and literally dragging me to the car. As we were riding, I heard her in the phone steady screaming **"WHERE Y'ALL AT???!!! WHERE Y'ALL AT???!!!"** My mama was swerving through the streets, losing her mind as she was getting lost in a neighborhood that she was all too familiar with. We ended up on Caldwell and Tamarind, where we found six of my brothers homeboys. His body had been found in some heavy grass. Niggas wasn't calling the laws just yet. They were doing their own hood investigation. Whoever did this to my brother had a serious personal vendetta against him. Through all the bullet holes, I saw that his wife beater was a stained yellow. The nigga, or niggas who did this had pissed on my brothers dead corpse, and that was the ultimate disrespect. The bangers calmed my mom down as best as they could, as I could now hear the sirens of the police coming up.

"C'mon Scooby. You don't need to see this shit." It was Rambo, one of my brother's closest friends. He pulled me away from the scene and took me to his house down some ways. My mama didn't even pick me up that night. She left me at Rambo's house, most likely so I wouldn't see her suffer. It was a day that changed my life. I hated the Fourth of July from that point on. I already didn't like it because I know my people weren't free on that day they signed the Declaration. Now, I had another reason for it leaving a terrible taste in my mouth.

I never liked being called Scooby after that day. Scooby was Carl's lil brother and everytime that someone called me that name, it reminded me of my big bro. The G's and everyone else in the neighborhood continued to call me Scooby. However, when I arrived at college, I just wanted to be Kevin. The only person who knew the story was Ty. He respected that and never called me Scooby since the day it happened. I got up and cracked his room door open. He was passed out sleep. He wasn't naked so that was a good thing. His laptop was still open, at the main page of Pornhub and he looked like he had one helluva beat session. I closed his laptop, but not before sneaking a peek my damn self. He had one of my favorite females on the screen, so I know he had himself a fabulous time. I walked outside, taking in the Sunday afternoon air. The police by now were long gone, but there was still caution tape around the scene. A few detectives or whoever they were still hung around, trying to gather evidence. I proceeded to head back inside and fix me a bowl of peanut butter crunch. Luckily, I got the last of the milk, because with how Ty ate cereal, it was surprising that there was any milk ever left in the house. I just chilled out, ate and conversed with my mama on the phone. She had moved out of Compton right after I had graduated and was now staying in Fontana. Trust, it was a major upgrade from The Hub. As the day wore on and turned into evening, the sleeping giant finally came out of his room.

"Sup fool?," I said.

"Man bruh. Why you let me sleep so long?"

"Look here man. I peeked in ya room and saw you in shorts, sprawled out all over the bed. Now, I don't know how good shorty sucked a dick or took a facial, but she must've done something immaculate. Don't no nigga bust a nut like that and sleep for half the day. Not even the baddest chick can do that."

"Shit man," he said, as he over exaggerated a stretch. "It be like that sometimes. I'll put some clothes on and go get some more milk. Laws should be gone by now." Ty put his clothes on and did what he said he was gonna do. I knew the laws were gone and everything was clear because it had been ten minutes and he wasn't back in here. I stayed chillin, watching 60 minutes. 20 minutes later, he was back in the house.

"Damn my dude. You said you were going to buy milk. Not feed the whole country."

"Well shit we gotta eat man. I was at the store so I said fuck it." I got up to help him with the groceries.

"No ramen, no polishes, none of that huh?"

"Look man. I cook. That's what I do. That's what you need to have me teach you how to do. I'm tellin' you man. That shit ain't gone be cool when you a grown ass man living with a woman and you can't even boil water. Trust me nigga. It's cool now cause you in college. This will be the last time you can fuck a bitch in a bunk bed and give her some shrimp flavored joints, and be good. But one day, we won't be young no more man. Trust me, let me teach you."

"Naw, I'm good. Too much work bruh."

"Have it yo' way my dude, but I'm bout to make some chicken marsala for tomorrow."

"What the hell is chicken marsala?," I asked him.

"That's exactly why you need to learn how to cook my dude."

School the next week was about as boring as going to a San Diego Padres game. My classes seemed to drag on as if they would never end. The good thing was that with the course load that I was taking on, I was slated to graduate a full year early. It was challenging and taxing at times, but it was something that I felt would be worth it in the long run. While my friends would be spending another year in school, I could be ahead of the game, already working in the field of my choosing. The good thing about it was that this was a short week, as Thanksgiving was Thursday night. I had plans on heading out to Fontana to chill with my mom and spend some quality time with her. I got back in the house late that night around six. Walking in, I just looked around the kitchen and said what the hell to myself. That's when I saw Ty coming out of the bathroom.

"Sup nigga. Shit a nigga coming out feeling 'bout five pounds lighter."

"What's all this man?"

"Oh all this? Man this Thanksgiving dinner. I thought you knew." "But I ain't staying here. I'm eating at my mom's house. I thought you were rolling with me?"

"You never asked me bruh and you know you didn't."

"Well I would've assumed that you would wanna roll, seeing how it's my mom and that we only got one car."

"Man, what I need the car for this weekend? I got food. The barbershop three blocks down. If I need to go somewhere, I got them. Enjoy the time with ya mom's man."

"What you cooking anyway?"

"Man the question is what don't I got cooking? Bruh, I got chitlins." And that's where I stopped him. "Hold the fuck up man. Hold, the fuck, up. Know you do not got chitlins cooking in here."

"Umm...ain't that what the fuck I just said? I coulda cleaned 'em in here, but that's what Ellick mama for."

"Who the hell is Ellick?"

"One of my regulars at the shop. His mama come in every now and then, bringing us some peach cobbler. So I asked her could she clean me thirty pounds. She said $45 dollars and I said you got a deal." I still couldn't believe that this brother was in here making chitlins. "Well, enough chitlin talk. What else you making?"

"Well, the macaroni already finished. The dressing in the oven. It's greens on the stove. The ham beans on the stove. The giblet gravy will be ready here pretty soon."

"Man what the hell are ham beans?"

"See, see. I should kick yo' ass man. All them brains and don't even know what ham beans are."

"Who you got coming over?"

"Don't matter. Niggas from the shop gotta eat. I gotta eat. Might get a breezy from ya school over here so who knows. I cook for the block nigga." I shook my head and walked into the living room, watching this dude go to work in the kitchen while Atomic Dog was playing on his beats speaker.

"A man can you turn that down?" He didn't hear me as he continued on dancing and stirring whatever he had in the pot. "TY!!!"

"WHAT NIGGA!!!"

"TURN THAT SHIT DOWN!!!" He turned around dancing, flippin' me the bird and lowered the volume a bit. I cut on the TV and ended up flippin' through the channels, finding nothing. I don't know why, but I was somewhat upset with him. Like, he really wasn't gone head to my mama house. It wasn't like he didn't know her or that she didn't like him. Hell, we came up together on the same blocks. I don't know. Maybe I was trippin', but the shit was mind boggling to me. Thanksgiving morning rolled around and I started off my day early. When I say early, I'm talking six in the morning. I was packing because I was gonna stay with my mama for the whole weekend. Ty was up, but I hadn't said anything to him. He was warming everything up from last night, drinkin on an A&W while reading a book. Time continued to pass and we still weren't speaking. As I finished up packing and prepared to load my car, I spoke.

"What you reading man?"

"The New Jim Crow."

"What's special about that?"

"Nigga I told you that the most valuable education is one that you will not find in a textbook."

"Aight. Whatever nigga. I'm out. Enjoy yourself." Ty chucked up the deuce to me and then took a drink of his A&W. I shook my head and bounced out to my car. The trip to my mama house wasn't far, seeing that it was a simple trip up the 91 to the 15. Fontana was beautiful to say the least. It had its moments, but overall, it was a very decent place to raise a family. It felt good to be out of the L.A. area and in the Inland Empire. Out here, it felt like you could breathe good air and just relax without having to worry about a million folks crowding your every move. I got there, stopping at the gas station off of Baseline for some pork skins. The shits were like crack to me. Seven minutes later I was pulling up in front of my mama house on Dodge Court, happy to be free for the next few days. I didn't even get my things out. I was gonna sleep before anything. Walking up, I didn't even get the chance to knock on the door, as she came out and greeted me halfway up the walkway.

"Hey my son." She was gentle in her words, but her embrace damn near took all of the air out of my lungs.

"Mom, can you let me go?" She loosened her grip.

"Let you go? Boy I used to hold your ass to sleep for hours and now you want me to let you go. Whats her name?" I started laughing.

"No one mama."

"Mmmhmmm," she said. "I bet she can hold you and do a lot more things to you and you won't complain at all. Where ya stuff?"

"It's in the car. I'll get it later. I just wanna take a shower and go to sleep."

"Well I don't see how you gone shower without a clean pair of draws to put on." She said that as she walked back into the house. Damn, she was right. I went back to the car and lugged that heavy duffle bag out, and into the house.

"MOM WHAT YOU COOK???!!!"

"I got some grits on the stove right now if you hungry." That was good with me. I just needed something in my belly besides pork skins. I put my bag in the upstairs room and went back down to the kitchen where my mom was already at the kitchen table eating.

"You got bacon too?," I asked her.

"It's on the stove under the napkin," she replied with her mouth full. I grabbed a plate and loaded up on the bacon.

"You ain't gone eat no grits?"

"I'm gone get some mom. I'm just putting 'em on a separate plate."

"Well just know that you washing dishes."

"I got it mom. Don't worry." I fixed my plate of grits and sat at the table with her.

"You don't want no sugar baby?"

"Ty said people who put sugar on their grits are bred from the devil." She dropped her fork at that point.

"Now what that boy know about cooking or some grits?"

"Actually, ma, he knows a lot. He cooked chitlins, greens, dressing, macaroni and a few more things last night for the holiday."

"And you didn't invite me over?"

"I mean, I figured you wanted to spend it with me out here. Not in an off campus apartment."

"Hell I done cooked for you for 18 years. I would've loved to sit back and watch my son cook me a good dinner."

"That's the thing mama. I can't cook. Ty doing all this

extraordinary shit. Oops, I'm sorry." She just stared a hole through me, chewing her bacon in the progress.

"Now I done watched you and Ty since yall were in Pampers. That boy still cutting hair I know. But you seem a lil off about him. What's going on between yall two?" I started playing with my food like a lil kid because that was the one question that I wanted to avoid. "Kevin West. Answer me."

"I'm sorry mama. I just feel like we going on two separate life paths. Like, that's my dude. Darn near like my brother. I figured we could ride this thing out together for years. Lately he been talking about leaving California and going to the boonies to do something. I don't know."

"So what's wrong with that?"

"Nothing, but why discuss this so early? I mean, we only 20. We shouldn't be thinking about far fetched life plans at this age."

"Alright," as she wiped her hands after scraping the plate. "Baby lemme tell you something. Me and your daddy split up when you were very young. He went out to Texas and you barely got a call. People grow apart sometimes and that's just life. In all instances, it's not bad. You left Compton for Carson. I left Compton for Fontana. And truth be told, I should've left a long time ago. However, I didn't because you had become so entrenched in Compton that I didn't wanna cause a traumatic experience and separate you for something that you may not have gotten accustomed to. So yeah, it's my fault that we stayed in that environment for so long and I apologize. But, we here now. You can't expect everyone to stay on the same path you on forever. Now, you in school. He cut hair. He has a profession. Been had one since he was almost 12 years old, when he was cutting your cousin "Boonie" hair in the backyard of his house on Raymond. It come and goes babe. Time and people. You'll be okay. Y'all just make sure to always have each others backs no matter what. Now, I'm not gone tell you what to do or how to react to the situation. Just don't do anything irrational that you gone regret for a lifetime. I love you and I'm going upstairs to take a nap before all these people invade my house like some crazy numnuts." She gave me a kiss on the forehead and told me to clean the dishes as she headed upstairs. I sat in the kitchen and didn't eat anything else. I just pondered on the words that she had told me. Life was starting to come around full circle and I had to get on its plan before it left me in the dark. But, one thing I needed to know. **"MA!!!"**

"WHAT!!!"

"WHO COMING OVER???!!!"

"BUNCH OF FAMILY!!!"

"Sup man?," Ty said, answering his phone.

"Man it's a lot of noise in the back man. Who all you got over there?"

"Shit Spoon and all the niggas from the shop. Told you man that someone would be here to eat all this food. We gucci over here my nigga. How you and ya moms?"

"Everything is everything bruh. Few of the family starting to trickle in, so we'll see."

"Aight bruh well tell ya moms I said hi and enjoy ya day. I'll see you back here Sunday."

"Aight boy."

"Fosho. Gone." He hung up the phone on his end and I headed back downstairs to the family room where I saw a bunch of my cousins that I hadn't seen in a long time. Moms didn't make anything out of the ordinary. Hell, for the most part, everyone's menu on Thanksgiving was pretty much the same. The only person whose menu was probably different was my Auntie Robin's from Fort Worth. Shit one Thanksgiving she bought five frozen pizzas and cooked those thangs up. That was our Thanksgiving meal. She was from an area in Fort Worth called "Stop 6." I didn't know what in the hell Stop 6 meant, but from the one time that I visited down there, I could tell you that the shit was hood. As I helped my mama set the table, the doorbell rang.

"Baby can you get that?"

"Sure thing mama." I opened up the door.

"HEY YOU!!!" It was my Auntie Robin.

"I ain't know you were coming through this year Auntie."

"Boy yeah," as she walked in the house flamboyant as ever. "I had to get out of Texas this holiday. Both the boys in college and the babygirl doing her own thang. I left ya uncle down there and needed some me time. Now, where my sister." My auntie actually made me smile with her shenanigans. It was good to see how family could brighten up your day with a lively personality. Eventually, we all sat at the table and enjoyed a hearty Thanksgiving meal. Catching up was good indeed and seeing my mom in a great place was more than refreshing. It wasn't always like this, but like she told me before, all that matters is now. Around 9:30, everyone started to file out and head home, and I helped mama in the kitchen with the dishes. We laughed as we talked about school and all my freshman year adventures that had occurred while I was there. Being a sophomore, there was a lot of experience that I had under my belt. That first year of college was a hectic one. Not knowing where I was going and trying to get used to familiar faces was a task in itself. I thought about joining a fraternity, but I didn't wanna roll with a large crowd of people just to say that I was a part of something. Also, I wasn't anti black, but it just kind of rubbed me the wrong way how brothers could pledge Greek when Greeks were the ones that fucked up Africa. In short, I just didn't wanna be associated with one specific group.

I even met a few beautiful ladies in my time there. A few of us had some conversations, but that was it. All my action had occurred outside of the campus. If dating in college was anything like dating in high school, then I didn't want it. High school was full of drama with females, and college was a bigger version of that. "When you heading to bed?" That was my mama, creeping down the stairs while I was watching television in the living room way past midnight. "I dunno mama. I'm nowhere near sleepy. Just gone watch these movies until I doze off."

"Ok. Well," as she let out the yawn of yawns. "I'm headed back upstairs to knock out. Goodnight baby."

"Goodnight mama." It felt good on this couch. I honestly didn't know what movie was on TV, but I could careless because I was comfortable. It was almost one in the morning and I still had energy. I started messing with my phone and logged into the book. Scrolling through my timeline, I saw Ty had posted a pic of everyone in the crib, drinking and getting full off of nasty ass chitlins. He had posted it about an hour ago, so I hit the nigga up to see how everything went. *"What's good. Look like yall had a ball over there,"* I wrote in his inbox. I got no response. I figured he had went to sleep, so I didn't trip. I scrolled through and through until my eyes finally got tired of looking at memes and ratchet statuses. I turned off the television and went to sleep. Arising the next morning at eight o'clock on the dot, I got up and put the Colgate to my mouth. There was nothing worst than walking around with bad breath. In the morning time, that breath could melt steel. At least mines could. I threw on a college hoodie out of my duffle bag and proceeded to leave the house to take a nice morning jog around my mama's neighborhood. It was calm and serene over here. No worries. This wasn't like jogging in Compton. Hell I did most of my running back in high school when I was running the ball for Compton High. We weren't anything special, but for the kids on that team, it definitely gave us an escape from the day to day struggles that we were all going through.

I continued on throughout the Heritage Village neighborhood for what seemed like forever. I ran all the way through the heart of the neighborhood, to Foothill and back to my mama's house. In the end, I had jogged for well over an hour and I was in need of some R&R. I walked back in the house and heated up some leftover food from yesterday's dinner. Mama was still sleep and didn't hear a peep when I came into the house. I figured I'd keep quiet and not disturb her, seeing how she probably needed her rest from cooking that big meal yesterday. The microwave went off and I sat at the table, eating my meal in silence. I felt good. It felt like it was just me and the world at this point. Out of the blue, my phone rang. I saw the 714 number, but I didn't recognize it, so I didn't even bother answering it. I continued on with my meal, until the number popped up again and my phone went off.

"Hello."

"A nigga. You forgot bout a nigga?"

"Who this?"

"Fruit Town Breezy nigga."

"Ahh shit waddup man."

"Nothing much. A, you holla'd at my relly Ty? I keep

calling this nigga but can't get a hold of him."

"Naw not since last night. I know the nigga at the house cause he cooked up a big dinner and had the whole barbershop over there. I'm at my mama house though in Fontana." We chopped it up for another ten minutes and I told him that I would get at him if I got in contact with his fam bam. I hung up, putting my dish in the sink, thinking about what I was about to get into this Friday.

"What you doing boy?" I shot around with my heart beating at 155 miles per hour. My mama had scared the living daylights out of me. "Man ma. You can't be doing that to me. You nearly gave me a heart attack."

"Now you know how I felt every time you left out of the house and someone called my phone. It's the same feeling. You'll never understand until you become a parent."

"So you wanna hang out today mama?"

"What you wanna do? I see you getting a lil pudge on you." I looked down at my stomach as my mama began to laugh. I grabbed my stomach and noticed that I was getting a chubby pocket down there. "C'mon mama. It ain't that bad." She laughed some more. "You wanna come as a guest with me to 24 hour?"

"Very funny. But yeah, I'll go."

"Ok. Let me shower and you do whatever you gotta do."

"Wait, wait mama. Why you taking a shower before we go to the gym? You bout to get sweaty and funky anyway." She gave me that look like she wanted to slap the taste out of my mouth. "Boy, I oughta slap you silly. I don't give a good *** damn. I ain't walking into no gym, no building of any sorts funky. Working out ain't an excuse to be funky to death. I am not trying to raise my arms and make people collapse. Boy I hope like hell you showering before school."

"I do mama."

"Mmmhmmm." I went upstairs to my room to get changed while my mama went to go take her shower. While changing, I texted Ty again. *"Yo fam? Whats poppin. How was last night?"* I got dressed and after five minutes, I still got no response from him. Why was this nigga ignoring me? I knew Ty and he was usually an early riser unless he deliberately said he was sleeping in.

"Your cousin Breezy hit me up last night. He trying to get up with you." Again, I waited and after five minutes, I still didn't get a response. Yeah, this dude was on something else. I just had to find out what it was. I sat there and started going through my phone, looking at random pics that I had stored in there, waiting for my mama to get dressed so we could roll.

"I'm ready." I looked up to see my mama standing in the doorway.

"Ma. Ma. You gotta take that off and put some clothes on."

"Boy what you talking about? These are clothes."

"Ma. You don't need to be wearing no yoga pants."

"Do you say that to those college girls you up there with?"

"Ma, that ain't the point."

"You right, cause the point is this. I pushed you out. I run me. The son don't run me. I know you don't want anyone looking at your mama, but I'm still young in my life and hell. If I meet a man in the gym, so be it. But don't knock me because I look good. Now C'mon." I shook my head and just stood there. My mama had literally just punked me. Who was I kidding? My mama was a knockout. Seeing pictures of her when I was younger, I see why my daddy had got her pregnant. But still, no man wants to live with knowing that many men wanna give it to they mama.

"BOY IS YOU COMING!!!"

"HERE I COME!!!" Man, I couldn't believe that I was about to do this. I just hoped that I didn't have to choke any man out while I was in the gym. We rolled out and headed towards the gym. The day was destined to be a good one. I had my crazy and goofy mama with me. Hell, we were somewhere where we could drive with the windows down and not worry about getting shot. This shit was real and the shit was fun. I could only wonder how much more fun that this weekend would have to offer.

2 TRUST THE PROCESS

"Wooo shit," I whispered to myself. I was feeling good than a muthfucka. I looked over to my left and seen that phat booty thang still laying next to me, passed out. I had been trying to get in Daria's draws since the day she had walked into the barber shop to get her three year old's hair cut. She wasn't no easy win, however. I was surprised that she came over with Spoon, Brody and the rest of the crew.

"Oh this is nice. Who cooked all of this?" I was smiling when she asked me that.

"Well why you asking beautiful? You see whose place this is."

"Beautiful?" That's when I know I had her.

"Of course. Did you want me to call you the other B word?"

"Boy, you trying too hard."

"Now why is it a brother is always trying too hard when he gives a woman a compliment? That tells me that you are used to dog ass dudes who grab ya arm in the club, shout out the window for you and other ignorant shit like that. I ain't like that, but I can't change what you are accustomed too unless you are willing to make that change." She looked at me dumbfounded, while I turned back around and stirred the macaroni on the stove to loosen it up.

"I think you got her panties wet nigga," Brody whispered in my ear, as he continued to make himself a plate. There were seven people in here and this was turning into a bomb Thanksgiving. See my Big Mama had taught me how to cook. Big Mama Cora Lee. She grew up in Hattiesburg, Mississippi, and moved out to California at the tender age of 19. She stayed over in Athens Park. I used to hate going over there as a shorty. I ain't fuck around over there. The most I did was stay in the house and play in the backyard with a few of my cousins. Before I could even think about playing outside or any video game of any sports, she always made me cook something. Now truthfully, I hated this shit with a passion. However, she didn't let up. She kept her foot on my neck when it came to cooking in the kitchen. "Boyyyy," as she always drug on the last syllable of the word. "Learn how to thrown down in the kitchen now. Because you gone mess around and grow up. If you end up with a woman who can't cook, you gone starve. And from what NaNa seeing, yo' generation of women ain't nothin but booty shakers and hoochies. Plus, baby. Women love a man who can cook. It means that they don't gotta give two hoots about being in the kitchen, slaving over a hot stove."

Ahh the stories of my grandmother. I prepared me a plate and went over into the living room, joining the rest of the crew who was watching the 32 inch with me. As we smacked on this good ass food and watched marathon episodes of Martin, out of the corner of my eye, I could see Daria kind of side eying me. Inside of my head, I simply laughed. I wanted to run my hand across my cornrows, but I didn't wanna come off as too cocky.

"A, a relly. This nigga bout to come out and sing with Jodeci," Brody yelled out. As we started rollin to the antics of Martin Lawrence, Spoon suddenly started to sing his rendition.

"Spoon, shut yo ass up," I told him.

"Boy please. You mad cause you can't sing like this."

"Nigga if that's singing, then Lebron James ain't a flopper." The crew cracked up.

"Well since you so good," Brody said as he cut the TV off. "Sing to Daria." Suddenly, you heard the roaches that were four houses away crawling around. I got put on the spot. My mans didn't have to do that, but I understood what he was trying to do. "My apologies, but I only sing at private shows for women." I then gave her that look and went back into smashing some of these turkey necks that I had smothered in gravy.

"So you singing or what?," she asked me.

"Ohh nigga she waiting," Dominique blurted out.

"I'm sorry baby. I don't do requests."

"You scared?"

"Not really, but what's singing to you gone do for me? I mean, you cute and all, but you ain't nothing special to ponder on." I heard Spoon cough as he damn near choked on some chitlins. I was staring at her and she was staring right back at me. Calmly, she laid the plate of food she had on my living room table and walked out the front door.

"Nigga what is your problem man?," Spoon asked me.

"What man? I ain't got no problem. I just ain't gassin no female head up. Especially if I ain't lying with her every night."

"Man you might've fucked it up for a lot of niggas with that one. Yo, man where the remote? Cut this TV back on." As Martin was back on the tube and everything was sort of back to normal, my phone began to ring. It was Kev.

"Sup man?"

"Man it's a lot of noise in the back man. Who all you got over there?," he asked me.

"Shit Spoon and all the niggas from the shop. Told you man that someone would be here to eat all this food. We gucci over here. How you and ya moms?"

"Everything is everything bruh. Few of the family starting to trickle in, so we'll see."

"Aight bruh, well tell ya moms I said hi and enjoy ya day. I'll see you back here Sunday."

"Fosho. Gone." Fam bam sounded a lil down, but it was what it was. At least he still had a mama here on earth to enjoy. Our night over here continued with laughing at Martin until it was time to slam some bones.

"BIG SIX TO THE BOARD!!!," Brody called out. Dominique dropped it and you know what time it was.

"Get that paper my nigga," I told him. I slammed six three on the table.

"THREE SWITCHES AND BITCHES!!!"

"Man fuck that big six. Going behind that hoe. It ain't my

41

guts," Brody said as he laid six deuce.

"Fuck it. I'll open the pussy up." **SMACK!!!**

"PUT MY NAME ON THAT PAPER NIGGA!!!," my nigga Sharif said, who was Brody's cousin.

"Well shit. Follow that cab cause it got my dope in it." **SMACK!!!** Brody followed behind and got the same ten with six blank. Now everyone was on paper and this shit continued on for the next few hours. See, for y'all that don't understand bones, it worse than spades. In spades, you can fuck over your partner playing out of turn or reneging. When it came to bones, you had to read the board, know when or when not to take money, play defense and most importantly, talk shit. The talking shit aspect of bones was just as important as matching colors. And shit, real G's didn't play with colored dominos if they could help it. That's what amateurs did, so they could know that they were matching. Either they were black and white, or one solid color and white.

In our case, we kept it black and white. Two of the niggas were ex Crips. One was an Ex blood. We didn't wanna cause tension on the table, so we kept it kosher. Plus, it was a reason Crispy Cutz was a diamond in the rough. Everyone who worked in there, or that was associated in some form of way, including the teen kids who would rotate cleaning the shop and running errands for us, they were from some pretty fucked up homes. So in order to counteract the streets, the shop gave them a chance to enhance at life. Not to mention, learn how to cut some hair in their spare time so that they could make some money when they got a lil older and become proficient at what they were doing. We slapped these bones for over six straight hours, only taking breaks to piss and eat some more. By the time I looked up, it was 12:30.

"Aight boy. You gone be in the shop tomorrow?," Dominique asked me.

"I dunno man. Depends on how I feel. I know no one hit me up bout a cut on the celly today. I'll let you know though."

"Aight bruh." I dapped Nique and the others up as they proceeded to exit my place and go on about their own business. I was pooped. Luckily, during one of the breaks we took, I had managed to clean up the kitchen at what seemed like warp speed, so I could get back to playing bones.

"**WOO SHIT!!!**," I let out, as I plopped down on the couch. My phone was on the arm of the couch, but I was too lazy to reach over and get it. The Martin episodes were going off at two in the morning, so I figured that I would let them put me to sleep. I got up to go brush my teeth to clear all of the chitlin smell I had in my mouth out. **BOOM! BOOM! BOOM!** There were three knocks at my door. It had been a good 20 minutes since all those niggas had left. I just figured one of them had forgot something. I rinsed my mouth out. "**COMING!!!**," I yelled out. On the way to the door, I saw that Dominique had left his head wrap. I knew how serious he was about his dreads being tied up, so I just knew it was him. I opened the door to see Daria. She was in some sweats and a wife beater.

"Daria. Whats up?"

"Are you just gonna leave me at the door or are you gonna let me come in?" I stepped away from the door and she proceeded to walk in. She shut the door and proceeded to stop where the kitchen met the living room.

"Did you mean it when you said I wasn't anything special?" Now, the right thing to do in this situation was to lie for a chance at the draws. But, being me, I was gone tell her the truth just like I had earlier in the night.

"Well, you asked was I just gone leave you at the door and I didn't. I told you that you were beautiful and you took it as a shock. I told you that you weren't anything special to ponder on. But then again, you ain't my woman, so why would I give you special treatment?" She bit her lip, shaking her head up and down.

"Well, if it's one thing I can appreciate about a man, it's one that's honest." Right then, she planted those DSL's on me and I happily obliged to this five foot seven, caramel piece of quality work. We made it back to the bedroom and it was all she wrote.

"Damn," I whispered. "I ain't even put on a rubber and I nutted all in her." Yeah, my pullout game was weak, but she sure as hell had some good kuda snap. I slowly got up, not wanting to wake her up. I went out to the living room, swangin, grabbing my cell phone. "What's good? Look like y'all had a ball over there."

"Yo fam. Whats poppin. How was last night?" I missed two inbox messages from Kev on my messenger, but he'd be aight. It was too much fun going on over here for me to worry about anything or any situation last night.

"Good morning." I turned my head to see Daria in her naked bliss standing by the door, looking like she wanted to go for a round two. I smiled at her.

"Commere," I told her. She walked over to me and sat next to a brother on the couch. She put both legs on the couch and just stared in my eyes. "What?," I asked her as I was chuckling.

"You know. They say never underestimate anyone. I definitely did that with you."

"You mean with what I did in the bedroom?"

"No, no baby. What you did with my mind. You know I left your house last night pissed the hell off like this nigga had the nerve to say what he said. But as I got to the crib, I started to think. Every other man, including my baby's father had always sugar coated shit. And I think that's the part of a woman that is fucked up. We say that we always want the truth. Always want us a nigga who keeps it 100 with us. But when a man does tell us the truth, we really can't take it. Our emotional balance ain't like that. What we say to do, we sometimes don't want y'all to do. And you did something no man had done to me as long as I can remember. And that was tell the truth."

"Well shit. That's just how I was feeling. It wasn't no reverse psychology type shit."

"I know it wasn't. That's why I drove back over to your crib. It was like ten or something. I drove pass, but I still saw Spoon and Brody car outside, so I said naw, I ain't going back in there with them niggas. So I actually went up the street to get something to eat. I came back and I parked across the street from your place and waited for over an hour. I was gonna come back and see had you felt the same way. Shit to be honest, I knew I wanted to give you the draws the minute I saw that you cooked. Speaking of eating, I'm hungry."

"It's a gang of leftovers in there baby. I'm good for the

next few days."

"Well let's eat." This shit was crazy. Not only did I get to dig into this sexy piece of work, but we were now eating soul food plates, butt naked at my kitchen table, laughing and joking about random ass things. We didn't even go back to having another session. I think the coolest shit about all of this was that she got to see a side of a man that she actually wanted to see, but never thought she would encounter. After our bellies were full, she showered up and left me to be. Of course I got her number, and I would be seeing more of Daria Thomas at a later date and time.

After she bounced, I cut on the music and thoroughly enjoyed myself. A good hot shower and prancing around my crib in my draws were the things made of legends. I peeped my phone and saw that I had another missed notification. Kev had hit me about my fam bam Breezy from Fruit Town. I hadn't hit fam bam up in a minute. I was gonna call him later, because I was gonna head into the shop and see if I could get some heads. Not to mention that I had to see when Serrita was gonna be available to rebraid my hair again. Had to keep the rows on point like Kawhi. I swear it seemed like no matter how much he would sweat, that nigga hair wouldn't be frizzy or anything. I needed to get my shit like that.

I got dressed in some blue jeans and a R.I.P. shirt from a while back, in memory of my fam bam Dre. I strolled with confidence this Friday afternoon. My nuts were empty, my belly was full and I was living my passion in life. I stopped at the store on the way there and picked me up some Frosted Flakes, a small plastic bowl and a gallon of almond milk, cause I ain't fuck with the parasite infested shit from cow's titties. I had to keep a stock at the shop, cause I needed my fix.

"Aaah shit man. Thought I wouldn't see you today," said Brody as I walked in.

"Yeah man. Everything good. Where the others at?"

"Shit I dunno. Maybe they ain't coming in today. I know I couldn't pass up no money. But it is slow today." He wasn't lying. Wasn't no one in the barbershop but us two and the head that he had in his chair. I sat in my chair and poured me a bowl, looking at the TV, chillin. "Man you look like you refreshed as hell. You must've needed last night."

"Yeah man. Last night ended on point." That's when he shut his clippers off. He stared at me and I looked back at him, trying not to laugh while having a mouthful of Frosted's.

"Nigga," as he shook his clippers. "Nigga you fucked didn't you?" I shrugged my shoulders. **"I'LL BE DAMNED NIGGA!!!,"** he yelled, while his customer joined in on the laughter. "She came back?"

"Damn shole did."

"Boy, boy, boy. You a slick rascal. I'll tell you that much."

"Yeah man. I wasn't expecting it. But she came over like 20 minutes after y'all niggas left. Then she came over and over. Then I nutted in her."

"Damn nigga. You was supposed to fuck. Not make love to the broad."

"Man I did fuck. Shit that pussy was so good though I said fuck it. My pull out game was non existent. You know when you used to play GoldenEye and Oddjob couldn't get shot, so you just said fuck it? That's basically what I did."

"Man," Brody said laughing. "I ain't fucking with you man."

"But I am." We both looked at the door to see this gentleman in a suit who had said that.

"Hi. Are you Wayne Russell?"

"Who wanna know?," I responded.

"Me. I assume you him. So lemme introduce myself. Im Eric Hans, master Barber from the Midwest." He stuck his hand out, but I didn't budge. I kept on eating my cereal.

"Continue on my nigga," I told him.

"Well, if you don't wanna shake my hand, then why continue?"

"Hold on blood," Brody said.

"Naw, I got this fam," holding my hand up in the air to Brody. "Nigga where you even from? Cause you roll up in here like you own the joint. You could be a fed. A set up. A payback. Nigga what do you want? I don't know what you Midwest niggas accustomed too, but out here, you'll get fucked up and not even thought twice about."

"Man look. I came out here because they say you one of the best. Now, I flew all the way from Indiana to make you an offer."

"Man what the fuck is there in Indiana? Yo, ain't y'all the niggas who produced Michael? Cause besides him, I ain't heard shit about anything else coming out of Indiana."

"Fly out. The best barbers in the land gonna go to some of the most random places on earth and make things happen. Gone take this shit to another level. Now, you can stay and continue doing what you doing. And by the way, it doesn't look bad at all. Ya man got ol' boy in the chair looking right and I assume the other guys are just as legit. But yo' name came up. So I'm gone leave my card on the ledge over here. Holla at me by Sunday if you want the opportunity. Y'all gentlemen be easy." He walked out and I sat there eating my cereal.

"Blood I swear I was gone knock his ass out," Brody said. "It's all good man."

"I don't trust that fam. You better be careful looking at that opportunity."

"Shit I ain't paying attention to that dude man."

"Now I said be careful looking at that opportunity. Not blow it off. Shit may be legit. Shit may not be. You ain't gone know 'til you hit that line."

"Yeah, but, something about that dude don't seem right. And again. Why would a nigga from Indiana fly all the way out here for me? Like really? Think about that shit my dude."

"Well, think about this. Is half the niggas in California from this muthafucka?" And that's where he got me. Fam bam was right. This state was overrun with out of staters who came out here and made a new life for themselves. Out here, this where the people came to challenge themselves amongst the best in the world. So why wouldn't ol' boy want to fly out West to get some of the best? I rose up and grabbed his card off of the ledge. I looked at his name and number for what seemed like 40 times. I could tell no one was gonna be in today. Ol' boy was now out of the chair and Brody was just sitting in his chair, playing on his phone. "A man, I'm a head off to the crib."

"Be easy my nigga." I walked on out, thinking about this proposal all the way to the crib. Once I got in, I did the typical thing and tried to decide what time I was gonna call him to arrange this. I told myself five o'clock. Then, I told myself as soon as possible out of fear that he may find another barber. I couldn't take that chance. I plopped on my couch and hit up this 219 number. "Hello," he answered. "When do we start?"

"Haha. I'm glad you accepted. A, sorry about earlier if I came off too brash, but I wouldn't fly out here if I didn't think you couldn't add any prosperity to the team. Send me your e-mail and I'll send you everything you need. My private plane will take off from LAX Sunday afternoon and land at Chicago O'Hare later that evening. The team is made up of four of us. Five if you come on board. Myself, and one from each side of the map. We gone go around the world, cutting hair in some of the most remote places. I started this about four years ago and it took off from a Midwest classic to a worldwide thing that has caused me and everyone involved to prosper. I know your cousin Breezy. I sliced him up one time when he was out in Chicago. We've stayed in touch ever since and he was the plug."

Me and him continued our conversation for the next hour, rapping about my upbringing and how I got started in cutting hair. I was excited. This is what I wanted in life. To get outside of L.A. and see some different shit. I was excited about going to the Chi. Deep down, however, I was hoping to go to the places that people did not hear of often so that I could make a name for myself. It was still early and it was time to celebrate. Wasn't going to be any clubbing with me, however. It was simple. It was Friday night, I had a pot full of chitlins and some beer in the fridge. Yeah, I know I was 20, but what 20 year old you know didn't have access to alcohol, especially in California. I grabbed me a cold one and heated up my pig guts until they were good and boiling. I slapped 'em in a bowl and flooded them with some Louisiana. I kicked my feet up, in my own world and then my phone buzzed.

"Man nigga. You ignoring ya boy or what?" It was Kev. I swear he acted like a broad sometimes. Damn near borderline gay.

"Man I'm chillin. Headed to Chicago Sunday for a barber gig I pulled today."

"Oh. Great." Man what was this dudes problem? I really couldn't fathom it. I mean, he just couldn't be happy for a nigga. Who is upset around Thanksgiving? You're surrounded by people you love. You got unlimited amounts of food at your disposal. Man, shit was gravy. I just didn't get my dude sometimes. He pretended like separation was a bad thing. Truthfully, that's why I think he took the scholarship to Dominguez Hills and not to one of the many schools on the East Coast that were vying for his services. I told bruh when we were in high school that he needs to venture away from California to see some shit. You ain't gonna make anything out of yourself being around the same people your whole damn life. In order to become comfortable, you must first make it through uncomfortable situations. That's how character and fortitude is built. I dunno. My mans was on some other shit. I called off the rest of the night, and the weekend for that matter. Sunday morning, I was hitting a plane headed for Chicago.

I landed in Chicago at 3:30 p.m. Midwest time. I had never been here, so it made me more excited to get my hands into what the Chi had to offer. I wanted it all while I was here too. I had a homeboy I knew from Chicago who always talked about pizza puffs. I had never seen one and could go only by how he described them to me. So before this trip was over, I wanted me a pizza puff.

"Sir, the limo is coming." I looked at the stewardess with a dumbfounded look.

"Limo?"

"Yes sir. Eric doesn't walk anywhere. This is private. The vehicle comes to you." I could've shat gold bars at that point. I felt like I was a part of the A list club. I stepped off the plane with a light jacket on, but I should've had on something thicker. It was colder than polar bear nuts out here. 24 degrees wasn't something that I was used too. I couldn't complain too much though. It wasn't snowing, so that was a blessing in itself.

"Welcome sir." A beautiful, thick, chocolate sister opened the door for me and I literally started to feel like a king. There were black assistants grabbing my bags and putting them in the trunk. The most impressive thing that I noticed out of all of this is that everyone was black. He kept the money with his own people. When I turned around, I even noticed that I had a black pilot. Yeah, this trip was going to be great I could see. I got comfortable on the plush seating of the limo and pulled out a bottle of Moet that was in there. I grabbed a glass and poured me up some. "Aaah," I let out with the first sip. 20 years old, sipping' some Moet, and possibly on the way to bigger and better things. *"Yo' where you at?"* It was Kev texting me.

"Man you wouldn't believe me if I told you."

"Where nigga?"

"Nigga I'm in Chicago. I told you that."

"Quit lying nigga." At that point I said to myself that I gotta really show this nigga that I ain't playin when I say I'm out here. I didn't know what part of the city we were in, but I know we were still near the airport. I waited for another ten minutes until I was stuck on whatever freeway this was. I saw a billboard for the Bulls, Cubs, Sox, Bears and Blackhawks. Immediately, I raised the window down and snapped the picture on my cell phone. I immediately sent it to him and awaited his response. Three minutes later, there it came. *"Nigga. for real? You could've took a nigga."*

"You wasn't invited. Plus, it was spur of the moment."

"What's the reason?"

"Major barber move man. I'll tell you about it when I get back on Thursday."

The text stopped after that as I just stayed focused on the task at hand. I was bobbin' my head to the music bumping from 107.5 WGCI. I was really here. My wire then got hit again. "Hello?"

"I hope you enjoying your trip so far man." It was Eric.

"Oh yeah Eazy E. Chi Town is definitely hitting so far and I ain't even made it off the freeway."

"Cool man. Look, the limo gone take you downtown to the Hyatt on Wacker Drive. I hope the accommodations will be to your liking."

"Man I already know bruh."

"Cool, well look. I got a business call to make here soon, so I'll pick you up at 9 a.m. tomorrow."

"Aight."

"Gone." Now, the shit was more than legit. I arrived about 45 minutes later, feeling like Derrick Rose instead of Wayne "Ty" Russell. Valet opened up the door for me and Eric's people took care of my stuff.

"Mr. Russell, Welcome. Here's your room key. Anything you need, our staff will take care of you." I grabbed the key from the hostess, looking at her through my shades like are you serious. "So there's no check in or anything?"

"With Mr. Hans credit to our company, any guests of his are treated as if it was himself sir."

"I'll take that." I walked off with my card and took the elevator up to the top floor. Shit, I didn't even wanna leave the elevator. I had never ever been in an elevator that smelled so damn good. It was like walking into a juices and berries spot. I was hungry for some damn fruit now. I got down to my room and just basked in the experience. The minute I opened the door, I was in heaven. There were suites, and then there was THE SUITE. All I needed was Nia Long up in here and I would be cool as a fan. I toured the room. It was everything that I could ever want. Then, I noticed a letter in the middle of my bed. *"Your tab is covered. Enjoy."-Eric.* He didn't have to tell me twice. I plopped down on the bed and scanned the food menu.

"**OH HELL YEAH!!!**," I yelled out loud. I grabbed the phone, calling in my order. "Yea lemme get the chicken cordon bleu and a peanut butter milkshake. It's already taken care of by Mr. Hans."

"We know sir. We have your room number." I hung up the phone like a boss. I laid back on the bed and looked up at the ceiling, smiling, knowing that all the G's whose heads I cut would be proud of me right now. I looked out the window and saw the amazing awe of Chicago. Right now, that's exactly what I was looking at. I was seeing Chicago. Not Chiraq. It would be easy for me to say what the problem was here. Truth is, unless you from here, around the area or in the streets everyday, you really don't know what the problem was. It was the same way with L.A. The first thing all the people wanna holla are Bloods and Crips. It was deeper than that shit. The same way that it was deeper than the P. Stones, GD's, BD's and Vice Lords here. You had many underlying factors that people wanted to ignore. The closing of schools and putting rival neighborhoods in one building with each other. The lack of funding and resources to the inner city. Those are just some of the obvious. But, even knowing that, I still couldn't speak on the problems here, because I wasn't here to see the inner workings on a daily. **BOOM! BOOM!** "Room service." I jumped off the bed and damn near did the negro skip to the door. I slung it open with the quickness.

"Anxious I see we are huh?" I chuckled at that.

"Sorry. Just in a good mood."

"Well sir, I'm glad. Here's your cordon bleu and your peanut butter shake."

"Thank you." He shut the door and I proceeded back to the bed to smash on this awesome goodness. "*** Damn." Man I didn't know if this was a specialty Chicken, or a hormone infused chicken. I had never seen anything this big in my life. I grabbed the fork and knife, cutting off the first piece of this poultry monster. Upon first bite, I almost passed out and went to heaven. This ish was beyond fire. It was an extinction level event. For the next half hour, it was this and the television. Once it was done, I just sat back and relaxed, enjoying the night before probably the biggest opportunity of my life.

I woke up the next morning at seven, as the Stevie Wonder alarm on my phone seemed to blare a lot louder than it usually did. I had my outfit laid out from the night prior so that I wouldn't be rushing like a madman in the morning. I sat up on the bed, absorbing the morning light that was shining into the hotel room. I got up and stretched, scratching my nuts with that morning wood that most of us men woke up too. I made that slow bop walk to the bathroom and pissed in my leaning tower of pisa stance. You know fellas, the leaning tower. When your dick is hard, you place that one hand on the wall and lean until you are a straight shot into the toilet. I let enough water go to refill Lake Michigan if it ever went dry. I then did the morning nigga shake. You know, no hands. Just shake up and down and let ya nuts clear any additional droplets. I cracked the shower water on and did the unthinkable. I became a female for once. You know as men, we like everything cool, calm, collective and simple. A luke warm shower will do the trick on any given day of the week. However, seeing how it was chilly outside and a brother needed to feel some good warmth besides the heat that was cranked on inside of the room, I slowly adjusted the water to what I call "The Brink." You know, the brink. When you put the water teetering between hot enough and what the fuck. I made it just right so I could enjoy it while not burning my soul away. I had this young tenderoni back in my senior year of high school who wanted me to take a bath with her after an awesome session of hot loving. When I put my toe in the water, it was like my nerves talked to me. "Negro, don't you do this," they said. I should've listened, because by the time both of my ankles were in there, I could see the dead skin of 17 years all of a sudden boil off.

"C'mon," she said. As a man, I didn't wanna seem like a bitch, so I slowly eased down, grabbed both sides of the tub for balance and quickly sat down in the water. It was at that moment in life that time stopped and I literally felt what hell was like. You could've added some andouille sausage, shrimp, okra, rice and made Negro Gumbo. That's how hot it was. I enjoyed the shower as I pondered on what the events of this day would bring. Finishing up, I dried off and went back to the bedroom to get dressed. I saw that I had a missed call and a voicemail alert. *"Morning brother. Be out in front at 8:45. Limo will be there. We'll see what you're made of today."* It was Eric. That sounded more like an initiation speech instead of a welcome aboard to the team. It was only 7:36, so I took my time. I put an extra crispy starched crease in my jeans and ensured that my button up was much of the same. It wasn't too dressy, but it was casual enough to tell whoever would be watching me that I meant business. I took a snickers from the snack tray that was in the room and indulged it as my breakfast. A sugar rush was exactly what I needed to get this day going. I headed downstairs once 8:30 hit. As soon as I hit the lobby floor, I saw it. A stretch white limo, sitting out front, waiting for me. I peeled out of the doors to the awaiting valet.

"Have a good day Mr. Russell." I nodded my head down to him as I entered the limo to the sight of Eric.

"Impressive. You were early."

"As I learned a long time ago E. If you on time, you're late."

"I likes man. I likes."

"So where we going?"

"On one of the biggest stages you will ever see in your life. We'll see how good you cut."

"Who is we?"

"You'll find out?" We stared at each other for about five seconds after he said that and then his phone rang. He took the call and I just sat back, taking the ride in stride. It was a long journey, as we were stuck in this morning mayhem traffic of Chicago. A cool site that I did happen to see was The White Sox stadium that was sitting right off of the freeway. Next to it, it looked like two big ass project buildings. Yeah, this was definitely the South Side from what I could see through the windows. Niggas think Compton is hard, but Southside Chicago was fucking nuts. Hell, the whole Chicago for that matter. E was in an intense phone conversation as I saw his tone go from cool to vicious with whomever he was talking too. It was crazy how business could be. I wasn't a businessman as of yet, but to see what went into it, it was something that I indeed had to prepare for if I wanted to separate myself from everyone else.

"We're here man. Gone get out." Eric stepped out and I followed out the opposite door. The drive was over an hour due to traffic, but it seemed like merely five minutes now. "East Chicago Central. You brought me to a high school?" "Not a high school. Thee high school." I looked around and observed this monstrosity of a building.

"Follow me man. We headed towards the gym."

"The gym. Man I get to cut hair and hoop?"

"Man please. This Indiana. What y'all call hoopin' in California is baby ball out here." I stopped him right there. "Say what? Aight, now I know you trippin. First, you calling this Indiana when it clearly says East Chicago."

"I didn't stutter. This East Chicago, Indiana."

"East Chicago, Indiana? Don't you mean the East Side of Chicago?"

"Naw. I said it right. East Chicago, Indiana. EC. Harbor. Calumet. The one place you don't wanna fuck with." He gave me a stern look and proceeded to head towards the doors. Now, I was seeing a side of Eric that I hadn't saw. That was the I'm not fucking around side. I followed him inside, walking through the black tinted doors. We proceeded down a long hall, passing the auditorium along the way. We kept going until we hit the gymnasium. All of a sudden, my life shifted.

"Man, this ain't no damn high school."

"You right," Eric said. "It's not a high school. It's a mecca." I looked around. I mean this place had huge bleacher sections all the way around. I mean, really. I had never seen anything like this ever in my life. Then, I saw the barber chair in the middle of the floor.

"So who gone be there for me to slice?"

"In a minute man. Just take this place in. This my hometown. This mines. That Cardinal right there on the floor. That shit mean the world round here. See Red. That's what we say. They say this gym holds 8,296. But, I clearly remember well over ten five in here during any given night. Especially when we played Gary West Side. I hate many things in life. I hate lying ass politicians. I hate people who put ketchup on eggs. But Gary West Side? Man whenever I see anything orange and blue, I'm ready to smack the shit out of it. **LITE FIRE INTO THEY BITCH ASS!!!** I still remember back in the days. Top, top row of the upstairs bleacher section at West Side. Them punk muthafuckas won 65–63. I'll never forget that shit. Had that shit been here, with being ranked number one in the state at the time, oh we would've destroyed their bitch asses."

"Were you playing?"

"Nah. I was out of school by then, but I still supported. Man, that was a long ass night." I was just looking at this dude with one foot pointing towards the door in case he started shooting.

"I'm sorry man. I had a moment."

"All good man," I said nervously.

"But yeah, here, we live and breathe this shit. EC the richest basketball city in the state. From the undefeated state champs of EC Roosevelt and EC Washington, to the combo when they turned it into EC Central. Legends, and I mean legends, have played here and walked through these halls. Ricky Wright, Oudie Baker, Marcus Jefferson, Corey Stokes, Juda Parks. E'Twaun "Smooge" Moore and cats like that. Man, they lit this building up many, and I mean many of nights. I brought you here, with all these bleachers open. With no class in here for the next few hours. I want you to cut here and imagine over ten thousand muthafuckas in here watching you. Its an adrenaline rush. Matter fact, here comes my man now." I turned around to see a tall brother walking in through one set of double doors. Brother man was clean as a whistle. Had his slacks and sport coat on, looking like he had just jumped out of a casket. "Whats up E?"

"Whats up L.A.?" They dapped up. "A L.A., this my mans Ty right here. He'll be slicing you up today man."

"So you gone take care of me huh?," he said as we dapped up. "Yeah man. I'm gone do that. But you from L.A. though?"

"Naw man," he said chuckling. "It's my nickname."

"LA3!!!," Eric shouted out. "Its short for Lamar Atteley the third."

"This guy," Eric said, stepping in and putting his arm around him.

"He my dude from a while back. We met in Vegas where he was working at the time. Now, he staying out in Asia somewhere."

"That's cool man," I said. "What part of Asia you in?"

"Guam fam bam. Now, I'm a businessman, so I need a business type taper. I need my 360's crispy. I mean I want them shits so clean that the navy start doing deployments on the top of my dome." He handed off his coat to Eric and sat down in the chair.

"There go your clippers all plugged up and ready," Eric told me.

"Do ya thug dizzle." Shit was amazing. I was somewhere different, cutting someone of obviously high importance and proving myself.

"Oh by the way, before you start. You slice him up right, and you'll be introduced as the last member of the team that's gone travel the world in January, slicing up heads for more than just fame and glory. I'm talking major impact bruh." I looked at him as I wrapped L.A.'s neck up and put the cover over him.

"Well tell team Eric that I'll see 'em later." He cracked a smile and I got to work. I was cutting with extra precision. I loved the challenge of making someone look and feel good. This wasn't pressure to me. Pressure wasn't nothing but chewed up grass. I relished this opportunity. Me and Lamar made lil to no conversation as I performed surgery on his head, giving him the tightest taper that he would ever have in life. Shit, I was making his taper look so fresh that I was considering cutting my rows off and going with the same style cut. I continued on, thinking about how this opportunity would forever change my life. How it would get me outside of California and more importantly the country. "You want the razor fam?"

"You the barber ain't you?"

"It's yo head ain't it?" We stared at each other.

"A Eric, you got a keeper man. Yeah fam, gimme that Steve Harvey, before we knew that shit was a toupee." We all laughed at that as I got the shaving cream and put it over his edge up. As I let it sit there for a minute while putting a rag in a bucket of hot water, I looked around the gym one more time. I started to see over ten thousand people in here watching me do what I was born to do. The shit got me up to a level that I couldn't even explain. I wiped the cream off and let that rag soak on his head for a good minute. Then, I proceeded to give him the crispiest lining he could ever imagine.

"How's that?," as I handed him the mirror. He looked all around, checking the sides, front, all of that.

"My nigga. Whenever I see you in Guam, if you make it there, your first thousand in Foxy's Strip Club is on me." He dapped me and Eric up, came back and slid me a hundred piece and left. I turned to look at Eric. It was obvious that I now had his approval. The shit was refreshing to know that I accomplished my goal. Lamar was long gone now, leaving only me and Eric.

"Here's the contract. Look at it." I skimmed it up and down. In short, it said I would be a part of the team of barbers going around the world, teaching others how to become masters with the craft. As a result, we will get a monetary gain with each place we go to. Six months traveling the world, hotels covered and individually, we would each see $250,000 at the end of the six months.

"Where do I sign?"

"You sure you don't wanna see a lawyer with this first?"

"Now I know I'm gone sign. If you were trying to fuck me over, you wouldn't have brought a lawyer up."

"My nigga." He handed me the pen and I signed my life to this. We dapped up and proceeded to clean everything up, leaving the chair and the clippers. I took one last look around this monstrosity of a gym as we were walking out.

"A Eric. Who John Baratto?"

"Thee Coach. That's who he is. The man." I chucked the deuce towards his name and proceeded to follow Eric out of the building. We stopped on Indianapolis Boulevard at a pizza joint called Toni's, with folks looking at us weird because we pulled up in the hood in a limo.

"Here man, when I was coming up, this was the place we got our pizza from before all the big fights on TV. You know, when everyone had the cheetah box."

"Fuck is the cheetah box?," I asked him.

"Aww y'all ain't have the black box? Man, we used to have this black box and get all the pay per view joints for free. All the Tyson fights and all that shit."

"Aww man we got the same shit. Except we just plugged into the neighbor's house cable. Shit was gravy." We enjoyed that laugh as a big ass sausage and mushroom pizza came out. We took it back to the limo and peeled off, smashing all the way until we got back to the hotel in Chicago. Upon arrival, we headed up to a private conference room. Once inside, I saw three other brothers waiting around at a table. "Gentlemen, gentleman. Y'all look like y'all having a good time."

"We are," said the stocky looking brother with a red polo on. "Aight cool. So Ty, here are your partners in crime for the foreseeable future. This brother right here who just spoke, this is Malcolm "Mook" Dunaway, originally from West Palm Beach, Florida. Over next to him, my mans from up North, Mr. Portland, Maine. Jeremy 'E.J.' Williams."

"Wait," I said. "Nigga you from Maine?"

"Yeah man. I'm from Maine. Like they say. Niggas is everywhere man."

"Last but not least," Eric continued. "We got Bryson Evans, from up North. That part of Michigan you forget about."

"And lemme make it clear my nigga. I ain't from Marquette. A nigga just went to college up there and stayed there in the city cause I opened up a shop near the university. I'm Saginaw all day." It was interesting getting three brothers from totally different backgrounds together for what seemed like an achievable goal.

"So where you from Ty?," Bryson asked me.

"Compton."

"Got a Cali nigga huh Eric," he told him. "Yeah man. He gone round us out. Gone have a seat Ty. I sat down at the table next to Bryson and listened to Eric explain everything to us.

"Top of the year gentlemen, we begin to travel. We hitting the world for one big ass party. Six months, cutting hair, teaching how to cut hair, international competitions and all that. We compete for pride and we get paid to show up to places. Easy money. So, it's maybe a month until we bounce out on January 3rd, 2016. Get your home business squared away, because when we on the road, it's just us. We going to Hawaii, Seychelles, Malaysia, Tokyo and The Philippines. In between those places, we'll fly off to some random joints and just have fun. Y'all all signed the contracts. You guaranteed 250 G's each, citing that y'all complete what y'all signed up for. Y'all the best from each side of the map. Let's make magic happen and make me proud that I picked you gentlemen." I wanted to say this was a dream and that this wasn't really happening, but I couldn't because it was. It's crazy how Eric had become rich off of cutting hair and creating competitions. Funny what could happen to your bank account with a few high profile sponsors and knowing the right people. Thank God I had a passport already. We had today and the next day to mingle in the Chi. For the next two days we partied, ate the marvelous food that only Chi Town had to offer and went to see Wrigley Field. From how Eric was talking, it was where the only real team in Chicago resides. The shit was gravy and Wednesday morning, I was headed back to L.A.

I got back to Carson around six Wednesday evening. I was tired and drained to say the least. Chicago had taken it out of me. Kevin was nowhere in the house from what I could see, which told me that he was still in class. I literally plopped down on the couch and left my bag right there on the floor. I didn't move for a good 15 minutes. I was just happy to be home. As I was getting up to finally get things situated, Kevin came through the door with an exhausted look on his face.

"Welcome back nigga."

"Yeah man."

"So how was that shit?," he asked as he grabbed some orange juice out of the fridge.

"Bruh, when I say I had probably the best three days of my life. I really mean that I had the best three days of my life. I cut hair, saw an East Chicago in a whole 'nother state, met a cool ass nigga from Vegas and partied it up in the Chi man. Bruh the shit was on some next level shit." As he pulled out a TV dinner from the freezer, I could see that he didn't wanna hear any good news right now. "What's wrong with you man? You looking like you lost your best friend or some shit."

"Man this overwhelming school shit man. It's tiresome. Not to mention basketball practice and all that too. I just feel burnt out you know. Luckily, we got a three game home stretch, so I don't gotta worry about traveling anywhere but to the gym and back home. Plus, I'm glad yo ass back. Gimme someone to talk too and destress with ya know." It was good to hear how much he appreciated me, but I knew all of it was about to take another turn. "A man. I'm gone after the new year."

"Oh you taking another trip out there?"

"Naw man. Like forreal, I'm gone." The buzzer on the microwave went off and he pulled his meal out.

"What you talking about Ty?," as he pulled the plastic off.

"Man look. I got an opportunity to travel the globe and cut hair in competitions. There's a guaranteed $250,000 if I hold it out for six months. Man, I can't pass this up. You feel me?" He just looked at me, all distraught and shit. "Yo man why you can't be happy for a nigga?"

"Man I thought we were in this shit together Ty," he said sitting down at the kitchen table. "Man I ain't hating, but I ain't see this shit coming. I got school, I got the apartment, shit we need for the living situation and now you say you bouncing. I don't need this right now bruh. You gotta say no man. We got bills around here and the scholarship money only cover so much of that."

"So what nigga. Get a job or move on campus." He looked up at me mid bite as if he were gonna do something. "Yeah I said it. Yo, you can't go around bitchin' because things ain't fallin' into play how you want 'em. Yeah, we made it out of Compton together. Yeah, we been niggas since we were yay high. Yeah, we always got each others back. But my nigga. We can't be tied to each other forever. You even said it yourself. You want the bright lights of the city. Well, I don't want that shit. I want something else. And beyond my control, it happened to have offered itself to me over the last three days. So either you can adjust to it or you won't. Either way, you gotta accept it." He got quiet as hell as I got up to put my bag in the room. I thought nothing else of it and began to unpack my clothes. That's when I heard the crash on the floor. I raced out the room. "Yo what the fuck are you doing man?"

"GET OUT MAN!!!"

"Man you must be crazy thinking I'm getting out of something that I put half of my money into. Fuck you nigga."

"Dog, get out of this house."

"Again, fuck you nigga. Acting like an old bitch. I swear sometimes you borderline gay my nigga."

"Man you got three seconds," he said, walking up to me and getting within a foot of my face. "One." I popped his ass dead in the throat. He started looking like ol' boy from He Got Game when Denzel popped him. That blow broke him down to 5'10 like myself.

"Get out you say?" **BOP BOP!!!** I gave him another quick two piece. "Fuck you nigga. This my life. You don't control shit round here bout me. I'll be out this bitch in a month. You must've forgot I had the passes in other hoods. You didn't. You got me fucked up cuz." As he laid on the floor holding his throat and his jaw, I calmly walked past him to grab my Frosted Flakes, some milk and my favorite red bowl. I poured up a big as bowl with the most gangsta finesse that you could ever imagine. He got up, still holding his throat, looking at me. As I began to walk past him, I stopped and took a big ass spoonful of my Frosted Flakes to the mouth. I walked off into the room and shut the door on his ass. He could sleep his bitch ass on the couch tonight. I arose the next morning around eight o'clock as I was getting ready to head to the shop on this Thursday. I walked out of the room to see that Kev was already gone, headed off to school. I wasn't comprehending it. None of what was going on. Nothing and I mean nothing was supposed to separate homeys. But it was obvious that this situation was. You saw this type of shit due to women and money. But to relocation? Like, who does that? The game ain't setup like that. Now, had I still been in the hood. Wait, let me rephrase this because Carson is hood. It's not outrageous as Compton, but it's hood indeed. If I was still living in Compton and I decided to roll out to better my life, I could expect it because others may be envious for the simple fact that I couldn't take them with me. Even the fact that they may fear that I may leave and start to think that I am better than them. That was how the hood operated and I understood that. But how could you be upset at a man when you are doing the same thing that you are crying about?

He was going to school to pursue a degree. I was cutting hair to pursue my passion. Either way, it was to become better than we once were. I shook my head at the thought and went to going about my day. As usual, I had to clean out my bowl and re-up on some Frosted's. All I had left in my life was to turn into Tony the damn Tiger himself and catch diabetes. I played some YG on my laptop and mashed my bowl, all while cleaning up the house at the same time. I wasn't gonna go in until around 10, so I had a good minute to do what I did. I started picturing how everything would go once January hit. I thought about two places he said in particular. The Philippines and Malaysia. I knew that there were high profile places within those countries. But, from hearing the stories of a couple of hood cats who went to the Navy, there were a lotta poor parts of those places that existed. If only I got over there, that would be a whirlwind of an experience.

"Ahhh shit, look who's back." I cracked a smile over Brody's words and went to my chair just to chill out. The shop was packed for 10 in the morning. All chairs were full and everyone was waiting for my story.

"A nigga," said Spoon. "So you gone tell us about Chi-raq or what? How them hoes out there man?"

"Man the boy just came back and the first thing out yo' mouth is about hoes," said Dominique. "Ask the nigga how he been or something."

"Man I'm good y'all. Thanks. And yea, Chi-Town got some bangin women."

"So what was that shit about man?," Brody asked me. "I mean my nigga. Dude is loaded. I mean he had a private limo. Hold on, lemme take it back further than that. I was on his private plane. Got picked up in his private limo. Nigga took me to the Hyatt in Downtown Chi. Put me in a suite. All the food and drink I wanted. Then, the nigga picked me up the next day in another limo. Took me across the border to Indiana, to a big ass high school gym. Shit fit like ten thousand. Nigga started talkin' bout a nigga named Oudie or some shit. But anyway, dude had a barber chair set up in the middle of the gym. Now mind you my nigga, kids is in school at this time, so to have the gym locked down, you know he got some clout over there. Then, his homeboy walk in. Nigga said L.A. So I'm thinking you know. Nigga from The Wood, Compton, Crenshaw, some shit like that. That was just the nigga initials. So my test is to cut the nigga hair 'cause he a big business man in Asia or some shit. I slice the nigga up. The nigga liked it and right there fam offered me a contract. We bounce in January for a world traveling barber competition. We guaranteed $250,000 and even more shit depending on what we win wherever we at. So yeah nigga. I ate Toni's pizza nigga, some of that White Castles shit, some Harold's, all that shit. Man, on some real shit, Chicago cool than a muthafucka." The whole shop was quiet, shaking their heads in astonishment.

"You know out of everything you just told us, the only thing I could put my finger around is that you told that story in true nigga fashion." The whole shop bust out laughing at Spoon, as my first customer had walked in and sat in the chair. "Man did y'all hear the nigga? Shit I was waiting for the fight to pop off. You know niggas can't never tell a story without all the extra dramatics." This shit was fun. My team was behind me, but then Dominique asked a serious question. "So what about your team here?" Things got so quiet that you could hear a rat piss on cotton.

"What you mean man? I ain't gone forget about y'all. I mean, y'all niggas just as important to me as all the niggas in Compton who let me work magic on they heads."

"I know my nigga. I know. But let me be real with you. Don't let every nigga know about your success. Like, I love all the niggas in this shop, even the ones I ain't cutting. But truth be told, one of them niggas could be plotting to tell the homies bout yo' come up and have someone come after you. So with that said, on Piru, bet none of y'all niggas be setting my mans up. This shit stay in this shop. It get out and I find out, y'all catching heat ya feel me?" Nique went from around his chair, flashing the two guns that he had in his waistband.

"Ain't no need for all that Nique. I think niggas respect us enough."

"I'm just making sure Spoon, and it ain't no disrespect to any of you niggas in here, whether you know me or not. But I gotta look out for my brother. We all niggas and we know how some niggas do." Everyone could fuck with that logic and things in the shop got back to normal after that. The heads kept coming in and we went well into the night time slicing. Man I cut one married nigga so good that his wife was gonna be mad at me. As crispy as his cut was, how could she not expect other females to come up to him?

"A I'm gone Brody. I'll see you tomorrow."

"Aight fam." I dipped out around 8:30 with a chipper attitude seeing that I had more than a killing today. The walk home was chill as no cars slowed down for the drive by and it was a nice night outside. Shit, Daria had even texted me, asking me when the next time me and her was gonna get up. I walked in the door and saw Kev at the table, face deep in his books.

"Whats up bro?," I told him. He got up from the table and extended his hand.

"Sorry bout the last few days bro."

"It's all good my nigga." We embraced. All greats got into it every once in awhile so it was nothing.

"Look my nigga. I'm happy for you and all that you do. I

just wanna make sure that we gone be good even if we ain't linked up."

"Man ain't shit coming between us nigga. Never has and never will. But umm...on some real shit. You have been acting like a bitch at times."

"Aww nigga please," as he gave me two or three playful punches to the gut. It was all love again as my boy had come back to his senses. I didn't wanna hit him. Yet at the same time, it was low key my payback for when he scraped me when we were eight. Nigga was whoopin' my ass in Mortal Kombat and I couldn't take that shit. I swung on fam and he smooth hit me with a game controller. It was one of the funnier moments of my life.

"Yo we got a game tomorrow at seven. You coming?"

"Who yall playin?," I asked.

"Shit we got UC San Dog."

"Yo. Ain't them those niggas that had the nooses and shit hangin in the dorms years ago?"

"Yeah that's them. I heard it be some fuck shit going on at that school. But truthfully, what school don't have fuck shit going on?"

"Yeah, you right."

"I mean, think about it. You see all these big time universities. It ain't too many of us at either one of 'em. They hate the shit out of us. But look at they sports teams and its nigga city. Take all the blacks out of every sports program in America, and they wouldn't be shit. Kentucky wouldn't be shit. Duke wouldn't be shit. Carolina wouldn't be shit. Indiana wouldn't be shit. None of them muthafuckas would be shit."

"Yeah, you got a point there my dude." It was amazing to see a black athlete like Kev understand the reality of things, even though he was doing something that he loved, which was play basketball. Sure, you got an education out of the deal. But, compare what the black athlete gets in a scholarship compared to what the school makes in revenue, and truthfully, they don't get shit. Granted, Cal State Dominguez Hills wasn't nowhere near caliber like a Division 1 Big Ten or ACC school, but the same principles applied. The money the schools made off the student athlete trumped what the student athlete actually earned. You give one star athlete 300 something dollars and change for food. Yet that same dude done brought you $1 million in concessions, $5 million in merchandise, $20 million in ticket sales, $50 million in television contracts, so on and so forth. Yet these niggas wanna get mad that these dudes taking money to go buy clothes and have fun with their friends? I called the whole system some total, unadulterated bullshit. That's why I didn't fuck with college as a whole. I thought it was the biggest white man hustle on earth. You come to my buildings to get a piece of paper and I'll get you a job where you can pay me back. But, when you pay me back, just know that even if you don't have a job, you gotta still pay me back. Even if you get a job immediately, but then fall on hard times, I ain't gonna forgive you. You are still gonna pay me back. That was that bullshit as we called it. They made Terrelle Pryor pay for getting some free tattoos, but they didn't complain when he was filling up The Shoe. They complained about The Fab Five, but they didn't complain when they had Michigan at the top of the college basketball world. And who could forget the infamous USC scandal, where the coach and that whole university fucked over Reggie Bush. If I was Reggie, I would've told those bitch made, pussy muthafuckas that if they want the Heisman Trophy, they can come get it from me. Even better, he should've put that shit in the middle of Southeast San Diego where he from. Tell those college football fuckers that if they could make it past all these Bloods from O'Ferrell, Skyline and Lincoln, then they could gladly take the trophy. That's how college did with their athletics. Chew you up and spit you out. They didn't give a fuck about the black athlete. They only cared about the green paper.

"Thank you for taking me to this game. I never been to a college game."

"Ain't no problem beautiful." Me and Daria had agreed to have us a quote on quote date night tonight. I didn't consider a basketball game a date, but if it was to her, then it was. We walked into the Toro Dome and took our seats close to the floor. It wasn't anything special in here, as there was maybe two to three thousand people in here, which wasn't even half of their gym's capacity. It was a way to watch my boy and let her experience something she never had. Plus, it would make it even better when I would be knee deep in her later. The game started off slow. To be truthful, neither one of the teams were really good. Ok, let me take that back. UCSD was decent, but CSDH had just two wins in six games so far. UCSD jumped out to an early 7-0 lead until my mans got a breakaway dunk and sent the crowd into a craze. However, as for the first half, that would be all the excitement that would come from the Dominguez Hills side of things, as they were trailing 41-27 at halftime. Kev had 13 of those points, but they would have to do more if they wanted to have even the slightest of chances. "You hungry beautiful?"

"Yeah. Could you go get me another thing of popcorn?"

"Sure thing. I'll be back." I went off to the concession stand to get her food. While standing in line, I noticed a gaggle of bad ones standing on the opposite end of the building. I wanted to go holla at let em know who I was, but I couldn't mess up that fine piece of work that I had waiting for me in the bleachers. I said screw it and kept focused, getting her the popcorn. I walked back in the gym to see that the second half was near starting. As I was walking back up the bleachers towards Daria, I saw some cat sitting next to her. He was trying to talk to her, but she seemed to be trying to shove him off. Walking closer, I saw it was Ralo. I thought nothing of it, as my mans was a jokester.

"Whats up Ralo? Here you go baby."

"Baby? Yo, you with my bitch nigga?" I stood up with the popcorn still in my hand.

"First off man, chill with the bitch callin. Second off, I didn't know this was your woman, cause judging from the other night, that's hard to tell." He stared at me like he saw the devil himself. "You fucking other niggas on me huh?," he asked her.

"You ain't my man Ralo now get the fuck out of my face." Voices were starting to get raised and I saw security heading over our way from the other side of the arena.

"Yo nigga. You need to raise the fuck outta here man with that bullshit," I told him.

"And if I don't nigga?," he responded.

"There a problem here gentlemen?," the officer came over and said.

"Yes sir," as Daria got up ecstatic as ever. "My ex is pestering me and my date, and deliberately trying to start a fight over here, and he needs to be out of here."

"Sir?," the officer addressed Ralo.

"Man fuck that bitch and fuck you." He shoved the officer and that became the biggest mistake of his life. I pulled Daria back as I watched this big pitbull built officer and his partner fuck Ralo up to the highest extent. I couldn't call it no race shit because both of them were black and looked like they grew up in the hood. Of course, the white folks around us were nervous and students were pulling out their cell phones recording everything. Game action had stopped as everyone had become distracted by what was going on here. People were running on the floor out of sheer fear. The more Ralo struggled, the more those two officers punished him. Finally, he was handcuffed and subdued. Daria had to calm me down and bring me back down to Earth so that we could enjoy the rest of the game. As hard as it was because I was so turnt up, we did. Things calmed down and the game eventually got back underway. Unfortunately, that scrum didn't give anyone from Dominguez Hills any excitement, because they took a disastrous 85–58 L. There were ass whoopings, and then there was just putting people out of the gym. Kev ended up dropping 31, but that was the only bright spot. Me and Daria left the bleachers, and went outside the locker room area to wait for him to come out. "Where you wanna go after this beautiful?"

"Umm. I know this is gonna sound sort of strange. But how bout we go out to the Mexican spot for some surf-n-turf burritos?"

"Girl, don't be bullshitting me."

"I'm not. I mean, that's how I got thick. I mean shit. I hate women who be wanting wine and dine on dates. I'm like, just keep it simple. Some burritos or anything simple. Specifically, burritos will do." This girl had just moved to my Sportscenter top ten list. I loved surf-n-turf burritos. Give me mines with extra shrimp and no pico de gallo, and I was good.

"Well what's good Muhammad Ali?," Kev said as he came out of the hall, dappin' me up.

"Bruh, I ain't do shit. That was the poes over there body slamming ya boy like they were the road warriors or some shit. Didn't throw a punch or nothing."

"You ok Daria?"

"Yeah Kevin I'm fine. I just don't know why niggas don't get when something is over it's over. I ain't been with him since late last year. He a fucking lame. Don't know why I wasted my time on him. Glad I ain't fuck him." We both got a laugh out of that.

"So what y'all bout to do?," Kev asked.

"She wanna go out for burritos bruh."

"**BURRITOS!!!** Yeah girl. You done made that niggas day. Only thing he love more than Frosted Flakes is some damn surf-n-turf burritos. I ain't never known anyone who eats more cereal or burritos than this dude. I swear I don't know how his asshole has survived this long."

"Aight man, you done fucked up the mood. We out." Daria was cracking up as she said goodbye to Kev. Me and him dapped up, and I headed out with shorty. "So you don't have your own whip. Why?"

"You saying I'm a bum ass dude?"

"If I thought that, then do you think I would be out with you?" Damn, she was good.

"Naw beautiful. I'm just a brother who is still in search of much. Like when I came out here with Kev from Compton, we went half on a lil get around vehicle. Nothing extravagant. Just something to get us from A to B. We decided to split the costs on it as far as maintenance and gas. Now, as far as my whip, could I get one, yes. Right now, it wouldn't benefit me. I am a homebody for the most part. I study and go to the barbershop. That's pretty much it. So I never thought about having one until I absolutely needed it. I mean. I got it tonight cause Kev got a game. He dropped it off at the shop earlier and got in a teammate's car. Most of the time, though, I just let him have it for school and I foot it wherever I need to go."

"Well, wouldn't it be nice if you just wanted to drive and take a trip somewhere?"

"Yeah, it would. But honestly, I don't need it. In January, I'm leaving for six months."

"And where you going?," she asked as we pulled up to a

red light. "I flew out to Chicago a few days back. Met with a barber team that travels around the globe and competes in competitions. Not only that, but they teach the art of cutting hair as well. We suppose to hit some interesting places along the way and that's cool for me. I always wanted to teach someone something they never had the chance to learn much you know?" She stayed quiet for about a block. I thought for sure I had fucked up telling her my plans. Here we go, I thought. She was about to blow up something serious. "I think it's a great idea," she said, as we pulled up to the drive thru, sitting behind two other cars. "I mean, look at you. You about to do something that very few people get to do, and that's travel the world doing what you love. I'm assuming you getting paid for this right?"

"Yeah."

"See. That's impressive. You just made me admire you even more. I can dig a man like that. I hate that you leaving, but self growth is valuable. The opposite sex will always be here." Her intellect was turning me on to say the least, but I had to ask her one question.

"So are you saying that being with someone isn't important?"

"Not at all. It's a million you's in the world. Referring to men. It's only one me. Why am I gonna spend all my time trying to grow with different men and never take time to grow for myself? I think it'll be good for you. Matter of fact, great. You grow as a man, and then you'll be ready to grow with a woman." I swear if I could, I would rip her clothes off and bang her back out in the damn drive thru.

"Hold on beautiful. Lemme make this order. **YEAH, LEMME GET TWO SURF-N-TURF'S, EXTRA SHRIMP, NO PICO DE GALLO!!!** You want some fries with that?" Oh, this nigga cupid must have struck me something serious. I was even offering her fries. We swung around to the window and I paid for her grub.

"My place or yours?," she asked.

"Yours beautiful. You've seen mine." We rolled back into the night, enjoying great convo and anxiously awaiting to sink our mouths in these tortillas full of goodness. We got to her house in a nice apartment complex. It looked like she had her stuff well put together from what I was seeing. "Hey

Kesha. Where my baby?"

"He in the room knocked out. You know how he gets after fish sticks and Finding Nemo. And who is this?"

"Oh, this my friend Ty. Ty, this Kesha, my bestie since grade school."

"Nice to meet you," as she shook my hand and looked at Daria. It was all funny to me.

"Girl, enjoy yourself. Nice to meet you Ty." She gave Daria that look like she better whip it on me and exited the house.

"Excuse my friend. She silly."

"No worries. It's all good. Where you want me to set this food at?"

"Just put it on the table over there in the kitchen and I'll be with you in a minute. I gotta check in on my lil man." As she went down the hall to her room, I started scanning the pictures on the wall. I mean shorty was gorgeous, but she had been a banger since her younger days in elementary school. I scanned everything from the high school diploma framed, to the associates degree from Chaffey College, to the picture she had with some guy who played college football. Then, I saw the one in the frame that said "I Love Mom." I had to take a deep breath and put my hand over my mouth. If she was an atomic bomb, then her momma was a full blown asteroid that could destroy mother earth. Her mama was just as thick and from what I saw, the pic was taken during her high school graduation. She didn't look a day over 25. I don't know what she had been eating all of her life, but man oh man oh man.

"You lookin' at my mama ain't you?"

"Huh," as I turned around, stunned beyond belief that she saw me. "Naw, I was just looking through everything."

"It's okay. I'm not mad. It's who I get it from. Everyone who come over here, including women, they fall in love with my mama. C'mon let's go eat." I walked over to the table behind her, mesmerized by that ass of hers. I had seen it all before, but I was now seeing her in a different light. We sat down and our conversation started to take a turn.

"So how you like motherhood?" She let out a deep breath.

"I'm sorry. I aint mean to strike a nerve."

"Naw it's cool. So...I got pregnant with Derrion right after I graduated high school by my then boyfriend. We had been together since our sophomore year. Long story short, it was gravy until I told him I had his baby on the way. Then, he disappeared. I had my baby and been holding it down doing school and everything by myself since. I stay out here, but I'm originally from Fullerton. I'm in school right now, working on my bachelors to give my son a better life. I don't get it sometimes. I'm a barely 22 year old, with a lot going. I'm just trying to figure everything out." As I took another bite of heavenly goodness, I was hoping that she wasn't trying to slick talk me a sob story about trying to have me be her baby daddy's replacement.

"Oh, by the way. Please don't take this as a me trying to lock you for a replacement. I was just being open. I'm not saying you were thinking that, but just in case, I didn't want you thinking that."

"Naw girl naw. Now why would I start thinking something like that? That would be crazy." If only she knew that my ass was crazy.

"Well, I'm glad. I just want to aspire for bigger and better things. Like you. When you told me your story, inside, I was like wow. He is more than just a barber. He has some serious ambition. Not to mention he's cute." I chuckled at her notion and just played along.

"So how you gone handle traveling the world? You know. Being away from America for so long don't seem like it'll be easy." I sipped some of the almond milk she had poured in my glass and just thought about the perfect answer to that question. In that moment, I could only think of three words.

"I don't know." She looked at me and smiled.

"Well, I think you'll be good. And to tell you the truth, I thought you had something special since the first time I saw you in the barbershop."

"So why you ain't never say anything?"

"I dunno. I mean. Like, I wanted to. But. Naw. I was just there for my son. I didn't want anything extra added on my plate outside of my son and school. Nothing personal. Please don't take it that way."

"I'm not." We smiled and continued our eats until we were good and full, and done with our crazy conversation.

"It's 11:37. I think I'm gone head home."

"You sure you don't wanna stay?"

"Naw. I mean. I don't feel comfortable you know. You got your son in here. I don't want him to wake up to a stranger in his house and get the wrong idea. I mean, I'm not saying he will, but I was that lil kid once. I know what it's like seeing different guys in the crib." A smirk came across her face.

"Ok, I'll make a deal. You stay here and leave at seven in the morning. He won't wake up before that. Trust me."

"Only if you agree to the fact that you're good with nothing happening tonight. Out of respect for your son."

"That's cool with me," she responded. We cleaned up everything and headed into the bedroom. Nothing went down. We just simply fell asleep like two respectful adults. For once, and actually, for the first time in my life, I laid next to a woman and was gravy with nothing happening. She earned some major cool points in my book. Aside from my momma, she was the first woman who I could call "woman" with confidence.

Saturday morning was here. Early December signaled the last days of 2015 winding down. People were getting ready for New Year's celebrations, New Year's resolutions, Christmas shopping and a whole bunch of other mumbo jumbo. As for me, I had to get everything together to make sure that my trip would come with little to no problems at all. I called my grandma and told her the news. At first, she wasn't cool with it. You know, your child leaving for six months to go to random places sounds too much like the military. And I say child because my mama was dead and she practically raised me, even though I stayed with my aunt in Spooktown. As the convo went on, however, she became more light hearted and happy for me. I think she knew that it would be good for me. However, a granny is always gonna worry about her grandbaby. That's just what they do. Kev, was being real helpful with my whole situation. He had the plug on some gift cards that one of his cousins sold for the low. Nigga got me $400 worth. And trust, I went into Burlington and cut the fool with it. I spent all $400 in one trip as I copped over 20 polos, 15 pairs of jeans and two pairs of dress shoes. Shit, all you had to do was look for the red tag when you went in there and you would be gravy. I may have been young, but I wasn't dumb. I wasn't breaking

$400 for a Gucci belt or none of that shit. I took everything back to the barbershop and decided to make me some money for the day. "Yo what's up man?"

"Ain't shit Spoon. Yo, who shit is this?," as I pointed to the new chair.

"Aww man, it's some new nigga we got coming here. He paid a rental fee, so we gone see what's up."

"Well, what's the nigga name?"

"Nigga call himself Cook. That's all I know. Brody knows that nigga. Ain't that right Brody?"

"Man don't bring me in this shit," Brody said, as he brushed off his clippers, preppin to line up his client's beard. "Dominique knows that nigga. He brought him in."

"Now hold on nigga," Nique stated. "I just met the nigga in the store. I just told him the booth fees per month. I ain't know that nigga was coming in here the next day. Shit, money is money, but don't say that I invited him in."

"So why all y'all niggas pretending like y'all don't know him?," I asked.

"Shit cause the nigga can't cut bruh. Folks been in here two days and done had three niggas in his chair. Two niggas he knew and that nigga Frito," exclaimed Spoon.

"Now you know Frito don't give a fuck. He done got sliced up by all of us. He figure shit, if this nigga in the shop with us, then he must be good. Man he FUCKED Frito's head up last night. They shoulda slapped a red tag on the back of his head dawg. I mean, Frito grabbed that mirror and just shouted **WHAT THE FUCK YOU DO TO MY SHIT!!!**"

"Tell 'em what happened after that," Nique said.

"Oh yeah. So Frito said what the fuck and this nigga Cook like what you mean? Nigga turned around like I asked for a medium fade. Not a *** damn Seminole chop. That's when the nigga tossed his mirror and the whole shop literally had to grab him. Like nigga, all of us had to get that nigga out. And what Cook ass do? That nigga just sat in his chair talking to himself. Telling himself that he did a good job. And shit, that nigga needed to sit down. Be humble. Really. Cause he fucked shit up. I don't know them other two niggas he cut, but they gone be his only clients." Damn, if homey was this bad, then I didn't even wanna meet him.

"Well where he at now?," I asked Spoon.

"I don't know, but wherever he is, he can keep his ass where he at. That nigga gone have the shortest stint of any barber I know." The shop laughed and right on cue, the nigga was seen in front of the door, on his phone.

"Uh Oh, here he come. Slice-n-dice." I held my laughter in from Spoons words as I continued to sit in my chair and chill.

"A what's up y'all?" The nigga what's up was met with mumbled what's up and head nods.

"Sup lil nigga. Who you?" The clippers cut off and I just looked at this nigga.

"A my nigga you just got here. You don't know me like that partna. Take that shit somewhere else."

"Well I ain't seen you nigga so I'm asking nigga."

"Yo who the fuck you talking too?," as I raised up out of my chair. Brody and another cat waiting for a cut came too me, holding me back. I was ready to steal off on this bitch ass nigga.

"Fuck wrong with yo boy Spoon?"

"The fuck wrong with you nigga? You popped off at him. Not the other way around. Now look, this been one of the 100 niggas way before you got here. So if you coming in here, then I advise you show some respect, or you can find somewhere else to work at. Don't make me no difference."

"So that's how it is?"

"Exactly how it is nigga." Ol' boy shook his head up and down, biting that crusty ass bottom lip of his.

"Aight. **FUCK Y'ALL NIGGAS!!!**," he yelled as he stormed out.

"Fuck ya mama," Spoon responded as he bounced out the door.

"You good man?," Brody asked, as he let me go.

"Yeah man. Yo y'all need to watch who y'all hiring. Y'all got niggas in here off the streets y'all barely know. Should've known he wasn't good when I seen he was a dark skinned nigga."

"And what that mean?," Nique asked. "Man c'mon. You know y'all dark skinned niggas crazy as shit."

"Ok, Ok, but tell me who always killin' bitches in the movies? **LITE SKINNED NIGGAS!!!** That nigga Michael Ealy in Perfect Guy, Perfect Man, whatever that shit was called.

Then, y'all had Cuba crying and shit in Boyz N The Hood. Umm, Umm. Shemar Moore ol' sensitive ass in that Madea movie playing captain save a hoe. Muthafuck y'all lite skinned niggas." The shop was rollin' and I had to clap back.

"Well aight, let's talk more about y'all dark skinned niggas. Start with Ricky punk ass. Y'all darkies dumb. Nigga done ran his ass damn near to USC and he couldn't start jukin' or hoppin' a fuckin fence. Nigga ran straight like a bullet was gone do twist and turns. Then, since you wanna go to Madea movies, you had ol' Blair Underwood beating on his fine ass woman 'cause he scared a lite skinned nigga gone take her. And I fucks with Michael Ealy. He killed Morris punk ass by running him off the road. As a matter of fact, if he y'all national spokesperson., then y'all losing, 'cause he get fucked up in every movie. He got shot as Ricky, nigga got ate by an anaconda, Taye Diggs fucked Mia, He died in a cave in that other movie. Then, the nigga broke the NFL rushing record and had his book written by the same nigga who fucked his wife. Then, she died. And then, I saw some play a while back he had with baby girl Michelle from Destiny's Child. That muthafucka got smoked in that bitch too. Y'all niggas losing." By this time, the whole shop was in a hysterical frenzy. Me and Nique continued going back and forth. It literally sounded like the Bernie Mac show up in here. All we needed was a few more muthafuckas and it would've been the closest thing to Kings of Comedy any of us had ever seen. We didn't stop. We were 10 minutes in and having a good ol' nigga time.

"**FUCK ALL Y'ALL NIGGAS!!!**" I turned to the door where the voice came from. That's when I saw the gun come out. I ducked behind the chair and heard at least nine get let off. I knew there was much more than that, but I think I literally blacked out after hearing all of those shots. Glass shattering and screams is all that I remember. When I did open my eyes, there was complete chaos, and I saw that Cook nigga on the floor.

"**SPOON!!!**" I heard his name being screamed out. I turned my head to see my nigga down. I rushed over to his side. The blood was everywhere. "**SPOON STAY WITH US MAN!!! CALL THE FUCKING AMBULANCE!!!**" I don't know who screamed that out, but everything was chaotic right now. The fuck boy was dead. But now, we had a bigger problem. Spoon was fighting for his life.

3 CUT IN MORE WAYS THAN ONE

"Say man. You gone be okay over there?" Ty looked at Kevin with a look that only friends can relate too when he asked him that.

"Yeah man. Just another chapter of life that I gotta complete. Now that Spoon gone, I feel more inclined to do right. Like, I wake up some nights and think to myself. Why? Like, why man?" Kevin hugged Ty. These two had been through it all. Death was something that was very familiar to them both. But, they didn't expect to have it hit them hard again when they left The Hub. Spoon fought for two days after catching two bullets to the stomach. Unfortunately, his fight wasn't enough. At the funeral, hundreds turned out for Spoon, as he was clad out in a pearl white suit, with his clippers on the side of the casket. He was killed over something petty and there was already enough of that going on in the hoods of America.

"Bruh, I leave tomorrow on a plane for Seychelles. I don't even know what to expect man."

"Just do what you have always done."

"What you gone do in Seattle man? I mean, it ain't like NY or M-I-A?," Ty asked Kev.

"Naw man. I changed my mind. I'm heading to the Bay." Ty gave him a look of disgust.

"The Bay? Yo, what's in the Bay man?"

"Frisco. I got the big city life I've always dreamed of. It's only a few days, 'cause you know, basketball season and our New Years breaks ain't nothing extravagant. I just wanna live it up man."

"But I've told you," Ty said, clasping his hands. "You can't always follow the crowd. You have to be your own individual. Now, not even a month ago, you were talking about going to Seattle because you wanted to be where no one is, but it was still bright lights and big city. Now, you wanna go to Frisco? You know how many rich dummies already up there? Yo man. You don't go where the trail is already laid. You go where there is no path and carve your own niche. They already winning up there. You hear about Frisco all the time. I say Seattle. But, at the end of the day, it's your choice and I hope you get what you want out of it." Kevin was starting to feel pressure now. He hadn't considered the consequences of the results of where he would go. It was starting to seem like Ty was turning into him, when he had told him that he was gonna travel overseas to cut hair.

"Well, bruh, I know everyone won't like what I do, but I gotta do this for me. We left Compton to pursue better things. So what's different with this?," Kevin asked him.

"You right man. Good luck." The two dapped up and embraced, knowing this would be the last heart to heart that they would have for a while in person.

"C'mon man. Let's get these bags down to the car and get you to the airport. I'll buy you a surf-n-turf burrito on the way down there."

"My nigga." That was music to Ty's ears, as they hauled off two huge luggage bags to the car downstairs, preparing to take their final ride together as roommates. The ride through the Carson streets were out of the ordinary for Ty this time, as his new adventures would possibly take him places where paved streets were a novelty item. They rolled up to the taco stand, where he ordered a surf-n-turf burrito and some carne asada fries.

"Damn man. I know damn well you ain't gone eat all of that," Kevin said.

"Don't believe me just watch."

"Aight, Trinidad Ty." As Kev proceeded to get back on the road, Ty didn't waste anytime. He dove into the carne asada fries head first as if he were a Japanese suicide bomber during World War 2. Kevin took turns driving and looking at Ty smash this food at a record pace.

"You ain't touch that burrito yet I see."

"Because man," Ty said with cheese dripping from his bottom lip. "You gotta save the best for last." The traffic on the highway was jam packed as usual, as traffic went from a standstill to flowing to back again. What was usually a twenty minute trip had turned into twenty minutes in almost one spot.

"Thank God for this traffic and three hours to spare." Ty said that as he unwrapped the meaty goodness he called a burrito and took the first bite in. He leaned back in the chair, chewing like he had bit into a slice of heaven.

"Damn man, is it that good?," Kevin asked.

"Negro yes. The only shit that could make it better was if it was wrapped in bacon."

"A bacon wrapped burrito? Are you serious man?"

"Hell yea I'm serious," Ty responded.

"What doesn't taste good wrapped in bacon? So peep man peep. I met this cat from Jersey in the barbershop one time. Dude name was Jeff. So you know me man. I be having to check cats temperatures when I meet them. I don't just trust anyone like that. But he seemed cool. So back in September, the weekend that I went to San Diego, I was with him. Man he took me to a joint called bacon festival. It was a week long, but I only caught three days of it. On the last day, man we was at this big ass park over on the good side of town. Hell, all of San Diego good if you ask me. Bruh, they had bacon upon bacon upon bacon. I know by the end of it I had six mild heart attacks and increased my cholesterol to an astounding level that no human should ever have. But it was the greatest greasiest moment of my life bruh."

"You know for someone who doesn't gain a pound, you sure as hell do eat a lot," Kevin told him.

"A man, I didn't hit 6 feet. But it went all to my dick."

"I didn't need to hear that shit man."

"Well you heard it nigga." These two were indeed some characters. Traffic had got to flowing again, but then slowed down once again. Finally, the LAX sign was visible. The car got quiet as both of them were pondering on what was about to happen. As crazy as Ty's trip had seemed, Kevin had his own experience to deal with. He was flying into Frisco for the next three days, coming back on the 3rd for basketball practice.

"I can't believe dawg you gone pay $24 dollars a day for parking up here."

"Rather me have my own way back and break bread than pay someone to take me."

"But that's what Uber's for man. You ain't gotta worry about driving."

"I just don't see how y'all find that legit man. You know what's even more crazy. When we were kids, we were taught by everyone and they momma not to take rides from strangers. Now, we literally pay strangers to give us a ride everywhere. Yo, I don't know if they got Uber in all those places y'all going, but I wouldn't trust it. You gone end up in a floating meat market in China chopping up cow hooves. You know they eat everything up there."

"And how would you know? You ain't never been to no China."

"But every hood got a Chinese restaurant and we know damn well that we done ate about forty pounds of rat and dog in our lifetime." They both laughed as Kev pulled the car into long term parking. They both got out, knowing that this was it. Their planes were located in opposite ends of the airport. Ty was flying to Chicago before anything. He was gonna spend the night there with the rest of his barber team and then they were all out the next day on an international flight to Paris. From there, they would catch a short flight to Seychelles, East Africa. Kev was a one shot flight into Frisco, where he was going to be staying with some buddies he met in college on the basketball court. They walked together to the Southwest terminal, checking in quickly. It seemed like Southwest was the black people's airline. Good fares and you knew you were gonna get where you were going on time, or before that actual time. You might not get shit to eat besides peanuts and some cheese crackers, but your flight would be A1.

"I swear man. I am not gonna enjoy this shit constantly," Ty said, referring to damn near getting naked when going through the security gate."

"Yeah, I feel you on that. I only gotta do this twice and I dread it." They made it through security and relaxed even more over a bite at a sandwich spot. Their talk lasted over an hour, with Kev enjoying a sandwich platter and Ty simply drinking a juice, seeing how he had indulged in the whole country of Mexico just a mere hour or so earlier.

"12:05 man. That's when we both bounce. What time is it," Ty asked.

"11:13," Kev said, looking at his watch.

"Well man, you think its bout time we start this journey man?"

"Loyalty my dude," Ty told him.

"What you mean man?," Kev responded.

"No matter what happens. We stay down with each other. Don't let the world separate us. Don't let the world tell us because we chose two different paths that we don't gotta be brothers. We built this shit from the ground up. We got this. Don't get trapped in our own conscious." They got up and hugged. Giving each other their last daps, they headed for opposite ends of the terminal to wait at their gates for their departing flights.

When we took off, I felt at ease. Once we hit 10,000 feet, I put my beats on my ears and decided to let Chicago music take me to Chicago. "Crucial Conflict's" first album was blazing through my speakers as I began this journey into the unknown. I looked out the window at the last remnants of California, as I wouldn't see this place for six months. Gone was the gangbangin, bad air, weed and terrible traffic. I could live without that and I was perfectly fine. At the same time, I couldn't forget what I had survived and came from. In a zoned out state, with Do or Die's "Po Pimpin" now taking its turn dancing in my ear drums, I lifted up the sleeve on my right forearm to expose my tattoo. I analyzed it more thoroughly than ever before. The word Compton sprawled across a city welcoming sign. A street sign rising from above it saying Raymond Street where I grew up. The word "THE" was on one side of the street sign and "HUB" was on the other side. The rest of the tat was pretty much fill in, but you got the picture. Compton was a part of me as much as I was a part of it. I would definitely miss it, but not the bullshit that was associated with it. I knew times were rough for my people and this was my way of helping them out. There was a dude who used to rap named Kia Shine who once said "How you gone rep yo' city if you never left yo' city. Go somewhere and make it, and that's how you help your city." That indeed was my goal. I was lucky, because unlike a lot of my homies, they didn't get to see a moment like this. Their lives were cut down way before their time. Everything, and I mean everything started in the halls of Compton High. They escalated to the streets outside. Spooktown, Park Village and Acacia Blocc were just some of the neighborhoods that made up the school. Niggas that went to Centennial were blooded out. We hated 'em. It was PIRU central. Somehow, someway, some event that was being held for high schoolers in Compton would see us meet up. I remember one day in particular. There was a basketball tournament being held in the city. I knew it was going to get ugly, but I didn't want to tell myself that. Me and two of my partners in the tournament were the heavy favorites. I was a Sports Guru and everybody knew that I have more skills than just with the clippers. So, to make a long story short, in the first bracket of the tournament, we ended up matching up with some cats from Centennial.

"Sup Blood. What's brackin?" That's all it took as the game had ended before it even started. Even with all of the security there on that hot summer day, it didn't stop the madness from happening. The rumble went from the concrete courts to well outside the barriers. It carried over from that day. As I sit on this plane and think about it, I realize one thing. Out of the six brothers that were supposed to play that day, I was the only one still existing on earth. As for everyone else who had jumped in, they were probably still in the hood doing the same shit. I had escaped it and I was grateful. However, I know the real challenge in life still waited for me.

"You've arrived in Chicago. We hoped you enjoyed your flight." Those words were music to my ears as I couldn't wait to get up and stretch my legs. Sitting on a plane for four hours was not the business. I was all the way in the back, so I had to patiently wait for everyone else to exit.

After what seemed like forever, I jumped up and let out the biggest yell heard to man.

"Feel loose sir?"

"Oh yeah," I told the stewardess. "I'm bout to get off this thang and cut the fool."

"Have fun," she told me. I walked off the plane, grateful that I wasn't at O'Hare. That joint was too big. I landed at Midway with this one. It may not have been a private plane, but the airport itself was easier to navigate, even though I didn't even have to navigate O'Hare. I arrived at baggage claim and saw Eric with a huge grin on his face.

"My nigga," he greeted me with.

"Glad to be back man."

"I hope so. This just a quick turnaround. We out tomorrow morning."

"I know man. I know. Paris, right?"

"Oui oui nigga." I got a good laugh out of that as we waited for my bags to finally come on the carousel.

"We going back to the Hyatt E?"

"Only the best man. Only the best." I pumped my fists in sheer joy. I enjoyed it the first time around. This time would be shorter, but I knew it would still be turnt. We got my bags and headed out towards the parking garage. I heard the car alarm beep twice. "Damn my nigga," I said.

"I told you bruh. Only the best."

"What you call this?"

"Black Pearl." It was a fitting name. An all black 350, tinted windows and black chrome rims, with the license plate reading BLKKING. I couldn't knock it. My mans was a king, as he handled his business. And truthfully, that's what made a man a king. Handling his business. It wasn't the money. Shit, if you picked up trash for a living, but you kept your house in order, your family fed and never had them want for anything, you were a king. As a people, money was always a goal. However, our mindset had to shift in order to truly reach our potential. To be honest, we didn't control the money that we actually had. So, in order to compensate for that, we have to elevate ourselves in other areas to truly ascend to the top. And those other areas involve things in which money is not involved. I was impressed by Eric's wealth, but from the first encounter I had with him, his intrigue and intellect impressed me the most. We rolled out to Cicero Avenue, making our way towards the highway.

"This shit here man. After you see what we will encounter in two days, you won't even think about this," he told me. "Seychelles right?"

"Yeah man. The Motherland. Its an island of the Motherland. I'm telling you. I ain't never been. But to know that five of us gone be in the Motherland doing what we do. Man. Can't no amount of money buy that. And we get paid to do it." I simply nodded my head to his words and enjoyed the quaint ride threw the chilly Chi streets. We hit the highway and once again, traffic came to a standstill. The city was fresh off of a good snowfall the day prior, so it was definitely having its effect.

"Yo, how do you deal with this?," I asked him. Eric just started laughing.

"Man everywhere got their good and bad. Y'all got earthquakes. The middle, middle of the map got tornados. Down south got hurricanes. Up here, we got snow. Sometimes blizzards. I mean shit, and look at this muthafucka right here." He was referring to an idiot who tried to jump in another lane, but ended up smashing into the car behind him. "Anyways, but yeah. We got that too. Dumb asses who can't drive in the snow. But that's the Midwest. I swear this city the only city that can have all four seasons in one week. Fuck around be 22 today, 75 tomorrow, springy 65 the next day, 50 after that, go back up to 95 and be -12 by the end of the week. I swear on my mama Chicago is bipolar when it comes to weather." This nigga wasn't lying either. I could tell by the way he was talking. Shit, this made me appreciate California even more. I'll keep the earthquakes. I wasn't built for this shit. It took us literally an hour to get to the hotel. Once there, it was all love the minute I stepped through the door.

"Look at this nigga," said E.J. "Fuck you doing here?"

"I was gone ask you the same shit nigga. Too many black people in one space for you. This probably the largest amount of niggas you ever been around." Mook, Bryson and Eric started laughing, only to fuel his ass up.

"A look. I told you. Niggas is everywhere. We in Maine, Rhode Island, North Dakota, South Dakota, Montana,

Oregon, all that. Nigga I'm just unique."

"Yeah you right," said Bryson. "Unique as you the only nigga in the whole state." Again, the laughter shook the room.

"A man, just cause I ain't come from a plethora of niggas, don't make me no less black."

"Now wait a minute," Mook interrupted. "Ain't no one questioning your blackness dawg. Don't even go that far. We love you my nigga. But shit, you know we gone fuck with you. Shit, I told you the day Eric introduced us that I didn't know niggas existed in Maine. Shit, as a matter of fact, how many sisters y'all had up there?"

"A Handful."

"See, see. That's the shit that I'm talking about," as I came back in the conversation. "I gotta have me a gaggle of sisters around me."

"But hold up Ty. You from California. Y'all got more Mexican ass than anything," E.J. said.

"That may be true, but we got enough sisters too to where I would never go nuts. Boy you better be careful with them bunnies man. One gone mess around and invite you home for the weekend and her parents might end up hypnotizing yo' ass into something that you don't even know."

"Aight, Aight, y'all," Eric said, trying to contain himself. "Forreal though, serious biz. Let's go to the table and talk." This was the cool shit about this suite we were in. This damn thang had an individual meeting room. If that wasn't no impressive shit, I don't know what is. We were all seated as Eric reached into the refrigerator and handed everyone water except for me. "I got you a case of A&W man. I know you and this shit goes together like Jamaicans and weed smoke." I cracked that thang open and chugged. I could drink these all day. "Aight y'all, look. Everyone passports checked out so we all good. Tomorrow morning, we up at 4 a.m. We hitting the limo at five for the ride to the airport. We bounce out at seven for D.C. From there, Paris. From there, Seychelles. It's gone be a long day tomorrow. And really, two days, seeing how it's gone be a day ahead once we reach the Motherland. Are we good?" Mook raised his hand.

"Yeah man. So tell us like forreal. What's going down man. I mean, all I know is $250,000 for six months and cutting hair. Like, I'm good, trust me. I just want a clearer picture that's all."

"What's going down in Seychelles is that we gone be there for two weeks, teaching a lot of young cats over there how to cut hair. Its East Africa man. We get paid to go teach our own. Hell, we get to learn from our own as well. I mean what the real culture is."

"So we teaching and competing for six months correct?"

"Yes man. Some places teaching. When we competing, you gone know, cause I'm gone be on a whole other level. Anything else?" We looked around at each other. No one had nothing but a look in their eyes saying let's do this shit. "Aight man. Let's head to Harry Caray's joint. I need to get me some act right in my stomach," Eric told us. We headed downstairs, drinking at one of the bars, sippin' Cognac as we waited for the limousine to pull up. Life was in the palm of our hands right now. As the drinks kept flowing, slowly, so that we all wouldn't get faded too fast, I looked at the muted television. The news crew was somewhere in Chicago reporting about a murder. Reading the caption, it said ol' boy was gunned down near 147th and Halsted. I shook my head. The destruction that was being brought forth on my community was appalling.

"You aight," Mook asked me.

"Yeah man. I'm just seeing this shit on the TV and it hurts me man."

"Shit tell me about it. I lost mo' niggas back home in one year than they lost niggas in Iraq it seems. When the shit gone end man?" I think that was the six million dollar question. The limo eventually arrived and we headed out to Harry's steakhouse. It was a quick fifteen minute drive. We all indulged in some good cuts of meat, all while enjoying the majestic mystique of the Chicago Cubs. I wasn't from nowhere near here, but I could only imagine that excitement and joy of what would happen if they ever won the World Series. I firmly believe that the Great Chicago Fire would have a part two. Here we were, five black men who were about to embark on one of the most impactful journeys of our lives. I would say treacherous journey, but seeing how we were all black, we were only one step away from being lynched. That journey would never be complete until we were in the grave. We finished up after a good hour and a half of eating and drinking, and patiently waited for the limo to return while indulging in great conversation. Once it came, it was back to the telly. Unlike the first time, there was no individual suite. We were all locked in together for this one. None of us could risk missing this trip, so Eric ensured that for tonight, we all stayed together. We were separated into two rooms each, with Eric sleeping on the pullout in the main room. Bryson was in the room with me. We were each kicked back on our own beds, watching Menace 2 Society.

"Aww nigga, here go my favorite part. O Dog 'bout to cuss his ass out."

"Naw nigga. When fam say homey you need some help and then blast his ass. Now, that's a gangsta ass nigga right there," I told him.

"So was shit really like that in L.A?" I looked over at my mans. "Yeah man. That Blood Crip shit is real."

"But let me get this straight though. Y'all niggas beef with the same gang though. I don't get that shit." I just shrugged my shoulders.

"That's just how it is man. I ain't write the rule book."

"So after this trip, you gone stay out there where you at?"

"Yeah man. Why not?"

"Why?"

"What? Is it bad that I try to help out the same people that I came up with?"

"No. Not at all, but I never said you weren't helping them out. I said are you gone stay out there where you at?"

"Yeah nigga. Why not?"

"Ok man," as he sat up on the edge of the bed.

"Sit up and look at me face to face bruh." I really didn't want too, but I obliged. "Aight look fam bam. The job is to get out of the hood and stay out of that muthafucka. That doesn't mean don't visit. That doesn't mean you can't help out. But, if you come up and still wanna physically live in the same shit that you spent your entire life trying to escape, you crazy. Look. Saginaw. It's far from Compton. But it got its shit like everywhere else. I'm from an area called H&R

Block, and muthafuckas got taxed up on a daily. No pun intended. I grew up fist fighting, seeing niggas get shot, drug addicts, all of that. I made it to Northern Michigan University up there where people forget that Michigan even exists. Four years, some sports and a degree later, and I kept my ass up there. Why? It wasn't that I hated home. Naw. Its cause it was much more chill, it had a better vibe and way less bullshit than home or a lot of other places. How I help niggas in Sag you ask? I invented 'em up. Showed 'em how I was living. Showed 'em a different way. That's how I helped them. Now, if they choose to go back and do the same bullshit, that was on them. I played my part. Nigga with $250,000, I ain't no L.A. or SoCal guru, but shit move out to Irvine or Fullerton. And the only reason that I know about those places is 'cause I had a homey play for Cal State Fullerton not even three years ago. I took one trip out there and was amazed. Open up your own shop, or link up with someone out there and y'all do y'all thing together. Invite cats from the crib to come see a different way. I ain't saying forget about those niggas. Naw. Not even close. But, show 'em another way, in another city." I got what he was saying, but I wasn't trying to listen to him.

"My niggas had my back all my life. I can't just leave 'em. I wanna help. I wanna be there. I don't wanna be cities away. I wanna be in the heart of the hood, where my hood can see me doing good."

"So you gone stay around the same mess and want hood stardom? Ok man. It's your call."

"You right man. It's my call." He got up and headed to the bathroom. I was glad cause I was on the verge of wanting to ring his bell. Like, I couldn't stand that. Cats didn't wanna go back to the hood after leaving. That shit was a sham man.

"Oh yeah," as he cracked the bathroom door. "Remember that I asked you why move back. I never said shit about visiting or forgetting where you came from. Don't screw my words up nigga." He shut the door.

"JUST SPRAY IN THERE WHEN YOU DONE!!!," I yelled.

"NAW!!! I'M GONE LEAVE IT SHITTY JUST FOR YOU!!!" Fam indeed gave me a lot to ponder on.

"Wake up man. Wake up." I heard the voice, but I swore to

goodness that I was dreaming. "Wake up man." I got up swinging, hitting Bryson in his jaw in the process.

"Bruh, I'm so sorry," I whispered.

"No problem," he said, rubbing his jaw.

"What time is it man?," I asked him.

"There's the clock right there," as he pointed towards the TV. It was 3:41. Surprisingly, I wasn't phased by the bright light coming from the lamp. I guess that punch had me on ten from the jump.

"Damn man. What time did you get up man?"

"We all been up since 2:30 man. Man we went downstairs and got it in at their 24 hour cafe. A nigga ate some fire corned beef and everything." I was lowkey mad, but not too much, because I didn't like my sleep interrupted at any point. And truthfully, I was totally mad that I wasn't woken up at four on the dot. 3:41 was nineteen minutes that I couldn't get back. I slow bopped it to the bathroom, listening to the sounds of everyone else in this suite getting ready to bounce. I loaded up the Colgate on them bristles and got to work. Not even ten seconds in, I stopped. I looked in the mirror. Actually, I was locked in on my reflection. This would be the last time that I brushed my teeth in America for six months. It was something that wasn't registering with me. I tried to tell myself that it wasn't real, but it was.

"A nigga hurry up. I gotta shit." I curled over the sink laughing. That what his ass get.

"Hold on nigga." I rinsed my mouth out and opened the door.

"Damn nigga can you wait at least 'til I move."

"Corned beef coming out nigga." I shut the door right on time as Bryson let out a horrendous fart that could've killed half of the human population on earth. I shook my head and went over to put my clothes on. Lesson #97979 when taking a long trip. Shower the night prior. You damn sure don't wanna be rushing in the morning. I didn't know what to expect out of this weather in D.C., so I threw on a sweater, and an old fur coat joint I copped off of Dominique before I left.

"My nigga. Is we going to do barber work or are you going to pimp some bitches?" I looked up to see E.J. staring dead at me.

"Man I don't know how that crazy weather gone be like bruh. I'm just tryna stay warm for the long haul."

"Man we ain't doing nothing but connecting a flight. **A ERIC!!! COME LOOK AT THIS NIGGA!!!**" Eric rounded the corner along with Mook and just started laughing.

"What the fuck is this man? You from the West man. Not Milwaukee."

"Man nigga it's gone be cold."

"Man we connecting flights, not putting hoes on the stroll," Mook blurted out, laughing his ass off.

"Man, fuck all y'all," I told em. Bryson came out the bathroom spraying glade in the air like he was brother man from Martin.

"My nigga. What the fuck is that?"

"And fuck you too," I told him. 4:45 came around faster than I could've ever imagined. It was crazy that this was happening. We all headed downstairs via the elevator and rolled to the limo that was already waiting for us outside.

"Damn Bishop Don," said one of the valets as I entered outside. I just gave him a stern look while the others were cracking up. We loaded up into the limo.

"Look at it one last time fellas," Eric said. "We won't see Chicago, nor the states for a long while after this."

"I can fuck with that," Bryson said, holding a glass of champagne up.

"Nigga it's too early to be drinking but shit, po' me one up nigga," E.J. told him. Bryson passed the bottle to him as I got into my own zone. It was time to do this. I just didn't know how I would maintain this for all this time.

We ended up taking off from the airport at seven and arrived in DC a little before nine. Switching airlines, we made it through security to our international gate for our flight headed towards Paris. Looking at the screen, it would be a seven hour and forty five minute flight. I barely lasted being in the car for an hour. How in the good hell was I gonna survive nearly eight hours in the air? I was skeptical about this one. I had flown before, but never nothing to this extreme. Plus, me and water did not get along. Like, you hear about all those planes that crash on the long international flights. I did not wanna be the next victim either. It was one thing to be flying over land. At least if the plane crashed, they may find my body intact and still looking somewhat presentable for the casket. However, if that ho crashed over the Atlantic, man I would be in a shark's stomach when it was all said and done. Don't let me mess around and survive either. Then, I would have to fight to stay alive and feel a shark killing me in open water. As we sat on the runway waiting for take off, I saw that all of our seats were in different areas of the plane. Immediately, once the flight attendants did their thing and told the passengers the usual about safety precautions and how long the flight would be, I put on my beats and zoned out to the one song that could put my mind at ease, which was Wale's "Nike Boots." Ironic that he was from DC and I was leaving this mofo for good. I felt the plane take off as I started to see Compton in my rear view mirror. I started to see my cousins and everyone else waving goodbye to me. I also saw a lot of dead homies beggin' for me to take them on the ride. Oh how I wish I could do that. How I wish I could go to the graveyard and raise 'em from the dead. How I wish that I could take the bullets back.

Then, you just had some homies who were giving us the example of success way before any of us could ever realize it. One of the big homies was named Quentin. Now, the only reason I knew Quentin was because I ended up slicing his brother head up a few times. See Quentin was bred in Campanella Park. Much like every young brother who came up out of there, he was Piru. However, unlike a lot of brothers who were from that neighborhood, he had a vision and a plan of action with everything that he put his hands on. I mean, if you asked this nigga to make a sandwich, he made a plan on how he would layer each piece of meat, ingredient or whatever else consisted in the sandwich. This would come in handy when he got a lil older in the game. See Quentin had a knack for cooking, much like myself. Except with him, no one had to show him. He naturally was inquisitive when it came to food. He was throwing together shit at a young age and just going to town with it. At least that's what his brother told me. So after graduating high school, he devised a plan and went out to San Diego. He linked up with a blood nigga from Skyline that he knew had gotten out of the game and became a chef. With the right guidance and proper teaching, Quentin was now in South Dakota, running his own restaurant business called "Dre Day." Now why would anyone name a restaurant Dre Day. Well, for two reasons. One, in Compton, niggas knew Dre was one of the best to come out. Two, Dre Day was a dis and involved one of the first times it involved Snoop on a track. It went hard. So with the same toughness that song brought to the rap world, he wanted to bring that same toughness to the cooking world. Dre Day's smoke shack was born and he set the state of South Dakota on fire. He went from one restaurant in Pierre, to nine throughout the Midwest. Classic items such as "Lincoln Park Greens, Spooktown Sandwich, Piru Playa Platter, and the world famous Skyline Strip Steak made his name one that you couldn't leave out of your households. To white folks, they just saw crazy names attached to some crazy, yet filling dishes. To the hood, we saw embracing of different sets, flipped to represent something that could attach to your soul. And food was something that could do that with anyone. I learned a lot just by watching him.

Seeing how he set an example by leaving the city and making a name for himself. It actually helped the city and helped me in the process. He is one of the ones who gave me the motivation to do what I do. To go out and actually become an asset and not a statistic. I hadn't made it out to one of his joints yet, but it was something that I definitely had in mind when I returned to the states. According to his brother, the best joint on the menu was the "VL5 popper" and the "7-4-14." What were those you ask? The VL 5 popper was a staple. Five jalapenos stuffed with bison meat, more peppers and two types of cheeses. But the kicker was that they were deep fried and smothered in a sauce he concocted called "Burning Asshole." I think the name is self explanatory. The 7-4-14 was a monstrous challenge. On top of a 1 1/2 pound bison patty, was 7 thick cut strips of beef bacon, topped with 4 jumbo sized fried eggs, with the yolks runny may I add and smothered in pork gravy. You had 28 minutes to finish it. If you did, you'd eat free for a year and get your name put on the wall. If you didn't finish it in 28 minutes, which most people didn't, you were coming $60 out of pocket. It sounded nutty and wild, but shit like that gave us hope in the hood. Quentin was my nigga if he didn't get any bigger. We were two hours into the flight and all was good to go so far. I was watching Saw 3D on the screen and just taking in the entire experience. Time constantly flew by as right after this, I would watch the original Saw. Once that was over, I still had over two hours of flight time left. I spent those next two hours the only way that I saw fit. Reading. I reached into my bag and pulled out a book that I thoroughly enjoyed. It was entitled "They Came Before Columbus" by Ivan Van Sertima. I think you can pretty much figure out what the book was about from the title. I marinated my eyes into this masterful piece of work for the next two hours until the words that would shake my soul blasted over the plane's speaker. *"We are beginning our final descent into Paris."* I literally froze up as those words played over and over in my head as if someone had told me that I hit the lottery for 100 million. I immediately put the book away and cocked my head back, trying to lower my heart rate. There was nervousness, excitement and anxiety all wrapped up in one. I was really about to be in another country. Like, that shit wasn't resonating with me. Not another state, but another country. The next thing I remember was hearing French Words while walking from the plane into the awaiting airport. "Oui oui nigga."

"E.J., chill nigga. You ain't French."

"Shit nigga. Dick don't discriminate. French pussy, American pussy, its all pussy."

"Where's Eric, Bryson and Mook?"

"Hell still stuck on that monster ass plane probably." No sooner than he said that, all three of 'em were coming off the plane.

"Gents. Welcome to Paris. Now, let's get our asses to this other gate, for this other long ass flight."

"Wait hold on," I told E. "How long is the flight there?"

"11 hours."

"11 HOURS!!!"

"Ain't that what he said fool," Mook chimed in.

"Don't worry bruh. We got two hours before we catch that one. But, I know my black ass gone be near the gate when they board us. Shit I told you it was gonna be a long day or two. Shit let's ride," Eric said. We began walking through this monstrosity of an airport. I was taking in the faces, sights and just different culture that I was now apart of. To add to that, E.J. wasn't lying. It was some bad ass French women in here. I ain't know if they spoke English or not, but they were fine. Shit, and the crazy part about it was that there were a lot of sisters. You could tell these were French sisters and not American sisters. When I say we are everywhere, we are literally everywhere. We made it down to our gate. To our luck, there was a restaurant sitting right across from it. I couldn't pronounce the name of it, but from the smell, we all figured it was gravy. Eric took care of the bill on his black card as we indulged in some wings, pastrami sandwiches and all sorts of other shit. Eating and looking at beautiful French women pass us woke us all up.

"Man I wonder how those sisters gone look in Africa," Eric said.

"I know damn well they gone be some beauties," I told him.

"Man," E.J. said with buffalo sauce dripping from his mouth. "What if them hoes like jungle bunnies, swinging from vines and shit?"

"You would think that shit you crazy muthafucka," Bryson told him. "Maybe cause you like them hoodrat jungle bitches swinging from dick to dick."

"A, I don't deal with jungle hoodrat bitches," E.J. responded. "I deal with big bitches. I need me an ass behind them legs and a least a good 180–190 on the scale."

"Man I don't see how you do it," Mook told him. "Easy nigga. Man don't nobody want these skinny bitches walking around. I want something thick. Something when you hit her once, she throw that shit right back at you. I wanna see the soundwaves in her ass. Like nigga, put a radar near her ass and detect the doppler radar of that shit." I spit my drink out and so did Bryson as we laughed our ass off. This boy was a plum fool. We kept at it for the next hour and some change, enjoying life in another country, even though we were just stuck in the airport.

"A Eric. What time we gone get there tomorrow?"

"Three in the afternoon."

"Shit ok," I told him. "I was just making sure. Cause we left in the a.m. and now we over here in the wee hours of the a.m."

"I can't believe this bitch still packed though my nigga," Mook said.

"It's Paris. I wouldn't expect anything less. You won't see this shit in America. Don't nobody wanna visit that ass clown of a place." They all looked at me.

"What you mean?," Bryson asked me.

"C'mon man. I guarantee that tomorrow and for the rest of the trip, we gone be treated like Gods. My peoples who been in the military done told me 'bout overseas. We're loved. Everywhere. People know our power and lineage. It's just in that corrupt ass place called America is where they don't love us."

"Well, we gone see," he responded. "We definitely gone see." We wrapped up everything when they called that they were about to board. Motherland, I'd be there soon. I was knocked out beyond belief until I felt someone shaking me something serious.

"What what," I got up saying, groggy as ever.

"Look at that shit man." I wasn't comprehending what Mook was saying, but when I looked outside, I immediately turned up inside something serious. I saw nothing but the sun's reflection off of the water and green everywhere. Not to mention that I could tell that it had gotten hot as ever. The A/C on the plane was cool, but I knew that I was about to walk into a tropical paradise. I had ditched the fur in Paris and boy was I lucky. We descended down and I felt the thump of the plane as we skidded across the runway. *"Ladies and gentlemen. Welcome to Seychelles, East Africa."* Those words announced by the pilot did us all justice. Everyone, especially black people felt an obligation to one day get to the Motherland. This was the birthplace of all civilization. Even if you didn't believe Adam and Eve were the first two people on earth, which they weren't, this was where civilization started. We were in the land where the great kings of Ancient Kemet built diamonds that still stood to this day. We were in the land of the flowing Nile River, the longest river on earth. In the place where the Great Wall of Zimbabwe existed. The place that has all the gold, diamonds and exotic animals. The place that the world wanted because they knew how valuable we were to this world. That is exactly why everyone wants to destroy the black man, because they know how powerful we are and that we are the true children of Mother Earth. All of us looked at each other on that plane with looks of excitement in our eyes.

"We got a private vehicle waiting for us y'all. This is it. This is what we worked for. For the next few days, we party and take in everything that Mother Earth has got to offer. At the same time, we show these people how to cut hair. Let's roll." Those words from Eric soaked into my cranial. One by one we exited the plane, but I was the last one off.

"Ooo Shit," I said as I stepped off that joint and into the blazing hot sun. It was at least 95 degrees over here. I pulled my sweater off with the quickness while watching the gentlemen place our bags into the huge Navigator that was waiting for us. Man talk about an introduction to the world. This shit was beyond savage. I felt like a damn king. We entered in and none of us said a word. We were all in amazement as the truck took off and drove us to the hotel. Looking through the tinted glass, I saw lush greenery everywhere. As we rolled through the winding hills, it looked like we were in a combination of Oregon having sex with Florida.

The villages we passed let you know that we were a far cry from the normal streets of America. It was unique, however. We winded past another hill and onto a gravel road. There was a school on the left sitting on top of a hill. To the right, there was a community center. We hit a quick right at the community center and continued on down the road. We then bust a left. At that moment, I saw one of the most spectacular courtyards the eye could ever imagine. Then, we stopped. Our doors were opened up by a black man in a tropical shirt.

"Gentlemen, welcome to your home for the foreseeable future. The Berjaya Beau Vallon Bay Resort and Casino." We exited out, with myself like on the plane, exiting out last. We were all speechless. I was wanting someone to pinch me to tell me that this wasn't real. They didn't have to, however. It was real. I did a full 360, seeing nothing but rolling greenery. The Motherland was more than beautiful. It was a hidden gem.

"Well I'll be damned," E.J. said.

"We all be damned," Eric said.

"I knew we were coming up, but I could never imagine this."

"Gentleman, right this way," the escort said. The middle aged brother led us to the lobby, where Eric begun the check in process. We handed him our passports to confirm everything.

"Thank you sir. Here are all of your room keys." I saw five keys being handed to him.

"Bruh, you mean to tell me that we all get our own separate rooms?," I asked him.

"Hell yeah. You think I come all the way to Africa to share a room with y'all? You must be crazy. I might come up tonight on the beach. I can't bring something back with one of y'all in there. Oh, sorry E.J. Ain't no heavy weights over here."

"Shid. I'll find one," he said. We all laughed as our bags were out of the car and on carts, with hotel staff ready to take it to our rooms. I looked at my room key 228.

"Where yo shit at?," I asked Mook.

"226."

"A," Eric said. "We all next to each other. 226 through 234. Close enough to keep tabs on each other. Far enough to do our own thang." E walked off with the staff who had his cart and I purposely waited for the rest of them to go upstairs. I gave it about five minutes before I told the agent to head upstairs. We made it up the three flights of stairs to the second floor. I was met with an unique smell that said "fun." I didn't even realize that there wasn't an elevator in here and that the staff had carried my joints up. I slow bopped it down the hallway until I made it too my room.

"WOOO!!!" I heard that scream in the distance. By the voice I could tell it was E.J. Either he had found a big one or there was a steak sitting on a platter, 'cause those were the only two things that he ever got excited over.

"Thank you sir. I'll take it from here." He nodded his head at me, leaving me with my two huge luggage bags. I took the key and unlocked the door slowly. Once I opened it up, I stood in amazement. I took two steps in, and hurried up and went back out to grab my things. Had I stayed in an amazed state, I woulda left my joints in the hallway. I brought them in and sat them by the door. Now, was the room a top tire suite? Not at all. However, how many rooms do you know have three beds in 'em? Three nigga. Three. I had two full sized beds, with a twin by the window, that was facing out into the courtyard. The bathroom was a bathroom, but the walk in shower was cold with it ya dig. I had a flat screen and a refrigerator, so everything was all gravy. I plopped down on one of the beds and just laid there for a good ten minutes. I was here. I was still in shock. I was really in Africa. **BOOM! BOOM! BOOM!** I got up to answer the door. I opened it up to see Eric.

"A, we'll meet downstairs in the lobby at seven. Gone rest up for a lil bit. I already told everyone else."

"Cool." I shut the door. I looked at the clock by the television and saw that it was 4:59 p.m. That left me two hours to just relax. I had already slept enough on the flights over here. As crazy as it may sound, I had already gotten used to the time and day change. I took the time to unpack my things and store them in the dressers and closet. I was situated totally around 5:30. Seeing how it was hot outside, I simply pulled out a white Hanes undershirt and some basketball shorts. I didn't see us doing anything extraordinary tonight. We had did enough traveling and I figured that we would lounge around the hotel tonight, getting our chill on at one of the bars they had here. I cut on the TV as I got comfortable in this bed of mines. Luckily for me, the TV channels were all channels that were common in the states. I found TNT and saw that Rush Hour 3 was on. I was now in chill mode. With more than an hour and some change left until we met up, I debated about making some calls. "Nah," I said out loud. I'd call my grandma in the morning. I'd call Kev in the morning. Tonight, I planned on getting good and fucked up. They could wait. They'd be aight. Wasn't anything gonna distract me from getting it in on my first night in the Motherland. 6:45 rolled around and I walked outside of my room.

"Man its boomin downstairs."

"Yeah Mook. I hear that shit. Hope it's some bad breezy's

to go with that music." We were both chillin, waiting on the others. As we continued to chop it up, one by one, everyone made their way out.

"Well skip the lobby then huh," Bryson said, as he was the last one to make it out the room.

"You right," E.J. replied. "Let's hit this bar up. A nigga ready to drink." We moseyed on down the hallway and to the stairs. Once down, we were welcomed with the sight of sights. It was packed like all hell on the beach. I mean, the sun had made its descent about 90% underneath the Earth, so all you saw was the bright and beautiful rainbow colors that were cascading over the Indian Ocean. To our right, there was one bar, which seemed to hold the older crowd. But near the beach, that's where all of the action was taking place.

"Well niggas. I say right there," as Bryson pointed to the beach bar. "I'd say that's where we gone get it in at."

"Well, y'all niggas head that way. I'm hitting this buffet over here. My fat ass gotta eat."

"I'm right behind you my nigga." E.J. and Mook took off for the buffet that was adjacent to the bar. The rest of us made our rounds to you know where. Once over there, it was bananas. I said I was gonna get fucked up, but I wanted to remember the night as much as possible.

"Gimme three mango pineapples," I told the bartender. Those other two fools went straight for the medicine cabinet, ordering the cure of all cures. Hennessey. As Coolio's "Fantastic Voyage" blared through the speakers, we were met with all types of women. We weren't the only brothers over here, but we were the only brothers from America. Man, we stuck out like a sore thumb. Me with my tight white hanes T on, exposing the muscles. The Nike basketball shorts and my Oregon State fitted. Eric with his white and blue Ralph Lauren, with the denim polo jeans and white with blue trim polo shoes to match. The fitted of his choice was a simple, yet classic New York Yankees joint. Bryson was thinkin' like me. Black Nike shorts, with the grey wife beater, exposing his arsenal of tattoos that covered his entire upper torso. On his feet, the grey and white Kyrie Irving's, with a steel grey and black Portland Trail Blazers fitted. As far as the other two, well, E.J. was being E.J. Black denims, a colorful polo, some pearl white ones and an all black Spurs joint. Mook, well shit, I forgot what Mook was wearing, but with his eating habits, he had probably spilled all kinds of food on his clothes by now. I sipped my drank as if it were alcohol, chillin under this cabana. The sounds of the ocean crashing seemed to mingle in with the music in a way that it felt like it became a part of the music. For the next hour, the three of us engaged in conversation with random people, all while satisfying our liver with what it needed. Only for me, mines wasn't alcoholic.

"Yo nigga. That shit was fiya."

"Damn E.J. Do you gotta lean all over me?," Bryson said.

"Nigga I don't know what some of that shit was called, but a nigga do remember crab legs."

"Yeah I know. So can you go coax that seafood breath somewhere else my nigga?"

"Fuck you nigga. Order me a drink."

"Yo, where Mook?," Eric asked him, a lil bit slizzard.

"Man that nigga met a bad bitch in a brown dress. I call her the brown dress wearing bitch. Nigga she had an ass so big, that muthafucka could eclipse the moon."

"Oh so y'all niggas getting ass and ain't tellin nobody huh?"

"Man if you don't turn yo' Compton ass around and finish drinking. All this scattered pussy out here and you asking why I ain't plug you. Shit nigga I was eating. Now, I go get bitches." E.J. clasped his hands and disappeared over into the crowd, looking for a victim.

"So my nigga," Bryson asked me. "How you enjoying this shit?"

"My nigga," as I threw my hands up when the DJ cut on Buy U A Drank.

"Nigga this is the life. I don't need shit right now. I got everything I ever wanted." Indeed I did have everything I wanted right now. I was in a foreign land, non alcoholic drink in my hand, surrounded by the ocean and thick ass women.

"You wanna dance American man?" We looked over to see Eric being grabbed by one of the baddest creatures any of us had ever seen. I didn't know what country she was from, but she was black and had the sexiest accent a nigga had ever heard. She helped Eric's almost drunk ass up and escorted him to the grassy area so they could get their groove on.

"Nigga I need some of that," I told Bryson.

"Nigga tell me about it. We got some time here. I know it's coming. Yo, look at this nigga E.J." I turned around as he pointed towards where the sand met the concrete walkway. That boy had his arm around two heavyweights. In a land of nice bodied, slim in the waist, thick in the ass type women, he found two big ones. He had each arm around them, looked back at us and chucked the deuces, signaling that he was about to head upstairs and slay those gigantic mammoths. Just then, some white girl just randomly came and kissed Bryson in the mouth, grabbing his hand and escorting him away. Now, it was me and me alone by myself at the bar, wondering what was gonna come and scoop me. I didn't wait for it. With my niggas gone, I said screw it and began to walk around the rest of this outside mecca. I got up and ventured east of the bar by one of the largest heated pools I had ever saw in life. Surrounding this pool was a plethora of bad ones. I slow strolled, making sure they saw me. I hit another bar that was attached to a restaurant. I didn't even know this was here. I noticed the buffet from jump, but this eatery joint was tucked away. There weren't many people in here, but the ones that were, they all were indulged in some pizza. I walked through and came to a sign that said private residents only. Just adjacent to the restaurant, there was what seemed to be townhomes. Now, this was the part that looked like the States. If only I could get in these, I know that whatever was in the hotel would be irrelevant to me. I began to make my way back towards the bar by the beach, when I saw what E.J. was talking about in the brown dress. My mouth dropped and I damn near dropped my drInk. This sister was thicker than a pot of grits with butter, salt and cheddar cheese. I mean, her ass was a good, round shaped, natural ass. You could tell that no botox injections hit that one. She was just blessed. I continued on with my walk until I made it down to the sand and just stared into the night sky. I wasn't going down into the sand, seeing how the tide had came in and I wasn't getting my shoes wet. I simply basked in the goodness of the ocean sounds and the good drink. It felt good to drink and not get lit. I toasted to the night sky, thanking the kings who came before me for creating such a magnificent place. I was on one and it felt good. I stayed out 'til around midnight, when most of the crowd started to file out. I hadn't come up on anything, but I was gravy. I made my way back towards the room. Heading up the stairs, you couldn't tell me nothin. I was in a world of my own. As I hit the second floor, everything seemed normal. I got back to my room, but noticed that room 232 was cracked open. I knew that was one of us, so I made it my business to see what was going on. I put my ear near the door, hearing nothing but the television. I cracked it open and saw two feet facing down from one bed, and two feet facing up from another. Walking in, I saw a beautiful sight in the far bed, as this chick was ass naked and glistening. Man it looked like her body had been made out of clay. She was knocked the hell out. The room smelled like padussy, so I knew some slaying had been going on in here. When I rounded that corner, shit got ugly.

"NIGGA!!! MAN WHAT THE FUCK YOU DOING IN HERE???!!!"

"C'mon Mook. Put that shit up."

"The fuck you doing in my room?" I caught this nigga rubbing his damn meat.

"Nigga you left the door cracked open. I was making sure you were gravy."

"Oh shit. Forreal?"

"Nigga you drunk, but I'll leave you alone cause I know you good now. Plus, I ain't trying to converse with a nigga who got his nuts out."

"What you come up on?," he asked me as I was leaving the room.

"Not a *** damn thing," as I chucked a deuce in the air and proceeded back to my room to call it a night. I slept by the window. I had two big ass beds, but I chose to sleep in the twin sized joint. Something about waking up and directly looking at lush greenery was amazing to me. Even better, when I pulled back the blinds, I saw stars like I had never seen before. I immediately jumped out of the bed, put my shoes on and headed back downstairs. I walked outside to the courtyard. With a crystal clear night and the weather feeling like heaven, I looked up. It seemed like the movie Bruce Almighty. It was like someone had put the stars in the sky individually and then pulled the moon very close to the earth, because it was beyond huge. I just stared in amazement. I had never saw anything this beautiful in my life.

"They're beautiful aren't they?" I turned around to see the woman in the brown dress in some boy shorts and a wife beater. "Are you from America?"

"Yes I am miss lady. Ty."

"Arita."

"Arita," as I shook her hand. "And what part of the world are you from?"

"Aussie. Come to have some fun you know." At that same moment of saying that, she gave me the look of wanting to have some fun.

"Well we can continue this in room 228 if you'd like. We can have a lot of fun."

"You lead the way." I grabbed her hand, laughing a lil bit with her as I cracked a joke here and there.

"So what are you here for Ty?" That accent was getting a nigga on swole, but I couldn't get brick just yet. I didn't wanna be walking up the stairs at attention. "Barber convention."

"Oh, so you like to play with hair I see?" She smiled as she said that and walked through the door to enter the second floor. I had to be careful. I didn't wanna snatch her shit out all the way. Just give her a couple of good and decent tugs to let her know who she was fucking with. We got to my room and I opened up the door. She walked in as I stood there. She stopped three steps into the room, took her wife beater off, covered her breasts and looked back, laughing at me. She ran and jumped on the bed. Oh yea, I was about to take down all 6'0 of her. Yes indeed. She was a sister from Australia and a brother was truly about to visit the land down under. I didn't give a fuck about her being taller, because we all the same size when we lay down. Around eleven o'clock the next afternoon, I heard the bangin of my room door. I jumped up out the bed, wondering who in the good hell was this beating on my shit like that. I grabbed a towel from the bathroom on the way to open it. "Yo," as I opened the door, still half asleep.

"Damn nigga. You must've had one helluva jackoff session last night." They laughed at E.J.'s gander, but I wasn't phased by any of it. Just then, they all got silent and their eyes wandered past me. I turned around. Arita had put on one of my oversized shirts and came into view.

"I'm sorry gentlemen. Am I interrupting anything?"

"Naw you ain't beautiful. Gimme a minute," I told her. I walked in the hallway with my partnas.

"Nigga when you get that?," E.J. whispered.

"Last night, while y'all niggas were handling ya own business. Shit don't even play ya boy. I put that Spooktown on her. These niggas bust out laughing, keeping their voices down in the process.

"Well look," Eric said. "Meet us downstairs in the lobby at 12. We catching a cab to a barbershop in Victoria. Time to do the other thing we came here for. But good job my nigga." Fam dapped me up along with everyone else and I rolled back in the room.

"A love. I gotta go cut some hair with my guys you know. We here to teach some guys the master aspect of barbering."

"Oh that's great," she said. "Are you coming back?"

"Yeah, we here for a few days." She smiled and came over to me, pushing me against the bed. She commenced to give me the most illustrious blowjob I had ever receive in my life. My eyes rolled into the back of my skull, my toes were curling and then, she did some shit I couldn't believe. This nasty broad cocked both of my legs back and proceeded to give a brother a rim job. For y'all that don't know, she started to flick her tongue in and out of my asshole. I didn't know whether to scream like a bitch or question my manhood. Either way, I didn't stop her. She had fun with that, came back up and got right back to sucking. After gulping down all of my kids, she proceeded to tell me her room number and to hit her up when I got back. Then, she left. I was in a trance on my bed. The head was no longer the issue. This freaky bitch really ate my ass. I didn't ask for that shit and a brother didn't like anything near his bootyhole. But I can't front, it felt good than a muthafucka.

It was something that I would never tell the boys about. After coming back to earth once my soul entered back into my body, I jumped up and took the quickest shower known to man. I hustled up and threw on some jeans and a black tee. I raced out the room towards downstairs because it was 11:56. Once there, I saw all those fools just looking at me.

"Well it's about time man," Mook yelled out.

"We was bout to leave yo ass. You know what 11:45 look like?"

"Indeed I do brother, but you ain't saying no to some deep throat. Nann one of y'all niggas. Shit I would've just walked to Victoria if need be."

"Nigga please," Bryson let out. "But I ain't mad at you though. That bitch was bad my nigga." Fam bam dapped me up and we all rolled out to the taxi van waiting outside. As I was the last one to enter, I put my head down and thought to myself. Wow, this bitch really threw my legs back and licked my asshole. I couldn't believe that shit.

We caught the cab down to the Victoria district of the island. I mean, when I say this place was something else, it really was. Coming down the hill leading to the Victoria district, the view of the Indian Ocean just amazed me. You could see it clear as day, sprawled out over the rolling green vegetation of the hills. Our cab driver was an elderly black man. He stated that he was 67. From the looks of it, he didn't look a day over 45. We conversed with him, doing more listening than talking. It was crazy what he was dropping on us.

"We're calm over here. Everything is natural. We eat natural, we birth natural. We embrace all of mother earth and all that she gives. So we give her back twice as much as she gives to us. She is the womb and we are all encased in her. You put into her and she gives back out unto you." His knowledge and wisdom was astounding to say the least. With all the American money that we hadn't exchanged yet, he stopped at an ATM near our drop off point. Hear, one US Dollar was 13 of theirs. When we were informed of this, I started to calculate in my head how much I had actually put on my card last night. 6 pineapple and mango drinks at 62 rupees a piece. I paid $24 dollars total for six drinks. Yea, that was more than amazing. I took out 6,800 rupees, which was $500 in American. We got back in the cab and was dropped off right in the the district. "Mon Kontan Sesel" was the name on the sign that we were dropped off in front of.

"The hell that mean?," E.J. asked Eric.

"Man you asking me like I'm supposed to know."

"Nigga you the one who flew us over here. At least I knew oui oui in Paris."

"Nigga everyone knows oui oui," Mook said. I just laughed as we walked and explored, looking for the barbershop. Upon our walk, I noticed a building that I had read about in one of my books.

"What the hell is that Eric?"

"E.J. why you keep asking me like I'm the fucking tour guide?" They may not have known, but I knew clear as day. This was the legendary Arulmigu Navasakti Vinayagar Temple, the only Hindu temple in Seychelles. We hit a right and got into the heart of Victoria. The sidewalks here were almost non existent, so we had to be real careful. None of us wanted to come here and get smacked by a moving vehicle. However, with what we were all seeing, that would be highly unlikely, as we saw a lot of people roaming the streets. The street was filled with side shops and boutiques. We kept going and that's when we spotted it.

"There it is. 1st floor. Room 104."

"Where you see that at Mook?," I asked.

"Right there," as he pointed out eagerly to all of us.

"Aight gents, let's make history," Eric said. We all scoured and searched until we found the stairs that were leading up to the floor. They were located in the middle of the building, and Mook ass almost got hit by a car trying to chase down a pack of females. I can't lie. They were some beautiful sisters. Ludacris was right. The most beautiful women in the world did reside in Africa. I had only been here for a day. However, all of the native Seychelles women that I had saw wore no make up. Their hair was natural and curly. It wasn't induced by relaxers, weave or any other chemical you could imagine. Their skin tone was smooth as if they ate right all the time and drunk nothing but the purest of water. There were no butt or lip injections. Arita from last night was just a glimmer. From what I was seeing while walking around, the ugliest woman here was an eight.

Joe McClain Jr.

"Welcome gentlemen. You must be our brothers from America." As Eric greeted the guy speaking, the rest of us were looking around this joint. I know none of us wanted to say anything, but this didn't look like much of a barbershop. It looked like more of a kids room with two chairs. Oh well, it truly didn't matter to me. Real barbers cut hair in all kinds of places. We cut in shops. We cut in basements. Hell, half the niggas I sliced up in Compton was in backyards, with homies lifting weights behind us. Eric introduced all of us to the four men who were in here and we started our training session. They had two young adults in here. They couldn't have been more than age 15. As E.J. and Bryson begun to cut the two kids up, with two barbers at each chair learning, me and Mook just sat back, observing everything. Eric was explaining to the barbers the techniques of everything. More than anything, the barber's over here were surprised that we had top of the line equipment. Their clippers did the job, but they weren't high quality like the stuff we had. We spent about two hours in there, taking turns cutting heads, to include the barbers. As we were getting ready to end our session, a young man walked in.

"Excuse me sir." I looked around.

"He talking to you man," Eric blurted out.

"What's going on lil man?," as I extended my fist towards him for a fist pound.

"Could we get haircuts from you too? You guys are gods." I just smiled and looked at my partners.

"Well, yeah. Who is we?" Lil man ran outside and shouted downstairs. In two minutes there was a line that was halfway around the building. What had started off with two teenagers and four adults, had now turned into a million kids it seemed.

"Oh sir. Sorry," the African brother said to Eric.

"We were not expecting this. We cannot pay for this."

"Don't worry," Eric told him. "What we have is enough. We'd be more than honored to stay and cut the people of this beautiful land up. **AIN'T THAT RIGHT FELLAS???!!!**" E.J. threw his clippers up like let's go. For the next several hours, we rotated, taking turns giving these kids free haircuts. Their ages ranged from seven to seventeen. The looks on their faces were priceless as I saw the power of what can happen when you simply make someone feel good with clippers.

"Excuse me sir."

"Whats up man?," E.J. said. "Can you give me the Russell Westbrook?"

"The fu–I mean, what's that?"

"You know. The mohawk. I want to dunk like him." E.J. looked up at me and shrugged his shoulders. I shrugged 'em back laughing as I was putting a star design in another kids head. The others were sitting back, laughing it up with the other elders of the shop. We got all kinds of requests during the day. From Russell Westbrook, to one kid who wanted everything shaved off so he could have his head shined like Michael Jordan. Eric got a request to give one kid who had a monstrous beard the James Harden lining. But the bread and butter came when we were down to only a few heads left and Bryson was slicing folks up.

"Sir, can you just fuck me up?"

"Excuse me," he said, stunned like the rest of us were.

"You know. The fuck me up. In America, they sometimes say that your head game is fucked up. I want the fuck me up." E.J. turned around in his chair trying not to laugh out loud. Everyone else put their heads in their shirts. I was more amazed that a kid actually asked for the fuck me up, as if it was a real haircut.

"Let me get this one Bryson," I told him.

"Yeah man. You got it." The kid had a mini fro, so I had to see what the hell I was gonna do without fucking him up.

"I got you man. Don't worry. I'm gone show you the fuck me up and have you be the hottest brother in the land with this one." Eric just start hollerin' and left out. The other two African brothers didn't have a clue what was going on. I started off picking everything out. Then, I hit the sides up for a good skin fade mid length. I went to work on the form. Picking it, shaping it into a box. Then, came time to part his head and slope it. To end it, I left a patch in the back of his head and put a rat tail in it. Now, his joint was fucked up, but he would be the freshest fucked up boy on this island. Shit, to tell you the truth, he would probably get more ass than any of the high schoolers. "Peep it out man." I handed him the mirror.

"Oh man. This is cool. What do you call this in America?" Everyone looked at me. I truly didn't know what to call this. "Umm, In America, we call this the Bobby Brown. Or, even better. Just say it's the New Edition and they'll be all on you."

"Cool cool," as he jumped out of the seat. "Thank you. Thank you."

"Hold on," I said.

"Gotta take the barber cape off of you. Can't run off with that." That was a good laugh as the kid took off out of the building. We all went outside to see hoards of kids who had gotten their hair cut hours ago still waiting. The oohs and ahhs that echoed in the streets were indeed heart warming.

"Boy do that kid really know what you did to him?," Eric whispered in my ear.

"Naw, he dont. But it don't matter. Look what we did collectively." We were just in awe as a group of fresh cut kids were running through the streets of Victoria, happier than a pig in a pile of shit. Who knew that something so simple could turn into something that was bigger than life itself.

"A y'all, come in here for a minute." We all walked back inside, where it was only one of the African brothers left. Eric went to a back room and grabbed a briefcase. Coming back and placing it on a circular table, he popped it open.

"The fuck is the money E?," Mook asked.

"Right here."

"That look like a laptop to me."

"Remember when I had all of you get Bank of America accounts? This is why." He logged in and showed us the money that had just went into his account.

"I'm $15,000 richer. As for y'all, you guys are splittin 475,000 Seychelles rupees."

"So how much is that?," I asked.

"$35,000 in cold hard U.S. cash."

"So wait wait," E.J. said. "You mean to tell me that us four cutting up some hair, we splitting thirty five grand?"

"Nigga that's near nine a piece," Mook chimed in.

"Gone head and log into your account Mook. Peep it if you don't believe me." Mook logged into his Bank of

America account. **"HOLY SHIT!!!,"** he yelled out. That's all that I needed to hear as I knew that everything was legit.

"So wait, wait, wait, wait , wait." It was E.J. once again, clapping his hands in front of his face.

"Nigga be real with me. Who in the good hell pay $35,000 for brothers to come slice some heads up and teach a few tips. This don't seem like them two barbers paid us."

"Not them. They government. You'd be surprised at what governments spend their money on. I dunno if some of them niggas got some bad cuts or what. All I know is that they put the money in the bank. Now, let's get in this van cab waiting downstairs and get ready for tonight."

"What's tonight?," I asked.

"Yacht party my nigga," Eric responded. We got back to the hotel at 6:14 on the dot. We weren't bouncing out until ten, so we all had time to celebrate and pre game here. Immediately, all them dudes went to the bar to start their drunken escapades. Me, I was hungry as shit. Those sandwiches they gave us at the shop were good, but they didn't fill me up. I hit the buffet up. Parrot was the name of it, but I was about to eat like a dirty bird. I loaded up my plate to the max and summoned my inner fat boy. Not to mention they had some African grits. Now, I didn't know the major difference between regular grits and African grits. However, one thing was common. There wasn't any sugar in these thangs. It was good to know that they weren't spawns of satan over here.

I spent a good hour in there and barely made it back to my room. I scrambled through my closet, looking to see what I was gonna wear tonight on this yacht. I didn't wanna be too laid back, nor did I wanna be overly dressed. So, In the end, I settled on some black jeans, a black tee and my black timbs. Fuck it, I thought. I was in the Motherland, so it was all black everything. I mean, I know I was young, but some niggas killed me with the notion that they thought they knew fashion. I couldn't see anything fashionable about jeans and shirts. When you say fashion to me, I think of suits, slacks, dress shirts, shit like that. Being fashionable in some jeans and a t-shirt? Nah. And what the fuck was up with some of those trends? Niggas wearing skinny jeans where their nuts couldn't breathe. Then you had cats wearing jeans with holes in em, or they were ripped. When I was coming up, if I had a hole in my jeans, it was cause mama was poor and she couldn't get anymore jeans for me at that time. She'd sew a patch over those things and call it a day. Now, cats were paying prices out of the ass for some jeans that were ripped up. It was like cats were trying to say at times, "I wanna be homeless, but not actually." The shit was crazy in my eyes. I starched the hell outta my joints and cut on the shower water.

"Fuck," I said. Just as I was about to get into the shower, I had to lock my ass up. Those grits were knocking on the door and it was time to release. I'm glad I caught it, cause ain't nothing worse than getting clean, only to turn around and have to shit. I pulled off one of those Chris Tucker shits in Friday. Y'all remember that nigga face when Ezell first saw him. It was like the nigga was releasing death out of his soul. It was one of those. I finished up, wiped my ass, but you know I didn't flush that thing. I wasn't trying to affect my shower water. And even if it didnt, I didnt wanna take that risk. "*** damn nigga. Them grits wasn't no hoe." I said that out loud looking into the toilet at the monsters that I released.

I got in the shower, getting crispy clean with the Axe snakeskin body wash. I felt refreshed than a muthafucka once I got out. I was by myself, so I just bypassed the towel. I went back into the room and plopped down on the bed that was closest to the fan. I cranked it on high speed and let my nuts air dry. The shit was so refreshing. I got dressed, throwing on a black Indiana Hoosier fitted and waltzed on out the door.

"Damn nigga."

"Oh shit man, you scared me." It was Mook. Like, the nigga was literally two steps outside of my door when I came out.

"Shit you kept it simple. I fucks with it."

"Yeah I did. But nigga what you got on?"

"Shit this my simplicity. Some slip ons, shorts and a tropical button up shirt."

"Yeah man, but what's up with the fedora? You trying to be Cam Newton?," I asked him. That's when the nigga opened his shirt up, exposing the superman undershirt. All I could do was shake my head.

"Let's roll my nigga. Gone super soak a ho tonight." I followed him and said a prayer at the same time.

"Lord, please watch over these crazy niggas tonight, for they know not what they do." We met up in Eric's room and chilled until about 9:30. We took a cab down to the docks where the boat was already packed and live from what we were seeing. From the minute we walked in, it was pure madness.

"A, A, let's split up," E.J. said.

"I'll take the top floor, cause you know, big bitches need room to move. Y'all niggas stay down inside here on the second and first. Peace." That fool shot up the stairs in search for his King Kong thickums. We didn't know what was up there, but from what we were seeing here on the second level, we didn't wanna go anywhere.

"A you man. Let's get it." That was one of the dudes who worked on the yacht, calling out somebody for something. People started converging to the front as these two dudes started having a dance off. Now, I wasn't much for dancing and doing all that crazy shit, but it had definitely got the females on here going and it was all I needed.

The next thing I saw was Eric getting a lap dance, Bryson had something bent over and Mook, as for Mook, this nigga was taking pictures. At 6'3 and clean shaven right now, they really did think this nigga was Cam Newton. If he was smart, he'd play that role all night and bring 'em back to the telly so he could hit 'em with the dab. I observed and walked around, noticing a room right behind the cats who had jumped off the dancing. I walked in and saw it was like a mini nightclub.

"Come here sexy man." I ain't know who shorty was, but she grabbed me and went to work. I wasn't gonna deny no ass shaking on me. Shit, I may have been from the West, but you could've swore I was from Chicago the way I took the juke. That word, juke. My partner from Chicago, "Milly," whose hair I cut often, used to say that shit on a regular. "Man, those hoes be juking something serious in the Chi." I used to just laugh when that nigga would say that. But, right now, I was embracing it. Baby girl was jukin and jukin it up to the highest degree. I stayed in there for about 20 minutes, rotating from chick to chick, until I went back out to the open second deck. It was party central now. I didn't even feel when the boat had taken off. I looked at my watch. 11:07. Damn, I thought. We had already partied damn near two hours. Just as I was about to make my rounds to the stairs and hit the third deck, that's when I saw it. Some cat was chilling near the edge of the boat, when pure throw up came down on him. Man, that nigga was hot. I looked in disgust at first, as did a lot more people. Then, I started to laugh to myself. At least I had one helluva story for my folks when I got back. As I proceeded to get halfway up the stairs to the third deck, I saw E.J. waiting up top with his arm around two thick ones. There were some rolls in that stomach, I can't front. However, the thickness of both of 'em was not to be ignored.

"A NIGGA!!! I'M BOUT TO EAT BOTH THEY ASS TONIGHT!!!," he shouted out loud. Lesson #09780. As a man, you never, ever, at any point in your entire existence admit that you openly eat ass. I didn't know if he knew, but he was never getting a swig of a drink from me ever again. From the looks of it, that was a lot of ass that he would have to eat. Boy, better him than me.

4 B.P.P.

"What's good man?"

"Ain't shit but the rent. Kevin."

"Brooks." Now my flight would definitely be gravy. I was seated next to a brother. You could never predict with planes. It was like playing Russian roulette. You could get the cool person, the talkative person or the fat person who could take up their seat and yours.

"So what you headed to Frisco for?," he asked me.

"Just to kick back man. You?"

"Shit I'm Bay all day. I just shot down to L.A. for a hot minute to watch my lil cousin in his homegoing."

"Aww man I'm sorry. What happened to him?"

"The streets my nigga. The streets." I was seeing through his dreads and gold rows that cat was a real down to earth dude. It was more than refreshing to sit and rap with someone like minded.

"Shit I know what you mean bruh. I'm from Compton."

"You from Compton or Bompton?"

"Compton man. I ain't no blood." He got a chuckle out of that.

"You a Crip?"

"I'm a school nigga. I'm in college man."

"You know what," he said, shaking his head. "I can respect that. I mean, I don't get it with a lot of niggas. Not saying you weren't affiliated or are affiliated, but I meet so many niggas that do positive stuff, yet wanna associate themselves with gangbangin. You ain't lie to kick it my nigga. You told me straight up. Yo, I go to school. I can respect that shit." Right then, the stewardess came to the middle of the plane as they started to explain the safety procedures to everyone. It was a full flight, minus the one seat in between us. I guess either one passenger didn't show or no one wanted to sit between two niggas. We slowly started to back away from the gate. "We'll rap some more in a minute man. I gotta get my Mac Dre on."

"Fosho," I told Brooks, as he proceeded to put his black and silver beats on. I just continued to look out the window, getting ready to spend one hell of a new year's eve in the city. I flashbacked to the first and only time I was on a plane before this, and that was heading to Mississippi way back when to see family with my mom. I wasn't six anymore. I was 14 years senior and I didn't have anyone holding me back. I watched the planes before us take off as I simply leaned back, getting ready for my plane to take its place on the runway.

I was finally getting my wish. Even though the saying be careful what you wish for because you just may get it was true, it wasn't in this case. I knew what I wanted out of life and this was the first step in achieving it. Our speed started to increase and everything started to fly by as we were just a few seconds from going airborne. **BOOM!!! "THE FUCK!!!"** That's all I could let out as the plane became full of screams and loud cries. Not in the air yet, and Thank God we weren't, a loud explosion had shook the plane to its core.

"GET ME OFF THIS MUTHAFUCKA!!!," I heard Brooks yell over everybody. In the midst of this chaos, I was still coherent and noticing that the plane wasn't full of flames. I did, however, peep out the window and see a cloud of black smoke. All I could think about was the movie final destination. The oxygen masks had come down as the plane grinded to a halt. The side doors opened with rafts. As crazy as shit was, the stewardess' were doing their best to get people off in an orderly fashion. The nigga Brooks had disappeared. Like, he literally jumped over people, went through people, all of that. I don't know if he had made it down the raft yet, but I damn sure didn't see him. This was the one time that I hated sitting in the back of the plane. The smoke was now starting to engulf the plane and things had gotten frantic. Finally, after what seemed like eternity, I was finally escaping, sliding down this huge yellow raft. I ran as fast as I could away from the burning piece of metal. I observed the fire trucks and security vehicles racing down the runway, coming towards us to put the blaze out. I was keeled over, in a secure area where all the passengers of the plane were led to.

"Hey man," as I felt the huge slap on my back. I jolted up and turned around, still out of breath, looking at Brooks.

"Sup man. I'm still trying to catch my breath."

"Man bruh. This just fucked up my whole day. I wanted to be out of this mofo. Now, I'm stuck here for another day."

"Naw. They probably gone get you on another flight up out of here. Me, I'm not messing with a plane anymore. If I go anywhere else, then I'm gone just take the train." EMT personnel were now over with us, checking everyone to ensure that we were okay. For the most part, we were, minus a few people who had received some cuts and bruises fighting through the crowd. One guy even had a laceration on his forehead. As we were finished getting checked, one by one, we were brought back into the airport.

The airline worked tirelessly to get people booked onto other flights, while at the same time getting luggage off the defunct airplane. Turns out that a fire occurred in the engine compartment underneath the left wing of the plane. Brooks had disappeared, as I didn't see him anywhere in the airport. Me, I said to hell with the clothes. I still had $80 in Burlington gift cards, so I could come up even better than what I was leaving with. I was only going to be leaving three pairs of jeans and four shirts. Besides, they would probably be mailing my stuff to me anyway. My trip to San Francisco was the quickest recorded trip in the history of man. The shit literally lasted 5 seconds and didn't even make it past the runway of LAX. I calmly made my way from the crowds and disappeared in silence. I was on my phone, searching UBER like I never had before. I walked at a frantic pace as if the FBI was following me. I just wanted to get up out of there and get home. LAX was more like a major city inside of another major city. I was telling myself it was only a missed flight. However, I felt like I was missing the opportunity of my life. Ty was gone and off to begin his own adventure, and I was still stuck. I made it outside of the airport and patiently waited for the UBER driver to arrive. Ten minutes turned to 20, turned to 30 and to 40. Finally, 45 minutes later, I saw the Red Volkswagen come up with an Angels flag flying from the window. I walked up and was greeted with a "Hey, are you Kevin?" It was a scrawny white kid with curly hair. I didn't know him from the man on the moon, but I appreciated the ride.

"Hey man, thanks again."

"No problem. You going to Carson right?"

"Yeah man," I told him as he began to merge into traffic to get up out of here.

"Yeah bro. When you said Carson, I thought to myself, cool. I know a guy out there who gives great haircuts." I wasn't trying to think too much into his comments, but his words left me very inquisitive.

"So what is his name if you don't mind me asking?

"He said his name was Wayne man. Yo, like, dude from Compton, so he intrigued me a lot. Like, I met dude at a party. It was real brief. We were all messed up, but I saw him in the party and thought he was cool. So I said hey man, I'm Grady. He tried to go around me but I just moved in front of him saying hey man, what's up. I lifted my arm to shake his hand, and all he said was I'm Wayne. I'm a barber in Carson. Excuse me. It was brief and I was intoxicated, but I thought he was cool."

It was a small damn world to say the least. I remember that night. That was that crazy ass party that we had went to in Anaheim, but didn't stay because it was too much weird shit going on. I listened to dude talk all the way in traffic as I just sat back and waited for him to say more crazy stories. Asking him more about the party that night, he told me everything that went down. Some stuff ol' boy could've kept to his damn self. I literally wanted to throw up from some of the stuff he said. But, that was white people. Rather, white college kids. They were know to do outrageous shit like setting themselves on fire and thinking it was the greatest thing in the world. I made it home around a quarter to three in the afternoon. I plopped down on the couch and looked forward to relaxing away on this new year's eve. The party scene was over with in my eyes. **"FUCK!!!"** I punched the couch repeatedly. Out of all the madness that had occurred today, the most madness had just hit my mind. I had just realized that I drove my damn car to the airport. I left it there. I had to be the dumbest sommabitch on the face of the planet. **"Uggghhh,"** I let out as I slapped both hands across my face. This was the shit that I didn't need. I was hot. I had no whip. I had no trip. I had no chick. Fuck it, I thought. I would go get that thing tomorrow via one of the homies that was at the school. This shit right here boy. Now I saw why people shoot up post offices. I pulled out my phone and began scrolling through the numbers, looking for someone to call. I had to get out and do something. I found my teammate Sky Matthews. Yeah, I know. It was funny to know a brother named Sky. I hit him up and asked him was he still in town. He said yeah and that he would have no problem scooping me up tomorrow. More importantly, he said that he would get me out for something simple and different tonight, whatever that meant. I had some hours to blow as he said he would come through by six o'clock. I showered up and ate me some of Ty's Frosted Flakes. It was odd eating my boy's shit. I poured it in a bowl and had to catch myself for a minute. I was getting upset thinking about whatever he was doing. For all I know, he was halfway around the world right now, doing what he wanted to do. Me, my dream was derailed. I poured the milk over the cereal and indulged in it. No TV, no music, no anything. I finished up, took a shower, followed by a nap, waiting for the activities of the night to show up.

"Yo what's up man?," Sky said.

"Man I'm glad you came through man. This been a rough one." I dapped my dude up and we took off in his Altima. Sky came out of Dallas, Texas by way of Augusta, Georgia. His parents were well off and actually pissed with him. I remember the stories he would tell me about how his parents wanted him in the Yales, Princeton's or Harvards. However, he just wanted simplicity. So he came to Dominguez Hills, where he felt he could be normal. However, this was the first time that I could really sit down and rap with him on the shit. "So you left your car at the airport man?," as he laughed.

"Yeah man. I was the dumb ass. That damn plane blew an engine on the runway and I thought it was a wrap."

"Yeah man. I saw that on the news. I was like man, I hope them folks alright. They said the plane was supposed to headed to San Francisco, but I wasn't thinking that was you on that thang."

"Yeah bruh. It's been a long, short day. I just need a release." "Well look man. I got something that you wouldn't expect for new years."

"What's that man?"

"You'll see."

"Naw man. I don't like surprises. You gotta tell me." He looked at me and laughed.

"We going to a midnight library extravaganza."

"Man what the hell you talking about a library?"

"A 24 hour library like I said. I mean, think about it. You got all these cats going out to parties, having wild sex, drinking their livers away tonight. And that's all fine and dandy. Nothing wrong with that. But, I know while I'm here, I'm trying to elevate my mind as much as I can. I'm 22, trying to think like I'm 52. Not saying I'm better than anyone, but I'm trying to be better in my mindset than people my age." I was intrigued and it actually blew my mind as we hit the highway.

"So where this library at?," I asked.

"Riverside. It's down by the college, at a coffee shop."

"Back to the grind," I said.

"Yeah man. How'd you know?"

"Well I had a breezy or two back in the day who did poetry and she invited me one night. It wasn't my forte, but I mean it was some bad bitches in there." My mans just laughed as we kept rolling on and on. Music started to accompany our conversation about a library as we inched closer and closer to Riverside. Finally, we got off Mission and I saw people out and about, gearing up for their big night.

"Yeah man. This is typical college. I wish it was somewhere else besides this."

"Besides what?," Sky asked. "This. College. I gotta see

these niggas everyday."

"But I bet they won't be in here tonight." We found a parking spot across the street from the shop and proceeded to make our way in there. The nightspot next to the shop was already poppin'. We walked into the coffee shop. It looked more like we were walking into a back alley. There were only three people here, messing around on their laptops.

"Hey Katie."

"Hey Sky. Your usual?"

"Two of 'em please."

"What you gettin us man?," I asked him, as ol' girl went back to start preparing the order.

"Two ham croissants and some hot chocolate."

"You gone have a nigga sipping some hot chocolate?"

"Better than sipping alcohol and destroying your liver right?" All we did was look at each other for two or three seconds as he hit me with another gem.

"$12 Sky."

"Keep the change as always," he told her as he slid her a $20. She smiled and I followed him down the stairs.

"Yo why we ain't sitting up here? I ain't trying to go outside," as I thought he was heading for the back door.

"We ain't going outside," he said as he stopped. "See, another flight of stairs." We headed down and walked through another door. What I saw was nothing short of awe inspiring. I saw stone, clay and brick walls. A small stage with a mic stand was entrenched in the concrete floor. Spread out throughout, there were tables and chairs. Not to mention, it was good and warm down here. It changed from the last time I was here.

"So where's the library?"

"Over here," as I followed him to the far corner. I saw a bookshelf lined with a lot of books. Whose books were they? I had no idea. "Yo man, this ain't a library," I told him.

"Why not?"

"Nigga you say library and I'm thinkin big building, millions of books, innocent looking people with glasses. This a coffee shop with a book shelf." I sat down with my food at a table as he just stood there lookin at me.

"You gotta learn the word game bruh. Library. Break it

down. Lie and bury," as he sat down with me. "That's where America buries their motherfuckin' lies. Here. We read real shit. We talk about real shit. It's a library that doesn't encompass lies. Happy new years my nigga," as he took a bite of the croissant.

"So you basically brought me here to talk?"

"Naw. I brought you here to open up. I mean, for both of us. Think about it. What's gone last more in your mind forever. A night full of women, liquor and possible fights. Or, or, a night full of conversation and enlightenment over good food?"

"We could've did this at my crib my nigga," I told him.

"We could have, but distractions are there. TV, music, the surroundings. Gun shots."

"So ask me something? Naw, matter fact, lemme ask you something," I told him as he sipped his hot chocolate like he was the Godfather or some shit. "Aight. What is it that I don't understand about you?" He shook his head up and down.

"You understand. It's everyone else who don't understand. They hear about me getting the offers from Princeton and Harvard, and like to think that oh this nigga better than us or so and so. What he doing in Carson? This ain't his life. Look. I grew up hard. I grew up part time in Georgia. Part time in Texas. Parent's both made over six figures. I get it. People think you privileged because your parents are well off. They divorced, and that's why I moved to Texas with my mama. Still got the good jobs. But I wasn't privileged. Now, here is where the kicker comes in. People see money. They didn't see divorced parents. They didn't see the kid who had to fly to see his daddy. Granted, he was there, but I needed him in the physical sense all the time. Because some situations as a man, the phone conversation can't do justice. You need the face to face. Now, something else they didn't see. The smarts. Why is it illegal for a nigga to be smart? Why can't I be book smart? See what cats gotta understand is that you have to master all aspects. The street smarts and the book smarts. Yes, I went to a good school. Yes, I grew up around good middle class people. Now, when I say middle class, Im talking about not super rich, but well enough to live somewhere where you can walk the streets at night. Sure man, I lived in an area of Dallas where it wasn't The Hamptons, but it was good and mixed. White, black and I just made it. But, I was simple. My mama and daddy didn't give me anything. But the perception is what kills us. I don't know man. I just don't get it. Every nigga that do good for himself ain't a coon who sold out to the white folks."

"Well," as I took the last bite of my fire croissant. "Damn. I gotta go get me another one of these. Anywho, I ain't never really seen that, cause you been an A-1 nigga since I met you. I aint gone lie. I was impressed when I found that out about you. Its like you don't meet people like that on a regular. You had the chance to go Ivy league, play ball and get a degree from somewhere prestigious. I just think it's cool that you put who you are over what your parents or anyone else wanted you to be. I think that's some shit that you don't see everyday. But lemme ask you, why did you turn those schools down?"

"Simple," he said without hesitation. "I didn't need that. What was going to Princeton gone do for me? Put me around some rich kids who nine times out of ten ain't struggled for nothing in their whole lives. Now, when I say that, it's not me talking about their parents. As a parent, you do wanna have a life for your kids that you didn't necessarily get. I get that. Nothing wrong with it. But, when you embed in a child that they are entitled, just because of their stature, that's when people get messed up in their heads. None of us are entitled to anything. Entitlement should be called decrement. It reduces the capacity of an individual's mindset, thus messing them up for the future." I took the last gulp of my hot chocolate and told him let's go upstairs to get some more. We went upstairs, getting two more drinks and another croissant for myself. I noticed that the three people who were in here before were now gone. We headed back downstairs and went right back to the same table that we were at before.

"Yo man. So what kind of books are over there?" Fam got up and brought one of them back. He handed it to me. It was a dark brown cover book with gold trim. The book was thick, but it had no title or author on it. I turned it around and there was nothing on the back. I opened the book and it was nothing but blank pages. "Man what the hell did you give me a blank book for?"

"It's yours man. Write your story."

"Man I thought we was gonna read some shit, rap and get intellectual, or whatever you said. You brought me here to a coffee shop that's full of blank books."

"Naw man. Its books up there written by folks that you could read. But, I purposely gave you that one so you could write your own."

"Man I ain't no damn writer. I ain't got time to write no book. I barely like writing reports for school. What make you think I'm gonna write a book?" I bit into my croissant and just looked at him like nigga really. He started laughing as I kept biting. "You a fool man. You really is."

"I mean shit nigga," with crumbs dropping from my mouth. "You really thought I was writing a book."

"Aight, so let me ask you this. You got a facebook?"

"Yeah."

"You got a twitter?"

"Yeah."

"You got an instagram?"

"Yeah nigga. What's you point?"

"So you put all of your thoughts, your business, your feelings all over social media. You put all your opinions for everyone to see and for everyone to criticize. And what you get out of it?" I was in mid chew when he asked me that.

"Nigga what you mean what do I get out of it?"

"Like what you get out of it?"

"Like nigga. I'm not getting what you asking me."

"Ok let me simplify this shit." That's when I knew he was serious, because as long as I'd known Sky, he had never used the word shit. "Why put all of your thoughts, opinions, poetic sentiments, feelings and anything else on social media and receive nothing but comments? Why do that when you could put all of those thoughts, opinions, poetic sentiments, feelings and anything else in a book, and get paid for it?" His eyebrows raised as he now had me thinking.

"Look man. You one of the most bipolar people I know. You go from chill to brash dude in the blink of an eye. In the same breath that you can uplift people, you can also kill 'em with your words. Put that stuff in a book. At least if people gone get pissed off at you, then that pistivity will get you paid. I think you should do it." I looked at him and saw two things. One, he was smart. Two, he was crazy as hell. Wasn't gone be no way that I would ever write a book. However, in the same breath, it was a time that I didn't think that it wasn't gonna be any way that I would ever make it out of Compton. By the time I had looked at my watch, I saw that it was 10:18, one hour and forty two minutes until the year 2016. "Maybe man. Maybe. But what other books over there for me to read?" He smiled and walked over to the shelf, grabbing two books. He dropped them both down on the table.

"Latonya S. Hicks. Who the hell is this?," I asked.

"An author you gone know about. Just read one and I'll read one. They poetry books. It's just a way to open up. Again man, I'm sorry if this ain't what you had in mind for new years. I just wanted to do something different. I like seeing my brothers being enlightened."

"It's all gravy man," as I dapped my mans up. I grabbed ol' girl's "Broken Lead' book while Sky took her "Life Through Brown Eyes" joint. We spent the next hour just reading through these magnificent writings and breaking down each line. I never had a problem with reading, but I had never gotten in depth with it like I was doing now.

"Yo what's that noise?," I said, as we both looked up at the ceiling. I looked down at my watch and saw that it was 11:59.

"They bout to turn up," Sky said. "Just think about it man. In less than a minute, a lot of people gone go into 2016 a lot drunker. We going into 2016 a lot smarter." He looked at me, and all I could do was stare back at him. Once I heard in unison the crowd yell ten, I put my head down and just listened. The countdown was one that I had heard all the time on this day. However, it was much different now. **"THREE, TWO, ONE, HAPPY NEW YEAR!!!"** That was the roar of the crowd going nuts above us in the venue next door. "Happy new year guys." We turned around to see the girl who had served us.

"A thanks Katie," Sky said.

"Sorry, but I have to close guys."

"It's all good. Just glad y'all stayed open late tonight so I could bring my boy down and kick it. Oh, and I'm sorry I didn't introduce you two formally. Katie, Kevin. Kevin, Katie." We shook hands and proceeded to head back upstairs.

"Umm Katie, this may be awkward, but can I get two more sandwiches before you close? Or, is the kitchen closed?"

"No, thats cool. As a matter of fact you can have em on the house. I close tonight, so my manager's not here." It was always good to get the hook up. Not to mention those croissants that they were serving in here were beyond fire. I took two of those for the road and we got back to Sky's car, heading back to my crib to rest up for the night. As we hit the road, while I was indulging in some swine goodness, I thought about everything that me and my boy had done tonight. He did teach me something very valuable. Time can not be repeated, so we must be cautious of how we spend it. True, I was only 20, and I could've spent this night illegally drinking and not gaining anything. However, I truly went into 2016 with something more gracious than a kiss from some random chick. That, simply, was mental enhancement.

I woke up the next morning in my bed. The light was coming through the small window in my bedroom and I for one was glad that I was waking up sober. I didn't feel like getting up and doing anything yet, so I did what a lot of us do when we first get up in the morning. I grabbed my phone and just started to scroll through facebook. Out of all my 2,000+ friends, I could see that a good 50 of em had posted their new years pics. Oh boy, you talk about thottin' to the tenth power. I swear it was like new year's and halloween were the two holidays were women had an excuse to wear no draws and be cool with it. I just shook my head as the more I scrolled, the more I saw bottles popped and hungover statuses. The homey Sky was right. This could've been me or even us. And hell, I loved to party my darn self. After last night, I was re-evaluating a lot that was going on in my life. I put the phone down and closed my eyes once again, drifting off into another world for a while. However, when I woke up hours later, there was Sky in my face.

"Dog, you good?"

"Yeah man. What time is it?"

"One o'clock. You ready to go get ya whip?" I thought he was bullshitting until I looked over at the clock and saw that he wasn't lying. "Aww man. I'm sorry bruh. I ain't mean to sleep in this long. I got up and then fell right back to sleep."

"It's all good man. C'mon so we can get your stuff." I threw on some jeans and an old raggedy t shirt, and headed down to the car with him. Hitting the highway, I was shocked to see that traffic was pretty clear today. There weren't any traffic jams going on. That was gravy in my book. As we got to the airport, fam drove me right up to my car.

"Here man. My parents always sending me spending money. Most of it I invest to collect interest, but here man. Use this $50 to pay for your joint. I know how college life is."

"Man I can't take this," I told him.

"Bruh, it's gravy. Between moms and dad, they send me at least $500 a month. Maybe even more."

"So man let me ask you something. I know your parents well off. Not rich, but doing good. I know the car is gravy. But, when I see you around campus, you always in the chow hall. You live in the dorm. I mean. Why bruh? You got the means to make it happen. I mean, yeah I live off campus, but you see what we got in our joint. Rather me now, since Ty gone."

"This how I look at it man," Sky said. "Let someone else do the service for me. Ok, take a business man. An entrepreneur. They don't do the physical work. They pay people to do the work for them and sit back collecting the benefits. All the while sitting in the comforts of their own homes. Its called outsourcing. Ok, moms and pops got me a nice car for school. Ok, moms and pops send me some spending change every month cause they know how difficult school is. Cool. But, I'm here on a scholarship. You gone pay for me to live in the dorm. I'll do it. You gone pay for my meals. I'll take it. Yeah, occasionally I'll get something off campus. You know, surf-n-turf burritos always do me right. The point is this. Let them pay for it. Like I said, most of the money my parents send me goes to investment. Let it cure some interest and work for me. I don't knock y'all who live off campus. You do you. As for me, I'm gone sacrifice now, so I can chill later. Then, I can have my fun. You feel me?"

"I feel you man. Thanks again."

"No problem bruh." I got out and headed to my car, keys in hand, happy that I had my baby back. The last 24 hours were interesting to say the least. I peeled out the lot after paying the over $40 fee for almost two days. As I shot out back towards the freeway, I hit Ty's number in my phone and put it on speaker. It rang five times and went to voicemail. Man, my dude must've been having fun in Chicago, if he was still there. I journeyed on back home, calling my mama next. She was upset with me that I didn't call her after the plane had its malfunction. She was completely oblivious to it happening. Plus, I should've called her anyway for new years. All was eventually forgiven and I made it to the crib. I planned on heading out there to Fontana to kick it with her the next day. For right now, however, it was football time. The college bowl games were on. I stopped at Buffalo Wild Wings and got me 20 of the most smell good, hottest wings you could find. Today, it would be me and the television.

"Hello?"

"WHATS UP NIGGA!!!"

"Yo who the hell is this?," I asked. I didn't have any 808 numbers in my phone and I didn't know who the good hell this was.

"My nigga I'm calling you on my laptop via google."

"TY???!!!"

"YEAH NIGGA WHAT'S UP!!!"

"Man, where the hell you at?," I asked him.

"Bruh, I'm in the Philippines right now getting ready for a barber competition. We did some time in Seychelles, East Africa and all of the surrounding islands. My nigga. When I say we were treated like kings, that shit is an understatement. My nigga. They love us over here." I was dumbfounded and shocked to say the least. Here it was, the end of January almost, and this fool had been to Africa and now the Philippines. I see why he didn't call. His ass was having a good ol' nigga time.

"So what is y'all exactly doing over there?"

"Man we gettin paid to cut hair, teach people how to cut hair and barber competitions. Yo like real shit, some of these cats on the international scene get down forreal forreal. Like nigga, after we left Seychelles, we jetted up to what I call the trifecta. It's where Egypt, Israel and Jordan all meet up. Yo, its some real niggas over there and they hold it down."

"Like what you mean? Real like what?"

"They fucks with us on some real shit. Like nigga, forreal forreal. We were in Jordan right, and we out there in Aqaba. Now you know what TV make you think. Terror in the Middle East. Man, we saw just the opposite. First of all, we all black. I don't care if they were Muslim or not. It was all love when we were up there. Yo, like, they listen to hip hop and everything over there. They got clubs, bangin' females, all that. But the crazy shit is that they have culture. Man, they kept it G with us. Our guide was a local cat who was good with the royalty of that country. I can't remember if you call 'em king, emperor, prince or whatever. All I know is that when we hit the barbershop over there, it was a palace my nigga. A fuckin' palace. Five of us and five of them. This wasn't about teaching. It was a straight up competition. Like, they made it a huge media event. And when I say them niggas can cut, them niggas could cut. It was like looking at clones of ourselves. In the end, it was all love. There weren't any winners or losers. They paid us for friendly comp, we both exchanged tips and nigga, we all went out afterwards. Aww man, they get down in Jordan. Even got me a pair of gold clippers. The shit was amazing." I listened to his stories and just dropped my mouth in awe. What he was experiencing was once in a lifetime. Me, I was just living the normal life, hoping to aspire to that level one day.

"So what happened in Frisco my nigga?," he asked me.

"Man nigga we ain't even make it," I told him.

"The damn plane engine caught fire right when we were about to take off."

"Damn nigga. Like when y'all was backing out from the gate?"

"Naw nigga. I mean like when we were taking off down the runway full speed. Nigga I heard that pop and swore that I was about to meet my maker." Fam started laughing.

"I'm sorry man. The shit ain't funny. But it's funny, 'cause I can see your face when that shit was happening. So did you catch another flight?"

"Naw man. I was so mad that I didn't even stick around. I left the airport and came back home. Then nigga, I called an UBER, completely forgetting that my shit was sitting at LAX."

"Yeah nigga you dumb."

"Fuck you nigga."

"Anyways man, how ya moms and them doing?," he continued on.

"She doing good. Niggas at the shop doing good. Brody cut my shit last week matter of fact. Umm, we suck as a team. Our record ain't good at all, but it's all gravy."

"You still good making the rent and everything?"

"Yeah man. I get covered by the school with some of it and you know, a nigga done started writing so I'm making some bread on the side with that. Plus, I got the bread you send me."

"And nigga what the fuck is you writing? Shit it was hard enough to get yo ass to read a book."

"I know man I know. But lately man, ever since new years, I just had a knack for it. So you know how white kids do? They don't wanna do something, so they'll pay me two to three hundred to write an essay for em. I don't fuck with the fifteen page type joints. But something within a range where I ain't gotta be up all night, I fucks with. So yeah nigga, I'm good."

"That's what's poppin my nigga. That's what's poppin. So yeah nigga. We here in the Philippines right now and let me tell you. It's more black and asian babies running around this ho than anything."

"Really my nigga?"

"Really nigga," he told me emphatically.

"I mean, you can literally tell that it's been quite a few niggas out here that done ran up in this sideways pussy. So peep. We up in Manila right now, but the first two nights, I was down in this joint called Subic Bay, where all the navy ships pull in. Man, so they got this area called The Barrio. Like, its crazy, 'cause all the clubs are owned by nothing but old ass, white men. Most of 'em use to be in the navy. Anywho, we walk down to the end of the strip and find this joint called EMU. Man so we walk in there right with a wad of $20's and $5's, cause you know, the shit cheap over there. The minute we walk in, mamasan trying to get us upstairs to the room with some of her girls. You know, for once, we weren't trying to hear that. We had heard about Asia and how crazy some of those countries could be. So nigga we go to the top of the club. Nigga I'm with a nigga named Mook. He decide to drop one five dollar bill down from the top. The minute they seen that down below, they literally started jumping up, trying to catch it before it hit the floor. And when they didn't get it, they literally started scratching and clawing at each other like cats to get it. Now, the other niggas I was with thought it was funny. To me, that shit was sad. I was like damn. They got a fight over a five dollar bill cause they all so poor."

Now, right there, that made me flashback to us when we were in the hood. That's exactly how you had to grow up when you were in the inner city. You literally had to scrap for everything that you had. See most people think gangbangin' just occurs from circumstances of growing up in an impoverished environment. Naw. A lot of times, it was because you were just tired. I mean, think about it. Let's say you were the non street kid growing up. You were the one who went to church, got good grades, had both parents in the house, etc. Imagine if you were that kid. Now, every time you went to school, somebody was always waiting there, ready to start a fight with you because the clothes you had on were ironed. The fact yo' shoes were clean. The fact that you had yo' daddy in the house. The fact that you even had a lunch bag to take to school. See, not everyone ran the streets simply out of necessity. Some people ended up running with the streets because they got tired of the streets fucking with them. I mean really. Who wanted to walk out the house knowing that they had to fight 30 niggas everyday just because they looked good? Shit, it was better to fight alongside those 30 niggas against some other niggas over some ignat shit than it was to fight those same 30 niggas everyday over some shit you absolutely didn't get. You realize when you scrap with those cats, you were scrapping for the $5 payout, like those young ladies Ty described were doing. $5 was a lot for people who had nothing. $5 could buy a pack of bologna, and we all know niggas can fuck up bologna sandwiches at an alarming rate. $5 could buy loaves of bread. In the hood, $5 could buy you a lot. So I understand their plight. I understood their fight, because I knew people who had to fight for a measly $5 just so they could eat everyday. I saw that shit everyday for 18 years. They say that if you don't live right, and you are a Christian, then you got to hell. However, they failed to see that hell was the blocks that we were walking on everyday. The only people who didn't know were the ones who sat up on their rich asses in the hills of America without a care in the world about poverty. Without a care in the world about whether or not the police were going to kill them just because they drove a nice car. Without a care of a liquor store, hair salon or a gun shop, popping up in their neighborhood, only to be torn down later for gentrification purposes. Those people had no worries. Boy, it must've felt good to be entitled, privileged and born with the biggest advantage you could possibly be born with. We finished up our conversation after another hour of talking. He had to go because they were about to get it in. He said he had met a shorty over there who was Black, Filipino and Sudanese. He said he was gone get that tonight.

I went back to doing my homework, waddling away in a hotel room. We had a game against Sacramento State tomorrow night up here. I kept my face in my books for the majority of the night until ten o'clock hit. I went ahead and drifted off to sleep. The next day, what happened was just what I imagined. We lost. I dropped 33, but it didn't matter. We just didn't have the talent. We lost 87–55 and were now 8 games under .500. We had no chance for a national tournament, so I just pretty much played to play. As long as I was getting my education, then I was gravy. We flew back the next morning and got back to campus around ten in the morning. I had class at one, which was a good thing for me because it gave me some down time. I went straight to the campus library and sat there in a side room thinking about life. Then, I thought about what Sky had given me when we went to Riverside almost a month ago. That blank cover book. Ever since that moment, I had wrote for everyone else except for me. I got paid to write for other people, but I wasn't getting paid to write for myself. Fuck it, I thought. Within the next year, I was gonna complete a book and sell it my damn self. What better way to make money for me than talking about me. I went to my one o'clock class which was my behavioral science class. Now, I dug this class. However, today was not the case. I was still tired from last night and just wanted to nod off in class.

"WAKE UP MR. WEST!!!"

"Huh?," I responded. The class let out a laugh as I got myself back together.

"Long night I see," the professor said.

"Yeah, you could say that sir."

"So you can answer my question?"

"What's that sir?"

"Well I'll repeat it seeing how your naps are more important than your lectures. Are we born into our behaviors or are they choices?"

"We choose who we want to be in life sir."

"So a man who is born with more female genetic genes won't be prone to being gay I assume with your theory. Am I correct Mr. West?"

"It's a choice sir."

"And how is it a choice?"

"Anything you can undo is a choice. Sir." The class was dead silent and locked in on our debate now.

"So you can undo your sexuality? Is that what you are saying Mr. West?"

"No, but you can choose who you wanna sleep with. If a guy wants to lay with another guy, it has nothing to do with genetics. It's cause he chooses too. See, everyone always likes to pinpoint the gay vs straight argument. Why do they choose that sir? Its simple. It's the easiest conversation to have that is guaranteed to get a reaction out of people. At the same time, it is the same conversation that many shy away from because they are scared to speak on it. And quite frankly, that's not challenging. No one is born a criminal. No one is born a rocket scientist. No one is born a *** damn pharmacist. No one is born a racist. You choose the lifestyle, jobs, places you live, everything. Sure, everyone has surrounding circumstances. But grown ass individuals make choices. You didn't even have to come into work today. You chose to come into work today. Don't say nothin' about not getting your check or anything. You chose to get out of bed. You chose to eat or not eat this morning. You chose to either walk, run or drive to work this morning. So sir, with all due respect to your PhD and your philosophies, don't give me no damn you are born any way. You're born with a gender, a set of parents, all the potential in the world, and maybe some health deficiencies. After that, 99.9% of your life is a choice. The same way a baby makes a choice to refuse a bottle when it ain't hungry. 99.9% is a *** damn choice. Just like you chose to ask me that question. Just like you chose to pick me to mess with out of everyone. Just like you chose to wear that wack ass suit. You chose it all. So miss me with the gay vs. straight bullshit. Cause that's weak as fuck. Anything you can undo is choice." The class was so quiet you could hear a wolf howl on the East Coast if you wanted to. Professor looked at me, closed his eyes and raised his eyebrows.

"That class. That right there. That's proof that we all have the power of choice. If you don't get it, then there is nothing that I can do to help you. Mr. West. For you. Class is dismissed. Get Out." I collected my things and didn't think twice. I literally drug myself to my whip and sat in the driver's seat for a good five minutes. I had practice tonight at six o'clock, but knowing that I could get me some winks in before hand was cool. I got home and simply dropped my ass right there on the couch. My phone began to ring. I struggled to get it out of my pocket cause I was sleepy as all to be damned. I ain't even look to see who it was when I opened it up. "Hello."

"Yo nigga where you at?"

"Man I'm at home sleep."

"Well hurry up and get yo' ass to practice man. Everyone here but you." First thing I did was look at the phone to make sure that this wasn't no prank. I saw it was Sky hitting my line. Second, I looked at the time on my phone, then looked at the clock in the kitchen. It was 5:47. "Yo, I'm sorry man. I'll be there in a good minute." I stripped my clothes off and threw on my basketball gear, racing to my car. I damn near did warp speed to the gym. With the way I was driving, you would've thought that the campus was five miles away instead of five minutes away. I pulled up and parked in the student lot at 6:07. I ran over to the gym, happy that I was just ten minutes late. Once inside, everyone on the court turned and looked at me. "Well, well. Everyone give it up for your late teammate." The whole team started to clap with a notion that they really didn't want to. I could tell that coach was really on one.

"Sorry coach. I overslept," I told him, as I jogged up to the huddle.

"Well since you so fast, gone head and run 25 laps around this gym. Then you can follow it up with 20 sprints up and down the sidelines. We'll be waiting. We got two hours of practice, so I'm pretty sure you'll still have time to dribble the ball." Man I wanted to slap the dog pis out of coach 'cause he aint need to be this harsh. Hell, it ain't like the team was going anywhere. We sucked big time. Fuck it, I thought. I just started running. Coach, he was going on and on about last night's game and the lack of passion that we all had. As I continued running laps, I really contemplated quitting this and going in a different direction. I understand that the school was paying for my education, but this shit was getting repetitive and boring. I wasn't getting any excitement out of basketball anymore. After about 35 minutes, I finished up and got inserted into the normal rotation.

"Wake your ass up and run the play." I glanced towards the side at coach wondering why he was still sweating me. Every single possession on the court, whether I was on offense or defense, he hounded me.

"Oh, he hit the layup."

"You were late on defense Mr. West."

"Wake up Mr. West."

"GET OUT Mr. West."

"Those women are gonna be your downfall Mr. West." Finally, I had enough of all his phrases.

"A coach, can you chill with that?" I stopped a play dead in its tracks, holding onto the ball. Coach blew his whistle and proceeded to walk out to mid-court where I was at.

"Son, you're a captain of this team. Correct?"

"Yeah."

"Well, what a leader does is take the fall for everything.

So with you being late, you gotta pay what you owe."

"The fuck you mean coach? I just dropped 33 in an L. 27 the game before, 39 and 14 the game before that. I mean shit. What more do you want me to do?"

"Hand me the ball," he told me.

"What?"

"HAND ME THE *** DAMN BALL!!!" I tossed him the ball.

"Gather around everyone. Commere Kevin." I hesitated, just tired and pissed off from everything that had occurred from me being ten minutes late. "See, this is a ball." He chucked it with one arm. "See, it missed when I shot it. Now, the probability of me making it was slim to none. One arm. Half court. Yeah, wasn't likely to go in. So what's my point? My point is if I want to increase the probability of my shot going in, then I should get closer, shoot in a proper form and the chances of it going in will likely increase. It's the same way with leadership son. Look around you. Just look at these guys. They are ride or die, much like yourself. See at the end of the day, it ain't all about points. It's about wins and losses. Sure, we having a terrible season, and the blame goes down from the top, starting with me. However, I know I can sleep at night because I give my all in preparing you guys. See my job is to coach more than basketball. It's too coach life. I don't care how many points you score in the end. I don't care how many game winning shots you make or miss. Hell, at this school, we ain't expected to be a national title contender year in and year out. Could that culture change, yes. But right now, it's not expected. But what is expected, from me, is that you graduate from this mofo. What they expect from you, captain, is that you be on time. You lead the squad off the court. You assist them in areas where they can't see off the court. Why? Because that's what makes you a man. If you late, they might think it's ok to be late. You from Compton correct? I'm asking you."

"Now you know I'm from Compton coach."

"Ok, the same way you know I'm from the slums of Jacktown, Mississippi. Your team follows your example. You guys," as he began to point at each and every one of them. "You guys follow each other's example. You a sophomore. Sky a junior. Red, Billy, Terry, Marcus and Gray, all y'all are seniors. Three of you have a C on your chest, but you all follow each other's moves. When the drug dealer was on the corner and yo' mama was barely scraping by money to eat, he was a God. You wanted to follow his lead because he drove the nice car. He had the good food to eat. He wore the good clothes. That's all fine and dandy. But then what happens when the Gangster Disciples pull up, the Vice Lords or even the crooked police pull up, and shoot the drug dealer. You gotta excel in being the example. You gotta be that example all the way around. Being on time is just as important as scoring points. Scoring points is just as important as making the decision to do your school work. Doing your school work is just as important as you making the decision not to do anything stupid in your free time that will affect you, the team or your family. Get my drift?" Coach blew the whistle. "Back to the grind gentlemen. We got less than 40 minutes left. Practice with pride." He walked off to the sidelines to sit back on the bleachers and he absolutely blew my mind. For the remaining time, our squad practiced with an intensity like none of us had ever saw before. Coach, he wasn't giving praises either. He was still being stern in his approach. In his eyes, a lot of us didn't deserve too much praise. It was our job to score points he said. Practice ended around eight o'clock and I was dead to the world. Sprints, laps and practice just killed my body.

"KEVIN!!!" I looked over and it was coach calling for me. Signaling for me to join him in the hallway. I drugged myself over, trying to figure out what he was upset about this time.

"Son. Understand what I am trying to convey here. Earlier was not about embarrassing you. Not at all. That ain't my job as a coach. My job is to mold you, shape you and make you leave a better you than when you came. Now, as I said out there, I don't give a damn if you play like Kevin Love, Kevin Durant or Kevin Garnett. What I do care, is what you doing off that court. How ya moms?"

"Good."

"How's Ty?"

"I mean, I talked to that ni–I mean. I talked to him earlier. I mean, he good. In the Philippines right now." Coach shook his head up and down.

"Lemme ask you something. How accomplished do you feel right now? Like, right now in this very instance?"

"I mean. Like. Not really nothing. The season is what it is. I'm trying to build something to where I can mob the big cities later in life. I just feel like I'm not there yet."

"That's what I wanted to hear. See, I know that feeling. I came from Jackson. I was intrigued by television. The L.A.'s, Miami's. All the bright lights, glitz and glam. But, I just want you to remember one thing. When you make it, and I say when because I know you will make it, be ready for all the madness and shit that comes with it. Lot of people wanna go Hollywood. Then, they get there and hate it. They forgot all about the pictures at every turn. People asking for an autograph when you in a restaurant trying to eat with your family. Turning on the news and everybody in they momma from TMZ talking about you. Just be careful son and be wise." He patted me on my shoulder and went on about his way. I comprehended everything that he said and walked back to the gym. I grabbed the ball and walked to the free throw line. I shot one free throw. Then, I shot another one. Before you knew it, I kept repeating the process until I was completely zoned out.

"HEY!!!" I turned around to see the janitor halfway across the gym. "I LOVE YOUR PASSION AND ALL, BUT I GOTTA LOCK UP!!!"

"WHAT TIME IS IT???!!!"

"TEN O'CLOCK!!!" *** damn, I thought. I lost track of everything. I shot one last free throw and then proceeded to hit the exit doors, going home for the night to rest and relax.

February 1st came and that meant Black History Month for the world and for the school. Now, deep down, I was like Morgan Freeman. I couldn't stand this shit. I mean, you can't regulate us to one month out of the whole year. It was an insult. Then, I had to deal with the woke muthafuckas. Let me explain. I get that you can always become enlightened. But damn, some people see one movie, or read one book, or in this case, our month comes around and all of a sudden, they are woke. I'm like get the fuck out of here with the bullshit. Reading a Malcolm X book and understanding it doesn't wake you up. What lessons are you entailing after that? If you read a book and understand it, then you simply read a book and understand it. If you watch a movie and get the message, then you watch a movie and get the message. Shit, a gangster can read a James Baldwin book, then turn around and kill five or six people. The shit was getting out of hand with the woke term and a lot of it was my people. My phone rang. "Hello."

"Nigga what's up man." It was Ty on the phone.

"Not a *** damn thing. Sitting down eating lunch, trying to figure out what I'm gone write for this black history paper for my African lit class."

"Write. Nigga you Picasso or some shit now?"

"Naw nigga. They want me to do some written shit. You know. Like some poetry shit."

"Man if you don't get yo ol' go sell it on the mountain ass up outta here. The fuck you gone talk about? Trap Kitchen."

"Fuck you nigga."

"Fuck ya mama."

"Nigga where y'all at?"

"Man nigga. We tore the P.I. up. I mean we killed it in Manila. But shit, it was like we were damn near facing brothers. Shit all of them looked like us. Dem niggas had cornrows and afros too. Shit was live."

"That's what's up man."

"Yeah. Now we having our own lil kickback in Macau, China. Eric know the nigga who in charge of all the talent that comes through here. It's like the Las Vegas of China. Shit we gone chill here for a few more days, mingle with a few celebrities and see what China got to offer."

"How that shit is man? I be reading on some sights that they real racist over there."

"Nigga please. That's for them niggas that ain't seen shit but TV or them foo chows in Chinatown. Man, over here, it ain't nothin like what they make it to be on TV. Nigga we mobbed out to Hong Kong the first night, and the shit was crackin' nigga. I mean, wherever we went, we were Kings. I don't know what other muthafuckas talkin about, but being black over here is damn near the equivalent of being a God. This nigga Stephon Marbury got posters and billboards galore here. Fuck Jordan. If it ain't Steph or Kobe, they could careless."

"That's what's up."

"Well my nigga, get back to your poetry shit. I'm bout to hop on this massage table. Bloods wear red, Crips wear blue, but she loves black."

"Bye nigga." I hung up the phone, chuckling at that foolio. I was glad my dude was having a good time. Here, I was doing some hard contemplating. Here I was again, with this brown book with blank pages. Why oh why did I agree to do this? I left my belongings at my table and got up, buying me a ham and cheese sandwich from the cafe. I sat back down, dumbfounded, twirling a pen in my hand. Then, as my eyes scoured the surroundings, I saw someone in a Marshawn Lynch Seahawks jersey. Then, without hesitation, I just began to write. It was like my pen mingled with my paper. I went into another zone with this one. Like, I literally lost myself in the train of thought. It was like a silent Lyrical Exchange.

"Mr. West. You wanna answer that question?"

"Cuz you bet not answer that shit." The class erupted.

"Jason, why must you always have something negative to say?"

"Man Mr. Lewis ,c'mon man. You a sub man. I mean, you cool and all, but we ain't trying to do no work in this muthafucka."

"Why not may I ask?"

"Man what the fuck you think man? Nigga we in Compton. What the fuck these grades gone do for us huh? They ain't gone feed my mama. They ain't gone put no clothes on my back. Nigga I dont give a fuck about this shit."

"So why you even come to school?"

"Shit to stay the fuck out of my mama house." The whole class started laughing hysterically.

"So back to my question. You gettin' up outta here Mr. West?"

"I'm tellin' you cuz don't answer that shit," Jason said yet again.

"Yeah man. I'm getting out of here Mr. Lewis."

"Academics right?"

"Yeah."

"What's after that?"

"SEE I TOLD YOU NOT TO ANSWER THAT SHIT CUZ!!!"
Jason had jumped up and jumped around screaming that shit, entertaining the class even more.

"Aight y'all settle down. Settle down. Look, I just want y'all to see beyond the scope of Compton."

"That's easy for you to say. You don't stay in this muthafucka," Daveisha said, another one of my classmates.

"You right. I don't. But, I know what it's like to be held back because no one expects you to do anything but wrong in life. Man look at y'all. Y'all walk these halls everyday. Cuz this and cuz that. But what's after this? Y'all seniors. Shouldn't nobody be working fast food or anything moms and pops after this."

"We ain't nigga. We hustlin' Mr. Lewis."

"And how you gone hustle Jason?"

"Shit nigga whatever I gotta do cuz. You or none of these crackers gone feed my daughter or put diapers on her."

"You right. I'm not. But, it's more to life than hustling corners and putting your life at risk."

"So lemme ask you Mr. Lewis, since you asking my boy all this shit. Why you subbin? Why you ain't a permanent teacher?" The class got quiet.

"What do you mean?," Mr. Lewis asked back with a chuckle.

"I mean nigga you subbin. You ain't full time. You part time. I mean shit. Even a gangster is full time." Mr. Lewis shook his head up and down.

"You right. You are absolutely right. But I don't have to look over my shoulder every two minutes. I'm just trying to get y'all to break the mold man. I wanna see all y'all in five years and not behind no prison walls. Yes Darrell. I see you got your hand raised."

"Can I shine yo head for a nickel Mr. Lewis?" Having a flashback to that moment in class way back when at Compton High propelled me even more to write. All them niggas I was in class with, except for two, were still doing the same shit. Jason was one of those worst, as he got killed a year after graduating, fucking around over there in Campanella Park, which he knew he shouldn't have been doing cause that was all Blood turf. I wrote with furious passion. I was discovering something that I never realized was in me. Out of everything from speeches to reading, to listening to YG in my whip, I started to truly realize that there was power in words. It was a reason it was called spelling. Words cast spells on people, just like Sky had told me in the basement of Back to the Grind coffee shop. A library is where they bury their muthafuckin lies. Police. They fuck with poor people leased out by rich folks. The White House. Nothing but white people in it. So on and so forth. Many had gotten it already. I was just catching on. But hey, it was better to catch a late train to a destination than to never get there at all. I finished up my joint and sat there, reading it over and over and over again. I wasn't in amazement at what I actually said. I was in amazement that I actually wrote it. I finished up my croissant, packed up my belongings and headed out for my car. Class was over with for the day, so before I went home, I had to make a trip to the barber shop. I had to get my hair game right. The fade was starting to look like a facade, and I couldn't fall off. With a quick stop at Jamba Juice for a peanut butter shake, I doubled back and made my rounds to the shop.

"O, look what the fuck we have here."

"Three mark ass naggas."

"Ay yo fuck all that what's up with my order for Friday night?"

"It depends on what yo' bitch ass get. The fuck you want some chitlins, cheese, spam, tuna, some tomatoes? What the fuck you want?"

"Man y'all watching this shit again?," I asked.

"Speaking of a mark ass nagga."

"A kiss my ass Nique," I responded. "Ha, ha. What's up college boy? Commere nigga. Ain't seen yo punk as in a minute." I went over and dapped my mans up, followed by Brody. "A yo Kev, this the new cat "Gristle."

"Sup my guy?"

"Sup man," he responded, dapping me up in the process. He was chillin' in his chair, watching the movie with the rest of 'em. Weren't any heads in here right now, so it was a much needed break for all of them. Gristle turned around in his chair to grab a bowl of something as I sat down.

"Yo what is that shit my nigga?," I asked him. "Pig Ears."

"And that's why we call that nigga Gristle," Brody said.

"Muthafucka came in the first day eating *** damn chitlins in this muthafucka."

"Menudo muthafucka," Gristle immediately responded.

"Whatever. I said damn nigga, you eat the ass too. He said nope, but I'll fuck up the gristle in a pig's ear in a minute. And ever since that day, we been calling that nigga Gristle." I just shook my head and laughed.

"So where you from Gristle?," I asked him.

"Southeast L.A."

"Aww shit," I responded. "What neighborhood?"

"Southeast Alabama. Roll, muthafuckin tide."

"Don't worry," Nique said. "That's how he got our ass at first too. This nigga came in here with a blue shirt on. Im thinkin' this nigga from one of the Sureno hoods out here. This nigga end up being from Alabama. Shit, I ain't know they had Mexicans in Alabama."

"Shit we everywhere man. Like roaches fool. You kill one and we pop up somewhere else."

"Kev, you see this shit?," Brody said. "How many Mexicans you know from Alabama?"

"One now," I said. He laughed.

"You need a cut man?," Gristle asked me.

"Yeah man."

"Sit yo' ass down. Let him tighten you up. He good as fuck. Real shit," Nique told me.

"Aight then." I walked on over and sat down, still being entertained by these fools and House Party 3.

"What you want man?" "Taper me up and keep my shits spinning," I told him.

"Aight"

"A man," as Brody interrupted. "You heard from your boy?"

"Who Ty?"

"Yeah, that M-I-A nigga."

"Yeah man. We rapped a few days ago. Shit he having hella fun from what he be telling me."

"Man fuck him dawg. Real spit."

"Whoa Brody. C'mon now. You know that nigga traveling and probably just lost in the experience."

"Man I know. I just wish the nigga would call once. Blow a breath or something. Like, I hope that money ain't clouding a nigga head up."

"Naw man," I said over the clipper sound as Gristle started to work on the back of my head.

"I mean. Nigga had called me from Africa and shit. Tellin' me how live it was."

"What? What he say about those African hoes?"

"Man nigga out of everything you could've worried about Africa, you would ask about some hoes," Nique told Brody. "Hell nigga. Everything else we see on TV is feed a muthafucka for 30 cent a day. Shit, what nigga you know can eat off of 30 cent? I'm trying to see what them hoes like."

"This nigga," Nique said.

"Naw man," as I came back in the conversation. "He said he learned a lot of shit over there. Like, it ain't what the world makes it out to be. He say it's live and beautiful over there."

"You know Africa ain't Africa at all man." I turned my face up and the other two turned their heads towards Gristle.

"Man what you know about Africa?," Brody asked him.

"I know it damn sure wasn't named Africa from the beginning."

"Well enlighten us all. Who they name it after? A Roman my nigga."

"Exactly. You ever wonder why when you see an African person, they always say I'm Kenyan. I'm Ethiopian. I'm Somali. I'm Sudanese. Never once do you hear 'em say I'm African. Pay attention to the word game man. Its serious."

"So. That may just mean they proud of where they from," Brody responded. Shit niggas from France is French. Italy is Italians. Spain is Spaniards. I mean c'mon dude. You thought you had one."

"It's a major difference though. What's the biggest difference between Africa and Europe?"

"White and black."

"Exactly. When you white, everything comes under you. Look at America. They robbed and polluted this land. Hell, they even stole Mexico. We in Mexico now. That's why when a muthafucka tell me to go home, I tell that puto I am home. You get the fuck out. But forreal," as he stopped the clippers. "Look how they divide everything up. African

American. Mexican American. Indian American. Do you hear European American? Fuck naw you don't. If its white, its right. They came from Europe and they try to keep it superior. So that's the difference. In Europe, they all one, regardless, because all their pigmentation is gone. Here, they have to deal with the problem. They're far away from the Caucasus mountains. So they are going to keep every race separate to stay superior. Heck, what happens every time one minority groups population increases to 13% or higher?" Gristle cut the clippers back on and went back to work on my head. At this point, we were all stunned and shocked silent. We really weren't believing what we were hearing. I don't know if it was because what he was saying was true, or because it was history coming from a Mexican.

"So lemme ask you this," Nique said. "What you think this shit gonna turn into?"

"Mass deportation," Gristle responded. "I can tell you what. Us. My people. They gone come hard for us. We at 16% of the population now. It's not one state in the union where you can't find a Mexican at. I mean, us in itself isn't the problem. It's cause we are going to random places, establishing neighborhoods and businesses for ourselves. We keep everything Mexican. That's the shit they don't like. See it was cool when it was just us in California. Now, we are establishing footholds in all 50. And no, it doesn't have shit to do with drugs. They are coming because we are a major threat in expansion. They already annexed Mexico's land. It's a reason why the border is beneath them. Now, look at the black man. You ever wonder why they can't send you back to Africa? It's 'cause you are disconnected from Africa. They can send an Iranian back. They can send a Mexican back. They can send a Pakistani back, Afghan back, Turkish back, all that. Can't send yall back. Why? They disconnected you all from the start. But more importantly, with that disconnect, they made y'all dependent on them for survival. Now, and I'll admit this with no qualms at all. The black dollar is the most powerful dollar circulating the channels of America's revenue stream, and I'll tell you why. Look at the three major sports. NBA, NFL and MLB. I ain't gone even say hockey because it's a speck of bruhs playing that. NBA 95% black. NFL 85%. MLB is maybe 10% black.

HOWEVER!!! If you include all the Latino races with African blood in 'em, from the Dominicans, Puerto Ricans, all the islanders period, now you have increased it to well over 50%. You see the music industry. Black artists command the most attention. The Beyonce's, Rihanna's, the Bruno Mars. Even hip hop, which is consumed by majority white America, is 98% black. You are the value of entertainment for this country and the revenue you all generate is fucking unbelievable. So, you never have to worry about leaving or getting kicked out. But, here's the kicker. They limit you all to only a certain percentage of who will get that slice of the whites only pie. Everywhere else, including us, they are gonna press you into dilapidated neighborhoods. No bank loans for business or anything. Entice you with cheap housing. Entice you with making cheap look good. Oh, you'll pay small amounts of rent, but they own the land. And when they are ready to kick you out, they'll gentrify that same land. You don't believe me, go look anywhere in America. Hell, look at Portland, Oregon, where no one expects any of us to be. All the brothers used to be in northeast. Then, they got pushed out and are now in the southeast part of the city. It's all a game man. It's all a game. Oh, but to answer the initial question, yeah. It was a Greco-Roman emperor or war leader, some shit like that who invaded Africa and had it renamed after him." By now, House Party 3 was irrelevant. This had turned into a schooling session.

"I got one more question though bro," Brody said, looking as dumbfounded as he wanted to look. "Man, what books were you reading coming up? Not knocking you, 'cause you just dropped some gems. But, I need to get my hands on that type of knowledge."

"Real talk," as he dropped the chair back, getting ready to put shaving cream on my lining, prepping me for a crispy one.

"Growing up in Alabama. Birmingham. With a city that rich in history, and a high black population. Man, you gone see some shit and learn some shit." He started to place the shaving cream across my forehead and down the sides. I think we had all learned a valuable lesson in here today. That was definitely when you assume, you definitely make an ass out of yourself. One's skins color does not equate to lack of knowledge of another's struggle. He wiped my forehead down with a warm rag. Slowly, and with precise precision, he took the razor and carefully guided it across my lining, making it sharper than a Steve Harvey suit. I had a new respect for this guy, even though I really didn't know him yet still. He had killed my stereotypical notion already that many did not recognize unless they were one of us. The shit was amazing to say the least. "Aight man. Check it out." Gristle handed me the mirror. I was highly impressed.

"Damn bruh. You did me up right," I told him.

"That shit kind of suspect what you said man." The other two laughed, as I kind of set my self up for that. I gave him $20 and dapped him up. I went and sat back in one of the waiting chairs and continued on watching House Party 3. "A man. Call your boy."

"Shit I ain't got no number for him man," I told Brody. "He call me through google, and I don't know what time it is where he at or anything."

"Man I'm telling you bruh. Gotta watch who you loyal too man."

"Cmon Brody. Stall him out," Nique said, obviously upset. "It ain't that serious. He ain't forget about us man. He just handling business."

"I'm just saying man. I hope he loyal to the soil when he come back. I'm glad the nigga aight. I just wish he'd let us in on what he doing."

"Wait, ain't you the same nigga who was gonna fight ol' boy who came in here and offered him the gig?," Nique asked him. "Yeah, but I also told him to look into it. Shit, the nigga at least owe me a call."

"He don't owe none of us shit bro. He good. He'll be home."

"I know man. That's my nigga. I'm just saying. Loyalty runs deep my nigga."

"Nigga, we cut hair. We ain't Nino Brown."

"Aight y'all. I'm out," I told 'em both. I wasn't about to be involved in that. I got up out of there before it blew up into a full blown argument. I got in my car and headed to the crib. Still with a lot of time to blow, seeing that it was just 4:57 in the evening, I decided to browse the internet on some upgrade shit. I began looking up some conferences or anything to get my mind right. With all the revolution talk that had been going down lately, I wanted to see what was good. Umar Johnson. Boyce Watkins. I was hoping just one black figure was headed to L.A. soon so that I could enhance my mental. Unfortunately, my search results netted nothing. I took a break during it all and actually went into the kitchen. As I was about to fix me some top ramen, I told myself fuck that. For too long I had been quick and in a hurry when it came to food. Truthfully, half the shit that I was putting in my body, I know that it wasn't good for me. So, I tried something. I heated a medium sized non stick skillet on the stove. I pulled out three eggs, cracked 'em and threw em in a bowl. With a fork, I beat 'em furiously. I started to think that I was one of those famous chefs on TV or some shit like that. Hell, I grabbed some pepper and even threw it in there. I was gonna murder this cheese omelette. I did a trick that I had always seen my mama do back in the day. I ran my hands underneath some running water and shook em off to the point that they were still wet enough to let some droplets fly. I flicked the water onto the skillet and immediately heard the sizzle. Oh yeah, I thought. This was gonna be a classic. I poured the eggs in the skillet and watched as it bubbled up quick. I figured that I had the fire too hot, which I did, so I cut it down just a tad bit. I took a metal spoon, and lifted up a part of the egg to get more of the runny yolk underneath to cook. I let it sit there for a minute as I was thinking to myself, how am I gonna flip it? I had never in my life attempted to flip an omelette, let alone cook one. I grabbed the pan by the handle and started to move the pan in a circular motion. To my dismay, the egg wasn't moving. I kept trying, but the damn thing wouldn't budge. I even banged it on the non heated portion of the stove, but the damn thing still didn't budge. I was severely pissed. And then, I wanted to smack myself. I had realized that non stick didn't necessarily mean non stick. You still had to put oil in the damn thing. This thing didn't even move anymore. Fuck it. I just scraped the egg out on the plate. Some of the egg went on the plate. The majority, however, was stuck in the skillet. I set the pan down and put some dawn in the skillet to let it soak. I had really fucked this up. I see why I couldn't keep a consistent woman. She comes out, gives me the draws, then gets hungry and her ass starves. I went about the rest of my night just flipping through the television and watching random stuff that I usually didn't watch. Big Bang Theory, The King of Queens and any other retarded show that I could find. I literally sat down and watched it. I kept this going until I couldn't take it anymore. It was only Monday and the rest of the week would be a long, drawn out one. Another basketball game, a test and even more bullshit to go along with everyday life. But hey, that's the price you paid when you became grown.

5 ALL SUMMER '16

I was finally back in the U.S. I mean the shit seemed like it was forever. Like I would never get back. But on June 7th, 2016, I touched back down. I had never in my life expected to see what I had seen. Do what I did. The shit was truly incredible. This Tuesday morning, I was making my descent back into LAX. It was so refreshing to see American buildings, American trees, all of that which was America. Now, don't get it twisted. This country was still fucked up in its ways on how it treated minorities, especially black people. However, I lived here and my family was here. It was indeed refreshing to know that I could be back in my own bed soon. I had about ten minutes until we hit the runway for our final descent. I leaned my head back in my chair and closed my eyes, reflecting on what was my most prized moment while traveling the globe.

"Yo man, how the hell did we get so lucky?," Mook asked.

"I dunno man." Me and Mook were by ourselves, drinking Hennessey in our hotel room on the 13th floor. Now, that was how you know things were going to be crazy. How many hotels you know had a thirteenth floor?

"Shit man. This the second to last stop before we get to the crib man," he told me.

"I know my nigga. What you gone do when you get back?"

"Shit I'm bout to head back down to Florida man and buy me a house. With 250 g's almost, not to mention all the extra money we made out here, shit why wouldn't a nigga invest and get a crib? What about you?"

"Shit man. I'm a do what I learned in Africa man and get me some land."

"Who you learn that from?"

"Shit by just looking my nigga. They owned everything over there. At least in that part of the country. So shit, this the way I see it. Why just buy a house? I can buy the land, and have others develop on it, all while I sit back at the crib and get paid."

"Speaking of paid. I know you ain't gone stay in Carson anymore are you?" That's where I was hit with the o-ke-doke. I had my partna in crime since birth and my barber team there. However, with what I had observed over the last six months, Carson was no longer for me. I wanted to always do shit in unexpected places and Carson couldn't give me what I needed.

"Crazy as it may sound my G. I'm going to Boise," I told Mook.

"Boise, Idaho nigga? Up there with the potatoes. Why?"

"Shit why not? That's cheap land. That's unchartered waters. That's something that many people do not know exist really."

"I mean. If that's you my dude, then I respect it. Me, on the other hand, I just wanna get me a crib. I left my two girls behind man, trying to give them a better life. And truthfully, I feel bad sometimes because in trying to give them a better life, I left 'em there. And right now, with both of 'em twins, at three years of age, they need daddy."

"Well, look at it like this my dude. You got ya own shop down there. When you get back, you gone have ya own house. You gone be gravy my dude. Just keep doing what you doing. You don't see too many positive examples of black men on television anymore. Shit nigga, just writing a book is a positive example. You give someone else knowledge, wisdom and understanding through writing some words on a piece of paper."

"Oh like Larry Hoover huh?"

"Who?"

"Hoover. You know, the nigga Rick Ro-nevermind. Some things ain't meant to be understood by others. Go on."

"Ok. Well, um, you know man. Yeah. You doing it. Just keep going man. We gone all be great in what we do. I mean shit. We survived out here. Africa, Jordan, Israel, Egypt, Philippines, Singapore, Japan, Malaysia, where a nigga bought all those fitted caps."

"Haha," he let out as he dapped me up.

"Man nigga I dropped so much money in Centre Point Mall out there. Can't believe all this time that I was wasting $40 on fitted caps, and the same ones, made by the same people, with the same quality over there were going for $5 a pop. Nigga you remember them Polo shoes they had over there for $20 a pop?"

"Yeah."

"Yeah you saying that shit kind of depressing. I told yo' ass to get them shits. You was like nah, I don't wear Polo. Shit nigga. Had my feet not been so big, I woulda grabbed all three. America hustle the fuck out of us."

"Yeah, they do. Speaking of shoes. Did you get those timbs for your brother in law when we were in Dubai?"

"Man nigga naw. I contemplated too damn much. For $65, I shoulda got two pair. I owe my nigga big time man. He cool as a fan." Just then, there was a knock on the door.

"I got it man." Mook got up and opened the door. "Where the big hoes at?"

"Not in here I tell you that," Mook told E.J., as he strolled in there in his custom made suit that he had got in Dubai. Eric and Bryson followed in behind him, with bottles of Patron and Ciroc.

"Where y'all niggas been man?," I asked them.

"Shit, you see how fresh these goatees are man? Its an Aussie nigga cross the street from the telly who slice up better than us damn near. Brother man got our linings so sharp we could cut steel," Eric said. "He a brother?"

"Naw. A white boy, but he might as well be a brother. How many white boys you know can cut like this?," as he ran his hand across his fresh mid level fade.

"I'll admit, he is good my nigga."

"Fuck all that haircut shit. Nigga where we going? I wanna see some big hoes."

"E.J., ain't nobody caring about you and your whale sized plush bunnies. Nigga we in the city. Sydney, Australia nigga.

You better head to the outback with all that shit," Bryson told him.

"Shit I might have too. I'm ready to lay this belly on her back while I beat."

"Yeah. 'Cause two fat people fuck and make sparks." We all laughed at Mook's comment while E.J. gave us the finger.

"Y'all ready man?," Eric asked us. We told him let's roll and we headed out the door, ready to tear the King's Cross district of Sydney up. We all pimped out the room, leaving the bottles in there. We were in custom made clothes. Laced up from head to toe. We were the gold watch wearing, jet flying, kiss stealing, wheeling dealing, son of a guns. We were the black four horsemen. Eric was Flair, I was Double A, E.J. was J.J. Dillon, Mook was Tully Blanchard and Bryson was good ol' Ole Anderson. "**WOOO!!!,**" I let out.

"Nigga why you screaming in an elevator?," E.J. asked me. 'Cause I feel WOOO!!! Like making some chick ride space mountain tonight. WOOO!!!" All these fools were quiet, just staring at me. "Man y'all can't tell me that none of y'all niggas don't watch wrestling."

"Nigga you love that shit a lil too much don't you think?," Eric told me.

"Fuck all y'all niggas man. Y'all just don't know." We stepped out of the elevator, through the lobby and out of the front door. We stepped outside to a perfect night. See, in the southern hemisphere, everything was opposite. America's summers were their winters and vice versa. It was fall out here. However, to be 60 degrees, that still was pretty good. As we hit the blocks, every woman within eye distance looked at us and marveled. We were clad out in suits. I myself had on the trenchcoat and the fedora, looking like Bumpy Johnson's offspring. E.J., he wasn't the suit and tie type guy. He came out in his Bill Cosby sweater, some black slacks, black dress shoes and a Kangol. Mook, well, you already know how the Southern boys did it. Gold grill with the sportcoat, jeans and tennis shoes on. Let's not forget the ATL Hawks logo hat he put on his head. Bryson, well, he had the classic Midwest shit going on. You know, in those Michigan, Indiana, Illinois, Wisconsin parts, they known for pimpin'. He had on a *** damn bright yellow suit, brown shoes, the brown fedora, with the off yellow trench coat. But let that nigga tell it, he was wearing lemon, with baby cocoa shoes and the mango trench coat draped him up. Then, there was Eric. Also from the Midwest, but he came out tonight lookin like Frank Lucas reincarnated. Kicked back with the fur coat that looked like it was made out of dead polar bear. **"FUCK PETA!!!,"** he yelled as some car drove by, screaming some obnoxious mess. I couldn't really understand what they said with that heavy accent they had over here.

"Where we going man?," E.J. asked.

"Shit we gone find something. It's only a matter of time. This supposed to be their party district," Eric replied back. We saw a spot tucked away in a huge building. We didn't even see a name, but we walked in there and immediately just took over the joint. We started at the bar, with women and men in general coming up to us, asking us where we were from. We all lied and told 'em we were American football players, here to have a good time in the offseason. When asked who we played for, we told them the Jacksonville Jaguars. Let's be honest. No one knows who the hell plays for the Jacksonville Jaguars. Hell they could barely get 10,000 people at a game. It was lively in here. People were snapping pictures. Women were dancing with us. Out of nowhere, not even forty minutes in, some random Aussie came up to us.

"Would you gentlemen like to go upstairs?" Shit, we were with it. We didn't even know that the club had an upper level. We jumped in the elevator, finding out that this random guy was the owner of the club. Once we hit the second floor, it was a totally different vibe than downstairs. Down there, it was party central. Dancing, drinking, pure ratchetness, all of that. Up here, it was a cool, calm, serene scene. It was an elegant bar and lounge type vibe. There were people up here, but like I said, it was much more mellow.

"Oh boy, you see her?" We looked to see who E.J. was talking about.

"Ahh shit. This nigga done found a heavyweight," Bryson said. E.J. took off and headed over to baby girl, while the rest of us just slid back at the bar, tossing 'em back like liquor was going out of style. Man, the night was going gravy. One by one, more people came up to us, intrigued by our dress and the overall glow that we gave off. Once again, the Jacksonville Jaguars lie came into effect. Hell my head was starting to spin as combined with the pre game, I was good and fucking lit now. Now, I was coherent, but my liver was screaming for me to stop.

"A man?" I turned around to see Bryson with one of the baddest damn females I had ever seen. "Brittany, this my mans Ty. Ty, this is my new friend, Brittany."

"Pleasure to meet you baby," as I kissed her hand.

"Damn. Y'all out here tryna be all classy and shit with these Aussie broads? I know y'all niggas." Now, I didn't get offended, 'cause she was a sister. I didn't know what breed of Aussie sister she was, but she was definitely black.

"What you mean girl?," I asked her. "C'mon now. The furs. The kiss on the hand. Y'all doing the most," as she laughed.

"Yeah baby," Bryson said. "Don't mind my mans you know. He from Compton. You know they don't have any manners out there." Her head shot back around to me. "Compton? You from Cali?"

"Yeah baby why?"

"I got family out there. I'm originally from Boston, but I gotta cousin named Kevin out there."

"Kevin who?"

"West. It's on my daddy side." Right then and there, I wasn't even thinkin' about Kevin in a general sense. I was thinkin' that Bryson came over here trying to be slick and lost his chick in the process. She continued talking to me and completely ignored that fool. He eventually disappeared, and me and her spent the rest of the night drinking. Turns out she was here for school, studying at the University of Sydney. E.J. had just fell in love with that big girl as he danced with her the entire night. We stayed in there for about a good two hours, mingling and everything. I got Brittany's email and number, and we mobbed back out into the streets.

"Where to next man?," Eric asked us.

"Shit we gone walk and see," Mook responded. For a bunch of drunk dudes, I can say that we were walking, conversing and acting better than most sober people. We mobbed off into the heart of Kings Cross until we found a new joint. It was called Club Empire. From the looks of it, we were in for another classic. We stepped in there, now thinking that we were the old Dipset and not the horsemen. I just wanted to holla out "KILLA" when we walked into the building. Ahh man it was on from the moment we hit the lower level. I mean shit. I really thought I was a fuckin' pimp. Muthafuckin' women kept coming up to us by the boatloads it seemed. Now, we were no longer the Jacksonville Jaguars. We were now the Seattle Seahawks. We were the Legion of Boom. My cornrows over the last six months had turned into dreads, so they were thinkin' I was Richard Sherman. I had never in my life felt like a superstar on this level. All I needed was a Super Bowl trophy to hold in my hand.

When I woke up the next day, I was passed out in my hotel room, ass naked, a rubber on the floor and by my damn self. It was 1:30 the next afternoon and hung over wasn't the word. I had literally been resurrected from the dead. I don't know who I had smashed, but she must've been good 'cause I was out for the count. I struggled moving out of the bed. I headed downstairs to the sixth floor too E.J.'s room to see what was good. I knocked on the door more than enough times. I knew his big ass was in there. Finally, he opened up.

"A nigga, what you want?," he whispered. I looked in there to see that heavy hitter sprawled out across the bed. It looked like a giant squid had gotten stuck on the beach. The cellulite rolls that I saw in her legs were so deep in her hamstrings that you could rob a jewelry store and hide all the jewels in 'em.

"Shit man I was just making sure everything was good. Where them other niggas at?" He shook his head.

"Man, them niggas got so fucked up last night that we literally had to drag them niggas to they room."

"Who is we?," I asked.

"Me and Bryson, cause he ain't drink shit after you took his bitch."

"Was I fucked up too?"

"Yeah. You too. You were fucked up, but you straightened up when that nigga Eric threw up on your trench coat."

"Man, where my shit at?," patting myself down as if that thing was gonna magically appear in my pocket or some shit."

"Man you had to charge that shit to the game." I couldn't believe it. I lost my Bumpy Johnson outfit. That shit was tragic. However, Australia was lit as fuck.

"Welcome to Los Angeles. We hope that you enjoyed your flight and that you fly with us again." That was music to my ears as I stretched my legs out under the seat. As always, I had me a window seat. I just looked out at the tarmac as people started to get up and get their belongings. I wasn't gone even tell Kevin that I was coming home. I was just gonna sneak up on him and surprise my nigga. Also, my niggas at the shop. Man, it truly felt great. I couldn't wait to share my stories with my niggas. As I finally exited the plane, walking felt more than good. It felt like a damn relief. I had flown in from D.C., where we all had separated. I wasn't used to the time change just yet. I was gonna be sleep for at least for the first two days. I got to baggage claim and patiently waited for my bags to come, all while hoping that I could catch a cab that would take me 20 minutes south to the crib. With all the money I had made, I at least wanted to get one of my brothers paid. That's what being in Africa taught me. No matter what country you were from, you were black.

Hands down. You had to look out for your own. At the same time, I was steady scoping out homes and available land on my phone. I was seriously moving off to Boise. I didn't even wanna waste any time, but I at least owed my people a month before I raised the hell up out of Southern California. My bags came and I was off to the cab area, where I got lucky with a minivan cab that could accommodate my baggage. It felt good to simply be riding on Cali roads again. Dude was Ethiopian, so it was even better to give my business to someone with the same skin tone as myself. I sat back in my seat. He didn't make conversation with me and that was just fine. I needed to relax. I simply soaked up the California sun rays. Just when we got into the meat of the freeway and hit a traffic jam,

Will Smith's "Summertime" popped up on the radio. I couldn't help myself as I began to dance in my seat. I saw the Ethiopian dude laugh at me, but I really didn't care. I was back home and during the best time of the year. "Where did you come from with all those bags?," he asked me. "One of those places was Africa."

"Oh really. Did you go to Ethiopia?"

"Naw. I was in Seychelles. But I did meet a lot of beautiful Ethiopian women." He laughed.

"Yes, we have some very gorgeous women to say the least. It's funny. When I first came here, people looked at me strange when I told them that I was Ethiopian. I guess they had this image that we were all skin and bones, and had never eaten a full meal our entire lives. We are actually normal people. Our women are some of the most beautiful on the planet. What is it you guys call it in America. Thick right?" I could've spit a drank out if I had one with that statement, but my mans was right. I had seen a lot of Ethiopian women when I was over in Seychelles and Dubai. Boy oh boy. Sexy wasn't the word to describe them. They were just immaculate. Hell, you could say that about all black women. I see why the world tries to tan and be like my beautiful sisters. They are one of a kind in an entire universe of life. How many women and people in general came in 50 shades? I know, I know. You can't think of any other race but us. In this moment, I was definitely proud to be black. We got to my place after all the madness on the road had went down. "Thank you brother," as I slid him $200.

"Sir, you do not owe me this."

"Trust me, I do. You did me a service and I'm paying it back ten fold."

"Thank you sir," he told me with tears in his eyes. "You don't know what this means to me." With those words, I reached into my pocket and also handed him another $300. "Lets just say this is good fortune returning to you. I don't believe in God, so I won't say blessings. But, enjoy my brother."

"Thank you sir." He got out and assisted me with my luggage. As he pulled off, I threw on my shades and began to just look around me. The sky was clear and the sun was beaming. No one was out and about over here, and for good reason. It was too hot to be outside in an apartment complex. This was the time where you wanted to be at Dockwilder Beach or some shit like that. "Home. I am here," I said out loud. As strong as my lil ass was, this luggage was no ho, as I had to use the assistance of the rail just to get up to my apartment. Finally, I was at the door. I had the key, but I wanted to see if Kevin was home. I rang the doorbell and put my ear to the door.

"Who is it?" Yup, the typical black response.

"HOUSEKEEPING!!!" The door slowly crept open, but my man's looked like he wasn't excited to see a nigga.

"Sup man," I told him as he opened up and let me in. Not being phased by his no response, I simply brought my bags in and set them in the kitchen. I had chalked it up to him being tired from school or something. He sat on the couch and I plopped down on the opposite end, seeing that sitting next to him like a clingy girlfriend would be a severe man law violation.

"So what's up man?," I asked him. "What's been poppin' round here?"

"I don't know man. You tell me." His voice tone was very uncomfortable with me.

"Yo man like forreal. What is going on?"

"Look man. You left for six months. I got the bread you sent for helping with the rent and I highly appreciate it. But. But. I don't want you here anymore man." I began to laugh as I knew my mans was just fucking with me.

"Aight man, aight. Cut the jokes. I see the room door closed. You got a piece of ass in there don't you?" He didn't respond. "Oh, you got a piece of ass for me. Yeah boy," getting up clasping my hands like birdman. That's when he got up and put his hands in my chest. "Yo what's ya problem Kev? You actin real feminine right now."

"I want you gone man. Like out of here."

"Ok nigga. What's your gripe man? Did someone die? Someone break ya heart? Whatever the fuck going on, I'm sorry. But man don't take that shit out on me."

"Bruh. You didn't do anything. You sent money for the rent. You called a nigga from every place you was. But, I don't want you here anymore." Just then, the bedroom door creaked open. I looked around him and saw a tall dude come out. He was about 6'7, young looking and real stocky. Nigga had a dusty black du rag on and you could tell he had just gotten up.

"Who's ya mans Kev?"

"Kev, who this?," he asked him. "Just an old friend. Nothing else." I went to dap my mans up and he didn't extend his hand out.

"Yo Kev," as I looked at him while pointing at his mans.

"What's wrong with ya boy?"

"Nothin man. A Grayson, could you give us a few?"

"No problem beautiful." That's when I saw the shit that changed me for a lifetime. I was already fucked up when he called him beautiful. But Kev reached up to kiss him dead on the lips.

"YO WHAT THE FUCK GOING ON HERE MAN???!!!"

"Problem nigga," ol boy said.

"Yeah nigga it's a major problem," I responded. I walked up towards him to an awaiting gun sitting flush with my forehead. I looked at this dude with a look of sarcasm. Cutting my eyes, Kevin was backed off from us, hands covering his mouth, in complete shock of what was going on. While he was in shock, I was steady trying to comprehend what in the good fuck was actually happening. As that gun was pointed at me, I started to think many things. First, I thought at any minute that the Punk'd crew was gonna pop out from the bathroom and these niggas would start laughing. They would rip the plastic off of their lips and say gotcha. But, that's why they call an imagination an imagination. This was forreal. I had really came back to find out Kevin was gay and now his nigga had a gun pointed dead to my cranial.

"I tell you what man," I told him. "You better use that muthafucker. Cause if you don't, its gonna be the biggest regret of your life."

"Don't think I won't do it nigga." I laughed at him.

"You think I'm scared of a gun? A fucking gun? Nigga I'm from Compton nigga. **SPOOKTOWN CUZ!!! DA FUCK YOU THINK THIS IS!!! PULL THE TRIGGA NIGGA!!! PULL IT!!!"** This bitch ass nigga started to cry while he was holding it still. **"DO IT NIGGA!!!"** He was making a face like he didn't know what he was doing.

"Put the gun down Grayson," Kevin told him. He gave no response. Then, as I stared at this big scary bitch, Kevin's hand came in and he slowly started to lower the gun. He stood in between us, looking dead into my eyes. He knew that I was about to go ham sandwich. If it was one thing that I had learned from the OG's in the hood, it was that you never pulled a gun out if you didn't intend to use it. I don't care if you were just cleaning the muthafucka. At least you were using it in some sort of fashion. Showing it off, threatening a nigga did not fly where I was from.

"Go in the room Grayson. I'll be there in a minute." He took his tall, lanky ass back in the room, crying tears. That's how I knew he wasn't really bout that life. "I'm sorry Ty. I'm sorry. It's something I been battling since we were young. I never wanted to tell anyone or anybody. That was the hardest thing for me coming up." I turned around and took a deep breath, staring at the ceiling with my hands on my hips. I looked down and took another deep breath.

"Ty man c'mon. We been friends since we were yay high. I just hope this doesn't destroy our friendship." I turned around and just gave this nigga the "really nigga" look.

"Bruh. Bruh. Bruh. You gay man. You fucking gay. Like, be honest with me right now my nigga. Did at anytime you ever look at me like you wanted me? I mean like really, be honest."

"No," as he shook his head. "We were always friends man. That's how I saw it. I couldn't do this shit in Compton. Niggas get killed for less. I just got tired of battling it man. I couldn't take it anymore. I was with a woman while you were gone, and I broke down and cried in the middle of our session. I couldn't do it anymore." I shook my head as I was still trying to tell myself that this was a dream. The whole time, his man child girlfriend was in the other room crying, as I could hear him clearly.

"Bruh, we been through alot, but this shit here. Wow. I came here with you to try and achieve a dream. Because we agreed to make this happen. I get back and you were anxious to kick me out. And for what. Another nigga? Like, even if you wasn't in a 'ship with him, you was ready to boot me for another nigga. He ain't put no rent money in this muthafucka I bet. You know what though. I'm good. You the one need that nigga Jesus you talk about." I turned around and walked out the kitchen, grabbing my bags.

"I thought you didn't believe in God."

"**I DON'T NIGGA!!!**," turning around, looking back at him. **"BUT EVEN HIS ASS LOOKING AT YOU LIKE WHAT THE FUCK!!!** Matter fact, I'm a go sit outside. My whip been delivered. And you know what, I'm gone pack this shit up and just drive. Take my ass to the Marriott or some shit like that. I gotta get this off my mind. I don't know where I'm gone end up. Where I'm gone lay my head tonight, but I gotta roll out from here." I walked outside. I really didn't know where to go. My new truck was just sitting there looking pretty as ever. A taupe colored truck, with mango and chocolate insides. Egyptian hieroglyphic symbols were sewn into the seat. I had always had a fascination about Egyptian history, so I figured that when I came up in this world financially, I would do it big. My mans picked it up for me at the Long Beach port terminal and dropped it off the night before I got back. But now, having what I wanted came at the cost of losing what I had my whole life. My best friend. My ace. My road dog. My partner in crime, or whatever you wanted to call it. I loaded up my vehicle with all of my luggage.

"Ty?" I turned around to see Kev standing right behind me.

"Yo what you want man? You kicked me out. You got yourself a female, of a different sorts. What you want man?," as I shut the back door of my whip.

"Look man. You my brother. I'm sorry that shit hit you like this." He took a deep breath. "I been fucked up ever since sophomore year man. Naw, I didn't get molested or anything. I simply got my heart broken. I saw my mama one night as I was coming home from school. Matter fact, it was the day "Greasy" got shot." Greasy was a partna of ours who grew up with us in Spooktown. The nigga was short as ever. 5'6 to be exact. But, the nigga had hands. I mean, he was vicious with it. Everyone called him Grease for two reasons. One, because he was always working on cars in the hood. Two, I wasn't there, but from what the hood says, he got into it with two blood niggas that went to Centennial. They ran up on him thinking it was an easy win and he ended up taxing 'em up. Said his hands were so fast that it was like the other cats were fighting grease, cause they couldn't hit him.

"So when we walked back from the park and them niggas came dumpin, I cut through some houses," I told him. "Yeah and he got shot in the ass I know."

"Yeah, in the ass. Why we call him." "Grease ass," Ty interrupted.

"I know. Keep going."

"Yeah man so. I race home after cutting through alleys and making sure them niggas in that white car were nowhere in sight. I ran 'round the side of my crib and came into the back door. I shouted for my mama as soon as I came in the house. She didn't hear me. So I ran to her room and literally pushed the door open. She didn't see me, nor did the other chick. She had her face buried deep in my mama pussy. I literally paused for a good minute, just looking at the bullshit that was going on. I slowly let the door back to an almost closed position and went to my room. I sat in dead silence for hours. My mama didn't realize that I had saw her. I went my whole life hearing my mama preach about how she couldn't wait for me to grow up and get married so she could be a grandma, and have a daughter in law. Once I saw that, it fucked me up. It made me look at women different. It made me wanna stay away from 'em. It opened a whole other side of me. Trust man. I don't wanna be dealing with this shit." I just looked at him, not believing what he was telling me.

"So you fuck him yet?"

"Hell naw. I'm skeptical 'bout having a dick in my ass man. Like, I'm knowing the shit ain't cool. But I don't know what to do bruh. I'm confused man. Help me bruh." I looked around trying to soak this all in.

"Look man," as I placed my hand on his shoulder. "It's some shit that as a man, another man can't help you with. I can't man. I'm sorry you went through this. But right now, this just some shit I can't take. I mean I come home man. I come home to this. How the fuck six months turn into some shit like this man? And right now, as much as I wanna scorn you because of what I believe. I can't. Cause you know what, while you were talking, I realized something. Friendship is friendship. But still, it comes a time that friends gotta go their separate ways. So I tell you this man. I know who you pray too. So tell Him from me, that I hope you can break out of this and come back. But, I gotta go my own way now. I ain't got a home. I gotta go make one." We both stared at each other. I could tell he was disgruntled and feeling helpless. Right then, he pulled something out of his back pocket. It was Spoon's liners that he had left over the crib one night a long time ago.

"So you just randomly carrying clippers in your back pocket?"

"Naw. I just figured since you came home today, that it would mean the world to you." I looked at Spoon's custom line up joints. His name engraved in them. I started to remember how much my nigga was a beast with the clipper game.

"Take them and go far with 'em bro. Wherever you end up at." I looked at Kev again and back down at the clippers. I then looked up at him once more.

"Look man," I said in the most low tone voice ever, eyes watery than a muthafucka. "You fight your battle. And I'm gone fight mines." I said not another word to him as I went to the driver seat of my truck and started it up. I adjusted all of my mirrors, only to see Kev looking directly at me from the driver side mirror. Didn't chuck a deuce or anything. I simply peeled off slowly, making one last glance in my mirror to see that he was still lookin. Though he said what he said, I truly believe at this point that I had lost my best friend. I pulled up to the barbershop just three blocks away and knew these niggas were just waiting for me. I got lucky and caught me a parking spot right in front of the joint. I threw on my shades as I was gonna go in and be hollywood on these niggas. I got out the car and waltzed on in.

"Wassup niggas?," as I threw up my hands. They all looked at me with no response, steady cutting the heads they had in their chairs. "Yo niggas what's up?"

"What you want man?," Nique asked me. I took my shades off.

"I know y'all fucking with me man. Good one man. So whats up?," as I plopped down in my old barber chair like I had always done. Brody shut his clippers off.

"Could you please get up out of Gristle chair?" I stood up, literally now seeing that these niggas weren't playing.

"Yo man what's up? Why y'all acting like this?"

"Why we actin like this?," as Nique shut his clippers off. "Nigga you the only one who been action this whole time. Yo, when Brody first complained about you not hitting a nigga up, I would tell him chill you know. He handling business. But then as time went on, it's like you forgot about all of us. Yo' niggas. Yo' partnas. Nigga did you forget that we gave you a chance to cut in this muthafucka?"

"Bruh. The shit wasn't like that. If I didn't care, I wouldn't came back as quick as I did. Nigga I just landed not to long ago. After hitting the crib, then I came here. What more do you want?"

"We want you to get the fuck up outta here and don't ever come back to our shop again." Brody had walked around from that chair and got in my face.

"Cuz, I think you need to back the fuck up right now cause you getting a lil too personal right now," I told him. He turned around and put his clippers down in his area, and came right back to get in my face.

"And what if I dont blood? What you gone do? Nigga don't think the gangsta disappeared because I went legit. I'll still get shit brackin' around here." I wasn't backing down, nor was he. I glanced over at Nique. He was out in front of his chair, balled up fists, waiting for some shit to pop off. I glanced at the two niggas in the chairs. They didn't know what the fuck to do, as they both just had the I just came to get my shit cut looks on their faces. I looked back at Brody. "What you wanna do blood?"

"You know what man," I told him. "I'm gone leave. I wish you niggas nothing but the best out here."

"We don't need yo well wishes nigga," Nique said. "Get the fuck out," Brody whispered, as he pointed to the door. I walked backwards, refusing to turn my back on any one of those niggas. I threw my shades on and bounced out the door to get in my truck. Once there, I cranked it up and just started to drive. I didn't know where I was going. I cut all the music off and just took time to myself to think. After all the travel and crazy shit I saw and did, I made it home.

Made it home to find out that my best friend was confused and my niggas, who I thought were my niggas had literally gave me the boot. I didn't think that I had to call everyone in they mama when I left. I mean, niggas must've forgot that work was being put in. Niggas didn't know that I was putting on for the barbershop in every shop that I went too. Naw, them niggas didn't see that or know that. Now I see why so many niggas who leave never go back. They are persecuted for doing better in a better environment. It's like they cool with you when you all are on the same level. But the minute that you start to elevate your mind and your career path, all of a *** damn sudden, it's a fucking problem. I was sick of seeing shit like that. But, at the same time, I had to expect it. As a youth, I would think the same shit. You gotta partna who was just a brainiac. He get's a scholarship to a prestigious private school and then you pretend like he turned his back. Naw, it wasn't that. His capabilities were just better suited for a school system that wasn't in Compton. As a youngin, niggas in the hood, including myself, couldn't comprehend that. Someone in the hood was doing better than us.

Now, as a grown man, almost, I was starting to see the bigger picture. Niggas didn't leave to make you look bad. They left because they wanted to be an example for the niggas they left behind. But, we made 'em feel like shit when they came back to the blocks. Hell, some even got shot down for trying to just enjoy the comforts of home. That made me go 5 north instead of hittin the 91. I didn't know where this trip was gonna take me. It was heading into the evening hours. I continued on the road, only taking a break when I needed gas and had to pee. This journey was scary to me. I had left everything that I ever knew once again. Only this time, I didn't know where this part of life was taking me. When it finally hit 10:37 p.m., I finally found myself in Oakland. The Bay Area. I didn't know shit about Oakland expect that it was killas up here. I journeyed into downtown, to make sure I would be somewhere safe. Crazy enough, I found a Marriott downtown and checked into it. I told 'em two days, which would give me ample time to just relax in my room and do nothing. I had no plans on leaving and exploring the city. I just wanted to relax and forget that today ever happened. It was damn near midnight when I had finally got settled in and showered up. The TV was off and I was lying on the bed, thinking about everything. I heard the ring of my cell phone and looked over to see a 503 number. I didn't know who it was or what that area code was. I simply let it ring until my phone didn't buzz anymore. Two minutes later, it rang again. I let it go three times before I finally got frustrated enough and answered the call. "Yo who this?"

"Nigga if you don't wake yo' sleepy as up. Whats going on man?"

"Yo like. Who the fuck is this? Like real shit, don't play on my phone," I told 'em.

"Who else you know like to fuck 'em if they weigh over 185?"

"E.J!!!"

"In the flesh nigga. Why you sound so depressed?"

"Long day man. Long day. Whats up?"

"Whats up is that I moved to Portland and the shit is good nigga. The weed, the thick white women, all that. The shit is good."

"I mean. You went back to the crib. Congrats."

"Naw nigga naw. Not Portland, Maine. I'm in Oregon my nigga." I jumped up and sat on the edge of the bed when he said that.

"What you doing up there my nigga?," I asked him. "Opportunity man. I co-own my own shop. It's a gold mine up here and niggas need to take advantage."

"So how you go about that shit?"

"Shit man. I doubled up and got smart. I met a dude from Portland, in the other Portland I'm from. So he said he was out there visiting family. I told him I was heading out to do what I do and he said he had a weed shop in Portland. But, he wanted to double up and make it into a barbershop slash weed shop. And that's what we got. Rip City Chronic."

"Man nigga, you ain't waste no time my nigga."

"Shole didn't. Remember. I left a week and a half early before the rest of y'all. I spent one day at home getting some of my shit from a friends house. Then, that opportunity presented itself and I booked a flight out to Portland. The rest is history. Not bad so far. It's damn sure worth it." I continued listening to how E.J. turned shit into sugar. I eventually told him about what was going on in my life and how I had no clue about where I was gonna end up.

"Come up nigga," he told me.

"You mean to Portland?"

"Naw nigga Georgia. Shit why not? Yo' ass done already drove up hours from L.A. to Oakland, which I know ain't no short ass drive. Come up man. It's a chair for you. You said you wanted to be around some small time shit right?"

"But Portland a metro area man. Got an NBA team and all that."

"Nigga it's 95% white. You a bruh. You can make it happen. If you really want it. Drive up tomorrow. I don't care what time of the night it is. I got you. Just let me know." I really took into consideration what he said. It wasn't Boise, but it sounded along the lines of it. I had traveled this far and it was something to contemplate. I googled the distance to Boise and Portland from here. It was almost the same distance. Nine hours and some change. I was contemplating a lot with this one and now the urge to sleep automatically left me. I got out of bed and threw on my ones to head downstairs. As I was walking through the lobby to go chill outside for a minute, I noticed a framed football jersey off in the distance. It didn't look like any pro team. I walked over to it, which was located adjacent to the entrance. It was a number 9 high school jersey, blue in color. "In Memory of Carlos." I looked at the 8 x 11 picture that was also put into the frame. The kid was dreaded out and almost looked a bit like Flocka.

"Interesting young man isn't he." I turned around to see a short sister standing behind me."

"Yeah I was sitting here reading all the accolades. First team all state in basketball and football. Newport Harbor a school out here?" She let out a chuckle.

"Naw baby naw. Trust, Oakland and Newport are two totally different areas."

"Oh. Oh he was in Newport? Like Newport Beach?"

"Yup. That's my nephew. His daddy came up over some time with his business and got Carlos and his mama up outta here, and off to greener pastures. He would call me and say he adjusted to it, but it was nothing like Oakland.

Man I mean he could catch the ball, run the ball, dunk the ball. My nephew was special."

"What happened to him if you don't mind me asking?"

"Well, they had a game up here a few years ago. His team had gotten really good and they were ranked in the nation. They had to play Antioch, which is a powerhouse school up here in the Bay. They were at Raider Stadium, which is right there pictured in the top left corner. They lost the game. I mean bad. It was 62-31. But, to see my nephew doing what he loved to do, aww man, it touched my heart. Then, they got back to the hotel and someone shot him." The whole time she was telling me the story, I was looking dead at his picture. He looked like a kid who had youth mixed with Black Panther pride.

"Why did they shoot him?"

"The stupid hood mentality. Someone felt like he left them to handle the worst in life. All because his father had did what any parent would do and give their child a better life. My nephew died for nothing. You know?"

"No ma'am. I cannot agree. He died for something and he just taught me a valuable lesson, and he doesn't even know it."

"What's that?," she asked.

"He died with a purpose. I'm pretty sure this was destined, but I was contemplating a major move. And now, with the story you just told me about your nephew, he has allowed me to make that move with peace of mind. I'm Ty by the way."

"Juanita. Nice to meet you. So where are you going?"

"Portland. To start a fresh life away from Compton and anything else Southern California."

"Well. I'm going to go back to my office, but I want you to remember something. I'm definitely proud to see a black man make it from dire circumstances to even have the chance to succeed in life. With everything that we go through from gentrification, police shooting us, death for our organs, we still hold fast and survive. Just remember. A Black Man Has 9 Lives. And right now, you are living one of them. Sleep well tonight." She patted me on the back, smiled and walked back behind the hotel lobby desk, disappearing into her office. I watched her walk off and then looked back at his picture.

"Thanks brother. I appreciate you," I whispered to his picture. I swore on everything I loved it seemed like he had heard me. I turned around and proceeded back to my room. I got in and gave E.J. a call. "I'll be up tomorrow evening nigga."

"I'll meet you outside of the Moda Center my nigga." That was all that I needed to hear as I was now ready to leave behind one chapter of my life and write another one. I set my alarm for six in the morning and crashed out. The next morning, I was awakened by some old Big Mike blasting from my android. Running off of less than five hours of sleep, I was uncommonly still feeling good. The talk with the lady last night set me straight. I took a quick shower and threw on a white tee and some jeans. I didn't follow trends. Clothes were clothes. Whether you think they were out of style or in style, the fact was that you needed something to cover your ass during the day. I cancelled my last night at the desk, paid for my stay and bounced out. I hit up Jack in the Box and got me two supreme croissants for the long road trip ahead. I calculated that if I could hit the 5 by no later than 7:15, I should be there by no later than five or six in the evening. I headed out towards the freeway. As I hit the light before heading onto the freeway, I witnessed a billboard. Flac City Poparazzi is what it said.

"It's an Oakland thing" was sprawled in black letters across the bottom. I didn't know who that was, but they had obviously made their niche in the city. That's the same thought that I had going to Portland for this new start. I wanted to lay my own path in that city. Actually, that was an understatement. I wanted to take that bitch over. I wanted my face on the side of the Trail Blazers arena, next to Damian Lillard's and CJ McCollum joints. I blazed through the light when it turned green and merged on to the 5 with no problem. I figure since I was in the Bay, that I might as well let Bay music take me out. I cranked on some old E-40. "Sprinkle Me." This shit was a classic and a hit no matter what part of the country you were from. I got into a zone and cruised at an even 75, minus the times that the traffic stalled. Yeah, I was indeed ready for this. I made it to the Oregon-California state line in what seemed like no time, but I still had a ways to go before I was even anywhere near Portland. It was all the way at the top of the state, near the Washington border. I went along, not missing a beat. I was sincerely enjoying the beautiful scenery that you could only find up here in the Pacific Northwest. I had not a soul in sight it seemed, as there was no congestion out here on the road at all. **"WHOOP WHOOP."** I heard the sound and looked in my rear view mirror. **"FUCK!!!,"** I yelled out. It was the *** damn police and they had caught a nigga doing 87. I didn't even realize it until I saw him either. There was an exit up in a half mile, so I would just get off there and let him do what he do. I pulled off the exit and made a slight right onto a side street, where I parked the car.

"SHUT THE CAR OFF AND RAISE DOWN YOUR WINDOW!!!" I didn't know what the hell was causing all this, but I did exactly what he said. The whole time, I am carefully moving my hands in a way to make it look like I was not reaching for anything. I raised down my window. **"THROW YOUR KEYS OUT!!! EXIT THE VEHICLE WITH YOUR HANDS UP!!!"** That's when I noticed in my driver side mirror that there were two of them with guns drawn. Now, I was on nervous mode, because I was outnumbered, and it was obvious that my skin tone was not the common theme around here. I tossed the keys far and put both hands out of the window.

"OPEN THE DOOR AND SLOWLY EXIT THE VEHICLE WITH YOUR HANDS RAISED!!!" I slowly reached for the door handle with my left hand, opening my car door and I got out with both hands up, looking dead at them. At the same time I saw another squad car quickly approaching behind them. It was turning to join us. **"TURN AROUND. CLASP YOUR HANDS BEHIND YOUR HEAD AND WALK BACKWARDS!!! SLOWLY!!!"** I put my hands behind my head first, because I didn't want any reason for them to think I had free hands to do anything. I turned around, mad as fuck, but I couldn't show it. I slowly walked backwards, thinking that whole time that this was it. I was about to be the next black man on the news from death by a cop.

"STOP!!!" I felt them come up on me. One officer grabbed one hand, then grabbed the other and placed me in cuffs. I saw the other two heading towards my vehicles. Everything was adding up like it always did in America. Black guy with nice whip, in an area where we weren't commonly seen. Yep, I had to be a drug dealer. He walked me over to the squad car. "You got any weapons on you son? Any drugs? Anything that I need to know about?"

"No sir," as I cut my eyes to see his partner with a gun pointed right at me. The other two officers who had pulled up began going through my vehicle. No search warrant or anything. They just started doing their own thing. The worst thing was that there was nothing that I could do about it. Absolutely nothing.

"Turn around." I don't know why he asked me that since he took it upon himself to spin me around. "Son I cut my lights on well over a half mile ago and you proceeded to not stop until you got to an exit. So why'd you run?"

"I wasn't running sir."

"Oh you got a smart ass mouth on you I see huh?" He then proceeded to put the gun under my chin. "Boy you know I could blast your niggerish ass right now. Now tell me, what were you running from?" I had nothing to lose at this point. I had one gun beneath my chin. Another gun pointed at me from not even three yards away.

"Sir. Years ago. I had a friend who is a state trooper back in the state of Indiana almost lose his life on the freeway. A car almost took him out while he was writing a ticket. He told me a long time ago that if I'm ever in a situation and near an exit, pull over on the exit. That way myself and the officer's life won't be in jeopardy. Sir." It took a lot out of me to say that as scared as I was. It even took me to let my pride go by calling him sir." I had to man up. Wasn't no point of crying. If I was gonna die, then I was gonna die. Slowly, he lowered his weapon down, as did his partners.

"Are you bullshitting me son?"

"No sir," I said, shaking my head.

"Well, don't meet too many smart ones like you around here. You got California plates. Where you going?"

"Portland. I'm moving sir."

"Moving up for what?"

"A better life." I heard the thud of my luggage hit the ground as the other two officers started rummaging through my clothes, looking for any and everything. But, they weren't gonna find nothing. "Now you just stay put against this car boy. Let my officers do their job and you'll be on your way." The other officer once again drew his gun, keeping it pointed at me. I watched as these men threw all of my belongings out. I had clothes everywhere on the ground. Shoes, electronics, you name it. They showed no regards for anything of mine.

"All clear sir," one of the officers said.

"Well now boy looks like you were telling the truth. So I'm gonna let you out of these cuffs and you're gonna go on about your way you here?"

"Yes sir." He unlocked the cuffs while his partner still had his weapon pointed at me.

"Now you gone head clean that up and ummm, enjoy my good state ya hear." His partner finally put the gun down and all the officers proceeded to get back in their cars and take off. They left me alone, with everything that belonged to me scattered everywhere. As angry as I was, all I could do was shake my head at the level of disrespect that I encountered. And they wonder why we are angry. I wanted as less time in this place as possible. So I literally stuffed my bag with my clothes and put 'em back in the truck. I drove off in a hurry. Thank God I had gotten gas some time back, because Lord only knows how it would've been if they had saw me at a gas station out here. Nothing could cure my soul right now but getting to my destination. I continued on my drive, in my now dirty truck. They left their dirt in there. Themselves. See sometimes, the most unclean things can come wrapped up inside of a clean package. In this case, it was four men in black uniforms. I proceeded on down the highway until I finally reached Corvallis. I was now literally an hour and a half out, but I was drained, tired and hungry. I stopped by at a local restaurant, which was located near the Oregon State campus. Pancakes. I needed fucking pancakes. It couldn't cure my anger, but it would definitely make me feel better. And this place, luckily, had an all you can eat special. I must have ended up smashing nine flapjacks in record time. I scraped the plate and appeased my gut. I proceeded to jump back on the road and head back towards the freeway. It was now 3:29 p.m. and traffic was picking up around here. I called E.J. to let him know that there was no way that I was gonna make it at five. I had to get through Corvallis and Salem, so my road trip would be extended. He was cool with it, saying to just call him when he got there. He was at the shop, slicing some heads. The hour and a half trip started to move faster once I threw on some old Nappy Roots. I took it back to the second album "Wooden Leather." Good God Almighty, the first single on the album, just put me back in a good place. I realized that I couldn't change ignorant people. They could hate me for the color of my skin, but I guarantee they were the first one in line for a ticket to see mines perform. It was all good. That was the price we paid sometimes for being black. But you know what, I wouldn't trade places with anyone else on this earth.

"Yo my nigga. I just hit the city limits," I told E.J. over the celly.

"Aight man. I'm leaving the shop now."

"Where yo' shop at?"

"It's over in northeast. Matter fact. Just meet me at the Lloyd Center. It ain't too far from the arena."

"Aight, I'll hit my google up."

"Fosho." I was finally here after hours on the road. Much like the drive through the state, the highway was lined up with nothing but trees. It felt good to be somewhere different than California. I would tell people all the time that everyone not from Cali wanted to get there. However, a lot of us raised there wanted to get out of there. Granted the life was great with beaches, weed and weather. However, didn't nobody wanna fuck around with those high ass taxes and wildfires forever. I was happy as hell to be out. I called my grandma from the road and to say the least, she was pissed. To disappear without a trace and not even see her, she had a right to be pissed. I told her that I would fly her up when I got settled in. But, she wasn't hearing that shit. She hung up on a nigga. She'd be aight though. I finally got to the Lloyd Center. I parked my car and just started to breathe a sigh of relief. I was finally about to take my first steps on Portland soil. I stepped out the car and just took a whiff of the summertime air. Man, the air quality up here was majorly different from L.A. You could actually breathe up here without inhaling every fume known to man. I walked inside the first floor and hit up E.J. on the cellular joint. "You here man?"

"Yeah bruh. I'm here."

"Come over to Build-a-Bear?"

"Da fuck you doing in Build-a-Bear?," I asked him.

"Nigga just come in the *** damn store." He hung up and all I could do was laugh. What in the hell was a grown ass man doing in Build-a-Bear? That nigga didn't have no kids. I walked through the mall on the way to the store. I didn't see too many brothers up in here. However, the two that I did see, they were with their girls. Them niggas mean mugged me like I was the enemy on some James Bond shit. I mean, I got it. The city was 94% white. Black folks up here were like sprinkles on a cupcake. I didn't want their girls, but they could take no chances up here, seeing how the sisters were limited. The Lloyd Center was a typical mall as I saw nothing out of the ordinary.

"A MAN!!!" That was E.J. outside of the store. I ran up and dapped my dude up.

"Whats up man?"

"Ahh shit you know. Met a thick ass sista girl out here when she came into the shop to buy some trees."

"How much see weigh nigga?"

"I'd say she about a good 150."

"150? Nigga that ain't nowhere near your price range."

"It may not be my price range, but sometimes you gotta go for the goods that's on sale for 70% off. Besides, she interested in my big ass. I digs it." All I could do was laugh. "Aight man. Look. We got us a house in northeast that I'm staying at with him."

"How many bedrooms?"

"Six. Shit is cool over there."

"Once I get you straight, we gone move into something even better."

"You trying to room together nigga?"

"Hell nah muthafucka," he said emphatically.

"I need all my space for 150. We can live next door to each other. See yo' ass and chuck you the deuce at any time. You ain't gonna mess up my pussy." Man I swear that was that niggas weakness. But, it was a good idea. I had done the roommate thing for two years with Kev and it turned out to be a disaster in the end. His name was on the lease and I technically didn't have my own. But now, I was a quarter million dollars richer. As soon as we were to get to my new home for a while, I was gonna sit down with E.J. to discuss how we can both invest 100,000 into something to make our money multiply. I may have been young, but I damn sure wasn't boo boo the fool. I knew that all that money sitting in a checking account wasn't gonna do me any good. I had to make my money work for me. Let the interest take care of me, all while managing things to make sure that I was good for the long haul. True, I got myself a whip, but that wouldn't add any value to me. Land was my key and I needed to have it. Once I got the scope of Portland, I would be gravy. I would definitely invest up here. See some black business grow. We needed to put our stamp on this place. I know some people would doubt that it could be done, but I wasn't most people. What do you do when there isn't a path laid? You make one. That was my whole plan. Compton, L.A., I'm sorry I had to leave you, but you weren't conducive to me anymore. I couldn't stay loyal to the soil when the soil that we were planted in produced no crop. I had to go where the soil was rich and fertile and grow into a tree that no one had ever seen. That's how you made the real change on the world. Give 'em something that they weren't expecting. People are always intrigued with the BBD. The bigger better deal. You have to be that deal and realize that staying put where you at for all the homies may be the worst thing that you ever did.

6 WHEN REALITY STRIKES

I watched my homeboy pull off. I finally realized that it was over. Over 20 years of having each other's backs and it was all down the drain. I sat down on the curb outside of my apartment and just went into complete shock. I sat there, head buried in my arms, trying to tell myself that this wasn't real. "Are you ok?," as I felt a hand touch my shoulder. I looked up to see Grayson. I stood up.

"Yo man. I can't do this shit," I told him.

"What?"

"Man this ain't me. Right now, I'm fucked up. Yo it was what it was. But I can't go around being a bitch in life my nigga. I gotta go." As I tried to step around him to my car, he got in my face.

"What you call me lil nigga?" "You bitched up with a gun in your hand and I know *** damn well you ain't gone pull no trigger. I'm going to my mama house. Have yo' shit out my crib by the time I get back." I mugged him for about two seconds more and then proceeded to walk back upstairs and get my keys. I walked out and he was in the same spot as before.

"So you just gone throw us away. After months of getting to know each other. This is what you want. That nigga over me?"

"Naw," I told him, as I hit the alarm button on my car. "I

don't want him over you. I want manhood over you. And right now, I lost my shit and need to go get it back. Ain't no such thing as a bi sexual nigga. You either gay or not. And I fucked up 'cause I was fucked up in the head. So muthafucka enjoy yo'self. I got some shit I need to fix in my life. 'Cause at the end of the day, pussy trumps all." I jumped in my whip and peeled the fuck off. I had finally woke up. The shit wasn't cool and it was time to face my demons. I called my mama on the road to let her know that I was on my way to the house to see her. She was happy as always because she knew her son was coming. If only she knew what she was about to get because she was about to receive something that she wasn't expecting. At the same time while I sped down the 91 freeway, I had to maintain myself. I had to think on how I was gonna talk to my mama. Granted, I had a legit gripe, but I was still black. Black mamas didn't play that bullshit. It's a reason that some parents tell you that I brought you in this world and I can take you out. Besides that, I was really contemplating whether or not if I was gonna be all the way truthful with her. Over the last two months, I had kept my life a huge secret to her. How would she react to knowing that her son had dabbled in the gay lifestyle? I've seen people get persecuted for less. But with being gay, it was a whole other ballgame.

I mean think about it. Back in the 80's and 90's, from the stories I heard and read up on, if you came out as gay back then, it was damn near like a death sentence. Your life was pretty much ruined. But then, the world changed and it changed very drastically. All of a sudden, gays and different people in general were suddenly accepted. Everyone seemed to be on the gay train. Now, if you weren't gay, you were looked on as the strange one. Even though I did what I did, I still knew the truth. The agenda was being pushed in everything from cartoons, movies and everyday life. Like, I respect people's choices, but don't be all out there with it as if to say **"YOU'RE BETTER LIKE THIS."** People like what they like. But, to push a lifestyle on people, that was totally unacceptable. The world had become PC and I truly believed that anyone who did anything for the gay community didn't do it out of love. They did it out of fear of losing money, because there are no morals in making money. However, morals will affect your cash flow if it doesn't follow the morals of the majority audience that you were trying to connect with. I got to my mama's house in a lil over an hour. She was outside watering the grass and looking like she was having a jolly good time. This wasn't the way I wanted things to go. I was hoping that she was in the house, still sleep, so that I could collect my thoughts before the talk of all talks. "Hey baby," she said as I exited the car.

"Hey mama." I walked up and hugged her, giving her a kiss on the cheek. "You out watering the grass? What has gotten into you?"

"Well baby. Your mama went on a date last night for the first time in a long time."

"Excuse me?"

"Yup. You heard me correct. Mama went on a date." I stepped back and made that face like "yeah right," but she was dead serious. "And what you wear?" She cut the water off and looked at me.

"I wore what the hell I wanted to wear."

"Aight mama. You know I'm gone let this one slide. But next time, I need to see your dress and give you a curfew. Can't be having you all out and about not knowing where you at?"

"Just like I used to tell yo ass. C'mon in this house boy and eat." That was music to my ears as I waltzed in behind my mama enthusiastically. I had no idea what she had thrown down on. Walking through that door, it smelled good as ever.

"Damn mama. What you got in this pot?" I opened that thang up and put the lid back on with the quickness. "Ughh ma. You cooking chitlins?"

"Hell yeah."

"Ughh nah. I can't do these."

"Good. More for me." I was hoping that she was gonna say that it was okay and that she would cook something else to my delight, but it wasn't happening. "I know you ain't expecting me to cook you something else. Hell to the nah. It's chitlins and that's it. Now, it's a bunch of sausage in the fridge, some bacon, some TV dinners in the freezer. But if you think I'm cooking you something else."

"C'mon mama. I thought I was yo' son."

"You are and I love you, but I still ain't cooking shit else."

"Thought I was yo' panda bear like you used to call me when I was lil."

"Boy you better panda yo' ass to Panda Express, cause I ain't cooking nothing else. But since you over there, fix me a bowl of those chitlins and bring 'em over here to the table." This was the most difficult thing ever. I swear I would rather rebuild a car engine than take a spoon and scoop these into a bowl. It looked like a bunch of old wrinkled human skin. I put a good amount of them in a bowl and took 'em over to her.

"Now was that so hard?," she asked me.

"Yeah mama. It was." She laughed as I sat down.

"So what bring you here today?"

"We needed to talk."

"What's going on?," as she stuffed another gulp of nastiness into her mouth.

"Ummm, mama. This is hard for me to tell you."

"Ain't nothing I can't handle. I'm a mother. I've heard it all. Go head."

"Mama." I paused for a quick moment, because I knew this would affect our relationship forever. "Mama. For the last two months. I been seeing a man." She dropped the fork and stared at me.

"What man? A therapist. Doctor. What?"

"Nah mama. A man. Like, in a relationship." She just leaned her head back.

"No, no, no. Kevin," she said so somber.

"But it's your fault mama," as I raised up from the table, grabbing my head. "Mama. I saw you. I saw you when I was a teenager. You and that other woman. Y'all were in the room doing whatever. It screwed with me for a long time. I never told you because I thought I was gonna get into trouble." We were just staring at each other at this point, and I was getting more nervous with each passing second.

"Mama. You always prided in me one day meeting a woman and having kids so you could be a grandmother. But every woman I been with since that day literally scared me, because all I saw was you and that other woman. So, like, after Ty left for his world travels, dude who was gonna play ball with us next season, he sprung me and shit happened."

"You have sex with him Kevin?"

"**FUCK NO!!!** I mean, no ma'am." I had to catch myself because no matter what you talking about, cussin' at a black mama could result in a death sentence. "I broke it off. Ty just left for God knows where and I pretty much lost my best friend."

"Sit down Kevin," as she pushed the middle chair out with her feet. This was it I thought. Here I go. I was about to lose my mother. "Baby. Let mama say sorry. As a parent. No, as a human, because we all make mistakes. I thought I was tired of men and they ways, so I randomly tried out a woman. It wasn't the deal. Trust me. I never did anything with a woman after that night, but I do regret it. Now, I regret it even more because of what it has done to you. Son, in life, we all have to find our way. I'll love you whether you gay, straight, whatever. If I had my preference, I prefer you to be straight. You know, 'cause that's how things are set up. A man and a woman make a baby. And I don't care what anyone says. Ain't nothin gone pleasure a woman like a real dick. Don't care if its a 9 inch or a 3 inch. If a woman wants plastic, it better be a ziploc. Son, I love you and once again, I'm sorry. I don't want you confused, but I do want you to live your life."

"Trust mama. I'm done with that shit. That ain't me. It was just something that fucked me up and I finally lost it."

"Are you saying that for me, or for yourself? I mean, you can't take back kissing a man baby."

"I know, but I'm willing to forget about that if you can."

"Well, that ain't something you can just forget. But I'll tell you what. You keep being the great son that you are and I'll try to be a better mother."

"You're a great mother." All she did was smirk and go back to eating her chitlins. "And to show you that you're great. Dang. I'll eat some chitlins with you."

"It ain't nothing but pork boy."

"Guess I'll find out." I got up and fixed about two spoonfuls of these ugly things. I don't see how in the good hell people spent time cleaning the literal shit off these things. I went back to the table and my mama was laughing at me in astonishment. She wasn't gonna believe it until she saw me actually do it.

"Can you pass me some of that Louisiana mama?" She slammed it down in front of me as if to say "here you go." I poured it over them. Not because it enhanced flavor of some sorts. But, this is what I saw the majority of black folks do when they ate these things. Bacon, cool. A pork chop, cool. These things, hell naw. But fuck it, here goes nothing. I put a fork full in my mouth and began to chew. I raised my head up, still chewing. I cut my eyes to see my mama looking at me, smiling, looking like she was ready to bust out in severe laughter. I swallowed.

"Well?," she asked me. I don't even know why she asked me that. Over the next 20 minutes, I ended up fuckin' up three bowls of chitlins. I can't believe I had been sleeping on these things my whole life because of a smell and a sight. I mean shit, I'm pretty sure when a cow getting cut up for a steak, it doesn't smell all hunky dorey in the butcher shop. Man, I should've slapped my damn self. "So negro. You know you gone have to buy the next batch for me to cook."

"Mama. If you want me to bring you a whole pig, you best believe I'm gone do it." She chuckled.

"Come here," as she stood up. I stood up and hugged my mother as well. Everything had went over smoother than I thought. More importantly, I learned that she accepted me for who I was. And truthfully, I was a man, even though I had a slip up. Sometimes, the worst circumstances could put us back in the right place. I felt manly again. I felt human again. I was lost for a minute, but everything was gravy now. I couldn't take back what I did, but I didn't have to live in the past. I enjoyed the next few hours with my mama until I realized that it was nine at night. I had to get back on the road. Shit, a nigga had class in the a.m.

"Love you mama," as I gave her a kiss on the cheek.

"You want some grapes to take with you on the road?"

"Nah mama. I'm good. I already ate bowlfuls of chitlins. I ain't tryna to be droppin' turds on myself in the car while driving."

"Aight baby," as she laughed. "Text me when you get home." I ran out to the driveway. It wouldn't get me home faster, but I was just glad the air had been cleared on a lot. I could only hope that one day if I was blessed to become a parent, that I would do a good job at it. I hit the 15 to the 91 with anger and fury, but in a good way. I had the music blasting and it seemed like no one was on the road for midweek traffic. At this rate, I would be home by a quarter past ten or maybe even sooner. Just as I thought, a nigga gas pedal work was so gravy that I made it back into Carson at exactly 10:01 p.m. I know I was a speed demon and I was extremely lucky that CHP wasn't out and about tonight like they usually were. I stopped at the burrito spot and got me a surf-n-turf to mash once I got in the crib. It was only right to complete this night with something so mouth watering and satisfying. I pulled up to the house, lowering the 2Chainz that was blaring out of my speakers. I didn't wanna wake the whole apartment building. I moseyed on up the stairs, singing to myself. Once I opened the door, the shock of my life was awaiting. I just stood there in the door, looking at my now trashed apartment. Tables, chairs and even my couch was flipped over. Plates were on the ground, shattered to pieces. I slowly walked around, with anger and disgust building up inside of me. Everywhere I turned, I saw more and more destruction. It was only one person who could do this and I knew exactly who the hell it was. I opened my bedroom door. In big red letters, the words **"YOU FUCKED UP"** were spray painted on the ceiling, meaning the nigga had to get up on my bed and do the shit. My mattress was flipped over, drawers of clothes pulled out and now, I had the highest level of madness I had ever obtained. "I'm gone kill this muthafucka," I said out loud.

"Here's yo chance nigga." I turned around to see this dude standing in my bedroom doorway. I don't know where he had came from, but he had obviously been watching me. "You think you were just gonna play with my heart and think that I was gone let that shit ride? Naw man." He shut the door. As he was doing that, I got slick and palmed some fingernail clippers off of my dresser. I wasn't scared of this nigga, but he had me by three inches height wise, so I had to strike him fast.

"The fuck you doing in here man? I told you. I ain't with this shit no more."

"Oh no nigga. You may not be with it, but I am. See, I got a real problem with people who play with my emotions," he said, taking two steps forward towards me.

"Stop walking up on me nigga." We were literally four or five footsteps apart.

"Oh don't worry. I'm stopping, because I'm gonna give your ass a choice. You played me for the fool. But now, I got yo ass. So I'm gonna be nice and give you a muthafuckin choice. We can do this shit the easy way. Or, or, we can do this shit the hard way. And I don't think you want shit the hard way."

"Muthafucka this ain't no *** damn Boondocks. Come up on me with that bullshit and I'll."

"You'll what nigga?," he said. He dropped his shorts and in that instance I knew one of two things were about to happen. Either one, he was gonna end up a dead nigga and I was going to jail. Two, he would have to beat me unconscious to get what he wanted. 'Cause if a nigga thought he was just gonna punk me and put a dick in my ass, that muthafucka had another thing coming. He began to take off his shirt and once it was over his head, I rushed his ass, stabbing him in the neck with the blade part. I caught him right in the middle where his adam's apple was and he dropped like Lebron James on a ghost foul. I looked to see him grabbing his neck, gasping for air, as I literally left the blade in his neck. I ran out the crib and called 911 on my cell phone. I was literally screaming into the phone that a nigga was tryna rape me. I know it wasn't a call that they got everyday, but indeed it was one that was very serious. I ran a good half a block down the street. To say I wasn't scared, I would be lying. Could I hold my own, yeah. However,

I wasn't about to wrestle with no nigga who wanted a piece of my ass, literally. Jailhouse mentality niggas were not to be fucked with. I literally was outside, down the street, looking back at my apartments, waiting for the police. Then, I saw in the distance a body come stumbling down the stairs. It was him and all his nakedness. Hurry up is what I thought thinking about the police. You could tell that I had stabbed him viciously. As he stumbled my way, I stood my ground. He wasn't gonna make it too me. And if he did, he damn sure wouldn't have any energy. As I saw him take a knee in the middle of the street, I saw the first cop car round the corner, followed by the second cop car. As they came to a stop and the first cop exited the vehicle, I began to run up. **"IT'S HIM SIR!!! IT'S HIM!!!"**

"STOP MOVING!!!," they yelled back. I immediately stopped moving. **"DROP WHAT'S IN YOUR HANDS!!!"** Immediately, I dropped my phone. I didn't care if I had broke the muthafucker or not, but it wasn't no way that I was gonna have Carson PD put 150 bullets in my ass like they did some of our other black brothers.

"I CALLED YOU!!!," I kept screaming as one officer steadily approached me, pistol drawn. My hands were up. I posed no threat. As the one officer radioed for an ambulance for Grayson, the other continued his march up to me.

"WHO ARE YOU SIR???!!!"

"I called you sir. That man came in my house and tried to rape me. I'm unarmed," as I dropped to my knees, not wanting to give him any ammunition at all to put a bullet in me. He lowered his weapon and came over to me, the other officers now following behind him.

"I'm gonna handcuff you just for my safety ok."

"Ok." I was paranoid to say the least. Another officer had stopped where Grayson was lying in the street while the other one came over to me.

"What happened?," as he stood me up, patting me down.

"Sir he goes to my school. He was upset that I wouldn't become romantically involved with him. He was cool though, and he was in my house earlier. When I got home from my mama's tonight, I found my house ransacked with graffiti on the walls. When I entered into my bedroom and turned around, he was at the door. We conversed, I grabbed a pair of clippers off the dresser that he didn't see. When he started to threaten to rape me and take his clothes off, I lunged at him, stabbing him in the neck. I ran outside and called you guys. That's the honest to goodness story." They both looked at each other. Then, they both looked back at Grayson. Now they understood why he was out in the street ass naked with nothing on but a du-rag.

"You play basketball for Dominguez Hills don't you?," one of them asked.

"Yes sir. He just transferred and was gonna play next

year. But he wasn't trying to slam dunk balls. Not basketballs at least." I could tell that this was really fucking both of the officers up.

"C'mon son. Go to the squad car with us and we'll sort this out." The ambulance was now here and frantically going to work on Grayson, trying to save his life.

"So tell me again. He tried to rape you?," one of the officers asked me.

"He threatened me too. He had me cornered in my own house. What was I supposed to do? Just lay back and let him destroy my asshole? That shit wasn't happening. So if I go to jail for defending myself, then so be it." They once again all looked at each other.

"Well, trust. We will investigate. But, right now, your apartment is a crime scene. We're gonna have to take you in for questioning." At this point, there were a million folks outside the complex, staring, chatting, trying to figure out what was going on. I was whisked away to the precinct and now in a whole new world. I imagined on the car ride it being like one of those wartime investigations where they throw water in your face, torturing you so they could get some information up out of you. One thing they weren't gonna figure out was that I indeed had a relationship with ol' buddy.

I sat in that interrogation room. It was well past midnight. I was tired, sleepy and damn near drained. I could pretty much cancel anything that I had planned for tomorrow, 'cause that shit wasn't happening. Finally, the detectives came in the room. They introduced themselves and I got to explain my story. "So, I knew dude from school for some months. He had transferred there from I can't remember. Anywho, we clicked off top. We hung out a lot. He said he was gonna be hooping for the squad next year so I said alright cool. So, about three months in, he told me he was gay and wondered did I feel a certain way about him. But, I told him I don't roll like that, but if that's you, then cool. Do yo' thang. So we were gravy. So earlier today, one of my partners came back from out of town. It was me, him and Grayson in the house. So I introduced them, told him this was my guy from way back."

"What is your guys name?," one of the detectives asked.

"Name is Ty Russell. He a barber. He had been gone for a while but came back just to say what's up." I saw the detectives writing Ty's name down and I just prayed that I didn't drag him down in the end with this one. "So me and Ty got to rappin outside for about ten minutes. He bounced. I go back in the house and Grayson was kind of upset. Like, he was tense. And I asked him was he good. He said he felt like I was drawn to my guy more than him. But I told him like yo, I dont roll like that, and me and my mans grew up together."

"Now, at what point was Grayson at your house and why?," I was asked.

"He spent the night officer. We kicked it and shit the day before. Like I said, I had no problem with his lifestyle because he didn't force it upon me and I don't judge anyone. So he was already there. So when he started to kind of get tense, I told him like yo man chill. I don't roll like that. Then, I told him, you could stay here longer if you wanna, but if you leave, just lock my door behind you, because I went to go see my mother in Fontana."

"And what time was this?"

"Evening. Sometime between four and five. So I was in Fontana until almost nine o'clock. I come home after ten. My door was locked so I thought okay, he left. No problem. I opened my house door and I saw my crib ransacked. I opened my bedroom door. I see the spray paint on the wall. I see my mattress flipped over, clothes everywhere and I'm like what the fuck. Then, I heard him say something and I turned around. He was standing in my doorway. So obviously, he had been watching me the whole time. So he goes on about how he can't hold his infatuation for me and that he gonna have me anyway he pleases. So in the midst of arguing back and forth, trying to figure out how I'm gone get out of this, I slid some fingernail clippers I had on the stand next to my bed in my hand. He didn't see it. He dropped his shorts. Exposing himself. He then proceeded to take off his shirt. And when he did that, I made a split second decision to lunge at him and stab him in the throat with the blade part of the clippers."

"So you initiated the physical attack?"

"Yes sir. And I don't regret it, because there was no way

in hell I was gonna let another grown man put his dick in my ass. And that's it." I said that shit with such fluency and efficiency that I should've gotten the Oscar for best performance. The detectives walked out of the room and left me in there to ponder everything by myself. I had seen too many episodes of the First 48 to know not to do two things. One, don't put yo head down on the table. Or, don't start making body motions like you been lying. I stayed in the same position that I was during the interview. Sitting up straight, hands folded, occasionally, looking around at the walls. I didn't give them any reason to discredit my story. They came back in.

"Ok Mr. West. This clearly sounds like self defense, even though you were the aggressor of the physical altercation. Mr. Marks is in the hospital right now, unable to talk. We will not be holding you tonight. But, we will need you to be in the area. Is there anyone you can call and stay with tonight?"

"I mean, the only person near here is my mom, but she is all the way in Fontana. If I can get access to my vehicle at the house, then it's possible that I could stay with a friend." Boy oh boy. How I wish this could all just be a bad dream. A week passed by and Grayson was out of the hospital. My apartment was still not cleared to be entered into. Graciously, the niggas at the barbershop had let me live in the makeshift crib they had in the back of the shop. Truthfully, to be honest, it wasn't bad at all. It had a fridge, a huge ass couch and a television. Brody set this spot up for the barber crew when they needed a place to just lounge and kick it for a good while. The police knew where I was and I cooperated with them fully. Grayson pretty much admitted to trying to rape me, but the crazy thing was that he didn't admit to the relationship part. I don't know if it was a pride thing or what. I guess neither one of us wanted to be looked on as odd. He was charged with a felony attempted rape charge and was gonna be looking at some significant time behind bars. It was crazy how this world works. We are surrounded by real friends who always tell us to be ourselves. Some of us are brash, bold, loud, reserved, etc. We have all these certain qualities about ourselves that make us unique in this world. However, when it is time to face the real world, a lot of us wanna shy away from who we are simply because we fear that the world may not accept us. I mean, think about it. They didn't like Muhammad Ali because he was one black and successful. But, he also was loud and proud. He told you that he was gonna kick yo ass and look pretty while doing it. America hated him for it. That and taking a stand. It wasn't until he got struck down by parkinson's disease and could barely talk anymore that he was so called labeled a legend amongst the majority of this country's residents.

That's the shit that irritates me. We tell everyone to be themselves, but when they are themselves, they are persecuted for it. Fuck that. I say if you are going to be someone, be exactly who the fuck you are. Life is too short to conform to the norm. If you wanna be a Jesus person and shout His name all through the halls, then do it. If you wanna fuck, suck dick, swallow as many men as you can, then fucking do it. Be you and don't give a fuck what anyone else thinks. Hell, people always talk about what celebrities do. Truth is, we do the same shit that they do. The only difference is that we don't have cameras in our faces 24/7. And that my friends, is the truth, the whole truth and nothing but the fucking truth.

"Yo my nigga. So when yo apartment gone be ready again?," Dominique asked me.

"Man they say another 2-3 days before I can go back in. I ain't impeding on y'all shit am I?"

"Naw nigga you cool. But I wanna ask you something."

"What's up?"

"Man you talk to Ty lately?"

"Naw man. I mean. I miss my nigga forreal man. I think I did the wrong thing shunning him away like I did."

"Y'all got into it my nigga?"

"Yeah. Sort of. Kind of had a falling out when he came back over communication. So like, I was in my feelings on some gay shit." That's when I had to catch myself because I didn't wanna expose myself. "I mean. I didn't understand his situation."

"Wait though. I thought you told us that he kept in contact with you."

"I mean yeah. He did. But not like he should have I felt.

Wasn't any how you is my nigga? You need something my nigga? How the fam, friends, bitches my nigga? You know. None of that. But I failed to realize that the nigga was so excited that all he wanted to talk about was his life adventures."

"Yeah man. We kind of did the same thing to him. I thought the nigga had changed up. When he came in here, he was showing nothing but love. But we were so upset that we hadn't heard from the nigga directly, that we took it as a slap in the face. Him and Brody were damn near about to go to blows. Then, he left. And we ain't heard from the nigga since. I mean we kinda regretting that shit right now cause we realize that he didn't leave the hood. He was simply putting on for the hood. But we were too small minded to get that shit. You know where the nigga at?" I took a sip of my Dr. Pepper.

"Naw man. He peeled out and ain't been seen since. You talk to some of his folks in Compton?"

"Yeah man. I hit his cousin up. But nigga said they ain't seen him round Spooktown or anywhere else. It's like that nigga disappeared off the face of the earth."

"I mean shit. Let me call the nigga right now." I hit my mans line and it rang three times. "Hello?"

"Sup bruh?," as I had him on speakerphone, signaling to Dominique to not say anything.

"Ain't shit."

"Where you at?," I asked him.

"I'm good. That's all you need to know man."

"C'mon bruh. I was trippin' that day. Like bruh, you my nigga. I ain't trying to lose our friendship over some dumb shit. Especially some dumb shit that I did."

"Man...you and them niggas at the shop was on some bullshit. Yo shit. I mean. Nigga. I'm still fucked up about that. But I'm a real nigga. I ain't gonna speak on the shit cause it ain't something that I fuck with. All I'll say is good luck. But the niggas in the shop, if only them niggas took the time to hear me out, they'd know a million niggas bout to flood the shop in the summer."

"What you mean?," I asked, inquiring on his words.

"Man Eric know all kinds of muthafuckas. It's a bunch of high profile niggas who was gonna come through in August for a day and just get cut up. But shit, now I gotta call the nigga and tell him to nix that shit, 'cause I damn sure ain't looking out for them niggas after they did me the way they did."

"So you just gone miss out on that opportunity?"

"Hell nah. Bout to rearrange and get niggas up here in Portland."

"Wait nigga. You in Portland?"

"See. I done said too much. Gone nigga." He hung up the phone, and me and Nique just stared at each other. I learned a valuable lesson in all of this. You cannot spell the word assuming without having the word ass. And when you assume, you make an ass out of yourself. I now had one focus and one focus only. That was to find myself and at the same time, bring my nigga back to where he once was. The night came and they were all out of the shop. It was a lonely nine o'clock as I had now gotten a crash course in life in just a matter of weeks. Things had been worst before, so I knew that I could make it through.

The days had passed as I was back in my place. Summertime was one of those times as a college kid where you were supposed to be relaxing, partying and getting laid. Me, I had just the opposite for this summer vacation. Things kept developing and I didn't feel like much of myself at all. I truly needed to get away, but in my mind, where could I truly go? I was a college student with just enough money to get by, but not enough money to live comfortably. I ended up writing news articles for magazine and many online publications to consistently bring in income during the summer months, not to mention essays for people who were taking summer classes. When I wasn't writing, I was busy reading the writings of others, trying to put myself in their world to better understand them.

"DOMINO NIGGA!!! GIMME MY MONEY!!!"

"Damn Key. Can you please stop feeding this nigga and handing over yo' draws?," Dyron said.

"Look dude," I said as I tossed over an additional fifteen points to Nate and prepared to curse Dyron out. "I told you. I ain't pull shit, ain't have shit and can't turn these dominoes into no shit. So dude. What you want me to do? You just want some magic domino pussy to show up in my hand?"

"You need to do something nigga, 'cause Nate tearing yo' asshole up inside and out. Look like a damn meeting with a hooker on Bourbon Street after winning the Sugar Bowl." Everyone around the table began to laugh. Bones was serious amongst black folks. I had been playing this shit since growing up in Long Beach. You would've sworn it was World War 3 when big six and company hit the table.

"30 more nigga. Wash my shit," Nate said as he pushed the hoard of 28 over to me.

"Nigga he only need 40 to rock. Can you please put yo' foot on this nigga neck?," Corey said. Corey was about as irritating as Dyron when it came to this game. Hell, every one of us in the room for that matter. But, the game we were most excited about was soon to come. We were all back, primed and ready for our sophomore campaign. The whole world watched last year as "The Rodeo Crew," dubbed by college football analyst Lee Corso, made history on a level that no other college team had ever experienced. Sure, you had the miraculous run of Colt Brennan and pass happy Hawaii in 2007. You had the many years that Boise State had crashed the BCS party. However, what we did in our freshman season, no one had ever accomplished. We jumped the year off with probably one of the biggest wins in school history, if not the biggest, when we went into Oregon State and won 34-31. What made that game so special is that it was a comeback for the ages. We were down 31-10 going into the fourth quarter. In America's eyes, it was the typical big dog beating on the medium sized dog. What they didn't realize though is that these dogs had some fight. After Dyron worked his magic and drove us down for two scores, including a 71 yard bomb to Corey, we were down 31-24 with 1:43 left in the game. Facing a fourth and goal from the two yard line, I was off on the sidelines cheering my boys on.

"TIMEOUT!!!," coach yelled. "RAMSES!!!" Homey sprinted down the sidelines to coach.

"Yes sir?"

"You want your big moment in life?," coach said.

"What you saying coach?," he responded.

"I'm saying get your ass on that field and get these two yards." Right then and there, Big Earl Wheaton, our monster of a right guard smacked him on the helmet.

"Follow me man. I'm gonna open up a hole so big that King Kong won't be able to say it's tight." If that wasn't some backwoods Wyoming shit to say, I don't know what was. As they broke and headed back towards the field, coach grabbed Ramses arm.

"For Carlos and Willie."

"Coach, how'd you know?," he asked. "Don't worry how I know about Carlos. Just go in there and do it for both of those young men." I was standing on the sideline hoping we scored. Defense had held it down in the fourth, and two sacks by myself on the Beavers previous two drives had stalled them in their tracks. As Ram made his way to the on field huddle, I saw Dyron call the play. Over 45,000 started to make noise like never before. I saw orange and black everywhere, screaming, clapping, doing what it took for them to build their team up for the game saving stop. I could only imagine what my guys on the field were thinking. As they broke the huddle, I remembered one thing that an OG had once told me. He said any man can perform when the crowd is cheering for him. Its how he responds to the boos that makes him legendary.

Corey went in motion. He was the speedster who had burned them earlier, so I knew they would key in on him. As the ball was snapped, Corey darted past Dyron. He faked the handoff to him and with a delayed step. Ramses took the rock and ran right behind Big Earl. Unlike what he said however, the hole wasn't as big as a whale's vagina, or however big he said it would be. He made a quick cut left, as I saw he did just enough to push their D tackle to the right. He took the hardest hit that I had ever saw in my life, but he stretched the ball across the goal line. I heard nothing. No whistles, no referee chatter, none of that. Our whole team was on edge on the sidelines. Suddenly, the crowd erupted in a roar as one ref signaled Oregon State's ball from the half yard line. Then, another ref came in and they all began to discuss.

"The previous play is under review" Hearing that from

the official did me no justice as I went back to the sideline bench, hoping and praying for a miracle. My teammates were giving each other love, but I wasn't trying to hear anything right now.

"A FOOL WE GOOD!! DON'T EVEN TRIP. WE GOT THIS SHIT!!!" I looked up seeing Dyron headed over. "That's what the fuck I'm talking about. Look at that big screen." He was now hovering over me as I stood up and looked. Sure enough, from the looks of it, the ball was extended before Ramses right knee touched the turf. How in the good hell did the camera catch that with all of those bodies in there? Truthfully, I don't know. I guess it was just an act of Christ that it did.

"After review, the runner's knee was not down before breaking the plane. The result of the play is a touchdown." The bench erupted. The small crowd of Brown and Gold in the south corner of the end zone went ecstatic.

"TWO!!!," coach yelled. I didn't think about the call, nor did anyone on the squad. We were so pumped that we could care less about not tying the game and opting for a possible overtime. Coach and everyone was on edge for this play. Once the ball was snapped, I watched as Dyron looked exactly like Vince Young on the 4th and 5 play from the national title game against USC. He dropped back, started to run, dodged one tackle and hit the corner of the end zone. I couldn't believe what I was witnessing. The ensuing kickoff was a touchback. On the very first play from their own 20, Oregon State went into a shotgun formation. They were five wide, with no back in the backfield. The ball was snapped right over the head of their QB. I don't know what was going on in the backfield, but me and Nate were running after him like he seen the police. He couldn't scoop it up and he only knocked it back further. Finally, one of their receivers landed on it in the end zone as I dove with him at the same time. Our bench erupted, as the signal for safety had been called. We held on our last defensive stand for the win and it felt like I was losing my virginity all over again. The next week, we followed up with an even bigger shocker by going into Tennessee and winning 27–17. We were playing Rocky Top all night long. Here we were, beating a Pac 12 school and a former national title school out of the SEC in back to back weeks. I know those two schools weren't Alabama, Auburn, Oregon or USC, but for a small Mountain West school to beat the Power 5 in back to back weeks, on the road at that, it was more than major. It was just some shit that you could never forget. The Oregon State victory didn't get us into the rankings, but the UT victory did. We saw ourselves bolt up to number seventeen in the polls. With that, we were more than motivated to make a huge run. We ran through our conference for the rest of the year and sat undefeated at number six in the polls going into the last week. Everyone from every other major conference, with the exception of the Big 12, had their conference championship games going, so we were hoping that anyone ranked above us would fall into the flames and increase our chances at getting into the college football playoff. Should we have been higher? I definitely feel so. With wins over Oregon State, Tennessee and Boise State on the road, I felt like it was a no brainer.

However, the powers to be in college football didn't show any love to anyone who wasn't in the Top 5 power conferences, so it put even more of a chip on our shoulder to prove the world that they were wrong about the small schools if we did get our big shot. We were certain that we were getting into the college football playoff. With that victory over Boise State on the blue turf, 40–13 midseason, we just knew we were about to make history. They were the Cinderella's that jumped off the conversation about a football playoff many moons ago. I know Utah had done their thing with Urban Meyer back in the day, but Boise started a wild ride with that shit. TCU over Wisconsin in the Rose Bowl, UCF winning the Fiesta Bowl over Baylor and there was no such thing as overlooking the small boys anymore. The University of Wyoming headed for a college football playoff? Well, that was a dream in itself. Football and Wyoming weren't supposed to go together in the same sentence. Neither was black and Wyoming. But, we became the second impactful group of black men to affect this campus. "Da Black Nine" made it happen. Finally, a week later, after all the conference title games were completed, we sat on campus in our giant film room, awaiting the results. **"PREPARE TO GO BOWLING BOYS!!!,"** Dyron came in the room yelling.

"SHUT THAT SHIT DOWN HOMEY!!! THEY TALKING!!!," Big Darcell said as only a brotha from Compton could. Or as he said, Bompton. I analyzed the team in the room. Everyone was on pins and needles. Coach was in the corner twiddling his pen along with the rest of the coaching staff. As for me, I pinched myself to make sure that I wasn't dreaming. And I wasn't.

"Ok college football world. What everyone has been waiting for. Here is the final Top 10 for the season. But you know, that big four is what everyone is waiting on." I had always admired Rece Davis, but I swear he was going to become my all time favorite analyst when he announced that we were going to the playoff. "So at number 10, we have Ole Miss. At number nine, we have Florida State. Coming in at the eighth spot, the SEC rises again with LSU. At the seventh spot, all hail the victors as Michigan comes in for the Big Ten. At number six, TCU takes the cake. And now, who will be the last man out." The room at this point was dead silent as you could hear an ant screaming in a spider web. Some people got up, but most of us just moved to the edge of our seats.

"At number five." I swear it seemed like time stopped in this moment. I was ready to jump out of my seat. "The Cowboys of Wyoming," he finished. We stayed quiet. From the reaction in the room, you would have thought we went winless instead of undefeated. We were pissed to say the least. No one in their right mind gave us a chance in hell to accomplish what we had done. Now, it's like all that hard work was for nothing. As the program wore on, and the discussion about the four playoff teams concluded, we sat there, anxiously waiting to learn who we would play to prove to the world that they made a mistake. It was already bad enough not getting in, but Kirk Herbstreit telling the world the truth was what really got us going.

"How Wyoming is not in the top four when you have a one loss Ohio State team, who even though they won the Big Ten title, still took a loss at home to an unranked Minnesota. That is going to boggle my mind and the minds of diehard college football fans for some time. Wyoming went on the road and won twice in the Power 5. All their major games were on the road and they won." He was definitely right. We were black balled and I truly felt bad for whoever had to play us next. "And Desmond the bowl game that I am most anxious to see will take place down in New Orleans. The Cowboys of the Mountain West. Wyoming. The 2014 season feel good story of the year. Versus the Bayou Bengals. Taking on the Tigers of LSU in the Sugar Bowl." Louisiana State University. The multiple time national champions. They were pretty much playing at home, down the street from Baton Rouge. The loyal fan base from Death Valley was coming. We, on the other hand, were just some country hicks out West to the rest of America. We heard the mumbo jumbo all year from ESPN, Fox Sports and any other news outlet that covered college football.

"Can this team shine on the national stage if given the chance?" That was all they were saying. Screw winning on the road in the SEC. Screw winning on the road in the Pac-12. Screw the other out of conference game we won towards of the end of the season on the road at Syracuse. That shit didn't matter to them. All they saw was New Mexico, New Mexico State, UNLV, Air Force, SDSU, Fresno State, Utah State and Colorado State. Once again it was show and prove time.

"Can you see it big dawg? All these empty seats gone have 80,000 bad bitches screaming my name. Dyron, Dyron, Dyron."

"Nigga shut yo ass up," Darcell told him.

"Man don't hate on me cause yo big ass can't get no hoes." They kept going back and forth as we passed the time by on the sidelines while coach was working with the special teams. It was 48 hours before the game and this was our last practice. The entire week out here leading up to the game had been more than hectic. "Media interviews, taking in the awe of New Orleans, running two practices a day." At this point, I truly didn't care if the game would be played or not. I felt drained. I just wanted to go back to the hotel and relax for a little bit. However, we couldn't, because we had one last session with the media after this. Today, I was put on the list to talk to the media. **"GATHER UP GENTS!!!,"** coach screamed as we headed out to midfield. "Keon,

Darcell, Nate, you all head over with Coach Brooks to the media room. Keep it kosher. Don't fall for any okedoke questions." Coach Brooks took us off to the end zone where hoards of reporters were waiting for us to sit at the table. This actually looked like something out of a movie. I tried to imagine them asking any and every part about how we planned to compete with LSU. I kept answering questions in my head to try and make myself comfortable.

"You can all begin," said a gentlemen on stage. As we sat there, we watched hands raised.

"You there, in the blue shirt." He arose up. A skinny brother who looked like a combo of Dwight Gooden and Rickey Smiley.

"Tevin Howard, Black Journal. It's no secret that Wyoming hasn't been this good in a very long time and that most of you are freshmen. It's also no secret that the meat of this recruiting class was all black. Do you feel an obligation to win this game for your people and not just the mere sense of trying to put a school on the map in a state where black people are almost nonexistent?" I was dumbfounded by the question. Where was the what's your game plan for their dual threat quarterback question? Me, Darcell and Nate all looked at each other with crazy looks on our faces.

"Excuse me, sir?" Coach Brooks had stepped in.

"This is not the time and place for political and racial questioning. Now, if you want to discuss race, I suggest you do it on your own time and in the proper setting. But these are my players preparing for a football game. Not a revolutionary war."

"So are you trying to say coach that you aren't concerned about these black issues going on in America, yet you have no qualms about recruiting these same black players to fill your agenda? Like this man here from Inglewood?"

"YO I'M FROM COMPTON HOMEY AND YOU AIN'T GONE TALK TO MY COACH LIKE THAT!!!" Darcell flipped the table over and security flew in fast. Coach was being held back by security and media officials alike. Meanwhile, me and Nate were holding Big Darcell back, trying to calm him down. It was complete ruckus now. I saw coach and the team running over to the scene. There wasn't enough of a security presence to quell what was going on.

"YOU DON'T CARE ABOUT THESE BLACK MEN!!! YOU DON'T CARE ABOUT THESE BLACK MEN!!!," the reporter kept shouting that as he was being pulled, rather dragged away from the media area by security. This idiot of a reporter, whoever the hell he was, had opened up a can of worms in a dirt field instead of a lake. It was no secret that the media session was over, but the drama from it was just beginning. One by one, coaches hauled us together and got us up out of there. We were whisked away to the locker room. Most didn't know what was going on, seeing how they were on the other side of the field at the time. The few of us that did, we knew shit had hit the fan. We waited in one of the locker room areas as a whole unit, minus Darcell. He was outside being calmed down by the coaching staff. One thing about Darcell was that when he got mad, he got mad. He was born and raised in Compton. The youngest of four boys, two of which had lost their lives to the streets and one who was doing a 12 year bid on weapons charges. With a single mom, he fell into the family business. That was being Piru. His mom was a Piru. His dad was an OG Piru who got locked up when he was only nine. So pretty much, the streets raised him. Luckily, they let him take out his violence with vicious hits on other people and not with guns.

After falling behind 17–0 in the first quarter, we rallied to tie the game at halftime, topped off by a 64 yard scoop and score fumble recovery by Ronald P. Clark, one of our fiercest DB's. The second half saw nothing but a bloodbath as hard hits, shit talking and yellow laundry littered the field. One particular play sealed their fate and took me to a place that they didn't wanna see me go. It was the fourth quarter with 5:32 left. LSU was up 37–27. We were at our own 46 yard line. The huddle was broke and the play call was a simple ISO left. Coach had put me in at fullback due to an injury, so it was both ways til the end of the game. Upon a seven yard gain into their own turf, my mans Ramses was met with purple and gold bodies, but also the words "Cracker ass black boy." The scrum was on as tempers flared and body parts began to move. Both teams were at each other jaw jacking.

"I GOT YO CRACKER!!!," Ram told their safety as the refs tried to keep us all from killing each other. **"I'M FROM THE JECTS! NEW ORLEANS! YOU AIN'T ONE OF US!"** Right there, time stood still. Everything around me went black. All I heard was "You ain't one of us." The rest of the shit talking became irrelevant. It was like they cut out the lights again in The Superdome. Except this wasn't the Super Bowl. They had attacked my mans once again from growing up in an environment that he had no control over. I started to see that melanin didn't matter to some brothers. If you weren't raised in the hood, you were inferior to them. My guy had come too far and didn't have to prove his blackness to anyone, especially not his own people.

"Gimme the rock Dyron. Straight up the gut," Ramses told him, walking back to the huddle.

"Naw fool. We down ten. We gotta throw this bitch."

"DAMMIT I SAID GIMME THE BALL!!!"

"Will you shut the fuck up Ramses so we can get this next play call?," I blurted out. I understood his frustration, but we couldn't afford to lose our cool, especially at this moment in the game. He shut up, obviously frustrated and Dyron called for the next play. It was a fade route down the side for Corey. We broke the huddle and all my focus was on taking out the first person that made their way towards me. As the ball was snapped, I saw the cross blitz coming through the middle. With everything that I had in me, I unloaded on the weak side linebacker coming through the two hole. I put him square on his ass. The next moment, I was looking up at the ball sailing through the air and Corey had a good three steps on the corner. **TOUCHDOWN!!!** This stadium had gotten loud from straight shock and awe. I sprinted down to the end zone with the rest of my teammates, but my intentions weren't to celebrate. I found him. He wore the number 9 which was ironic as all to be damned.

"My man's from Newport and blacker than you fuck boy," I said as I jogged past him, turning around, hopping up and down. Then, he launched his fist straight into my helmet. I played it off and should've gotten an award for best flop. Even Lebron James would've been proud of me. The ref caught him and a fifteen yard penalty would occur on the next kickoff. That was all a part of my plan, along with letting him witness who I was up close and personal. As we lined up for the kickoff, they prepped for the usual. Then, we hit 'em with it. I watched from the sidelines as an onside was recovered by us with room to spare. On the next play, Dyron hit 'em with a play action and found Corey in the back of the end zone for a Sports Center Top 10 one handed grab. It was the smoothest shit I had ever seen in my life. A late interception from my mans Michael Carter out of Lincoln High in San Diego sealed everything, as we had now achieved the biggest win in school history with a 41-37 upset over LSU in their own backyard. We had done it. 13-0. "The Black Nine" as we referred to ourselves had made history and had reigned supreme. No one had seen anything like this since Jalen Rose and the Fab Five crew stormed on to the scene back in the early 90's at Michigan. We finished the season ranked #2 in the nation, and the next go round, we were looking for that #1 spot.

"THE CHAMPS ARE HERE LADIES!!!" That was Nate screaming as we headed down Bourbon Street in The French Quarter, celebrating the win as only brothers could do. The night was lit as we took in the entire New Orleans atmosphere from the crazy jazz bands on the street to the occasional pairs of breasts that were flashed at us. Along the way, we saw our peoples from back west everywhere. They were clad in brown and gold. You could tell that they weren't use to this atmosphere. Wyoming was quiet and serene for the most part. Down here, it was a party every damn night. Yeah, New Orleans was the lick. We continued up the street, high fiving folks who were proud of us and taking in the obscenities of obvious LSU fans who were pissed off that their squad lost to us. **"GO BACK TO THE COUNTRY YOU FUCKING QUEER BOYS!!!"** We all looked up to see some drunken idiot hanging over one of the establishments patio railings talking mess.

"I hope that nigga fall," said Dyron. Deep down, I was hoping the same. We got to the corner of Royal and St. Peters Street, where Juvenile had shot his "In My Life" video with Mannie Fresh, and that's when I knew life was about to take a turn for the worse. **"WHAT'S GOOD NIGGA???!!!"** It was homeboy from the game, along with his Tiger bunch as we rounded the corner.

"**TELL ME NIGGA!!!**, big Joe, our massive O lineman said, pushing his way through all of us.

"I'm here for that nigga right there whodi."

"Fuck that I'm here Joe," Joe responded. He was out of Chicago and them niggas said Joe after everything. Let me see that Joe. Bout to bag this bitch Joe. A Joe, hand me a pop. Shit, he said Joe so much, I started to think that everyone name was Joe. Before anything else got said, Darcell just fired off on one of them and the fight was on. I heard screams coming from the crowd as we fought tooth and nail with these boys. There were fist a cuffs everywhere. I know someone who wasn't even involved in the fight was probably getting taxed up right now because they were in the way, but oh well. We fought for a good minute and a half before the police arrived. They came in so deep that I can't even give you an exact number. Commotion was everywhere as bodies were pulled and snatched.

"**STAY DOWN!!!**" I felt a knee on the back of my neck. I struggled to breathe, as I didn't know how many police were on top of me. I was already bloodied up from the scrap so that just made things a whole lot worse for me. Through all the commotion, with my hands behind my back, I saw through my obscured vision someone else on the ground with laws on top of them. **POP!!!** It was the gunshot heard around the world. My life literally stopped. Nothing else mattered at this point. Not me in these handcuffs, not the Sugar Bowl, my girlfriend back home, nothing. All I wanted to know is who caught that bullet.

"Bout to bust your head open once again."

"Nate," I said.

"What you want man? Don't distract me from splitting yo culo open again."

"**NATE!!!**" That definitely got his attention and things got quiet in the room. "Nigga who you yellin' at?," he asked.

"Don't have a domino ass whoopin' turn into an official one."

"A man, remember that shit that happened after the Sugar Bowl?"

"Bruh. I ain't trying to talk about that shit no more man. Just play bones nigga," he responded.

"MAN FUCK THESE BONES!!!," as I threw 'em on the table.

"That shit still don't fuck with yo conscious? Man we being hunted on a regular, filling up prisons, police shooting us damn near everyday for no fucking reason. I mean, let's rap bout this shit?" Nate was obviously pissed. He had a look in his eyes that said he wanted to kill me. "Well since you fucked up the game nigga, then speak on it. Speak on the shit nigga," Dyron told me.

"Fuck that, I will. You think I'm supposed to be scared to live my life 'cause these faggot ass laws out here fear for their safety? Nigga if they scared like that they shouldn't be cops."

"But D I'm sayin."

"Naw, fuck what you saying," as he cut me off. "Look nigga. I know you ain't stupid 'cause you grew up in Long Beach. Matter fact, you ain't nigga. But here's the real. It's us vs. everybody else. Now I don't give a fuck how many games we won. How many trophies we have. If we weren't running 'round with a fucking pigskin in our hand, making these crackers millions of dollars, we'd be public enemy #1 in this muthafucka. Hell nigga, we are no matter what the fuck we do. That nigga, that nigga and all these other niggas in here know it," as he pointed at multiple people in the room.

"You worried 'bout shit in Louisiana? You need to worry 'bout how the fuck we gone survive out here til' our time is up. At least you can go down there and see niggas, and it ain't abnormal." There was so much tension in the room that you could cut it with a butter knife.

"So what Keylo?," Nate asked me. "What's plaguing you about that shit?"

"Bruh, we fought our own brothers and watched one of them get smoked by the damn police. The tape came out and showed he didn't resist, yet they still shot him. But, but, I have a hard time sleeping at night because had it not been for me, nothing would've jumped off. So I don't know 'bout the rest of y'all brothers, but the shit hurts me. Like muthafucka for real. It does." Big Darcell came up out of his chair.

"Bruh, it ain't no secret I'm from Compton, and we don't fuck with no laws. Just like y'all LBC niggas don't fuck with 'em either. I don't give a fuck who the fight jumped off with.

Shit my nigga, I'm actually glad you did. I was ready to get shit brackin. Had it been a bunch of white kids though, they would've just de-escalated the shit. But naw. WE were fighting. A bunch of black men. So automatically, tasers, pepper spray and guns become the first option. I don't give a fuck what homeboy told me or any other nigga in the game. That nigga still shouldn't have been laid up in the middle of the street with three in his back. It's four niggas on him and they still need a gun? Fuck that. They whole plan was to kill a nigga that night. Man...**FUCK THE POLICE BLOOD!!!**"

"Darcell, I know man, but we gotta do better," I said. "I mean, yeah they were wrong, but we brought that attention on ourselves. We got into that scuffle. We stirred up the crowd. We drew the attention to ourselves."

"DA FUCK YOU MEAN NIGGA???!!!," he yelled at me, flippin' the table, sending dominoes flying everywhere. He was up in my face now as I sat back in the chair.

"Nigga are you stuck in that white ass honkey ville that we get spoiled in? You a deep nigga. I commend you. But right now, you ain't seeing the bigger picture. You sounding like one of them coons asses who say well what about black on black crime. Nigga blacks kill blacks. Whites kill whites. Mexicans kill Mexicans. Asians kill Asians. If that's who you live around the most, then that's gonna be who does most of the murdering of that culture on a daily. I may not be all philosophical and shit like you, but one thing I know is this. I grew up in the motherfuckin' gang hot bed. Bloods, rips, ese's all that. Nigga that's life in Bompton. You ain't gotta do shit to attract attention. All you gotta do is be black. Be black nigga. I got dreads and I'm 6'3, 295 with tattoos nigga. Fight or no fight, I'm already in the image they fear. And the scariest thing about this image is that it's backed with a 3.7 GPA and I can smack the shit out of niggas on the football field. But they don't see that. They see big, black and a threat. Hear this clear and soak this in," as he put his finger in my chest repeatedly.

"A cuz," as I got up, along with everyone else in the room. "We can speak on a lot, but if you ever put yo' finger in my chest again, it's gone be like World War 3 in this muthafucka," I told him. We just stared at each other. I saw this nigga starting to cry out of sheer anger. Darcell wasn't no bitch, so I know these weren't bitch tears. He was just passionate right now.

"Look nigga," he said in a low tone. "Welcome to the real world. No one cares about us man. It's US. That's it." Big Nate got up and put his arm around me. The rest of the squad came in as well. I stood up and joined my brothers. A minute ago, we were damn near going to blows. Now, we were damn near all in tears. Here we were. Safe in our own bubble. Eventually, however, that bubble had to burst and it was back to square one. Differences make us all unique, but for a black man, we really gotta embrace the fact that we all are the same. Targets. Disagreements and fights will happen, but the point ain't to kill each other over the disagreements. The point is to understand each other and come up with a better solution.

"I love y'all niggas man," Dyron said, as we embraced in this moment. Just then, someone knocked on the door.

"I got it man," Nate said. He opened the door and to all of our surprise, it was coach.

"Sup coach?!," Big Joe blurted out.

"I see you all are having a hell of a time in here. Table flipped over. Chairs down. Dominoes all over the floor."

"Nah coach. We put a big ass pork chop on the table and watched Flex and Darcell wrestle for it." As we laughed, Darcell gave him the finger, wiping his face. Even coach was cracking up.

"Aight look guys, something I need to tell you." He then shut the door, which let me know that it was about to get serious. He grabbed one of the seats off of the floor. "My father once told me that you sometimes have to revisit the past in order to step into the future. What I realized growing up is that sometimes you have to step in someone else's shoes before you can walk their path. Guys, I'm nothing but an almost middle aged man who was born in small town Idaho. I played small town schools all my life and never met a black person until I went to college at Boise State. To tell you the truth, it was a culture shock for me. I didn't understand the culture or anything. Like I said, I'm small town Idaho, so TV was pretty much irrelevant. My social networking came from the other kids in a town of 700. I graduated and moved down to Cheyenne, coaching local high school ball. Years later, I went on ahead and moved to Colorado and became an assistant for the Air Force. There, I met military men whose job it was to make men of all creeds into professionals. It humbled me. Then, I took the job here eight years ago. I said to myself that I was going to do something special here, but Wyoming and college football don't necessarily go together. We struggled my first three years, not winning more than five games in a season. Then, we progressed and finally got to six wins and then seven, but no higher than that. Two years ago, Dyron, that crazy man right there was the number 10 QB coming out of Dunbar in Washington, D.C. Hell, I didn't look for major recruits because no one wanted to come here. However, he shocked me when he said he wanted to visit the school. He told me all about the crime and everything that plagued him coming up, and how he just wanted to get away and start somewhere fresh. He took a full ride to come here. On national signing day, every major college critic scratched their head. Two years later, as a true sophomore, he led our school to its most impressive season in history. How he impacted us is great. How he impacted those folks in D.C. is even more impressive. He gave them hope. So, we are a month and a half out from the start of the season. Mando work starts soon for the ultimate prize. However, mando work starts now for us to all become better. Gentlemen, in two days, we go to New Orleans for a week. Not just to practice and get in shape, but to better us all." He stopped talking and everyone in the room was quiet. We all looked around at each other until Ronald said something.

"But coach. Why we going to New Orleans? Because the last time we were there something happened that I will never understand. I've seen hoards of white kids get into brawls, fights, mosh pits and all the police do is de-escalate the situation without weapons. The minute we got to fighting, I saw more guns than a damn Jesse James flick." Coach just shook his head.

"A decade ago, Ronald, Katrina hit and I saw a country call people refugees in their own *** damn country that were built on the backs of your people. I want three things out of this trip. One, we condition in a place that's uncomfortable for a lot of us because of what happened. Two, we help those who need help in areas where they still need it. No cameras. No glorification bullshit that the media can sell. Three, I wanna understand you all. I wanna understand you. College football ain't shit without the black athlete and most colleges don't give a fuck who they bring in, as long as they can make them millions on a Saturday. Now, I care about my players. Hell, as you all know, I slide you guys pocket change so you can enjoy yourselves. What kind of individual would I be if I'm pulling in 1.3 a year and you're not seeing shit but cafeteria food? And again, that shit is to never get out. But, I know one day, you won't be here under me. You'll be back in a world where stats show police shoot you more than most, people hate you for your skin color and that you'll have to work twice as hard for what you want in life. I wanna understand the places you guys grew up in so I can have a better understanding on how to help you with anything in this world you have to deal with. I'm not black and I can't be black. I can never truly say I know what you're going through because here in America, white privilege is real. But not every one of us is a Klansman in a polo shirt. Every white person doesn't have an agenda to kill you. A lot of them do, but not me. You've helped me become a better coach. Now help me to become a better man. Because if it's one thing I know, is that at the end of the day, we all bleed red. So with that said, who is going?" Again, we were all silent, looking around at each other, not knowing what to say.

"Do we really got a choice coach?," Nate asked.

"You always have a choice Nate," coach said twiddling his thumbs. "That's the beauty of free will and being a grown man. Now, who's going?" One by one, we all raised our hands. "Good. So Sunday, we can all get up out of here."

"What about the rest of the team coach?," I asked him. "They'll all be there," he said, as he got up from the chair. I, however, was still in awe about something.

"Coach," I called out as he opened the door.

"Yes Keon?"

"So what made you come to one of our dorm rooms? How'd you know we'd be here?" He started to laugh.

"The best way to learn something is through observation.

You guys roll together because you are a unit. It's a speck of blackness on this campus and you stick together for protection and just because you all relate to each other. Wherever one of you guys are, the others aren't too far behind. Plus, I had been outside the door for a while listening to how Nate was kicking your ass in dominoes." As the crew laughed at me, coach smiled and walked out. Here was round two again I started to think. Back to the Dirty South. New Orleans, we would see you soon.

I was amazed at my cousin "Keylo" writing skills. He had literally put his life into a story and that to me was something that was easier said than done. Unlike myself, he made it in football. He had six major big shot schools calling for him. USC, UCLA, Oregon, Texas, West Virginia and Washington State. In the end, he bypassed all the glitz and glam for simple playing time. He went to the University of Wyoming. Now, when he first went, I was scratching my head why. But, he said, that when his man's Darcell, a big defensive lineman who played for Dominguez rapped to him about a group of brothers who were plotting to change the whole landscape of college football, he bought into it. Now, he was at the University of Wyoming turning it into a mini HBCU. Yeah, I know I was exaggerating, 'cause the only brothers you saw at universities like those are the sports players. Wherever bruhs went, we turnt things up and we turnt them out. I started to see my writing as a gift while reading that of others. I didn't know what would become of it. Maybe, just maybe, it would take me to places that I could only imagine. I mean, I watched Ty take a pair of Clippers and have it result in visiting some of the most beautiful places on Earth. If he could do it, then why couldn't I? I debated on calling my mama to have someone to talk too. But, I didn't think she would understand. So, out of the blue, I hit up Daria. I know I hadn't talked to her a long while, so I was hoping she was receptive. "Hey, what's up with you girl?"

"Nothin. Caring for my youngin and enjoying these next two days off. Whats up?"

"I just needed someone to talk too about some things."

"Well come on over." That threw me for a major loop. I

thought I was gonna just talk on the phone for maybe half an hour and get my mind right. I was never expecting an invite. I said fuck it and threw on my clothes. I got in my whip and hit the store before anything. A nigga was thirsty as all to be damned, so I got me a mango nectar drink and dipped up out of there. I made the ten minute drive over there. **BOOM! BOOM!** I unloaded two strong knocks on the door.

"You the police now huh?," as she opened the door. Now, opening the door wasn't the issue. It was what she was wearing that boggled my mind. Boy shorts and a tight wife beater, exposing her hard to death nipples. Now, inside of my head, I was making sure that she didn't think I was Ty, 'cause he the only nigga I knew personally who had wore this thang out.

"Oh shit. I'm sorry," I said as I waltzed in her house. "I'll make it quick since you got company coming over." She laughed and chuckled.

"Fool, you are my company," shutting the door and giving me that look. "The baby sleep," she said, as she walked up on me. I know this wasn't real. I just knew it wasn't. At any moment now, I was gonna wake up in a crazy dream. However, that wasn't the case as I realized that when she came up and kissed me, playing wrestle the tongue with a brother. Now, it was always a man rule that you never fucked your homeboy's girl. But, this wasn't his girl. The more she kissed me, the less I worried. I was hoping that her boy stayed sleep for hours on end. We made it to her bedroom and plopped down on her full size, removing clothes in the process. As I got on top of her near naked body, with nothing but her boy shorts remaining, kissing all over here started to become difficult. I began to see my mama and that woman in her bedroom many moons ago. With each of her moans, it started to play back more and more inside of my cranial. I was scared to say the least, as she was now on top of me, unbuckling my belt. My heart was starting to pound as I realized that I was once again with a woman and my demons from the past started to eat away at me. Then, like all greats do when under pressure, I simply said fuck it and went for broke. I pushed her head down on my dick, making her hold it there. As she came up drooling, she yelled at me to do it again. I happily obliged. The next thing I know, I was knee deep in Daria. I could see why my nigga Ty dug this girl. She had some good pussy. With each stroke, all that fruity pebble shit that I once struggled with, it was quickly dissipating. I beat the breaks off her thick ass. I didn't know whether or not I had kryptonite in my veins or that I was just on cloud nine, but I fucked her like I had never fucked a chick before. Hell, I didn't even realize that I was hitting it raw until midway through the session. Finally, after what was forever, we came at the same time. Her for the millionth time. For the five seconds of glory that I had, I felt like I was hitting the game winning shot in Game 7 of the NBA Finals. Shit, if she thought that I was gonna pull out, she had another thing coming. We lay there, looking at each other. I was rubbing my fingers through her hair and she was just smiling back at me. I didn't know what to think, but all scenarios crossed my mind. If she did this to get back at Ty, I hoped she realized that Ty never has and never will give a fuck about a woman's feelings. The way he saw it, pussy was a football. It was meant to be passed and shared with the next nigga. If she was in a mode of needing a quick nut and wanted me to leave shortly afterwards, I wouldn't trip. I still fucked. If she had been eyeing me the whole time for a relationship, but just never had the heart to say anything, then I hoped she didn't try it, because I wasn't trying to be in one. What I could thank her for was bringing me back to reality. Yes, my mama left me confused. At the end of the day, however, everybody got choices. So today's choice definitely made me realize why a man and a woman is supposed to be together. There was nothing like that sweet Georgia peach, that ripe apple, that snapper, that bite back, kuda snap or whatever the fuck you wanted to call it.

"You impressed me," she said, still looking dead in my eyes, satisfied to the max. Shit, she had brought a nigga back to reality. Hey, if y'all brothas wanna have other brothers, more power to you. As for me, naw, that shit wasn't flying anymore. I learned my lesson. I had my downfall. I would regret that shit for the rest of my life. However, you damn well better believe that a nigga wasn't gone live in the past. Checkmate bitches. I listened to what

she told me and turned on my back laughing, grabbing my
dick.

7 503 REASONS

"Yo man, so lemme tell you. Nigga, I swear. These white bitches gone be our downfall."

"Yo ain't yo black ass fucking a snow bunny right now?," I asked E.J.

"That's besides the point my nigga. I may fuck em, but I ain't being with one." Here we were again. It was another classic E.J. and Ty moment. Man, we always had conversations, but this one here was taking the cake. As usual, it was a chill day. July 4th was the day to be exact. Niggas were coming in at a slow and steady pace, but we were getting business. Me and him were the only ones in here slicing up heads today, as the other barbers had taken a vacation up out of town to God knows where. It was just us and a few of our niggas from around the way who had come to get right for the fourth festivities.

"So what you expect us to do?," E.J. said.

"Nigga we surrounded by white, in a state with legal green, and they women love niggas that's black."

"Nigga you tryna taste the rainbow muthafucka? I'm forreal E. Yo, them girls. Them white girls gone be yo' downfall nigga."

"Aight whatever nigga." My mans Felix was in his chair was just smiling, doing everything in his power not to bust out laughing at our asses.

"Aight so, lemme ask Felix," I said. "A bruh, what you

212

think? Is it a conspiracy for a brother to be with a white chick? I mean. Can you tell this nigga all pussy is pink?" I cut off the clippers and just looked at the nigga, along with the head in my chair.

"Well, I see it like this. We da minority and whenever they see us, it's a goldmine to them. Shit, we all probably Damian Lillard and CJ McCollum cousins. I just wouldn't trust 'em as far as I could throw 'em you know?" I let out a big laugh and E.J. moved around to the front of his chair.

"NIGGA WHY???!!!" It was even more funny now, cause the boy was so animated. At this point, we were all laughing hysterically.

"Yo nigga," Felix said through tremendous amounts of laughter. "You in love nigga." Oh we were making this nigga hot now. We were letting out that Bernie Mac laughter.

"You know what. FUCK ALL YALL!!!" He roared back around to his chair to continue giving Felix a line up.

"Stop laughin nigga. Tryna straighten out this nappy shit in the back."

"I know you ain't talking with the kinks in yo beard nigga. Bet all kind of fruit flies and mealworms living in that muthafucka." I had no choice but to shut the clippers off and holla. My partner Stone from Unthank Park had fell out the chair dying laughing.

"NIGGA I KNOW YOU AIN'T TRYNA ROAST!!!," E.J. said.

"Naw, but it look like yo fat ass done ate a few roasts. Nigga gone cut yo' belly open and watch horse hooves fall out that muthafucka." Aww shit man. This was exactly what I needed. A good ass roast session, and E.J. was being ethered.

"A, man. A. A." I couldn't control myself as I spoke. "A nigga stop. I'm trying to cut this nigga head straight." The laughter continued, but things calmed down and got back to the normal shit talkin'. If we would've all kept roasting, then none of us would've gotten any work done that night. Shit finished up early for us as our last heads were both done around six o'clock. We were closing up at seven, along with the weed spot in the very front. Once it hit 6:20, we knew we weren't getting any more business for the night. We were both sitting in our chairs, kicked back, watching the television.

"How you adjusting out here bruh?"

"Shit man. I mean. It's different. Way different. But, I'm maintaining bruh. But what you putting yo' money in?"

"Besides an IRA, not nothin. Just living frugal. How that shit over in Tualatin? I aint never really fucked round over there since I got here myself."

"Aww shit it's cool fam. You know. Got a townhouse over there. Got another brother over there, which shocked the shit out of me. We work out together when we can you know."

"What's his name?"

"Nigga call himself Big Los. Cool ass nigga from L.A. I mean shit. That nigga took me too his kinfolk house over off Killingsworth one day and *** damn. Nigga his momma cooked up some shit."

"And you ain't invite a nigga?"

"Nigga I can't just go round and tell you to drop in on people's houses. White folks might do that shit. But you can get yo' ass killed fucking round with niggas." E.J. certainly had a different operation than myself. You could chalk that up to him growing up in Portland, Maine, where a lot of us didn't exist. I started to understand that with each passing day that went by in my short life. We were all different. My nigga was far from a square bear, but there were some ways that he had to drop because he had got accustomed to that shit. Is that saying I'm better than my nigga? Not at all. Shit, we all black and the government want us both dead regardless if we were raised on Bloody Broadway in Phoenix, AZ or Barrow, Alaska. However, the hood just prepared you for more shit that life had to throw at you. See it was easy to make the transition from broke to stable to rich. You start from the bottom. But, you don't hear too many people who go from rich to stable to broke. When the wealthy lose money, prepare for one of those niggas to start going postal and shoot up buildings. See when you start off broke, the only way to go is up. And when you are up, life is gravy. But, if you ever falter and have to bounce back, it's nothing because you have been in that situation before coming up, so surviving becomes second nature. If you start rich and you lose it all, then you will lose your entire mind. Just look at how wealthy people who play the stock markets get when they lose everything. They flip out, start shooting themselves, beating their wives, kicking their dogs and doing crazy shit like that. And why? It's because they don't know how to handle the downfall. See, this here ain't about black or white. This is simply about the rich and the poor. The have and the have nots. I'm not saying at all that E.J. was privileged, because he for damn sure wasn't. However, he was surrounded by many that were. Whether people wanna admit it or not, when you are born white in this country, you are automatically born with a privilege. It is easier to avoid long prison sentences. It's easier to get access to great education. It is easier to get access to business loans to prosper in this country without much added scrutiny. America didn't wanna admit it, but there was and always will be a racial disparity when it comes to the lifestyle of blacks and whites. It goes deeper than the black neighborhoods having more hair shops, liquor stores and churches than youth centers, health centers and quality housing. We are put in a hole from the time that we come out of a hole the size of a lemon.

Our bodies are already diseased with diabetes, high blood pressure and heart issues. Many of us have to battle missing fathers or young mothers who are not yet ready to face parenthood. So a lot of us grew up calling our momma's by their first names and our grandmama's mama. We end up calling every male who visits the house daddy. We take the weight of outer space on our shoulders by the time we are five years old. We aren't set up to survive mentally until the age of 36. Hear what I said, mentally. Anyone can survive physically. But to die mentally, means you simply do not exist. Our mentals our destroyed with the images we are presented with. We are presented with death through our music. We are presented with death through the drug dealers and gangsters that we grow up seeing. We are presented with the illusion of freedom when we are actually limited in what we can do. At least in America that is the case. I heard so much from homeboys who went into the military and told me how we are treated overseas. For the most part, I heard nothing but great stories about black men wherever we land. The world knows the truth. We are Gods, Kings, everything. Look at Ancient Kemet, which the world calls modern day Egypt. They thought we were stupid. Why would we try and take wealth into the afterlife? But if they were smart, they would think outside of the box. The greatest treasures they left behind were in the monuments they established. The diamonds constructed in the soil. The pharaoh face that was etched on the body of a lion, which represented power in ancient times. So, if their greatest treasures couldn't be taken or duplicated, then why would they truly bury wealth? Could it be that they knew people would come and rob them? Well, isn't it ironic that many grave robbers end up cursed and pass away shortly after their thievery? Maybe, there was a deeper lesson in it all. Maybe they were warning us, the future generations, the black people of the land, that they will come and take from you like they did from them. Think about it. What if the prized jewels they wanted weren't the actual jewels? What if what they really wanted, which is a foothold in Egyptian land, couldn't be taken or duplicated? They attempted to build a pyramid, but man couldn't do it.

So since they couldn't duplicate the land over there, they simply took our land. We call it gentrification. They take our jewels and convert it into their own personal gain. They move us out and force us farther out so they can move in more of their own kind. Now think about this. The jewels stolen from Egypt are taken out and pushed through museum after museum after museum. Well, unfortunately, we are the museum. We are put on display, and when we falter, someone comes in and transfers us to another place and time. Are you getting the drift now? Do you see where I am coming from? This plan of action was created way before me or you were even born. This goes way back in the time when they were upset that the great Moorish empire of over 800 years lasted. They didn't like black people in power. They didn't like black people organizing. You wonder why the Black Panthers have been dismantled and not the KKK, or any other Neo Nazi group? You wonder why Tulsa, Oklahoma was bombed and not any other affluent white neighborhood in America? It's because if we come together, they know the power which we yield and they will do anything to see it come crashing down. See you never attack anything inferior to you. A lion will never attack an ant because it is a waste of time. However, a pack of hyenas will always try to take out a lion when they can. You know why? Because that lion is superior to them. That lion does not need the hyenas approval to eat. That lion can come in and take what it wants. See the hyena has to separate the lion from the pack, much like they separate us from each other. Gangster Disciples vs Vice Lords. Bloods vs. Crips. And now, they done got so slick with the shit, so they have the gangs fighting with each other. This block GD's vs. this block's GD's. This block's Vice Lords vs. this block's Vice Lords. If we all are apart of the same gang, then why in the good hell are we all fighting with each other? Well, it's the same mentality now. They pit us against each other. We get jealous easily over others who may have more than us. See it's a reason that they call it the hood. The neighbor aspect is gone. Watch MTV Cribs, Lifestyles of the Rich and Famous or some other flashy show showing off houses. You always notice that they say so and so stays in this NEIGHBORHOOD or that NEIGHBORHOOD. We limit ourselves to the hood, because we don't wanna see our fellow brother or sister as a neighbor. We would rather see them as an enemy because we have been processed to think that way. We fail to realize that if we bought up the land and everything in our neighborhood, then we could control everything in our neighborhood. But, we don't. Hence why we have gigantic church buildings being the only beautiful buildings in the hood.

So should the pastor be in question? Not necessarily. The community should be held responsible. I mean, it's their church. They allowed it. They attend it. Now, if we obtained the land, then we control what comes on it. But how much of the hood do we really own? See building assets are fine and dandy. However, owning the land is where the real cash flow comes from. But, we don't get schooled on that. Not enough of us are thinking about that. We are strictly thinking that having the house and the cars is good enough. But when they purposely GENTRIFY, like they did majorly in the northeast section of Portland, Oregon, then all of a sudden, we like to get up in arms. Why? Because now, we have nowhere to go and have to struggle adapting to other areas or cities ways. Then, with that, comes more violence because we are all trying to survive and eat. Before you know it, they gentrify that area and now we are stuck repeating the process again. See, contrary to what they want America to believe, a lot of these cats in the 80's didn't move strictly to sell drugs in an unaccompanied area. Sure, some saw easy money. However, the majority of the people moved to different areas because they were trying to escape the madness of some areas. But, with our migration comes white flight. And after a while, they finally let all of us in one area. Some even tag irrelevant titles on the neighborhood like historical black district, or give it some funky name to attract more people. Knowing all along that once the property value drops, they will swoop in and see us gone. That's unless you have the few kids who can play sports and then they may help the family out. The offer to move the family to another area of their choosing. Let them help a primarily white school out in exchange for housing and security. I've seen it and everyone has heard about it, but don't nobody wanna admit that it's wrong.

The parents get too wrapped up in my kid may get a scholarship to so and so school to play basketball. The white folks who know it's wrong will simply say "Well, he's helping us win." They aren't caring about the individual in any way, shape or form. And I say they because the black parent, even though they get to live comfortably, is doing so at the expense of their kid. I don't care how talented your child is, your dreams should not be lived through them. It is one thing to push your kid to do their very best. That is fine and dandy. In fact, I wish more parents did. But, when your child gets to that level where they become big time, rather if they become big time, then you're pushing of them shouldn't become "I."

"I" was the reason my child is successful. "I" am the reason they are in the position they are in today. "I" gave them everything. Ok, we get it. You worked with your child. You helped develop them in some ways. But, at the end of the day, it's up to the child to apply what you have shown him, along with other valuable help, go out there and get the job done. We sacrifice our child's health for our wealth, and that is totally and morally wrong. But, at least those parents love their kids. I say that because America doesn't value the black child. They don't value the black man at all. An animal's life is way more important than the life of any black man. Michael Vick should have never stepped foot in jail. Period. For dog fighting? Something that dogs do naturally. Shit in Compton, watching a dog fight was like a fish swimming in water. It was an everyday thing. Dogs naturally fight. Dogs naturally wanna go at each other, because they are protective of their owners as much as a parent is of their child. But, you know why he went to prison? Its simple. The government didn't get their cut of the deal. See, the gov't is a cold muthafucka. So much illegal shit goes down with individuals on a daily. However, the high life guys as I call them, they can pretty much piss on Jesus's grave if they wanted to and not see a day behind bars. Why? Because Washington will be getting a cut. The 1% only go to prison when they steal from the 1%. If they benefit off of the 99%, and it helps the 1% in return, then everything is fine and dandy. Sure, the occasional story leaks and they pretend to do some damage to a person's reputation. However, in the end, they walk home happy, scott free, sippin' their wine, cognac or whatever it is that they drink. You don't get that opportunity if you are black.

You must automatically pay for the crimes that you commit. See, being black is something that everyone wanna be, but don't wanna be. Let me say that again. Everyone wanna be black, until it's time to be black. We created damn near everything, but yet, they take the credit for it. Chuck Berry invented rock and roll, yet they give the title to Elvis as the King of it. We created hip hop in the streets of New York City. Now, we have no more hip hop, as actual hip hop music has been replaced with the brainwashing of get rich quick schemes in which they dumb down the art through the use of cats who don't know any better. Is that totally their fault? Yes. See they planted this seed called money in the roots of our blackness. Contrary to belief, money is not the root of all evil. If anyone says that, slap the shit out of 'em. The LOVE of money is the root of all evil. Well, it's the same thing is what some people will say. Nah the fuck it ain't the same thing. You can be lustful, but only to a wife or husband. Nothing wrong with that. But if you have a LOVE of lust, you could see yourself trying to fuck everything walking. Dreaming about fucking ya homeboy or home girl spouse. I could go on. So make sure you know what that love aspect entails before you go talking like you know some shit. Love is a powerful thing and they don't love us at all. I mean shit, I can look at this love in so many ways. Just like they love us in colleges across America.

SCHOOL. Now, let's get on this college thing for a good minute. I'm gone delve into the athlete perspective soon, but let me just talk about college. Every year, we see it play out from the inner city to the white picket fences of suburban America. A group of high school seniors walk across the stage and receive their high school diplomas. Four years, rather twelve years of hard work has finally paid off. For every one of them that walk across and receives their actual diploma, you can believe there are two that didn't. They are just walking across a stage to get the hell out of school. For the ones that did though, they take a long summer break. We have all been there, so we know what it consists of. Kicking it with friends, expressing feelings to the person you were too scared to talk to in high school, crazy summertime parties, etc. Basically, you are getting all of your last excitement out before you head off into your new world. Some prepped for a military career, but most teenagers are preparing for college. YES!!! You are preparing for college. Let me say it one more time. YOU ARE PREPARING FOR COLLEGE!!! You will finally be away from your parents. You will finally have your own freedom. There is no more living by mama and daddy rules. There is no more walking in the house at whatever time they designated. You can have any and everyone you want over at any given time. This is your time and your own life now. It is about to be party central. YES!!! Fraternities dancing around with candy canes and barking like dogs. Goofy students will be busy pulling goofy pranks on people. Wild parties that you know your liver will regret the next morning. You will be part of the crowd who cheers on your university team, hoping that they make it to the big game. This is the coolest thing in the world to a 17 or 18 year old child. However, there is one thing in the midst of all this celebration that most kids tend to forget about. There is actual school work that must be completed. Reports, lectures, study halls, individual study time, midterms, finals. YIKES!!! This college life will have some stresses involved with it. Then, on top of all that, one huge factor remains. What is it you ask? **MONEY!!!** That is the answer to the six million dollar question. Yes, money is the determining factor. College can be an expensive son of a bitch. Wait, let me take that back. College is an expensive son of a bitch. It is even more of a pain in the ass for out of state students. If you received a scholarship, then you should be fine. A few things you will have to come out of pocket for, but overall fine. However, if you didn't receive a scholarship, you will be trying to pull money from each direction that you possibly can. Student grants, loans, family members. Anything that will help you pay for this quote on quote higher form of learning, you will do it. You will do it all for obtaining a small piece of paper that will read either Bachelor's, Master's, or maybe even PhD. After four (or longer depending on your goals) strenuous years, you will finally be done and ready to once again walk across the stage. Congratulations, you have now completed college. You can let the picture taking with the ten to fifteen people who came to celebrate with you begin.

You have now obtained that degree that you so diligently worked your ass off for. Not only that, you also have great memories of all the wild and crazy things you did in those four years. Of course, you will have to keep some of those memories hidden from mom, or else she will go crazy and whoop your ass because she never would think her daughter or son were so off the wall. Hey, I know what you are going through. I am in the United States Navy and I have had my fair share of memories in 22 countries. From wild parties in Australia, to playing the role of "cameraman" in Hong Kong. If my mom knew some of the crazy stuff I did overseas, she would disown me and exile me from the entire family. Now, again, you have graduated college. What is the next step in your life? Of course, you desire to enter the workforce. The next hurdle you ask? Finding a job. You would think with all the money that you gave that school, the least they could do is help you obtain employment. Now, some schools do and I give them a hand salute. For the most part though, you get a kick in the ass, a good luck and you are told to go on your merry way. Now, let's say you can't find a job immediately. Now, you are back in the house with your parents. You are back to living under their rules. You are back to square one and it sucks. It is hard as hell adjusting, because for the last four years, you have been doing it on your own. It shouldn't be this hard for you or for anyone. You put many hours in the classroom and study hall. You should have a job waiting in your lap as soon as you are finished. Ok, so you found a job finally. **CONGRATULATIONS!!!** Your salary starts off as something that you are comfortable with. Actually, I will take it one step further. You start off with a salary that you are VERY comfortable with. Now, you saved up some money, got your own place, own car and a few nice things. You are finally settling in and becoming an adult. You have your own stuff, with your name on the dotted line of whatever you purchased. Life is freaking good ain't it? Now, just when you get comfortable, guess what happens? That first letter arrives. You have to start paying back all of those student loans you took out for this quote on quote higher form of education. Let's really dissect this though. What are you exactly paying for? Why is education not free? Hell, a university's basketball team can pull in over $10 million dollars in revenue off of jersey sales alone (See Fab Five Documentary). They can pull in even more millions from ticket sales at the same athletic events. There are several former alumni who generously donate back to their alma mater for top notch facilities. So really, what are you paying for when you go to college? Education should be free. You are being charged to look through a textbook, do reports, hear someone else talk, all something that you can do yourself. America is a cold son of a bitch ain't it? We have billion dollar Navy ships, million dollar airplanes, million dollar satellites, billion dollar defense systems, million dollar landmarks, but you mean to tell me that education cannot be free for every person in this country? Hell, every year, we donate hundreds of millions of dollars in aid to some poor country who we swear needs our help. We are big brother America and we have to save the world. Hell, I am surprised that the stars and stripes haven't been replaced with the Superman logo. We can do all that, but we have to pay to get an education? A degree? Really? I have to pay to receive a funky piece of paper? Ok, let me get this straight once again. I have to pay thousands upon thousands of dollars to obtain a piece of paper. Meanwhile, the coaches for the athletic teams are getting millions per year to call plays and bark out orders at the athletes. While I'm on athletes, hell, let's not forget they are students too. They are making the university millions of dollars, but they don't even get 1% of that in return. The President, AD, chancellors are getting hundreds of thousands a year (millions in some schools). I mean really? This is truthfully a mind boggling thought that I am trying to wrap my head around. This is sad on so many levels. I don't care what background you come from. Whether you are from the tallest project building or an area where white picket fences were common. No one and I mean no one should have to pay to get educated in this world.

This is the biggest hustle occurring in this country right now besides the government bringing in drugs, selling it on the streets and imprisoning men to run their billion dollar prison empire. This scam called the college hustle is truly demoralizing. Do we all see this or are we too blinded by our favorite school being able to be ranked #1 in basketball and football? Are we too blinded by the rivalries we obtain with these universities? He goes to Ohio State (BOO). He goes to Michigan (YAY!!!). Let's not worry about these kids education. Let us worry about who will have bragging rights for the next 364 days. No one thinks about this. Or do they? This hustle has been going on for decades and it will continue because we as a country are too stupid to do anything about it. Welcome to the American hustle. **COLLEGE!!!**

NFL. The good old NFL. The National Football League. For over 85 years, this sport has produced numerous, legendary athletes and some of the greatest memories known to man. I mean, where do we even start? How about Otto Graham, who went on to win seven NFL titles in 10 years with the Cleveland Browns as their quarterback. Let us remember Richard "Night Train" Lane, who was Deion Sanders before Deion was ever born. His 14 interceptions in one season is still a record that stands to this day. Gale Sayers, whose career was cut short by injury, but still made one helluva impact in his six years professionally. Many more names come to mind when you think about professional football. Joe Montana, John Elway, Jack Tatum, Jack Lambert, Alex Karras, Bruce Matthews, Willie Roaf and a slew of other greats past and present. I know they call baseball America's pastime and maybe it once was. However, I personally think football has taken that over within the last 15 years or so. Sure, Roger Goodell has turned the game into flag football with all the BS rule changes, but it's still very entertaining to watch. While we can't see men hit like men anymore (like the great Lawrence Taylor did), we are now entertained by high scoring offenses that light up the scoreboard like a tree on Christmas. Me personally, I liked football for what it used to be. Even though I think it is watered down now, I can never shake the love for the sport I played from high school through the military. It is something special about lacing up your cleats, lining up with ten of your teammates and going head to head in a battle of testosterone with eleven other men to see who wants to punish who more.

That is the game of football I remember and that's all it should be remembered for. Punishing hits, blood, sweat, people getting trucked, amazing catches, coaches who could voice their feelings towards a ref without a ridiculous fine. Now, **THAT IS FOOTBALL!!!** Ruckus crowds such as the Dawg pound in Cleveland, or the infamous and legendary Black Hole of the Raiders had us all taking pride in our football teams. **THAT IS FOOTBALL!!!** However, in this new age, things have changed. We have seen social media and a growing media market in general put player's lives full circle for everyone to see. A player can't even go on vacation without a camera being in their face. Hell, I'm surprised that I haven't cut on ESPN and seen a breaking news story of Peyton Manning taking a shit in his luxury home, with Ed Werner reporting on the size of each turd. Johnny Manziel partied in Vegas with a bunch of hot women and it made major headlines. It's so sad how we expect these guys not to be human. I personally think the only people who got mad at Johnny are guys who never had the chance to live that life. I'm not even talking about the money. I'm talking about being surrounded by hot women. Hey, it's not our fault you couldn't get laid in your younger days. You shouldn't have been so lame in your younger years. Now, we were all shocked by Michael Vick's dog fighting incident. In one instance, I understood him. Growing up in the inner city, especially in an area like Newport News (Bad News), VA., dogfighting was a natural thing to see. That was the equivalent of getting up on a Saturday morning and watching cartoons for us. It was just something we were accustomed to. I was more so upset at his family members who put the blame all on him. That, in the hood, is what we call some bitch shit. I don't know them personally, but they are some bitch ass fools for that. Ok, I can hear someone saying right now as they read: So you are one of those no snitching idiots? No and yes. No, I don't have a problem with a person reporting a crime or wrong deed going on. What I do have a problem with is ratting out people who weren't there when you get caught. We all grew up as kids with a bunch of buddies we hung around with. We all did knucklehead things at times. However, I understood that if we all went down as a group, then we all went down. If one of us got caught, then that individual got caught and not anyone else.

That is why you must be smart when you do what you do. In the other instance, it was sad to see a group of animals tortured and beaten like that. I am an Animal Planet junkie. I love animals' period. To see that torture was sad, but I didn't use it against Vick in my opinion of him. I still think of him as an excellent athlete who thought he was doing something normal because of the environment in which he was raised in. It was a mistake. True, no human or animal deserves to be treated like that. He did his time, but you have numnuts who can't move on from it. Only in America do we as a whole society treat animals better than human beings, and that is just downright sickening. Kids are getting molested on a daily by sick minded adults. Mental illness (or just sheer craziness) is causing people to kill in mass quantities. Do we go crazy over that? Of course not. Animals are so much more precious than a human life. I mean how many times have you seen a dog being carried and a child being put on a leash? Yeah, it is downright sickening I know. Any who, we all know Vick's story, but what about countless others? We have Matt Jones and his cocaine addiction, even though he got to play an additional four games after being caught (I wonder why). You have Riley Cooper, who wasn't suspended after saying what he said (I wonder why). The original word that came from the NIGER region of Africa meaning KING. However, people stripped our culture and downgraded us with a word that was never wrong. Now, with our loss of history, we had a positive word turn negative, only to turn around and have a more degrading meaning. Off that, there have been a lot of issues with players in the NFL. Ray Lewis, Michael Irvin and a slew of other guys have been far from perfect. Desean Jackson's case kind of intrigued me though. The Eagles claimed they cut him because of his alleged gang ties with the Crips. Hey, growing up in Long Beach, I'm pretty sure he knew a lot of them. I mean hell. Long Beach is one of my favorite places in Cali. I myself call it Crip city, because that's what I mostly see up there. It is one of the roughest cities in America. Young black men bangin are common in these cities. However, contrary to what is believed, for everyone who goes down the wrong path, there are two who go on a right path. However, any NFL team judging a player by where they are from is absolutely absurd. If this is the case, then shouldn't every NFL player from the inner city be cut? I'm from the Harborside of East Chicago, a majority Gangster Disciple hotbed. I grew up in the vicinity of one of the most notorious cliques of GD's which were the DSG (Dark Side Gangsters). Hell, half of the section I was related too so it was nothing to associate with them. I partied with GD's, ran with GD's and fought side by side with GD's at times. That's just how it is. You roll with who you grow up around. If I had grew up in the West Calumet section of the city, then guess what, I woulda been running with Vice Lords, breaking my hat to the left and other stuff. That's how it is. You can't be faulted for where you are from. Even with all of that, I was a three sport athlete and managed to graduate high school with a 3.8 GPA. Taking pictures with guys you grew up with is not wrong. I do it all the time when I go to the crib. I've got simple pictures with all smiles. Then, I have those hood pics where the homies I am around have guns and all. I saw the quote on quote signs

Desean threw up. I laughed at the Eagles saying they were gang signs. I laughed even harder when they claimed that throwing up the deuce was a gang sign as well. If that's the case, it's a whole lot of people, including nerds who are gang affiliated. The tiring part of all this is that the Eagles organization gave off the impression that you must be faulted for where you come from. Hell, get rid of the 80% black NFL, because most of them come from the inner cities. Some know Bloods, Crips, GD's, Vice Lords, P. Stones, or whatever other gang. Hell, a lot of them probably banged in sets with either one of these gangs, but were given a pass when the leaders recognized that they were too talented to be out and about on the streets. If you are from the inner city, then you dealt with gangs. There is no way around that. It wasn't anything that we could have done to avoid it growing up. That's just the way things were. With that said, I personally hope the Eagles never win anything for the foolery that they showed with the whole situation.

Furthermore, I hope every time that Desean plays them, whether in a Skins uniform or not, I hope he lights there ass up. This isn't a knock on the city of Philadelphia, because I have nothing against the die hard, rough, rugged, I will kick your ass for messing with my city people of that city. Hell, any fan base that tosses snowballs at and boos Santa is good with me. I actually like that. The Philadelphia fan base brings a lot of fun to the No Fun League. I mean NFL. Being proud of where you are from is great and Philadelphians exemplify that. However, the organization that runs the city's football team is full of shit. City of Brotherly Love? If it is, I sure as hell don't see it at Lincoln Financial Field. I hope fans toss snowballs at the owner's house one day. Now, that would be cool. Welcome to the NFL, which abruptly stands for **NIGGERS FOR LIFE**. Don't believe me? Ask Colin Kaepernick.

HIP HOP. The rise of hip hop throughout the 80's and 90's went from actually spitting rhymes, to creating war and dissension between our fellow black brethren. Let's take a walk down memory lane. In the late 70's, it started with the Sugar Hill Gang. In the 80's, Big Daddy Kane, LL, Biz Markie, NWA, Rakim and a slew of other artists who actually had rhyming skills and something to say came through. NWA was a trigger point for hip hop. They gave the voice of the inner city and America for damn sure wasn't ready for five black brothers to take the country, if not the world by storm. I know we all remember the timeless hit *"Fuck The Police."* Public Enemy was still pumping its revolutionary rhymes throughout the speaker boxes with hard hitting singles such as *"Fight The Power."* From there, the craft only grew. Wu Tang just became legendary, with Inspectah Deck, in my opinion, giving the greatest opening verse in hip hop history on *"Triumph."* Then, came along a man by the name of Tupac Shakur. Now, when it came to lyricism, Pac wasn't someone who would blow you away with his lyrics. What I mean by that is this. Listen to the majority of Pac's rhymes. He didn't say a lot of metaphors and similes that would make you say ooh and aah like a Nas or Talib, but he spoke from the heart and just gave you real life spit, on real life topics. To this day, *"Brenda's Got a Baby"* is my favorite Tupac song and an all time classic. He explained real life struggle in a way that even the whitest man from the suburbs could get. The raw emotion that he spit with made you believe every word that he said. He could've said Big Bird was slangin crack next to Oscar's garbage can, and you would've believed it.

Pac was indeed ahead of his time, but his mind didn't go with him at times. Personally, I think his downfall came when he signed to Death Row. You can see how he changed a lot. Yes, he could flip on a lot of subjects, but one struck a nerve with me. How can you say we need to make changes and love one another, but start a war with a group of other men from the other side of the map? That is a pure contradiction. Now, I know the brother had good intentions, but at the same time, he was still very young. I believe people got in his ear, and the thug persona overtook that revolutionary persona. In the end, we saw what that did. Five shots. No, he was not assassinated. That brother was shot by some other negroes. Six months later, B.I.G. met the same fate. From there, you saw hip hop take a very drastic turn, as more and more artists became more than thugs on wax. However, now we have gone from thugs on wax, to lil hippy songs with men wearing women's clothing, kissing each other in the mouth and all other sorts of foolery. This is what I call the brainwashing of hip hop. Now, step back real quick to the Pac/Biggie war. The media had a field day with the whole story. The war was only one example, as we have seen many wars in hip hop cost lives. If you thought No Limit and Cash Money was just on wax beef, you better think again. You have to remember that all of those dudes were legit gangstas from the projects of New Orleans. I have never been to New Orleans in my life. However, with my dealings in the Navy with cats from the N.O., I can tell you they are indeed bout that life. There were some bodies dropped due to that beef, so you know it was real. Moments like this are when I believe the media saw money to be made by the warring of individuals behind a microphone. Their influence has stretched beyond belief as conscious rappers like Common, Lupe, Talib, Mos Def are barely even mentioned anymore. Yeah, people still knock them, but not on the level of those who quote on quote live in the trap. If I had a dollar for every rapper who was a trap king, I'd be a millionaire. Slowly but surely, the quality of the music has not only diminished the craft, but it has also diminished the minds of those who have listened to it. This does not relate to all. It only relates to the ones who cannot separate the fantasy from reality. I was able to listen to God knows how much gangsta rap, but still have enough mind control to know that I didn't want to go out and murder 10 people. Unfortunately, everyone mentals aren't equipped like mines. All it sometimes takes is one song to get them going and that's it. The trouble is not in the music solely. The trouble is in the man whose mind is to adolescent to receive it. Until we can collectively separate the two, then I really don't see an end to the brainwashing effects of what we called "Hip Hop."

DEHUMANIZATION. On October 28, 2002, I sat in a hotel in Rosemont, Illinois, awaiting the next morning for when I would take off to Navy boot camp at Recruit Training Command Great Lakes(Located in North Chicago, Illinois). I vividly remember me going to sleep at precisely 9 p.m. This was planned ahead of time. As I lay in the dark, I thought about how my life was about to change in the next 24 hours. No longer would I be catered to by two parents. No longer would I be roaming the streets of East Chicago, Indiana. There would be no more hitting River Oaks mall in Chi-town with 4 or 5 of my partnas chasing after women. No, not at all. Those days were over. The next day, I would take my first official step into manhood. I thought about old girlfriends, friends that didn't make it due to the streets, my family, etc. Most of all, I thought to myself, *"What in the good hell am I getting into?"* The alarm I set went off at precisely 12:05 a.m., the morning of October 29th. I can't remember what movie it was that I watched, but it seemed like the slowest two hours of my life. I cherished this because this would be the last television that I would watch for quite some time. 2:15 a.m. quickly approached and I went into a daydreaming zone. I was trying to imagine exactly what boot camp would be like. To be real, I was angry at the same time. I felt my dad had shafted me out of college. The money was there, but he did not want to assist on paying for it. I really hated my pops at that point in my life.

I felt like he was selfish. I thought to myself that I was a good student. I graduated with a 3.8. GPA. I never did anything that was too crazy. I had my hardheaded moments, but damn. Why couldn't I go to college like I wanted to? As crazy as this may sound, even though I love the fact that I signed the dotted line, I wish I could have still went to college straight out of high school. I say this because I felt that this was a forced choice. I felt my father pushed the Navy thing on me because he went. Yet, the only reason he even went in was because the judge gave him the choice of either the military or jail. I didn't want to be anything like my dad. Growing up, there was a lot of stuff that went on inside those walls in that bright blue house on Ivy Street. Adults sometimes don't think kids see things, but trust me, they do. There is too much stuff to talk about that went on inside of my childhood home. However, when I had to choose the military as my new life, I initially went to the Air Force recruiter. Like I said, I wanted to distance myself from the essence of my pops and not be anything like him. As I walked out of the Air Force recruiters office one day my senior year, one of the Navy recruiters who went by *"Boats"* stopped me. He said *"Youngblood, what they giving you to sign up?"* I didn't know what the hell he meant, so I told him *"A new life outta here."* He said no, I mean, how much money? I told him nothing, and then he said the words that would change my life forever. *"If I guarantee you $10,000 to sign up, would you roll with us?"* That's all I needed to hear. Two weeks later, I was signing the initial papers for the Navy. I know the Air Force recruiter was pissed, but hey, I got 10 G's. Trust, knowing what I know now, that incident doesn't surprise me. The Navy is like any occupation. **CUTTHROAT!!!** It is all about numbers. Anywho, back to the hotel. 4:45 a.m. on October 29th, 2002 rolled around. By then, I was on the bus outside of the hotel about to take a short ride to the military entry and processing station (M.E.P.S.). I was dead tired and expecting to be shipped out as soon as I got there. However, it didn't happen. For the longest, me and a select group of people sat in a lounge, watching TV and eating free food. I thought that was cool. I mistook this treatment for how boot camp would be. The time ticked and ticked away until 6 p.m. rolled around. The second oath had already been sworn and we were escorted to a bus. We were told to shut up as we were driven to O'Hare airport. I thought wow, here we go. We arrived at O'Hare in probably 30–45 minutes. There, I was made to sit indian style with a whole group of folks that were about to take this journey with me. Finally, we boarded a bus, got told to stay quiet again and we were on our way.

I arrived through the gates of RTC Great Lakes a little after 9 p.m. No one came on the bus yelling and screaming as I expected. A first class calmly came in and told us to exit. Once outside, he gave us instructions of what to do. I went through what seemed like everything that night. I got to make the one minute phone call to my mother. I then proceeded to get my head shaved and made to put on the ugliest sweatsuit I had ever seen in my life. I became a part of Division 906, headed by MSC Milligan, PO2 Wood and AS1 Alden (MSC is now an officer. PO2 is now Senior Chief Wood. AT1 is now retired ATC). Over the course of those nine weeks, we were pushed to our limits. When I say we got beat (exercised), we got beat. Also, in a 900 division, you had the duty to perform for graduating ceremonies. We were state flags division, so we were the division who would hold up all the flags during commencement. Also, we were responsible for the color guard. On top of already trying to cram everything about the Navy inside of our thick skulls, we had to entertain folks. Boot camp, was dehumanization part 1. In this case, it was a great thing. The object of boot camp is too break you down mentally and force you to rely on each other to pick yourselves up and complete a task. It wasn't done out of spite, but this is what was needed in order to make future sailors. We operate in some stressful conditions and this was the first step into preparing us for that life (I will get more in depth later). They made us feel less than human. Yelling in your face. Talking about you. Trying to make you feel like you were the scum of the Earth sometimes. However, that was their job. They made you feel like you weren't human in order to accomplish a goal. I knew it wasn't personal. It was just business. Finally, on January 3rd, 2003, the goal was accomplished as I graduated boot camp and was no longer a recruit. I was now a sailor in the world's finest Navy. My journey would then take me right down the street to the Navy Training Command, where I would learn part two of dehumanization in the form of "The Purge."

Now, if anyone has ever seen the movie The Purge, you know it is simply a movie about free chaos and reign allowed for twenty four hours. Any and every crime you can imagine can occur. They dehumanize folks by allowing them to take from other humans. Well, NTC Great Lakes was sort of the same way. It has changed dramatically over the years since 2003, but when I was there, they allowed free reign. We were now sailors, but we weren't cared for. That ended up being a good and bad thing. Good, because I was 18 years old and feeling free like a rabbit who had just got uncaged. Bad, because of the same thing. There was a club on base called Club Liberty. It was like any other nightclub you went to, except it was just on a military installation. Oh my goodness. Everything and anything took place in this club. Drug busts, fights, you name it, it happened. It wasn't confined to just the club. The corpsmen (doctors of the navy) were on the other side of base. Over there, there were wild sex parties, some including instructors and students. It wasn't uncommon to hear about underage drinking or an attempted rape. This was the Navy I was starting to see myself accustomed too now. It was like, I go to school for eight hours a day to learn my job, and then it was "*PURGE*" time. I will not drop any names, but I remember one specific incident vividly. There was a wild rave party near base one weekend. Nearly 70 sailors who were in school ended up being charged with every drug count you could imagine. All of them were found guilty and the majority kicked out of the military.

Now, how is this dehumanizing you ask? Simple. There was no control. It was like fuck it. Let the kids do what they wanna do. If they make it, they make it. If they don't, they don't. I can only speak about my experience, but as I look back on it, I was pretty fortunate not to get caught up in a lot of things that occurred there. Had I got caught up, I probably wouldn't be here writing this book for you guys and gals. It may not have sounded like much to you guys, but I look at it like this. The military is a professional organization. No, they do not restrict you from having fun. However, back then, they let their sailors run wild and basically allowed them to destroy everything they touched. In a strange sort of way, I believe it put the wrong mindset in a lot of young folks my age around that time. That is why now I ensure I do all I can to make sure every sailor I come across makes proper decisions. Even if they screw up, at least I can say I did my part and didn't just leave them as a chicken crossing a pasture full of wolves.

Now, dehumanization part 3 comes in regards of the last five years I have spent in the service. First off, before we get into anything else, let me take this time to acknowledge and thank all those who have served. Yes, this even goes for you guys who were booted out of the military for whatever dumb crap you pulled. I find it amazing that a lot of guys who get kicked out of the military quote on quote hate the service life. However, I guarantee they never tell any negative stories about it to their friends back home. Ok, now that I have that out of the way, let's get to part three of dehumanization. It is simply when military members forget they are simply human. Let's be real here. Yes, there has only been one percent of Americans who have served this country. However, since when did doing that make them better than the man who did not? First off, let me speak on the *"I'm responsible for everything you do"* people. These are the people who take responsibility for everything that goes on in America, all because they served. Fact, there has been no war on freedom of anything since the Revolutionary War. Let's throw that out there right now. Secondly, so because you don a uniform, you are all of a sudden responsible for every American's success in this world? I ask you this. How is it that you are responsible for everything all humans in America do? Those types of people kill me. Because of you, the doctor in the hospital is performing surgery. Because of you, the NFL player is running the ball. Because of you, the car salesman can sell his cars. You are that elite because you are the 1% right? This is the first step in brainwashing. Remember, as military members, we work for the U.S. Gov't.

The tactic to make folks think we (governmental organization) are responsible for everything is a brainwash man. Then, you wonder why people are so dependant on the government and think nothing is wrong with it. True, there have been wars where military might was highly needed. However, the last real freedom war was the Revolutionary War, as I stated before. WW2, we had to defend ourselves against enemies who tried to take us out. I don't consider that a freedom war. I consider that you fucked with the wrong people war and now we are going to stomp 100,000 tons of a democracy illusion down your Axis power asses. Vietnam? Iraq? Afghanistan? What freedom was being fought for over there? I could go on. The brainwash tactic has a lot of folks clueless. These folks feel because they are the 1%, they are better than the other 99%. Well tell me, who protects your family while you are gone? Other family and friends who don't serve. Who grows the food that is sent to you so you can have a hot meal? The farmer. Who is teaching your kid in school? That teacher. Yes, all the people who are in the other 99% are doing that. Realize this. You are human. Humans need to depend on each other. There is no one person better than the other. Especially not due to the fact that one dons a uniform. Let's face the facts.

All y'all ain't been in the sands. All y'all ain't living by the UCMJ. You face the same problems that everyday human's face. Yes, there are drunks in the Navy. Yes, there are those with financial burdens in the Navy. There are rapists, gangbangers, drug addicts, drug suppliers, crazy people, all in the United States Navy and the military as a whole. When you put the uniform on, it does not exclude you from everyday problems. Tell me when has a bullet stopped and went around a person because they wore a uniform for whatever branch? Tell me when a bill collector said you don't have to pay this outstanding debt because you wear a uniform? Tell me what judge has said you don't have to pay this DUI fine because you don a uniform? Some of you really have life screwed up. This is the biggest dehumanization of them all. To actually make a human feel less like a human. I remember one incident. There was this young lady who was in the service. She went to Foot Locker, but that particular store did not give military discounts. She went off on a rant about she is the reason they can sell shoes, so forth and so on. At that moment, all I could think of was *"Why didn't her mama swallow?"* Stuff like that makes people dislike us. If you don't get a discount, then you don't get a discount. Either pay or leave. I consider myself 100% human. Always have and always will be. I realize that this uniform does not make me who I am. The man I am makes me who I am. There are so many people who currently wear, or have worn the uniform of the United States Armed Forces, but they did just that. They only wore it. They didn't define what it is to be a soldier/sailor/airman/marine.

They were in it for themselves and not to truly enhance everyone else around them. Furthermore, let me give my feelings on reservists. If you went from active duty to the reserve, I have nothing but respect for you. You know the game and just want to play it part time for however long. To the full time reservists, I have no problem with you for the most part. I only have a problem with those reservists who talk shit as if they do this everyday. Remember, there is a big difference in doing something one weekend a month, two weeks a year and doing it for 24/7. 365. If you recognize this, thank you. However, to you reservists that don't, please get off of your high horse acting like you do this all the damn time. Remember the word reserve. It is like insurance. In case shit happens. For the most part, active duty got it. When you do work with active duty as well, please don't mess things up. I really never had a problem with reservists until 2009. When they had their drill weekends at my shore duty command, a simple note saying *"please don't reboot computers"* was obviously not read. Now, who does that mess things up for? You guessed it. The active duty folks who had to go in and fix things, while they sipped coffee from their comfortable civilian jobs. There are some agreeing with me. Some are saying I am off my high horse. That's fine and dandy. You want happy times, go to Thailand and get a happy ending massage. To all military past and present though, thank you. I hope you are still human though. Unfortunately, many of our brothers and sisters aren't.

GROWING UP ON THE BLOCK Isn't it an amazing feeling when a baby is born into this world? It is the creation of new life. You don't even have to be a parent to appreciate a child coming into this world. Watching (or not in my case. That is some nasty mess to watch, lol) a woman go through impervious pain to deliver another life into this world shows you the true definition of strength. Then, after all the grunts, screams and maybe a few curse words here and there, the baby finally arrives. I mean, such an innocent life that has all the potential to become something great is finally here. Whether black, brown or white, it really doesn't matter. There is no hate in their hearts. No bigotry, no guilt, no anger. There is nothing but innocence at its finest hour. You look at the mothers of these children. They are lying in a hospital bed, exhausted from the strenuous effort that it took to push this magical creation out. The smile that stretches from cheek to cheek. The tears of joy and pain that travel down their cheek bones. The instant gratification that overwhelms her as she holds her newborn in her arms. Thank God for these women. Lord knows us men could not even fathom the thought of carrying a child for nine months and then pushing it out. I don't know if any of you have ever seen the viral video that shows two gentlemen simulated having a baby with electro therapy, but it isn't a pretty sight, especially for us guys. Again, thank you ladies, because we could not do it. This world would be more than under populated. Finally, doctors congratulate her as they finally relax after doing this for probably the millionth time. For one doctor, it was probably their first time involved in a birth and they are just happy that it is over. The other doc looks at it as business as usual. Then, we wait for the dad and his chance to hold him. We know how men are. They for damn sure aren't going to touch something slimy and covered in blood. We may be some hard creatures, but we aren't that tough. When that creation they helped make is fresh and clean, you see a totally different look in that man's eyes. But wait, where is dad you ask? He should be here. Maybe he was on a plane stuck trying to get back. Maybe he was bogged down in a shift at work that he could not get out of in time to make it to the hospital to see his son or daughter born. Maybe he was fighting through traffic, as I have known some men who were actually in that situation. Hey, things like this happen. Where is the daddy you ask? Unfortunately, daddy isn't anywhere around. No, this isn't the case of the dad being away on a business trip that he couldn't get out of in any way. No. This is the case of the father who never had plans to be there in that child's life. It isn't even the late shift or stuck on the plane that I just said. Unfortunately, this is the sad case for many black families in this day and age. Now, let's get this straight. There are fatherless children of all races and genre's. It is not just a black thing.

Truthfully speaking, unlike the stereotype depicts, active black fathers outnumber the deadbeats. However, as a black individual, this is seen far too often in our society. Where I'm from, a fatherless child is as common as the bullet that gets loaded into the gun to murder a rival gang member. I was fortunate to say the least. I grew up in a household in which I had both parents. It wasn't peaches and cream for the majority of my childhood, but at least I had them both. A lot of my friends on the other hand did not have that same luxury as I did. I saw the crippling effects of what happens when a father is not present in the home. The little boy grows up to be rebellious and live for the streets. The drug dealers, pimps and gangbangers become their new father. They teach them life in another way from the in house father. This life will lead to the jailhouse, unstableness, severe struggle or early death. The little girl grows up cursing at the age of five. She will probably evolve to be a twerker at the tender age of nine. She might be pregnant at the age of 13, have 4 kids by the times she is 20 and living off of government assistance in an housing project riddled with negativity. This is not uncommon at all. Hell, I remember in my four years of high school, seeing a pregnant teenage girl was as normal as the 90's Bulls winning an NBA title. That shit was like going to the water fountain to get a drink if you were thirsty. I am so serious. That's how common it was. A fatherless girl can end up going down a very treacherous path. A young man growing up without his father can be a death sentence from birth.

My homeboys without fathers were the worst of the worst. Gangbanging, drug dealing and the whole street aspect of life was their father, and they were dedicated to him. Some even lost their lives defending their favorite parent. I can't count on my hands how many of my partners died before I was 18 years of age. I can however remember the funerals or wakes I attended. I didn't go to them all, but I did make my presence felt in a few. I remember one in particular. I had a partner, who out of respect for the family I will not reveal his name. He was shot in a house a few cities over from where we were from. He was from the hood and everybody loved him. He was your typical hoodstar as we call it. The funeral was at Allen Funeral Home. Right across the street for the funeral home was the Harborside Apartments, better known as Guthrie Street. If you grew up in East Chicago, or any surrounding area, you knew about Guthrie Street. Guthrie Street was death. Guthrie Street was rough. Guthrie Street was where you did not want to be caught slippin. So many negative things happened over there. Shootings, stabbings, drug deals, fights, etc. You name it and it happened on Guthrie Street. It didn't even seem ironic that a funeral home was directly located across the street. I don't know if the owner did that purposely, but the residents of Guthrie had to have had an eerie feeling looking at what may be their final place they would end up at every day. As I watched my folks lie in his final resting place that day, I could only imagine what life would have been like for him if his father was present in the home. By having Joe Sr. in the house, I was guided in a different direction than most. Trust, it made a huge difference. See my dad was a full time steelworker. However, as a part time gig, he served as a pallbearer/mortician at Guy & Allen Funeral Home in Gary, Indiana. As a child, I really didn't fear anything. I would run up and down the funeral parlor, looking at dead bodies. I can't recall it, but my dad told me one time he caught me playing with the arm of a dead guy he was working on when I was five. He just stood back and laughed as my curiosity overtook me. Now, as a grown man, I start to wonder. How many of those young men were the victim of the streets, all because they didn't have a father in the home to guide them in the proper direction? More than that, what ever happened to the theory that it took a village to raise a child?

What happened to the men in the community who would take these fatherless young men under their wing to ensure that their inspirations weren't the thugs, gangstas or the fantasy that was played out on the television screens on a daily? Those days are long gone I know. More than all of that, I think about why did God place me in a family where the funeral home was common? I saw death on a regular, so maybe that's why it was hard for me to cry when someone I knew passed on. I probably will never know, but what I do know is that I am different from most. Coming up, I had five mothers. My own, my grandmother Mary Washington, Mrs. Perkins, Mrs. Winfield and Mrs. Jelks. I had many more, but those were the four besides my mom that I did not want to piss off in any way, shape, form or fashion. We all know how classic a grandma ass whoopin could be. I caught quite a few of those when I stayed over my grandma's and acted up. They did however result in some bomb ass naps though. You know you got yo' ass whooped good when you slept for a good three to four hours afterwards. If my mom or grandma wasn't around and I screwed up, I could expect my ass to get chewed or beat by the other three as if they pushed me out themselves. Mrs. Winfield was the mother of my homeboy O'Bryan. She was tall and I always had this image of her dunking on me and dropping me with a three punch combo. Mrs. Perkins was the mother of my best friend Dennis. He and I had known each other since preschool. She was more quiet and reserved. I think that's what made me scared of her the most. Even at a young age, I learned that you never mess with the quiet ones. I'm sure Mrs. Perkins would leg drop me and catch me with a Macho man flying elbow if I got out of line (I say that because Dennis and I were wrestling fanatics' as kids). Mrs. Jelks, she was what I called the calm before the storm. She is the mother of my other childhood best friend Doug Jelks. Like Dennis, I had known him since preschool. Me, him and Dennis made the trio. I interacted with Doug's dad a lot. He was the coolest adopted dad since sliced bread. His mother though? Well, she was cool, but you always knew that if you screwed up, the hammer was coming down on you. Hell, to this day, she still snaps off on me. Doug got a tattoo as an adult and she snapped on me as if it was my fault (I love you Mrs. Jelks). When her youngest son Johari got a tattoo, oh boy did I catch some serious hell. I guess she thought my 17 tattoos were what made them want to mark up their body (probably). Y'all all see where I am getting at though? They are the women who kept me in line back in the day. Everyone doesn't have that. The former adage of "It takes a village to raise a child" lifestyle has almost completely disappeared and it is truly sad.

In America, one out of every three children are born without a father. Also, in America, one in every three black males will go to prison in their lifetime. Now, sit back and imagine that. The next time you are out with your friends, partnas, homeys or whatever you may call them, imagine two of them gone. That is what it's like. Trust, I am not making this solely a black issue, because it is not. I am just speaking on the black perspective because I am a black man who has to deal with everyday problems that mostly black males face. Hell, do you really think someone cares that I have served in the military for over a decade with an unblemished record? When people look at me, most people see ignorance, trouble and thuggery. I remember taking a trip to Palm Spring in 2013. I stayed in the Hyatt and got a bomb suite. The second day of my trip I was entering the elevator, and there were nothing but middle aged white people and two children. I could tell that having on a wifebeater, a fitted cap and exposing 14 tattoos at the time may have been intimidating to them. During the ride down, one gentleman asked me sarcastically *"What brings you here to Palm Springs?"* With a smile I calmly said, *"I'm active duty military and I just returned from overseas."* Oh boy, you would've swore that I was the finest thing since sliced bread after that. The thank you's and normal conversation I got was astounding. I knew it was a bunch of cover up racist bullshit, but I rolled along with it, because I was enjoying myself and I refused to let anyone's judgment of me affect my trip. Long story short, that is how the events of the world have molded people's images of us into. I don't worry on it because I know who I am. However, it does not take away from the fact that the notion is still there. Now, I will go back to the aspect of the children that I was previously talking about. Personally, I believe no child should be made outside of wedlock. However, there are many unwed couples who have created life and the fathers of those kids have been an exceptional example of what it means to be a father.

These little girls need fathers more than ever. I look at this new age of technology and I see how it plays a factor in these kids development. Little girls, eight or nine year's old making twerk team videos. Fighting on camera and thinking that it is the thing to do. Cursing, dressing half naked, saying F the world and a slew of other ratchet things. What's even wilder and crazier are the mothers who think that is cute. They actually support this kind of lewd behavior. Words of *"Ain't my baby cute"* are accepted by laughter and jokes from her female acquaintances. Then, the mother is shocked when her fifteen year old all of a sudden has a huge stomach. All of a sudden, things get real. All of a sudden, the mother is wondering where in the good hell did she go wrong at? Her child is a child having a child. When I think of this situation, I automatically think of 2pac's classic song, *"Brenda's got a Baby."* If you are unfamiliar, it is the story of a young 12 year old runaway who got pregnant, did drugs, ended up being a prostitute and eventually she was killed. That may have been a song, but that situation plays out every day in the world that we live in. Being a father is imperative to a child, but especially to a young lady. Trust, you do not want any other man showing your little girl the way of the world. His way just might lead her down a path of destruction. Yes, there are single mothers who have done it on their own. That still does not mean that it was supposed to be done. Like Chris Rock said in his Bigger and Blacker stand up: *"You can drive a car with your foot if you want to. It doesn't make it a bright fucking idea."* A lot of things can be done alone, but there are some things that are better off when a team is involved. Parenting is one. We need more fathers to step up to the plate and handle their responsibilities. Black fathers really need to take heed to this message more than anyone.

"YO NIGGA WAKE UP!!!" I arose to E.J. screaming in my face.

"Huh."

"Man I'm bout to lock up the shop bruh. Unless you wanna stay in here and not go home for the night."

"Nah, Nah. I'm good. Shit I ain't even know that I fell asleep. What time is it?" E.J. looked at his watch so sarcastically.

"Nigga it's five minutes from the time you closed your eyes. Fuck was you dreaming about? Telling America what they didn't wanna hear so they could execute your ass later?"

"Naw nigga. I was dreaming bout a book I read where another nigga was telling America what they didn't wanna hear. His story." I knew I was tired then and needed to rest up. I got my shit and headed out to my whip. I sat there, sitting in my Egyptian baby, reflecting on all the shit that I had just thought about. I felt I was serving my purpose as a barber, but I needed to do more. I wasn't complete. Only one half of the dream had been complete. I needed to add another layer to the success. Instead of heading straight to the crib, I made my usual trip a little different. I hit up my man's Big Los mom, who stayed right off the 5 in northeast. I wanted to rap with her for a bit about some stuff. She obliged over the phone and I made the drive over to her crib. The sun setting was signaling another day down, but another day of learning had yet to occur. I pulled up to her crib, which was on the narrowest street you could imagine. Man, this was the crazy thing about Portland. This was a one way, but they had so many narrow two way streets that it would drive you nuts. I'm like who in the hell designed this city? Did they know that a two way street was supposed to have room for two cars at the same time? It was what it was though. "Hey boy. How you been?"

"Mama Los. What's happening?" She greeted me with a hug and I strolled in the living room, taking a seat.

"Boy come on over to the dining room table. I just finished cooking."

"Ahh snaps. What you cookin' up over here?"

"Ahh well." Black folks rule #90786. When an elderly black woman starts off a sentence with "Ahh Well" and it refers to cooking, you know the answer will be soul clenching.

"I made some green beans with white potatoes, neckbones smothered in gravy, mac and cheese with ham and bacon in it. Umm," as she turned around to look back at the kitchen stove. "Oh some deviled eggs and some fried cornbread patties." My stomach started to do the dab inside of my body. Shit it would've made Cam Newton proud.

"Gone in there and make ya'self a plate. Get as much as you want." Before she even finished the sentence, I was out of my seat and in there. I was still mannerable and washed my hands, because I swear that was my pet peeve. Folks that didn't wash their hands before a meal. I lathered my hands up and commenced on fixing me a huge plate. I was hungry from cutting hair all day and this meal would give me instant gratification. I sat back down at the table with moms. "So what is it that you wanted to talk about?," she asked.

"Well," as I scooped a fork full of well seasoned green beans in my mouth. "I just wanted to know how did you make it up here in Portland? You know. It's almost all white. The bruhs here are darn near in one area. What I'm really trying to figure out is how do I carve my niche in the black community with there not being much of a black community up here?" She shook her head up and down.

"Hold on," as she excused herself from the table. She walked into another room which was connected to the living room. She came back about two minutes later with a newspaper. "Read this," she told me as she plopped the paper down in front of me. I picked it up and began reading. The story read of a young brother who was living in the city. His name was Percy Hampton. The date was May 24, 1969 when he got arrested on the corner of Cleveland Avenue and Northeast Going. The police were assaulting his brother. Getting wind of this at his home, he ran towards his brother's aid, where he was met with force by police. They beat him, not allowing him to get to the officers who were assaulting his family.

"So is this brother still alive?," I asked.

"Yes he is, but it goes to show you that this city isn't all peaches and cream. For years, this city waged a stealthy war against the black residents of this community. They call it the Rose City. I call it a thorny thistle. Most black folks when they came here, they moved to the Albina neighborhood. No one wanted trouble. They just wanted the same opportunities as anyone with fair skin was afforded. But, as the American way goes, black folks had to go twice as hard for what we wanted and what we deserved. So to answer your question. How do you carve out, or give a niche back to your people? Remember this. There are 350 degrees of Loyalty in each person alive." I was dumbfounded and not getting what she was saying. "I see that look and know what you thinkin. What in the good hell is this old woman talking about? You want some wine?"

"Umm. Sure," I said. She smiled and got up, yet I was still confused about the phrase she had just said. She came back with two glasses in her hand.

"Here. Sip this. Tell me what you think?" I took a sip and my throat tightened up. My nerves were ringin' bells and my vocal cords became nonexistent.

"Damn mama," I let out in the raspiest voice ever. "What in the good hell is this?"

"I call it Dafukup."

"Dafuckup? Like, one word?"

"Yup," as she took a swig and wasn't phased by the

strength of the wine. "It's one word. Because you drink enough of it, it will shut you dafuckup." It had definitely done that to me.

"Anyways, here it goes. You ever heard of an angel number?," she asked me.

"Nah."

"Well. An angel number is something like a spiritual awareness. It's like having a message delivered to you through numerical sequence. As for the number 350, in basic and simple terms, it means to remain true to your values and beliefs. That's loyalty. You are loyal to what you believe. You are loyal in all aspects. You believe in family and love. You are loyal to that. It's for spiritual growth and positivity. When you are loyal to positivity, then you are loyal to growth. Now, don't get this twisted as relating to anything. You might have some folks talk about they loyal to the hood or the drug game. But what does loyalty to those two things bring? Not a damn thing but death. See people have to be weary of what they are loyal too. If it doesn't promote growth, then it's not worthy of your spiritual energy. Your spiritual energy transfers to other people. So you have to choose wisely. In the case of helping your own people, you have to ensure that you are dedicated fully to helping them. Your **COMPLETE** energy will transfer **COMPLETELY** over to the residents of those communities, whether it's Unthank Park or even a community of homeless black folks. You give **PART TIME** energy to the people, and you will get **COMPLETE** hell in return. If it's one thing about black folks, we can tell when someone is genuinely in something for the long haul, or if they're looking for a quick come up. If you get into something, stick to it. Your life and the lives of many can and will be depending on it." I sat back in amazement at what I had just heard. It was a reason that we had two ears and one mouth. It was because we were supposed to listen twice as much as we speak. And now, I understood why. I understood why E.J. had gave me the call and I drove to Portland instead of Boise. I understood why I was supposed to meet Big Los and get put on game. I understand why it was critical for me to delve deep into the issues at hand and put on for my people. Not saying that I don't have love for anyone else on this earth, but when worst come to worst, my people came first.

"Thanks mama. I needed to hear that."

"No problem. And that's another reason why I am still in this house. I'm loyal to this soil. They can gentrify a lot up here, but I'll be damned if they get me out. I been here from the start. I seen 'em put it together and I watched em take it apart." I busted out laughing.

"What you know about Jay Z mama?"

"Hey," she said, pointing a fork at me. "I ain't that old. Don't get it twisted." With a smile on her face, we ate, drank and chilled for about another hour before I decided to make the half hour trip back to the crib in Tualatin. As I got in my car, I sat there for a good minute and started to reflect on everything. I heard the noise boomin in the sky as I looked out my window and saw small remnants of fireworks shooting above the buildings. Fireworks were never intriguing to me, but right now, they were. It was like someone or something was telling me that my life was about to start anew. Even though July 4th didn't mean shit for my people, it still had an underlying meaning on this night. I pulled out my phone and made a call. "Hello?," they answered. "Hey bruh. What's up?"

"My nigga. My dog. It's been too long. Let's rap."

8 GAME 7

"Man bruh. Where did we go wrong man?," Kevin asked me. "It was me fam. Friends are friends. Shouldn't shit come between us. That was all me. And bruh. I'm sorry."

"Naw fam. Let me apologize to you. It ain't every day a man hits his best friend with an o-ke-doke. I fucked things up and I need to make everything right my nigga." It was refreshing on this July 4th day to hear from my nigga. Portland was a ways away from here, but I was determined to see us both put in work like we did way back in the day. Only this time, we weren't watching each other's back for survival. We were now trying to elevate ourselves to something we never were. Our convo ended after 30 minutes as he pulled up to his crib out there and was in need of some major rest. Me, on the other hand, I was here at my mama's, outside, watching the fireworks light up the night sky over here in the West Heritage section of Fontana.

"What you thinking about?," as I felt a hand grasp each of my shoulders.

"I dunno mama. I'm thinking about quitting school and actually pursuing something even greater." Her grip then dug deep into my shoulders as it gave me that negro I'll kick yo tail pain.

"Ahh mom. That hurt." I shouldn't have said that as she popped me upside the back of the head.

"Mama. I said a thought. Not reality," turning around

facing her, holding the back of my head.

"Boy what is your problem? You got all this opportunity in the world and now you wanna throw it away? You got a full ride, you playing basketball and you doing something you love."

"Nah mama," still rubbing the back of my head. "I'm living someone else's dream. Like seriously, what am I to that school? I'm a number. In a few years, someone will take my place for another number. I'm gone graduate, just to get another job, so I can pay the few loans that I owe. I don't want my life to be about that mama."

"So what you gone do?," she asked me. As I looked back up at the fireworks, I was thinking what is the answer to that question. What am I gonna do?

"I'm gonna do what I wanna do mama. That'd be me."

"Me don't pay no bills. You need money to survive."

"That's what we've been taught mama. Everything needs money. They condition us to live to survive and not just live.

"I gotta question mama. And by the way, I am not disrespecting you, because I see you have that look in your eyes like you wanna kill me. I am not that crazy mama. But, do you own the land on this home?" She gave me that "*Da Fuck*" look like black folks were so accustomed to doing.

"No, and what's your point?"

"You living to survive mom. You are a tenant. If oil got found right now in the backyard, the bank would put you out and put a big drill in the backyard. Hell, this whole block would be gone. See, this is the one thing that doesn't discriminate, and that's money. Money don't care if you white, black, green, yellow or brown. It will move you out of the way just so it could multiply."

"You still ain't told me what you gonna be doing boy," as she crossed her arms.

"Simple. Bounce out and live. Goodbye mom."

"COME BACK HERE!!! KEVIN!!!" I completely ignored my mama, got in my whip and drove. I knew that she was gonna kill me the next time she saw me, but right now, none of that mattered. I didn't drive home. I simply drove around the corner to the lit up basketball courts at the park. There, I just parked my car and thought about what I wanted to do. Big city life was calling and more prosperity was yelling at me constantly. I sat there, pondering my thoughts, well past midnight, as I watched suburban American kids enjoy their play outdoors. You couldn't do this shit in any part of Compton, whether it was Spooktown, Fruit Town, Nutty Blocc, Kelly Park or any other area. I was amazed how these kids just played outside without a care in the world. No threats of Bloods or Crips comin' through and shooting their game up. At about one in the morning, I returned to my mama's house and was greeted with her sitting in the living room with the lights on.

"Mama, what you still doing up?" She just sat there for a minute, staring at the floor. "Mama. You aight?"

"When you left and didn't say anything, I found myself not being able to sleep. It reminded me of times when you would be playing outside back home and I couldn't sleep because you weren't in the house yet. But, when you took off, after saying what you said, I truly realized that my boy is grown. Look Kevin," as she got up and walked over towards me. "Realize. I will always be a mother. I only want the best for my baby. But, I can't tell you what to do with your life. You have to figure it out on your own. Now, I don't want you to drop out of school. But, if you feel that you need to do this to advance in life. Then there is nothing that I can do about it." She then grabbed my face and kissed me on the cheek. "Get you some rest. Mama going to sleep." I watched as she walked up the stairs to her room, not once looking back at me. I walked into the kitchen and poured me a glass of cranberry juice. From there, I headed to the couch and just placed the blanket over me, heading to sleep. The next morning, I arose to the smell of mackerel and grits. I looked over and mama was getting down in the kitchen.

"You make enough for me mama?"

"Mmmhmmm," She said. "Yup. Figure I'd give you a good meal to make a decision on." There go ya plate right there. It was gravy that she had finished right as I was getting up. I really didn't have a choice, however, seeing how she had no problem waking me up at all whenever she cooked. I sat down at the table, mashing my plate with a glass of almond milk. Her on the other hand, she had disappeared back upstairs, eating alone in her own world. I ate slow and steady this morning, really contemplating about what I was about to do. My mind was already set. She just didn't know that yet. Then again, that was my mother and she knew me like the back of her hand. I finished up, throwing my plate in the sink, seeing how I had scraped that thang. I grabbed the last two mackerels left on the counter with a paper towel and walked back into the living room. I started looking at all the pictures that my mom had up of me, her and other family members. It was kind of eerie how I was just going through these pics like I was living my last days on Earth. But, to me, it was like looking at a framed graveyard. A lot of my family members in these photos were long gone from this earth. Aside from my grandmothers, who both died of cancer, I could literally point out the death that ravaged my people in typical hood stories. Uncle Buck, he died from a heroin overdose in a trap house. Cousin "Skink," he got shot eight times fucking around in Mona Park. My cousin "Double Deuce," who was nicknamed that from always throwing up both middle fingers at everyone as a kid, he got murked while serving time in Folsom by some Mexicans. Aunt Carol, well, she was just a bitch. Couldn't stand her ass whenever she came around. Always swore that the world was supposed to cater and revolve around her ass. Naw, she wasn't dead, but no one knew what she was doing because she was always on the move. And from all standpoints, I could give two fucks if I ever saw the bitch again. I shook my head and went to grab my keys, heading out to my car.

"**BYE MOM!!!,**" I yelled.

"**OK!!!**" Just like a mama to respond like that.

"**YO!!!**" My nigga Ty looked up. "I'll be *** damned. **COMMERE NIGGA!!!**" I walked across the barber shop and embraced my nigga. It was a long time coming. "Yo my nigga. You lookin good man," as he wiped me down in my black tee. "Man shit. I'm tryna be like you."

"Naw nigga. I'm tryna be like you." We looked at each other and just smiled at each other.

"Yo, so is you gone introduce yo' partna or stare at him like you in love?," the other barber said.

"Man A. Don't pay that nigga no mind. Nigga just mad cause he ain't seen his dick in 20 plus years with that bowling ball sitting under his chest."

"Fuck you nigga." I walked up to ol' boy.

"Sup man. Kevin."

"E.J.," as he dapped me up. "Yo, this yo best friend?," he asked me.

"Yeah man. That's my nigga if he don't get no bigga."

"And unlike yo belly nigga, I ain't growing no more," Ty said.

"A, A, A nigga. Shut yo' ass up. Lemme finish a head right here that ain't shaped like a deformed cantaloupe." We all got a good laugh out of that one.

"C'mon on over nigga. Lemme slice the back of that neck up," Ty told me. I walked over to his chair as E.J. was going to town on another cat's head. "*** damn nigga," as Ty removed my hat. "Nigga when the last time anyone put some clippers to this shit?"

"Man it's only been like 3 weeks."

"Nigga the shit look like 3 months. Look like an episode of National Geographic about to be filmed on the back of yo neck."

"Nigga just cut me up," I told him.

"I'm gone have to do more than that." I watched as E.J. and his client laughed as I just analyzed everything in here. Man, this shit was legit. Huge glass panes and a glass door separated the barbershop from the weed shop. Who in the good hell would think of a concept like that? Like, this was making me start to think about odd combinations that I could possibly take back to the hood one day. Shit, who wouldn't love to knock out two birds with one stone? Shit would be tight if Compton had some shit like this. Or, I could even put a chicken and waffle house with a nightclub. Have niggas getting full meals after sweating it up or in between a good couple of twerks. That energy reboot would be a monster.

"So man what made you shoot up here?," said Ty, cutting the liners on to clean up the back of my neck.

"Man you motivated me bruh. I saw how you got up out of your situation and went around the world. I was like man that shit was impressive. Then, after everything went down, you just came up here like it was nothing and did ya thing. Like what I wanna know is this. Were you scared?"

"Scared of what?," he asked, taxing up the side of my dome.

"I mean. Just disappearing into something unknown."

"First off man, you gotta realize something. Its niggas everywhere. Traveling round the world, you'll see that. You make connects everywhere. See E.J., he was on the road with me for those six months. He was upgrading just like I was. Shit went down with us. I honestly didn't know where I was going. I said I was going to Boise, but forreal forreal. I had no damn clue about where I was going. Then, my nigga over there gave me a call. Told me to come up here to Portland. Rip City. Start fresh and new. You know, it was different. It was unknown. But I said fuck it. Why not? I had went 'round the world to different joints. If I survived over there, then I could survive here. Came here, got my bread up. Clientele up. A nigga live in the 'burbs. Got a hunnid stacks collecting interest. What else do I need?" I closed my eyes, taking in every word that my nigga said as he continued to work his magic on my head.

"Where you staying at man?"

"I got a telly downtown. Nothin' expensive at all."

"You uber here or rent a car?"

"Uber."

"Well, after I finish up here, which gone be after you. You checking out. You staying with me bruh. I can't let my niggas struggle knowing that I got the means to help."

"You sure 'bout that man?"

"Is a pigs pussy pork?," he asked me, as he stepped in front of me and hit me with the stepback.

"Aight man." Fam bam handed me the mirror and sho nuff, my shit was on point.

"We good man."

"A yo E.J. A nigga. I'm out for the rest of the day," Ty told him.

"Damn nigga. It's barely three."

"A man. My peoples here. I gotta bounce."

"Aight." We took off out the barbershop and through the weed shop. The smell hit me even more than when I first came in.

"Later Wayne," Ty said to the guy behind the counter. He gave him a two finger salute as we waltzed out the door. The summertime air of Portland was just amazing.

"Damn man. It's more trees out here than niggas it seems."

"Yeah man," Ty said, as we got in the car. "Literally trees nigga." He fired up the whip and we rolled through the streets of the gentrified northeast to the highway headed downtown.

"Man, so it's only two of y'all in that shop?," I asked him.

"Naw, it's three. Other dude is a brother named Lilo, but he only come Monday, Wednesday, Friday and Saturday. But, we good. We hold it down."

"Man y'all got a shit ton of bridges out here." Ty laughed.

"Yeah man. Trees, bridges and white girls. But, it's gravy man. A nigga can ride around here without a care in the world." We kept cruising, hitting downtown until we hit my hotel, which wasn't anything extravagant. I checked out, losing some money, but I didn't trip. I'd rather lose money and stay in comfort than lose money and just be basic.

"Yo nigga. What's this for?," as I returned to the car. Ty was holding in his hand a thousand dollars.

"I figured you could use it while you up here."

"Man I can't take this."

"Nigga shut the fuck up," he told me slowly. "It is what it is. Nigga I'm good. I got money multiplying and I'm eating good. Just relax and enjoy the ride. Tomorrow, I'll take you to Pine State Biscuits. Right now, we go to my crib. See if Big Los at the house. Maybe we can do some shit tonight." I listened to my dude and just rolled to the sights and sounds of the Oregonian world. The window was halfway down and the breeze was hitting. A lil traffic mashup here and there, but for the most part, everything was A-1. We got to the crib 'round 5:15. We would've gotten their sooner, but we made a stop in Tigard at a joint called Elmer's. Man, I didn't know what the hell some Tillamook was before I got here. But, I swear for goodness that when I had my first bite of it, it was the greatest shit I had ever tasted. There was cheese, and then there was Tillamook.

"Yo my nigga. This shit is gravy," as I looked at this beautiful townhome.

"Tell me about it man. The good life." I walked into Ty's townhouse from the garage and the shit was unlike something I had ever seen before. I walked through the kitchen and into the living room, just in awe of how my mans was living.

"Yo. My nigga. How much you pay for this joint?"

"Man you'd be pissed if I told you."

"How much?"

"Damn near the same shit we were paying for that rinky dink one bedroom in Carson." That's when I knew I was in the wrong place. Our one bedroom in Carson was $1200 a month. This nigga had a three bedroom townhome in Oregon with a two car garage, and was only shelling out $1130 a month. I know you could get a lot more for that price in some other states, but compared to California, this was heaven.

"Man my dude. This shit is crazy yo," as I sat on his big ass sectional. There was then a big knock at the door.

"I got it my nigga." Ty got up and walked towards the door.

"HaHa," I heard. It was one of those long ass laughs. "What's up nigga," as Ty dapped up homey who was at the door. Fam bam came in with his Money Mayweather hoodie on.

"Sup brother. Big Los," as he walked over to me.

"Kev mane." We dapped up like brothers do. "You from Spooktown too?"

"Yeah man. Just up here kicking it with my nigga. Seeing what's up with this Portland life."

"Aight. Aight. Thats whats up. Yo nigga what you got to eat?"

"Shit man, I was hoping we could all go out and get us some grub man. This nigga new so I'm tryna get him out and about. Unless ya lady cooked up something."

"Naw man," Los responded. "She ain't cook shit. Plus the girls in there tearing shit up, so hell nah." Big Los followed that statement with that crazy ass laugh of his.

"Shit I can handle them," I told him.

"Man please. The five year old by herself will kill you and my three year old would bury ya body. They bad bruh." That crazy ass laugh of his followed his statement.

"Fuck it then," Ty said.

"B Dubs?"

"Shit I'm good," Los responded. Ty looked at me.

"Nigga let's go," I said.

"Aight cool. Lemme run and piss, and we'll be out. Me and Los rapped for a minute while we waited for Ty to finish feeding the fishes.

"Damn nigga. You made another ocean in there?," Los asked him.

"Yeah man. Had to let that juice loose. Let's roll." We bounced out to Ty's whip and peeled out for the quick five minute drive to B Dub's. I was hungry as hell and had an inkling for nothing else but some hot ass buffalo wings. The fine ass waitress came over and boy oh boy, the flirting began. Man, I was starting to not care about the whole thing of black men dating black women. Why? Because the white girls I were seeing were thicker than a pot of grits with butter and salt, with some cheese and shrimp added. Even with some mackerel on the side.

"Yo man. Los. Tell this nigga 'bout up here man. I don't think he believe me."

"Bruh. Like. First off. I know y'all grew up together. Even though I been knowing this nigga for a short time. This my nigga. Like, real shit man. Don't ever let shit come between y'all. But nah man, forreal, forreal. I came up here from L.A. a while back. Had a gang of Cali niggas with me. Man, when we first got up here, it was like man what the fuck is this? It wasn't L.A. It wasn't no hustle and bustle. Shit it wasn't no niggas. But man, over time, we just embraced this muthafucka. Like, a nigga got a family now. My kids. My ol' lady. Man this shit forreal now. The young boy days gone now. We men up here." We were then interrupted by our grub being brought to us by that fine baby once again. Ahh the smell of a plethora of wings and fries spoiled our nose hairs to the millionth max. We kept talking and maxin' on our food something serious. We were headed into the evening on a cool, calm and collective tip.

"Yo. Who that?" Ty pointed over to a cat sitting in a corner by himself, eating what looked like a buffalo chicken sandwich.

"Man nigga looking like he got a lot of shit on his mind," I said.

"Call him over bruh."

"Hell naw nigga," Ty told me. "I don't know that nigga."

"Man it's cool," Los said.

"**HEY MAN!!!**" He raised his head up slowly and looked up at us. We all gazed over at him as Los started to signal for him to come over. "**BRING YO' FOOD TO THE TABLE MAN!!!,**" Los yelled at him again. He just stared at us. And kept staring for a good minute.

"Yo, this nigga gone kill us," I whispered. Finally, he got up, grabbing his food and walking over. He made it to our table and stood over it. His eyes started to travel and look at all of us. Back and forth his eyes went.

"Well, are you gonna sit down or what?," Los asked. Five seconds later, he slid in next to me.

"This Los who was just rappin to you. I'm Ty. This my guy Kev sitting next to you." He once again looked around at us as he took a bite of his sandwich.

"Tep man." Los and Ty looked at each other. "Tep. Like, Imhotep," Ty said. He looked up at Ty, shaking his head up and down.

"Yeah man. Like the pharoah. So y'all from up here?"

"I'm not," I told him.

"My two partnas' with me stay up here. I'm just visitin'."

"Lucky you. Cause life ain't nothin' good for a brother up here."

"Whatchu mean?," Los asked, biting into one of his wings.

"Man. I'm getting away from here after I finish school. I can't stand this shit."

"Whatchu mean bruh?," Los asked again.

"It's obvious my dude. I see the tint on ya skin. I mean, you mixed with something, but it's obvious you got some black in you," Ty said.

"Not everyone saw it that way though man. Shit, I remember a few years back. I went on this school trip down to Alabama. Some shit about meeting different kinds of backgrounds and staying with a family for the time we were there. We were supposed to be helping the community. But them fugazi ass folks only helped themselves. I ran across a brother named Ramses. Ramses Osiris Martin. I remember him like the back of my hand. Dude was from Newport

Beach. And I was thinkin' to myself. Man, ain't no brothers in Newport Beach. But, to my surprise, he was. Anywho man, we stayed together in the same crib. Stayed with some detective ass dude named Fred. Shiesty ass dude man. One minute, he was cool and calm. The next minute, he had us on missions helping his fam out. Man, I saw the shit that you see on TV in Chicago, Gary and shitty places like that. Don't none of that shit happen here. Man this Portland. Ain't shit thug up here. I mean, you got a few cats who migrated here from Cali, Chi, a few more places and bring some noise. But for the most part, it's chill up here." He bit into his sandwich once again and we all continued to listen.

"I'm tellin you man," as he wiped buffalo sauce off his mouth. "Being a half and half wasn't cool with some of these folks. My mama Egyptian and my daddy caucasian, so all my life, I been hostile to these privilaged ass white kids who thought it was cool to crack jokes and shit bout me and my family."

"So you born and raised out here?," I asked him.

"Yeah man. I mean c'mon. This Tualatin. The Blazers live out here. Some over in Lake No Negro."

"What's that?," I asked.

"Oh that's Lake Oswego," Los told me. "It's the uppity up up area 'round here. Ain't too many niggas over there if any. I mean, Stoudamire used to stay over there when he was on the Blazers, but you ain't gone find too many of us."

"Man, as Tep continued. "When I saw y'all, I thought fuck. Some city niggas tryna start shit. But, once I analyzed y'all, I was like ok, this may be straight. I'm just glad to see more of my kind round here."

"So what happened to the partner you told us about?," Ty asked him.

"Who?"

"The pharaoh nigga. Umm. Ramses."

"Ahh shit. Man he play for the University of Wyoming. Football. Saw his ass when he first came out and balled on Oregon State." As he said that, I thought about the memoirs or whatever you wanted to call it. That shit that my cousin Keylo wrote when he played for them niggas. I knew the world was small, but it couldn't be that small. It was only one way to find out.

"Hold on, hold on man," I told him. "This may sound like an oddball question. But, umm, did yo' man's introduce you to some of his teammates? 'Cause I gotta cousin who played for them."

"What's his name?," Tep asked me.

"Keon Lorick."

"**KEYLO!!!**" The whole restaurant turned and looked at us as he was louder than Big Los when he was shouting for him to come over to the table.

"Oh shit. I'm sorry. You mean Keylo?," he said in a whisper.

"Yeah man. That's my big cuz from."

"From the 20's," as he cut me off.

"Yeah I know. He let us all know. Also let us know that he came out of Long Beach Poly. Yeah his big ass got a mouth on him, but I wasn't fucking with him man. He was crazy and I could tell. Damn man. Small world." It was indeed scary how small the world was.

"A man, you got his number or anything?"

"I can text my man Ramses and ask him. Let's exchange joints before we bounce."

"Fosho." We spent the next 45 minutes all just rappin' to each other, figuring out how we were connected, or seeing how we were connected rather. We all bounced out, hitting the crib around eight o'clock.

"A man, everything is yours. Gone head and get settled in, and let me know if you need anything," Ty told me.

"Aight fam. Fosho." Ty walked into his room and shut the door. Me, I simply dropped my leftover wings in the refrigerator and headed to the living room to just relax. It was amazing to see what my nigga had came from to where he was at now. I plopped down on the couch and started going through my phone, looking for Keylo number. Man, it was a long time since I had rapped to my fam bam and I had no clue what was still going on in his life. I knew he was loyal to the soil. More than likely, he was back in the Beach, relaxing 'til it was time to go back to school. For some reason, however, I was hesitating to call him. Something in my spirit was telling me something was wrong and I didn't wanna face it. My hands started to shake and my nerves got all bad. I closed my eyes, flashing back to my days in

Compton. I was seeing days of walking to elementary school with Dino, Jamie and Ray Grant. I saw days running from the corner store when niggas got to bustin'. I started to reflect on watching the big homies hanging outside apartment complexes blasting old West Coast music, C-walkin to everything, even if it was some bullshit rap that their homies recorded. I felt like I was distancing myself from the hood in a negative way, but I know that was just my conscious fuckin' with me. I sent the phone back to the home screen and tapped the phone icon. I had memorized my fam bam joint. It was just better that way. That's how shit was back in the days. When you fucked with a nigga, you embedded their number in your head. This new age shit was cool, but it was distancing us at the same time. If you lose your phone nowadays, niggas ain't know nobody number by heart. Niggas was disconnected. When we used to see a bad chick, we holla'd at her face to face. Now, we send a message to her inbox. All addresses were streets addresses and not ones with dot com added to the ended of it. I put the phone down for a minute since I had gotten into a serious thinkin' mode. I ran upstairs and grabbed my laptop from the room.

"Yo Ty?"

"Sup nigga," he said from behind the closed door. I cracked open his door to see him smoking a fat ass blunt.

"Damn nigga what you blowing on?"

"Nigga this the reggie. Just like the sandwich." My face frowned up. This nigga must have really been high.

"Nigga you know reggie is boo boo right?"

"Nah. Nah," he said, laughing and coughing. "This shit named after a sandwich. You'll see though." Yeah, my homey was done. "What you need though?"

"What's the wifi code?"

"It's downstairs by the television, on an orange piece of paper." I went back downstairs, leaving him to his lonesome to handle his business. I hit the living room, grabbing the paper off the shelf underneath the television. I sat back down, popping open my magic book as I called it. I connected to the net and decided to search my nigga up on the book. I loaded his name into the search bar. "Keon Lorick." About six of 'em came up. I browsed until I saw the obvious sign that it was him. The letters "LB" in blue bandana type patterns. I clicked on his page, browsing through his pictures. I saw the days of the wrath he caused on the field for Poly. There were the obvious photos of him being on the block with his 20 homies. Then, I came across what made me proud to be called his family. There he was, dead in the middle of a group, excited as all to be damned. He was holding up the Sugar Bowl trophy from their monumental victory over LSU. It was amazing to see the greatness that he had achieved. I went back to my phone, scrolling through until I found his number. Here goes nothing I thought. It took forever to just hear the first ring.

"Hello?" I just paused. "Yo. Hello?"

"Cuz what's up?"

"Yo who dis?"

"Man this yo cousin Kev."

"Kev? Spooktown Kev?"

"Yeah man."

"Yo. Wassup nigga?" That's all I needed to hear. We were back on the same page. We chopped it up for the longest, but when it came to one question, I got something more than I expected.

"So cuz. When you wrote that shit on your blog. Was it really going down like that in New Orleans?" He took a deep breath.

"Man. After that game man. The shit was just terrible. The police were down there fucking with us all. When I say everyone, I mean all black folks. They cleared the whole French Quarter out. Anything that had a dark skinned complexion was getting snatched up. It wasn't just about a nigga getting shot. They made that fight an excuse to go all out full force on us. And that's when I realized cuz. No matter what we do. No matter how good we are in anything. When it all boils down to it, they want us extinct. I ain't tryna give them niggas any reasons to put me off this earth. I saw everything like wolves on a hunt. Once they smelled blood, they went in for the kill. So ever since I got back, I been on nothing but uplifting shit. I go home to the block. Try to rap to the homies about what I went through and how I saw the master plan they have created. And you know the bad thing is that we know the plan. It's sort of like lions on a hunt. You know, the female lions get into different positions. One chases a gazelle or some other animal out. The chase begins, and right when that gazelle thinks it's gonna escape, here comes another lion. Now, it shifts course, going for an alternate route out. But then, that path is soon cut off as it runs right into another waiting lion hiding in a bush. It's the same with us cuz. They see us go in one direction. Then, they hit us with a roadblock, making us take an alternate route. But then, right when we think we scott free, they come in from another side. Now, we are boxed in. Trapped. We can fight, but the fight will only wear us out until we can't fight anymore. You wanna know why Italians, Jews, Chinese, all them niggas can keep all of their own everything?"

"Nah."

"It's simple. We bred to leave the hood. They are bred to return and keep their own. We leave and don't come back to invest in our own. They know this. So they come in and take what we don't own and make it theirs. Asian man leave, come back to the same block and double it into another block."

"But you said they trap us."

"They do. Listen to what I'm saying. How do you trap a black man? Give him the illusion that he is safe. We make it out the hood, we hated in the upper middle class hood. We get hated there, but keep grinding, and then we move to the richy rich parts of the world. But then, nothing changes. Your skin is still black. And then, we are trapped. You can't be poor. You can't be in the middle. You can't be rich. It doesn't matter. Your skin overrides all that. That's what I learned. We made a university millions. We went to a major bowl and won. We all maintained grades and carried ourselves well without incident. None of this shit gone matter when we leave. That's what I realized. So, cuz, it was less about the fight, and more about the realization that no matter where we go, its an opportunity to get at us. Feel me?" Indeed I did feel what cuz was saying. Long gone was the mindset of blue raggin. Now, I saw a man being formed inside the skull of a freshly graduated 23 year old. I ended that night around midnight as we stayed on the phone gossiping like two old hens. He was headed back to Laramie in a week and a half to start getting ready for his postgraduate Master's courses. Me on the other hand, I was headed to dreamworld in a minute. I stopped playing on my phone long enough to go outside and catch a good whiff of the Oregon air. I started to think about life in another sense. I thought about the biggest lesson that I had just learned. It wasn't necessarily about loyalty to yourself. It was about loyalty to your people. That's what the Latinos, Jews, Italians and Asians had. Why not us? In that instance, I was trying to figure out a way to stop asking why and start asking what, as in what is the role I need to play?

"Wake yo ass up nigga." I rolled over to not only notice Ty, but also that I was in all of my clothes from last night. Man, no wonder I was sweating profusely. Thank God I wasn't on one of those plastic wrapped couches from back in the day. I woulda been damn near dehydrated and in need of an IV.

"Take a shower man so we can hit the city and get some grub."

"What time is it?" Ty looked at his watch.

"It's 10:02. Time to get yo' ass up." He smacked my foot and headed upstairs. I got up and headed upstairs myself to get my clothes so I could shower up and roll out of here. I didn't know where we were going, but I do know that I was hungry as a hostage. I went on head and showered, throwing on a hanes tee, some blue jeans and an X fitted cap. Crazy enough, as Ty came out the room, he had on the same shit, minus the X cap, as he had on a blue Charger fitted.

"Naw nigga. One of us gotta change. I ain't going out looking like a couple. And since I'm driving, it's on you."

"Man ain't this a bitch bruh. I was trying to be comfortable today," I told him.

"Just throw a regular shirt on over it. Matter fact. Nigga I got something for you." He walked into his room and I heard him rummaging through the closet.

"Here nigga." I unballed the shirt and looked at it.

"Man where the hell you get this from?"

"The old African shop over in southeast. You know every hood got an old elder in the hood that sell everything from shirts to incense." He wasn't lying either. I threw the shirt on, which was an airbrush of brother Malcolm's face and we peeled out. We hit the freeway on this lovely Friday afternoon. The weather was a nice 77 degrees and it just seemed like this day was destined for greatness. After about 30 minutes of driving, we came up on Northeast Alberta. It was one of the most narrow damn streets that I had ever seen. We parked on the main road that came off of Alberta. As we made the block and a half walk to the restaurant, I analyzed my surroundings and really saw what Los was talking about. It had the look of the hood, but it definitely wasn't. There were white people out walking in droves. Walking their dogs and out jogging.

"Yo Yo man. Let me get a pic in front of this mural?," I asked Ty.

"Man what you think this is a photo shoot?"

"Shut up man and take the pic." Ty shook his head as I ran over to the wall. It was very colorful, with blue, yellow, orange, black and other joints. In one section of the artwork, there was a repeat of men in suits and fedoras standing in a line. A big ass state of Oregon graced the wall as well. I liked shit like this and I appreciated art.

"You done superman?"

"Fuck you nigga," I responded to Ty as he laughed at me. We crossed the street and jumped in the long line that wrapped around the block.

"Damn nigga. Is this shit gone be worth it?"

"Man I wouldn't have brought you here if it wasn't. Be patient foolio." We sat there, seeming not to move more than an inch per hour. However, it wasn't that long at all. After about 25 minutes, we were at the register.

"Get the reggie," he told me.

"Man what if I want something else?"

"Bruh. My dude," as he put his hand on my shoulder. "You know what. I got it. Yeah can I get two reggie deluxe joints and two sweet teas?" He gave his card to the cashier, took the number and we headed off to the back patio area. The shit was a cool spot. I couldn't even front. I looked around. It was like hippie meets modern day and everything in between. It was definitely different, but difference is the greatest thing about life.

"Here you gentlemen go. Two reggie deluxe sandwiches."

My eyes literally popped out of my head. I mean, I saw greatness in my life. But *** damn. Talk about a muthafuckin' sandwich. This thing had a big ass, deep fried chicken breast, fried egg, some God blessed bacon and cheese, topped off with being smothered in some bomb ass sausage gravy. The question that I was asking myself was how in the hell was I gonna demolish this? I looked at Ty, but he paid no attention to me because he was tonsil deep in that damn sandwich. I had a fork, but I couldn't be no bitch man. I managed to get my fingers underneath the bread on the plate and I leaned my head down to take a bite. I started to float in space. I saw the sun, the moon, the mountains and the rivers. I swore I was like the old R&B group Az Yet with this shit. Man, neither one of us even talked unless the waitress was coming back to give us another round of sweet tea. Once I was finished, unlike Ty, I began to do the finger scoop. I took my middle and index finger, and scraped every piece of sausage gravy off the plate.

"Damn morpheous. Are you good?," Ty asked me.

"Yeah man. Yo. I need to take this thing back to the crib with me man. Man how in the good hell did you find this?"

"Like everything else man. Word of mouth." We sat there not out of wanting to take in everything. But, we sat there because we had the case of the itis. It took about 15 minutes for us before we got up. When we did, it was straight to the car and another 10 minutes of sitting in there before the boy even started up the car.

"Where we going?," I asked him as we got back on the road.

"I'm taking you to meet up with a cool ass brother of mines man. When I say the networking game is on point. I mean. It is on point." I truly didn't know what he was talking about, but I was damn sure about to enjoy the ride. I was on vacation and I had not a care in the world until Monday morning. I let the seat back and just enjoyed the Portland scenery. Also, I was kind of a weird dude in a way. I always observed the highway and street signs along the roads, just to see how each state differentiated from the others.

"So we headed to the airport man?," I chuckled. Fam bam looked at me with a smirk on his face.

"Yeah. Exactly." I knew my nigga was bullshittin', so I just sat back and enjoyed everything. We got to an outdoor strip mall called Cascade Station.

"What we doing over here?," I asked.

"We, My nigga. We gone, rather I'm gone run up in Ross for a quick minute to see if they got some simple brown dress shoes. Then, we headed to the airport to bounce."

"Wait a minute. Hold on," I said. "Like, I was just joking when I said we were headed to the airport. Like we going there for real?" He looked at his watch.

"Bruh. We flying out at 2:40 my nigga. It's already after twelve. We full off eats. Now, I'm bout to run up in here and see if they got these shoes. You wanted a vacation. I got you. But at the same time, I had plans too. Now, you can roll with me. Or, I can get you an uber back to the house and you can chill for the next two days in a different state." I was trying to contemplate everything he was telling me as he parked the car.

"But man. I ain't got no plane ticket. How the hell I'm gone get on?"

"Yo," as he shut the car door. "I got this. You coming or not?"

"Do I have a choice?"

"You always got a choice. The same way you making a choice to walk in here with me. You could've stayed in the car. You could've walked over there to Famous Dave's or Jamba Juice. You got choices." We walked into Ross as I was still scratchin' my head at the fact that this dude was really about to fly out and didn't tell me anything.

"Boom. Right there. In the size 11 section." He found what he wanted from a distance. He walked up, grabbed 'em and looked in the inside of 'em one time. "Yup. Size 11. Nigga let's go."

"Damn man. You aint gone get nothing else? I mean you were on this place like you were gonna get something major."

"I'm a brother foolio," he said as we got in the short line. "I know what I want. I see what I want. I get what I want. Then, I get the hell out. He walked up to the register and I just walked outside the door to wait for him. He had a point with what he said. That was the good thing about being a man. We knew what we wanted when we got to a joint. Whether it was the supermarket or the mall. A man's shopping trip is 15 minutes and five of that is finding parking. I wish I could say that shit about women. My mama used to kill me coming up whenever I would go to the mall with her. I mean, we weren't breaking the bank, so I could never understand why we would spend hours upon hours in the mall. She'd buy one thing out of one store, and then we were walking around for the next two hours in each and every store, like she was gonna buy the joint up. I didn't get that. Then again, as a man, we just don't get women sometimes because they do some crazy mess sometimes.

"Aight man," he said, as we entered back into the car. "We flying private. This ain't Ty from Compton who cut hair in the hood. This Ty. The grown man. The one who takes private charters when it comes to business. It's a lot of stuff you gone learn about me. Hopefully, it can help you in the long run."

"Man how did you establish all of this man?"

"Easy," he said, stopping the car for some pedestrians crossing the parking lot. "I followed a blueprint. Check this out. When I went to cut hair for those couple of months, the brother Eric, who ran that shit, he challenged me. Nigga had me come to Chicago and cut a brother head in a high school gym the size of a damn fortress. I was wondering like yo. Why in the good hell would a guy have me cut a random brother head in an empty gym that fits over 10,000? It took me a while, but I realized he was delivering me a subliminal message. Expand your mind. Expand your expectations on yourself."

"So you expanded your expectations based on cutting a guy's hair in a gym the size of The Forum?"

"You *** damn right I did. I cut that muthafuckas hair like my life depended on it. And the whole time, I imagined ten thousand plus muthafuckas lookin at me."

"I hear you man."

"Naw you hear me muthafucka, but you ain't listening. I spent six months. Six months cutting people's hair, competing all over the world with other muthafuckas who thought they were better than me. Taking money, making money and all that shit paid off. The shits chess not checkers."

"Aight Denzel," as I looked over at him sarcastically.

"Oh you caught that shit too?," laughing after he said that. "Naw but forreal nigga. This shit has opened doors. I'm taking you with me. Follow my lead. In two years. You won't care about a college education. They making money off of you in athletics and you don't see shit. Hell, make money for yourself and you'll be good." We pulled up to the airport long term parking terminal and Ty began making a phone call.

"Yeah man. Bringing my mans with me. Teach him the game. The business." I was just staring at him while he was on the phone. "Aight man. We'll see you at about five." It sounded more like a drug deal call instead of an I'm coming to see you call. "Let's roll man," he told me. We got out the car and started walking towards the airport.

"So what we gone do about clothes?," I asked. "No worries. We'll be taken care of when we get there. Draws, deodorant, all that good shit will be taken care of. Food, everything. Just enjoy the flight homey." I had no choice now but to really inquire about what Ty was really into. Shit didn't seem real that you would make a quarter million in six months from cutting hair. Have a custom made car for you when you get back. Live in the suburbs of one of the fastest growing cities in America. Something wasn't adding up and I just hoped that the feds wouldn't be coming for us any time soon. We got to the section of the airport where the private charters flew out of. "Afternoon Mr. Russell."

"How you doing Anita? This is my man. From way back. Mr. West."

"Sir," as she nodded her head down. I waved back, because I really wasn't comprehending all of this. That itch in my stomach was one that I was trying to scratch. "No bags today Mr. Russell?," another gentleman said.

"No not this time. I have a partner with me. No bags for him as well."

"Ok. The plane is gassed up and ready to go. The pilot still has a depart time of 2:45. And as last time, your complimentary meal is ready for you in the lounge, courtesy of Mr. Atterly."

"Thank you Scott," Ty told him.

"No problem." We walked over to the lounge where waiting for us was the smell of great food being cooked. "Juan. How are you?"

"Nothin much Mr. Russell. Lamar gave the call that you were near so everything is almost ready."

"Okay, okay. But Juan, this is my partner from back home Kevin. Kevin, Juan. He's an outstanding chef."

"Nice to meet you brother." He reached across the marble counter and shook my hand. I felt like I was in the presence of big money, but my nerves were still on edge.

"C'mon have a seat man." I obliged to Ty's request and we sat at a table. Before we could even say another word, our food was being brought out to us.

"Thank you," Ty told Juan.

"Scrambled eggs dawg?," I asked him.

"Yeah man. You ain't think we were gonna eat a full meal after mashing those big ass biscuits not even a few hours ago."

"What's in these joints man? This don't smell like normal eggs, nor look like em either."

"Its an ostrich egg man. Organic cheese, white wine and cajun seasoning. Just try it." It was crazy the things that I experienced sometimes, but this was something that I never expected. I mean, these were a lot of eggs. I grabbed my fork and took a bite into it.

"Damn man. Not bad."

"See. I told you. Open your mind up to different things man. You never know what you might like."

"Aight bruh. Enough of the food. I need to know what's going on from a friend to friend standpoint. What are you doing besides cutting hair?" Ty literally looked at me while still smashing on his eggs. "You gotta tell me bruh," I told him. He wiped his hands and mouth with his napkin, still with his eyes locked on me.

"Kevin. We been knowing each other for over 20 years. In all that time, I have never put you in a spot to where you had to fear for your life. If we were fearing for our lives, then we were running home together. From bullets. See me leaving wasn't about clippers. It was about learning how to be financially independent. It was about learning how to be my own boss. Pay my own way. Wake up and decide what did I wanna do each day of my life. See, what they don't teach you in college and us in school in general, is that the smart ones figure out how to do something one time and make money in their sleep. We are conditioned since birth to do something many times over and make money every two weeks. We are taught to buy homes and not land. We are taught to spend money and not invest it to make it grow. We are taught that everyone works, when that's not the case. The best shit you ever did to me was turn your back on me. And even though all is forgiven, I can never forget that shit. But, if you didn't do that, I would probably still be a nigga cutting hair in Carson. At the same shop. In the same environment. See all you know is that I got a call from my guy to head up here. All you knew was that I was around the world partying. Being in barber competitions. You didn't see the morning meetings on money management. You didn't see the marketing classes Eric made mandatory for us. You didn't see the millionaire and billionaire gurus who were flying in from different parts of the world just to get a damn haircut. You didn't see all of that. And all of that, is why I am at where I am today. See I took a blueprint and followed the directions. The majority follow directions without knowing the blueprints. Therefore, they don't know what they are building. For every bottle I popped, woman I screwed and picture I took, it was twice the time learning the money game. My investments, my clients, my marketing. They all allow me to do what I do. You wanna know why I'm going to Vegas? Rather we? It ain't just for a homey. Who by the way was working for the U.S. government in Asia not even a year ago and now is worth over seven figures. It's for expansion, networking and ensuring that my family will never have to worry about a damn thing. You *** damn right I left Compton and I ain't looked back. 'Cause what you didn't know is that I went back about my fourth month gone. I tried to rap to those niggas about what I was learning. When I started to see my money grow. And you know what they told me? Naw cuz. Too much work cuz. Sound like some underground covert shit cuz. Pyramid scheme cuz. That's all I heard. But let a muthafucka come out with a new gangsta rap album, and they will listen and hang on to every word that muthafucka gotta say. But you don't wanna listen to the homey who dodged the same bullets as you. The same nigga who went to high school with you. Fuck is that about man? Nigga I'm going to cut three rich, white folks hair for $3,000 a pop. Do you muthafucking hear me Kevin West? That's nine G's for maybe an hour and some change for cutting on some clippers. And I'm trying to take you to show you. That's why I didn't bring no clothes. I would've had you not came, but since you did, now I can show you how to spend without spending. See don't let these rap niggas fool you on TV. $5,000 bottle of champagne. Throwin $50,000 in a strip club. Muthafuckin' platinum and diamond chains running at a hunnid to two hunnid thousand. The fuck is the point of all of that? Four or five cars. Two or three mansions. 100 *** damn pairs of shoes. You see the shit they instilled in us? Pointless shit. Now, look at me. One car. Decked out, so you can talk about me. First gift to myself. Simple townhouse in the burbs. Invested money growing at more than 6% interest. Clients paying me thousands to cut they hair. You know E.J., The muthafucka who in the shop with me? He bought land in Maine. In the city while we were gone. Mofos paid him $15 million to develop more college buildings. Now he owns land in ten states, in areas that will be developed on within the next year or two. You gotta decide whether you wanna be normal, or whether you wanna be extraordinary. It's your choice."

I had never in my life had something broken down to me that complex. That stringent. My mind was immediately shifted in the matter of minutes. Ty said that and went right back to eating his eggs like it was nothing. That's how I knew he was serious about what he had said. I couldn't even eat anymore, as I was now in deep thinking mode. I no longer wanted the American dream of the house, family and the white picket fence. It was a reason that they called it a dream, because you had to be sleep to see it. I wanted the actual factual reality. We boarded the plane an hour later and took off. In the air, Ty was knocked out. Me, I was busy looking at the clouds through the window. I had never in my life been on a private chartered flight. Hell, I had never even been to Las Vegas in my whole entire life. This wasn't what you called becoming a member of the mile high club, but being a mile high privately over the sky was something that many didn't get to experience in life. See I wasn't just looking at this as a random trip anymore. I was now looking at this as an life altering event. I knew about the glitz and glamour. Vegas had the celebrities and the bright lights. The big time casinos and the underground mobs that controlled the city. The murder of Pac on the strip. Vegas was as mysterious as it was glorious. But, I wanted to learn everything about the money behind it. Fuck the partying. It was time to become a grown man.

"Hey guys. We are descending down into Vegas. Go 'head and strap up." Ty popped up with the quickness.

"Damn bruh. Were you sleep or just resting your eyes?," I asked him.

"Bruh, you know I'm a light sleeper. I'm well rested though. How you enjoy the flight?'

"Shit was gravy man. I didn't sleep at all. I was too busy thinking about the opportunities that await me as soon as I touch down."

"How many times you been here though?"

"Twice since I got here. And I'll be flying out a lot more in the future. It's too much money out here bruh and I for one am not gonna miss it."

"I feel you on that," I told him. We touched down and landed as smooth as Michael Jackson's moonwalk back in the day. We unbuckled our seats and arose to the opening of the plane doors.

"Welcome Mr. Russell. Glad to see you again." I was right behind him watching as he was greeted by a very beautiful woman.

"Sir," as she reached out and shook my hand. I nodded in agreement as I then looked up and saw a tall, clean cut brother in a bomb ass blue checkerboard suit standing next to a baby blue Phantom.

"My man Sly Ty."

"Mr. L.A. and I ain't talking 'bout Los Angeles. What's up boy?" They dapped up as I was standing at the base of the plane steps.

"You just gonna stand there slick rick or you gone come over and introduce yourself?" I didn't know this brother from the man on the moon. I wanted to say he was being disrespectful, but I kept my cool, seeing how he was with my homey and all. I walked on over, watching Ty's boy take off his shades as I approached. "Kevin," as I extended my hand out.

"Lamar. Marketing and millionaire guru. Thanks for coming down. So how long you and my mans Ty been rocking with each other?"

"Since Compton days man." He shook his head up and down.

"Compton. A jewel indeed. Bunch of red and blue niggas who can't comprehend coming together to see that the color green is more powerful. Don't worry though. It's the same shit in Detroit. Eastside Warren and Chalmers. Niggas don't comprehend over there either. I hope you do." The nigga definitely came off with an appeal as if he was brash and overconfident. But again, I didn't wanna jump to any conclusions before I really got the chance to sit down and mesh with the dude.

"Let's get in man. Go get y'all some gear." We got in the whip. Of course, Ty was in the front and I jumped in the back.

"Yo nice car man," I told him.

"Thank you," he replied back.

"Gimme six months and I'll double up. And you gimme one day and you can do the same." I simply soaked in his words as we rolled off into the hot Vegas summertime. Thank God for A/C, because it was hot as hell outside. I'm talking at least 105 degrees. On the flip side, it was dry heat. It wasn't like that Midwest and South heat with humidity in the air. It would have probably felt like 120 then.

"So how long you been out here bruh?," I asked him.

"Over ten years man. I lived in Asia the last two. Actually, you heard of Guam?"

"Nah."

"Well, it's a U.S. owned island, but that shit is a part of Asia. Anyway man. I went out there for a government job and did my thang for a while. Then, I met a nigga named Puncho. Puncho challenged me to do better. Puncho challenged me to enhance my mind. He was into direct marketing and he put me on game. I was kinda skeptical at first, but once I got the aspect on how to draw niggas attention, then I was gravy. I built up my clientele, my word game and my dress game. And that was all she wrote."

"So where's Puncho?"

"My nigga went down to Houston to run things down there. I came back here."

"Shit I thought you two niggas was gonna end up killing each other the way you told me the story the first time," Ty told him. Lamar let out some extreme laughter.

"Yeah man. That's what I thought too. It was days that I wanted to kill that nigga. And I'm pretty sure he was gonna try and kill me. Hell, I thought he would sneak up on me in the lil coffee shop over there and murk me. But two great minds gonna butt heads. Now, look at us. Shit nigga, look at you." I sat back, analyzing everything about ol' boy. His demeanor, his mannerisms, everything. We hit up a spot not too far for the airport. Lamar called it "The Lick." When we walked in, him and the dude behind the counter dapped up.

"A Marley, you know Ty. But this his man's Kevin. He on the team too. Plug my guy with a G worth."

"A G worth of what?," I asked.

"Clothes nigga," Ty said. "You ain't got shit to wear."

"You ain't got shit either."

"I know I don't, but I know what I'm getting in here and I can pay for it. Don't question it man. Just roll with it." Marley directed me to the back of the joint as Lamar and Ty stayed up front. Ol' boy measured me from head to toe, then took me back out to the front.

"I got some shit for you man. Italian cotton looks good on you. Breathable and comfortable. He provided me with three short sleeved button up joints, all with different colors and design patterns. I also got three different pairs of jeans. They didn't look like anything special, but when I tried everything on, it felt good. I definitely didn't see all of this adding up to $1,000. "$900 even L.A.," Marley told him. Man my eyes got big upon Marley saying that. I mean, I looked at my mans hand him the black card like it was nothing. Three jeans and three shirts costing $900, all because of material. Man, this was some next level shit. I mean, I know niggas paid bukoo prices for Tru Religions, Gucci and all of that, but that was just because they were paying for a name. I guess I had to just get used to this. We rolled back out, hitting the strip. Man, cars galore wasn't the word. It was almost a parking lot out here.

"Yo' first time here right?," Lamar asked me.

"Yeah bruh. Never seen no shit like this ever."

"Trust me. It'll grow old if you live here. But the cool shit is that you will always meet new people from all walks of life. It took us about a smooth 25 minutes before we got through the strip. Fam turned off and hit the road again, headed out to God knows where. About ten minutes later, we were entering into a gated community, with some phat ass cribs. These weren't no Beverly Hills mansions, but they were some extravagant homes. We pulled up into the garage of a clad out brick home. I'd say it had to have at least five bedrooms.

"Yo bruh. How much you pay for this?," I asked him.

"The house or the land? I own both. Lil lesson for when you get big. Always own the land you live on. Don't pay attention to that shit that you got a house so you the owner. The bank still own your property so you renting at the end of the day. People just been programed to think they own for their own peace of mind." It was like deja vu all over again hearing about this land shit. I walked into the home with my clothes and my mouth just dropped. This place looked like a gem.

"Welcome to my joint Kevin. Five bedrooms, four bathrooms, a game room and a pool. All built from the ground up." This shit was something that you saw on the television on Lifestyles of the Rich and Famous. I had never been in something so magnificent in my life. I wanted to tell myself that it was a dream, but I know it wasn't.

"Just two years ago, brother, if you would've told me that I would be living the high life, I would've told you that you were full of shit. Now, it all came to."

"So how all this happen man?"

"Put your stuff upstairs in the first bedroom you see once you hit the top of the stairwell and meet me in the man cave downstairs." Lamar walked off and I looked over at Ty.

"Hey man," he said to me. "I been here before. I seen it all. I'm just waiting for clients. Go hear my mans out." I looked back up at the top of the stairs for a quick second then went up to put my things away. The first bedroom in view at the top looked more like a mini lounge. Plush couches, pictures and a flatscreen lined the walls. A picture of the great Muhammad Ali and Joe Frazier when they had their epic *"Thrilla in Manila"* bout sprawled across the furthermost wall over the king sized bed. I hung my clothes up in the main closet and headed back down. Ty was out of sight, as I didn't know where he was. I walked around, looking for the steps to the man cave area, but with every turn, I just walked into something more magnificent. *"NEXT TO THE KITCHEN!!!,"* I heard Lamar yell as I was standing directly in the middle of what seemed to be a mini restaurant. I walked down the stairs and into a true man cave. It had movie theatre style seating with a huge screen that was at least 84 inches. He had Detroit everything down here. Framed Red Wings and autographed jerseys, which were autographed by Chris Chelios and Megatron. Replica Stanley Cup trophies in glass cases. Yeah, it was nothing but hometown love. There was also a football jersey in a frame that wasn't NBA or college.

"Whats this?," I asked him.

"Man thats my old basketball jersey. They closed my high school a while back, but it's always gone be Finney in my eyes. I give two fucks what they built and call it now. East Village some shit, or whatever the fuck its called."

"So you can hoop huh?"

"Yeah man. Oh don't think you the only one who can get it in. I got down in my day. But I traded in basketball for bucks."

"What's up with the number 7 football jersey with no name? That's yours too?"

"Yeah man, and it's just sheer symbolism. The number seven has always mystified me. Vick got fried, but Ben didn't. I'm tellin you. That number been a downfall for our athletes. Kevin Johnson, Lamar Odom, Brandon Roy with his fucked up knees. Trust. It's gone be another nigga soon. Trust me. Nigga gone probably throw it back with a fro and a black fist."

"So why did you wear it?," as I sat down two seats down from him, kicked back, just looking around at everything.

"Cause I break curses. So what you in school for man?"

"Behavioral science."

"Good. Good. So lemme ask you. Is that job gonna allow you to be stress free and do everything that you wanna do in life?"

"Well," as I cleared my throat.

"You need a drink man?"

"What you got?"

"Take yo' pick," he said, as he grabbed a remote and pressed a button. Just as he pressed it, a portion of the wall slid open and bottle upon bottle appeared.

"I got everything from simple wine to Henny to Gem Clear."

"The fuck is Gem Clear?," I asked. "Man trust. You don't wanna fuck with that bruh unless you a hardcore vet in drinking. I had a homegirl in Guam gimme a shot of that while I was living there. Let's just say that was the first time I became drunk off of one shot."

"Umm," I said cautiously. "Let me get some Henn bruh. You got Coke?" He gave me a look as he began to get up.

"Man that's like asking a fat man do he have clogged heart arteries." He strolled over to the wall, grabbing the bottle of Hennessey and continued over to the refrigerator to get the Coke that was sitting in there. He poured me up a glass and brought it back over.

"Thanks bruh."

"No prob," as he sat back down. Damn I told myself in my head. My nigga had fixed my drank up right.

"Whew that hit the spot. But man, yeah. I wanna make money with it, but I wanna help the hood more than anything."

"That's cool. I can fuck with that," as he sipped a drink himself. "But. No matter what you do. You gotta remember at the end of the day, you gotta be happy. Now, I ain't saying nobody should work. We need doctors, lawyers, dentists, all that shit. But I'm trying to make as many self employed brothers as I can. I mean look. Who would've thought marketing would've taken me as far as it did?"

"Who's that," I asked him, as I saw Ty let someone into the house on the camera feed.

"Just one of three million dollar clients who need their hair laced up."

"Million dollars?"

"Yeah brother. Million dollars. As in over $200 million worth." I stood up slowly in that moment and really just stared at the camera screen. That was a handsome ransom and something that you just couldn't ignore.

"And how much you say Ty getting paid to cut this man's hair?"

"Three G's, with probably a couple hundred in tip." I just shook my head and sat back down. "See man," as Lamar got up to pour himself another drink. "I had to decide what's better for me. The hood or this. I ain't been back to Detroit since 2014 and I don't plan on it."

"Why not?"

"Hell why? Aint shit there. Niggas dying and shit for no reason. Niggas ain't got no jobs. No hope. No nothing. Why would I wanna surround myself with that negativity?"

"But shit happens everywhere man." He laughed when I said that and took another drink. "What's funny bruh? It's true," I asked him.

"Man, that's the biggest cop out that people use everywhere. Oh shit happens everywhere. Niggas try to justify anything to stay in an area they know ain't conducive. You go to Detroit. Niggas still shooting up clubs. You ain't gone catch that shit out here. Every club cost $25 and up to get into. You gotta dress. Ain't nobody tryna act up in a suit and tie. But niggas will act up in baggy clothes and fitted caps. Ok, what's next. Its crime everywhere. That's gone be the next shit. Cool. What's more prevalent? A nigga getting killed in Detroit or a nigga getting killed here? I mean, Vegas got hoods, but you gotta helluva lot more escape options out here. The fuck you gone do in the D? Go from the Westside to the Eastside? I learned over time that people say that bullshit it happens everywhere to justify and make themselves feel good for staying in a terrible situation. Not me bruh. Fuck all that hood shit. They can keep it." Our conversation continued on throughout the night, going back and forth from talking about direct marketing, and watching sports classics on the huge screen.

"What y'all niggas down here doing man?" We both turned around to see Ty walking in the room.

"Shit man. Chillin' and hoping ya mans come on board."

Ty walked around to sit down and looked at me.

"Well man. You down?"

"I gotta think about it bruh."

"That's cool," Lamar said. "It's what. 9:43. A Ty, how much you get for the two heads you sliced up?"

"Total it was eight grand." Lamar looked over at me. "And all that was achieved by marketing and direct approach. Now tell me one job in the hood you gone make that amount of money in one night without looking over your shoulder or running from the cops?"

"Man I ain't say I wasn't down. I just gotta think about it."

"Too me," as Lamar finished off his drink. "That means you don't wanna expand your life. But hey, if living financially free ain't important to you, it's gravy man. No knock on you. At least while you here, party it up with a nigga. Let's go get showered up and hit one of these clubs." I really didn't wanna bounce out anywhere, but I was on someone else's time, so I rolled with the plans. At eleven o'clock, we were all cleaned and pressed up. We jumped into the Phantom and headed down to the strip.

"Where we going Lamar?," I asked him.

"TAO. Inside the Venetian. One of my favorite spots. Got a few A listers in there tonight." We pulled up in front of the hotel, automatically getting valet parking and stares from on lookers. We were all clean as a whistle and I had never in my life felt like this ever. I really thought I was on a red carpet without a red carpet. I was slicked out in khaki and black Italian everything, with some gator shoes to match that Lamar let me use for the night, seeing that we wore the same size.

"Lamar. My guy." He dapped the bouncer up as we walked ahead of everyone and straight to the entrance. "A man. I got two of my partnas here. I need my usual."

"You got it." The bouncer let the rope back and we walked inside. We made our way through the night crowd and headed for a private table. The DJ had the music hitting and we were indeed living the highlife. She was fine too.

"YO WHO THAT DJ???!!!," I asked Lamar over the noise.

"DJ LADY P!!!," he shouted. **"FINE THAN A MUTHAFUCKA TOO!!!"** I saw next to us a few of the Warriors were in town, sitting in the V.I.P. section next to us. The way Lamar chucked up the deuces to them, it was like he knew them personally and not like a hey how you doin' type. I had never experienced life like this ever. We weren't carded for anything. All of our needs were taken care of. Crazy enough, we didn't even drink alcohol while we were here. It was straight cranberry pineapple mixed drinks. A few lovelies joined us throughout the night and that's when I knew that this life was something amazing. I thought back to a long time ago when I told Ty that I always wanted this life. But deep down, I saw that we had switched roles. He was now living the high life, cutting millionaires. Me, I now wanted the simpler life in helping people in low privileged areas. I really didn't wanna tell myself that, but I saw that the shift had occurred. I let myself loose for the entire night, occasionally dancing with a lovely and mingling with the high life as I called it. I couldn't believe I was here at this point, but then again, we never know what life will bring for us day to day.

I woke up the next morning, tired and still in awe of everything that happened. When I looked over at the clock, I saw that it was only 7:35 a.m. I could've swore we didn't make it into the house until at least 4 o'clock. I didn't drink or anything, but it was troubling that I couldn't remember a lot of the events from the night before. Unfortunately, as hard as I tried, I couldn't fall back asleep. I arose from the bed and walked into my bathroom. To my surprise, a brand new toothbrush wrapped in plastic was waiting for me. Man, this trip was something else. I slapped that AIM toothpaste on there and gave my teeth a good bathing. After that, I slipped on my tennis shoes and walked around the house. It was quiet as a mouse in here. I slid downstairs and towards the backyard. I let open the huge patio door and caught some of the Vegas heat. I said some because it was still early morning and I know the heat wasn't at its peak yet. I walked around the monster backyard of his in amazement. I walked next to the pool looking at the basketball rim that was sticking out of the water. This was truly crazy. It really had me contemplating my life's purpose now. Stay loyal to my people and help bring them out of a situation that I escaped. Or, look out for myself. Cause lets face it. You can't do anything impactful in this world if you do not have the ability to take care of yourself. I really had a decision to make. And whatever I decided to do, I really had to be able to live with myself. Five o'clock came and the house was now packed like a muthafucka. The pool party was on. There was a gaggle of white girls here. Now, myself, I was pro black, all black, all the time. I wasn't into white girls like that. But, for Lamar, it was like he came out here and caught white girl fever. This pool looked like something that should've been happening down on the strip. He had private cooks on the grill, a DJ blasting music from his own equipment. I mean, this shit was beyond fun. I simply rolled with the punches and enjoyed myself the entire time everyone was over here. And seeing how this was a private residence, wasn't no such thing as bikini tops. There were titties hanging out everywhere and wasn't nann one of them sagging or anything. I mean, I was giving piggyback rides, taking wild pics and shooting girls with old ass super soakers. We had been at it since 12 o'clock. For a Saturday afternoon, this was a great one. Portland was far out of my mind.

Vegas had me going. The best thing is that there were only about 20 guys here, but there were about 60 girls. I wasn't a mathematician, but 3 to 1 ratio meant that there could be a good amount of threesomes going on in this mofo. Nighttime fell and everything was still poppin' around ten. There were less people in the pool, but everyone was still here. As I walked in the house with a bangin' snow bunny on my arm, I saw that it was one huge orgy going on. I scratched my head on the inside because I was really trying to tell myself that this wasn't real. I was dreaming all of this. And like all the other times I thought that, I realized that I wasn't dreaming. This shit was on and poppin'. Me and baby girl, we made it upstairs to my room, and it was all she wrote from there. Well, let me take that back. One of her friends joined us up there and I had the greatest damn sex session in my whole damn life. Shit, I didn't have a care in the world. I was in my young twenties and I'll be damned if I wasn't living the life, even if it was just for a weekend. We flew back to Portland early the next morning. Seven o'clock to be exact. I was dead tired on the plane, but a private joint is definitely different from a commercial joint. I didn't have to fight for space with someone else. I had all the room in the world for myself. I slept the whole flight back, along with Ty. When we awoke, which was two minutes after nine, we jumped in his whip that was waiting for us and drove the 40 minutes to Tualatin. I needed all the sleep that I could get, seeing how I had to jump on another flight at five o'clock this Sunday evening. We made it to the crib after ten, feeling refreshed, but still damn near completely out of it. Walking in the crib with clothes in my hand, I threw everything down on the couch and plopped down on it.

"So what you think about that trip man?," Ty asked me, raiding the refrigerator for whatever he was looking for.

"Man," I said in the groggiest voice. "It was wild. Informative, but wild. What you bout to cook up in there?"

"Top Ramen and hot dogs. Oh don't get it twisted. Just because a nigga live in the 'burbs, don't ever think that I ain't too good for some wax noodles and crap rolled up into a piece of meat."

"So wait a minute. I thought you were into the big baller lifestyle?"

"Man, fuck that shit. I mean Lamar, the nigga cool, but I for damn sure ain't forgetting who the fuck I was for the majority of my life. It's one thing to move somewhere that is conducive to your growth. But, to just forget that you came from the struggle, I can't fuck with that."

"So why you fuck with him?," as I sat up on the couch. "Easy nigga. The money is good. Someone gone fly me down to cut a rich dummy hair for a few G's. I was born at night, not last night."

"But ain't you selling yourself short for a quick buck?" He put those noodles in the pot and came into the living room. "Nigga who selling themselves short? Nigga I ain't selling shit but some clippers. Shit, you got YG and Nipsey Hussle making money together. One's a blood. One's a crip. The one color they both have in common is green. Shit he black. I'm black. He know how to make green and I know how to cut hair to make green. You ain't gotta like the niggas you work with. But, if y'all got the same goal, then you make it happen. Shit look at Kobe and Shaq. Niggas hated each other to the core. But they made the shit work for three championships. You better get on board man and get up on the game. The shit chess, not checkers, and no this ain't a funny Denzel segment right now. This some real life shit. I love the hood, I ain't forgetting where I came from, but I damn sure ain't going back. The shit ain't conducive to me. You feel me my nigga?"

"As a friend. Nah, my nigga. I don't feel you."

"So what would you rather me do? Huh? Go grab a nigga by the hand and walk him thru the process?" With a quick thought, I answered him.

"Yeah. And you know what, as much as I love you like a bruh, I gotta tell you the truth. You've changed man and I can't feel it."

"Hold on a minute," Ty said as he walked back into the kitchen to pour himself a glass of water and cut the noodles off. He came back and sat on the opposite side of the living room, in his reclining chair. "Lemme tell you something. Bruh. I can't rep my city in my city. I can't put on for my city, in my city. This is it. This is life. I ain't a dumb nigga. But you are. You got the world twisted. Yeah you wanna go back. Be a counselor to the kids in the hood. Yeah, that's fine and dandy. But how you gone change the conditions of the hood? How you gone tell a child to be everything they wanna be and be a father figure to them, yet not change the environment? See I realized that with all the teachers we had. Oh sure, it was cool for some of them to actually be there and hear about our problems. Talk to us. Let us know that it was more on the outside than this. But what changed after we left those walls at Compton High? Not a muthafuckin' thing. Still had niggas with no dads. Still had niggas with no clothes or food. Still had niggas who had to sleep in the bathtub on a night in and night out basis. Still had niggas being scared to walk up and down East Caldwell out of fear of getting shot. Where they at nigga? Nowhere but the fucking hood. And you think I'm gone go back and talk to kids. Guess what? **THE FUCKING ADULTS DIDN'T WANNA TALK TO ME!!!** So what make you think a kid gone listen? Huh? Like really? You wanna teach kids something. Teach 'em to keep everything black owned as possible. Teach 'em the art of financial responsibility and freedom. Teach 'em the art of investment. We got a city of 90,000, and don't nann nigga, including the *** damn Mexicans own a muthafuckin' thing. See we happy with lil shit. A nigga put some computers in the school, we good. A nigga put some new basketball rims in the park. We good. And yes nigga, I read history. I know every time black people established their own neighborhoods, they destroyed them. Tulsa 1921. Central Park in New York, which was formerly Seneca Village. Rosewood, Florida. Now, where we the majority, all they do is put liquor stores and gun shops. So you say, oh we can get rid of that. No we can't. That shit embedded in our neighborhoods. Niggas so accustomed to mediocrity that it will literally take 100 years to break that mold. It's been embedded in at least three generations. Man, I ain't got time for the dumb shit. So if you think I'm dumb, so be it. I love Compton, but Compton don't love me. Ain't no loyalty to the streets. It gets you the grave or prison."

"But there is loyalty to your people."

"Again, ain't no loyalty. 'Cause the same niggas you give to, they'll turn their backs on you the minute you quit giving. And teaching a nigga is irrelevant, because everyone always want now, now, now. And if you can't see that, then I don't know nigga. I just don't know." I shook my head. That's all I could do. He cut the television on as I sat there chillin, watching local Portland news with him. Suddenly, a segment came on about a shooting that had occurred out there involving a counselor who worked at a youth center.

"See man. That's the shit that I'm talking about. I bet my mans was trying to help and niggas still tried to smoke him."

"C'mon man," I told him. "You can't base shit off of one incident."

"The fuck I can't. And I fucks with the hood, but the mindset of the many ain't there man. Like how the fuck you shoot the help? That's like a plumber coming to your house to fix your pipes but you smoke him for doing a good job. Man, you just don't see it."

"Naw. You just forgot where you came from." Ty cut the TV off.

"Man nigga fuck you. You the same nigga who flipped on me for doing better. You the same nigga who fucked around with a dude, but I ain't say shit. I could've been ended yo' hood pass a long time ago. But I didn't. 'Cause real niggas don't do that shit. But since you wanna be all happy pappy sappy, nigga get yo shit and get the fuck out."

"Really nigga?"

"Get the fuck out. Call the *** damn Uber. Matter fact, I'll call the muthafucka. Nigga if you think that I'm gone sell myself short for any nigga, you got me fucked up." I didn't even say shit. I simply went upstairs and packed up the rest of my belongings. Ty was steady going off downstairs as I heard his rants and raves going over a phone. I don't know who he was talking too, but I could careless. I had to get away from niggas who weren't conducive.

"A NIGGA!!! YO RIDE HERE!!!," I heard him shout from downstairs. Good, I thought. I had just finished and everything was everything. I got downstairs and he jumped up off the couch. "Hold on nigga. I'm a hold the door open for you." He held the door open for me. "Nigga lose my number. Don't ever call me again. Nigga forget that we even existed. I don't care about yo' family or anything else related to you. Fuck you nigga. Peace." I looked up towards the door. Neither one of us had even noticed Big Los was standing right there.

"Umm. Y'all niggas ok man?"

"Yeah," Ty said.

"My mans was just leaving." I gave that nigga an evil look and he responded with much of the same.

"A Big Los. Pleasure meeting you man."

"No doubt," he said, looking confused as ever. I walked off with my luggage around to the front of the garage where my Uber was waiting on me.

"Kevin," said the nerdy white kid out of the window.

"Airport." He popped the trunk and I threw my bags in there. The ride to the airport was a very quiet one, except for the driver telling me some stupid stories. I didn't wanna be rude and tell him to shut up. I simply said a few *"Ok's"* and *"Yeah's"* to make the time go by. I arrived there sometime after midday, meaning that I literally had five hours to just sit around and do nothing. My gate area was dead for this Sunday afternoon. All there were me, the two airline officials behind the counter and solitaire on my phone. Time was moving by slow and so was my life now. I took a break and discarded everything from my phone relating to me and Ty. Our pictures from parties, his number and any of his family. When I cut niggas off, I cut off everyone related to them. I ain't wanna fuck with you. That was just how I operated. Time passed and no one was filling up my gate area. By four o'clock, it was still a low crowd. I was thinking to myself that I know damn well a Southwest flight wasn't gonna be full. However, once boarding time was called, I saw that it wasn't. It was a good feeling, yet a somber one at the same time. I thought that this was a subliminal spiritual message to myself from something higher than me. It was like someone was telling me that my life was being emptied as well. I didn't know man. I just didn't know.

9 2018

"Kenny Man. You have to stay focused and bring yourself above your circumstances. This ain't life. What we see around here, this ain't life."

"But man Mr. West, what do you expect me to do? I ain't got no daddy. I ain't got no momma half the time. She working two jobs. Shit I ain't sayin ain't shit out there, but I gotta do what I gotta do to survive. I mean shit, you know what it is. You came up in Spooktown right?"

"Yeah I did."

"Ok. So you know what I mean." It was more than a difficult task getting these kids to try and listen to a different perspective. But, I understood it. When you are in dire situations, it doesn't look like a bright future is ahead of you. Times were harder than they ever were. No one wanted to be OG's anymore. What I mean by that is that people now calling themselves OG's weren't teaching proper principles to these kids. It was nothing but teachings about rob this nigga, kill this nigga, stay true for your family. The old head old heads, they actually taught you some shit. Hey, be book smart and street smart. Don't be afraid to read and expand your knowledge. Those niggas actually taught us how to make it in life and not just how to make money. That was the major difference between today and the yesteryear that I came up in. I was trying to emulate the times of yesteryear, but days like this, it seemed damn near next to impossible. I left Centennial campus that day and headed off to the crib in neighboring Long Beach about 30 minutes away. I split my time between Poly and Centennial, and also as an advisor at the campus of Long Beach State University. It offered me a challenge like no other. It allowed me to impact the hood, while at the same time to keep people who had made it out the hood to college on track. Life had passed by in a blur. Graduating early, as in after my junior year, I simply played basketball while working in counseling services for these children during my senior campaign. The job at Long Beach State I obtained allowed me to outreach past the campus. It was Friday now, however, and it was time for me to unwind and let my hair down. Off was the shirt and tie, and on was the jeans and t-shirt. I may have been in a better place mentally, but I still liked to relax. Tonight, at 9, I was gonna head to a conference at the Honda Center that I was invited too. Some of the most innovative minds in the world would be there speaking on life and how they overcame their challenges to get where they are today. I enjoyed seminars like that and it would definitely be worth making the drive, even though I was dead tired from the many adolescent fiascos I had to face. The shit was a chess match. Bloods, Crips, Ese's, even a lil brother who moved out to Long Beach to stay with his mother. It was even harder for him because all he knew was Chicago and life was very different from where he was from. Kids, they were indeed a handful, but they were definitely worth the fight because they were our future.

I walked into the Honda Center as soon as the doors opened at 8:15 p.m. My V.I.P. tickets ensured that I had two front row tickets to soak in all the knowledge and understanding that I could. Even though it wasn't a basketball game, they had the concession stands going like it was the NCAA regional finals. I got me some nachos with extra cheese, ensuring that I doubled up on the usual amount of napkins, because I damn sure didn't wanna spill anything on this sport coat of mine. I mingled around for a lil bit, talking to random people, networking and making connections. Once 8:50 hit, I hurried over to my seat in the first row. This was $100 that was well spent. Looking around, the stadium was now packed. It wasn't filled to capacity, but there were at least 6,000 people in here and I could dig it. Talking with kids in an office was one thing, but speaking to masses on a stage with you as the sole focus was a gift indeed. "Ladies and gentlemen. I welcome you to the great minds conference. Where legends become immortals." That introduction right there let me know what I had in store for the next two hours. I learned one thing from speaking with kids that translated to anytime you spoke to people or a single person. If you didn't get them locked within the first 15 seconds of making a speech, then until the time you were done, you would just be blowing hot air and the listener wouldn't be listening to you. It would simply go in on ear and out of the other.

"Ladies and gentlemen, presenting our first speaker. Originally from Compton, California. He is a major six figure income earner. He is going to share his story and the power of marketing and an open mind. Presenting, Mr. Wayne Russell."

My eyes got big as the crowd erupted. To the world they saw Mr. Russell, but I only saw Ty. And actually, I didn't see Ty. I didn't even recognize who he was at this point. He had ditched the cornrows turned dreads for an all even with a nice line up. His usual thin mustache was now accompanied with a huge beard as seen on CT Fletcher. Times had changed and indeed he had with them. As he walked out, waving to the crowd, mic piece attached to his ear, he crossed the section of the stage which was in front of me. While the crowd continued to clap, he stopped dead in front of me. We locked eyes. We were seeing each other again for the first time in almost two years. It was a look of shock and awe. What we were seeing were two totally complete strangers. He took his focus off of me and began to say thank you repeatedly.

"I grew up in Compton. There, you are taught that loyalty to the streets is more important than loyalty to self. Where loyalty to the homies is more important than loyalty to self. And lastly, I was raised in Compton. Where." He stopped and looked at me. He then walked up to the front of the stage and looked directly at me. "Where hot cheetos and nacho cheese are a flippin' good meal." The crowd let out a laugh and I went back to calming the tension that built up inside of me. I had just known that he was gonna take a shot at me in that moment. To my surprise, he didn't. He stayed on stage for about 20 minutes, speaking of his humble beginnings of cutting hair on the block and in the school bathroom, to moving around the world and becoming world class at his craft. He ended his speech with the same response as he entered with. Waving to the crowd, he pointed at me and exited the stage. I had joined in the standing applause. Not out of how great his speech was, but simply out of respect for what we once had. Over time, as we become grown, you learn to just let some shit go. Almost two years ago, we ended on a sour note. No communication had occurred from either one of us. In that time, a lot had changed. My mother was recovering from the numerous chemo sessions that took her energy from suffering from a rare form of cancer called sarcoma. As for Ty, his grandma was gone. Brody, the barber that he once cut with in Carson, he went back to the penitentiary, serving a 25 year sentence for second degree murder. As for Dominique, he ran the barbershop and had a whole new crew that was slicing up heads. Gristle, the Mexican brother, he left Carson after a year of cutting and went to Miami, opening up a barber joint called "Island Cutz." Him, a Dominican, Cuban, Haitian and a Trini had come together and they were now the #1 barbershop in Southern Florida. Baseball players were some of their biggest clients. As the crowd dispersed, I took my time trying to see if Ty had stuck behind along with the other big wigs. There were still a grip of people in here talking, networking and all of that. I got tired of looking and simply went back to my seat, calmly waiting. I pulled out a book in the meantime "There Goes The Hood" by Lance Freeman. I simply read through it passing the time by when I felt a tap on my left shoulder. I looked over to see Ty.

"Bruh," he said to me. I rose up. We simply looked at each other face to face. It was like looking at your own blood that had just gotten out of prison.

"Is it Wayne or Ty?," I said.

"Its family." We hugged and it felt like no embrace I had ever had with the homey. We were back and the shit felt good.

"Man yo," I said, as we sat back down. "Like man when you came out on that stage, I was like yo, this nigga really made it." He laughed.

"Yeah man. I mean, I came out and saw you, and in that time, my life froze. Like, it seemed like a few seconds to everyone else. But man, I literally went back to the days coming up on the block. From Kennedy Elementary, Compton High, to both our black asses being dragged to church on occasion by Mrs. Porter."

"Yeah nigga," I said, laughing at the Mrs. Porter line. "Them were the days. Yo. Where Mrs. Porter old ass at?"

"Man you know she still ticking at 97," Ty said.

"Get the fuck out," I responded.

"Nigga I ain't bullshittin. I went back two days ago man. She still at the same crib off Johnson. Still got niggas respecting her. Still saying *'Baby, pull up them pants before you trip and fall.'* And like always, them niggas do." Mrs. Porter was in Compton the majority of her whole life. In the same house she was raised in. She was an inspiration to all of us. She was there when The Hub was a majority white folks city. She didn't let them push her out or anything. She stayed right there and helped us out whenever she could. It was pillars like her in the community that we had to ensure stayed good.

"Wait man. You went back?"

"Nigga I'm from there. I was never scared or abandoning niggas like you thought. My whole thing where we all got misconstrued at was simply stating the fact that you can't waste time on those who have a closed mind. And just like I thought, I came 'round in a suit. A nice car. I know niggas were plotting on me. Few of the youngins were some years older. They asked me how I did it. They couldn't believe me when I told 'em that it was simply cutting hair and broadening my scope of people and things in general. I got met with the nigga you lyin lines. Cuttin' hair don't get you that. Nigga who yo' Mexican plug? All of that. So man, it wasn't me turning my back on anyone. It was that I know that once someone has their mind set to a certain degree and lifestyle, nothing that you tell them will be able to make them change it. Just like old people. They're stuck in their ways."

"Man bruh. Like, when I graduated school, I saw the shit first hand again. Like I was working for Long Beach State, which I still am. I started to branch out and help the kids at Centennial twice a week. I remember when I first started man. It had to be about three weeks in. A bunch of senior cats up there were waiting on my car when I left from there round four o'clock.

"Yeah man, Mr. West. Heard you were raised over in Spooktown." Now you know the first thing I'm thinking is that oh shit, these lil niggas bout to kill me. But, I just kept cool with 'em. I told 'em yeah I was raised in Spooktown. Then, one of the young niggas asked me so why I'm working in they hood. You know what it is. Why even put yo'self at risk? And I told them. You can't change an adult when they are grown, 'cause they are an adult. But, when you're young, your mind is still growing. I told 'em to see beyond all that blue and red shit, because I could easily take 'em to Chicago and show 'em savage life."

"So you lied to em?"

"Naw nigga. I did a quick lil venture for one of my classes. Man they sent us to the Chi to get a down to earth urban experience away from L.A. Man lemme tell you. Now that's hard life. Shit you think L.A. crazy? Go to Chiraq as they call it."

"You forgot I been, but I didn't get too deep in the streets."

"Yeah man. I mean, I rode around with one of the counselors one day. He was a former gang chief out there. Man we coming down some block and he tell me that he has to drive his car a certain speed or else the young niggas would shoot him, even though they knew his car, his family, all of that. It was so many rule changes out there that I had never seen. You wear your hat a certain way and they on you. I didn't even wear one out there. Those two weeks showed me what really is plaguing our kids man. And I'm hoping, just hoping, that you using your money for more than to live. Not knocking you, but just hoping." Ty then pulled a card out of his wallet and handed it to me.

"Whats this?," I asked.

"C.U.T.S Cultural Upliftment To Succeed. It's my business

man. I uplift these kids, culture wise, so they can do bigger and better shit. Why just cut hair you know?"

"But you said years ago that you don't teach."

"I don't teach niggas who don't wanna be taught and that's the majority of the hood. Plus, I don't teach basic bullshit. Again, most of us teach kids to go to school, go to college, give back. Fuck that. How you gone change an environment if you don't know anything about that environment except for the buildings? Think about it. We judge the hood by landmarks. Yeah nigga this the traphouse. Yeah this the park where so and so got shot. This little pathway right here, so on and so forth. Everything is a landmark for something negative. You never hear someone say this is the high school where I learned life management. This is the job that I learned the aspect of savings and interest. That's what I mean man. You uplift these kids out of something they are not accustomed too. You can't uplift a muthafucka out of something they see everyday. What I'm gone uplift someone in the hood with? A two bed to a three bed in the same environment. You gotta change it all. The dress, the look, the demeanor, the people, all of that. So again, It wasn't me being disloyal to the soil. But, I had to change everything around me to change the results in my life." Everything had started to come full circle now, as not only I had a full understanding of my mans methods, but a general understanding on how life in general went.

"Wanna grab a bite to eat? My treat," Ty asked me.

"I would hope it's yo' treat man. You got the mega bucks big time speaker and shit." We shared a laugh and rolled up out of the Honda Center. "Where we going?," I asked Ty.

"Shit to the waiting whip. And there go my bitch." I was in awe as I saw the Aston Martin sitting on the street with two men in black suits on each side.

"Damn nigga, that's us?"

"HELL NAH!!!," he responded. "Fuck I look like driving a sports car round this ho? There she is right there," as he pointed. What he pointed too was a tinted out, blacked out Escalade. "C'mon bruh. Hop on in. Take you to my mans suite in the telly. Introduce you two." We walked in the truck, doors held open by the chauffeur. Man, the shit smelled like money. Me and Ty conversed the entire time on the road. At no point did I even inquire about where I was going. Truthfully, I didn't care. We kicked back, drinking on some cranberry-pineapple drink as we pulled up into the front of a building.

"Where we at man? All I see is ritzy people through this tint."

"Beverly Hills Wilshire man. Only the high rollers stay here." Our door was opened and we were met with the highest quality greeting I had ever heard. We walked in the hotel and were actually escorted to the elevator. In that moment, so many thoughts ran through my head. I was literally trying to think who in the good hell did this nigga know? I mean, we were getting escorted, so it had to be major money up there. Crazy as it sounded, I thought Obama and his kinfolk were up there waiting. We hit the top floor to the penthouse suite. The minute we stepped foot off of the elevator, I just stopped and put my nose in the air.

"What you doing man?," as Ty looked back at me.

"Man," I told him, still with my nose in the air. "You remember The Rock when he used to wrestle and he would say you smell what the Rock was cooking?" I took a good inhale and whiff.

"Aaahhh," I let out. "That's what I'm doing. I ain't never experienced no shit like this bruh."

"Okay man. Do ya thing, but c'mon. You can smell other shit like food when we get in here." The escort knocked on the door three times. We patiently waited for someone to open up. No answer. The chauffeur again knocked three times on the door. **"ONE MINUTE!!!,"** we heard from inside the room. We were all quiet out in the hall as we stood and waited. Ty knew who it was but the suspense was killing me. Finally, the door started to slowly creak open until it was fully opened.

"Ty man, what's eating up ya plate man?"

"Ain't shit man. Trying to grind bones and make dollar bills. You know how it is." These two dapped up, taking ebonics to a whole new level. From what I was hearing, I would probably assume ol' boy was from the Yay area.

"Yo bruh. This my mans Kevin West. He works out of Long Beach State, assisting in the teaching of Behavioral

Studies. He also helps out the inner city cats in Compton."

"You from the same parts of Compton as my mans here?," dude asked me.

"Yeah bruh. We came up together." He gave me a strange look that was kind of throwing off my vibe.

"C'mon in here. Grab a seat." Ty directed his hand as I entered first. As cool as this shit was, this shit was still uneasy.

"You gentlemen want something to drink?"

"I'll take something to eat if you got that," I told him. He turned around and looked at me.

"Shit man. In the other room, I got a platter of buffalo wings hot off the press. Take ya fill." I got up and obliged, because I wasn't gonna turn down no free food. I grabbed 16 of those joints, along with four breadsticks and made it back to the primary room, which was a fortress. They were sitting down and I joined them.

"So Compton huh?," he asked me. "You know any niggas from Leuders Park?"

"Yeah," I responded, biting into a wing.

"Damn man slow down. Don't chew your finger off," Ty told me.

"Ahh. Leuders Park," the guy responded. "Amazing how you can go from damn near getting your ass whooped for trying to be accepted to now your own people not wanting to accept you because of your status."

"So what's your name man?," I asked him.

"Ramses. Ramses Osiris Martin." I looked over at Ty with a crazy look on my face. All Ty did was shake his head. The Portland trip had now come full circle. I was starting to see just how small the world really was. All I had was one question.

"So man. How was that night in New Orleans? You know, after y'all beat LSU in the Sugar Bowl." My man's leaned back in his chair, hands folded, tilted his head back and took a deep breath. He came back up in a normal sitting position.

"Hold on bruh," he told me as he got up to go pour himself a glass of some high end champagne. Me and Ty looked at each other, not knowing what I had truly triggered. Ramses sat back down and took a sip. "Aaahhh, that's some good shit," he said, sitting his drink down on the table in front of him. "My parents truly know how to live and this gone be all me one day. Welp. New Orleans. New Orleans. New Orleans." Each time he said New Orleans, his voice tone got lower and lower. "Well," as he seemed to have gotten his second wind. "It all started with my nigga Nate yelling in the streets **THE CHAMPS ARE HERE LADIES!!!**"

ABOUT THE AUTHOR

With his seventh release, Joe McClain Jr. has become an internationally known author. With two Best Sellers on his resume, he has ventured out through the entertainment industry to implement the importance of reading and writing throughout communities in America. Notable stars who possess his books are NFL Hall of Famer Jerry Rice, billionaire Mark Cuban, Actor/Director Duane Martin, Grammy award winning R&B star Eric Bellinger, Wu Tang pioneer GZA and other impactful people in the entertainment industry. Further information about him can be found on his website www.authorjoemac.com

ALSO AVAILABLE

When his father passed at 12, Mr. Terrelle Washington grew up fast and survived the dangerous streets of East Chicago, Indiana. After finding out his deceased father left him a large inheritance, he decided to leave for California and achieve his dream of becoming a published Author. However, the land of Hollywood stars was soon transformed into a maze of unforeseen obstacles he never expected on his way to the top. How will it play out??? Will he achieve his dream, or will it be shattered into a nightmare of failure

UPROCK PUBLICATIONS PRESENTS

BANDAGES

JOE MCCLAIN JR

A hard life in the inner city. Made it through. About to prepare for the next step of most young men. College. That was all until one fateful night to where freedom was taken away. Now, in the battle of his young life, a young man has two options. Die in prison, or snitch and possibly get another chance. Either choice will draw consequences, but what will he choose??? What wounds will be healed, and what wounds will be re-opened???

Star Jackson is pregnant and seeing her husband off for a six month deployment to The Persian Gulf. With Carl gone, Star will take herself out of her comfort zone and go search for the answers to her past which she so desperately seeks. However, during her journey, she will get many answers that she was not prepared for. In turn, it will open up many memories that lay dormant that are now seeking to devour her. With her husband gone and no one to lean on but herself, she must overcome the opening of old wounds and heal new ones. In a race to find the truth, she will learn that the biggest threat to healing is facing yourself.

Ramses Osiris Martin wasn't like the typical black kid growing up in America. He had it made in life. He lived in a good neighborhood in Southern California, with wealthy parents and went to the best schools money could buy. However, even with all of that, he still faced a challenge that no doctor or amount of money could cure. That was simply trying to face the reality of what it is really like to be Black in America. Separated from his culture due to where he grew up, the young 16 year old is now on a journey to see who he really is. A simple trip to unfamiliar lands will test him to the very depths of his soul. Throughout it all, it will take him through hell and back. From the football field, to the country, the inner city and beyond, what lessons will stay entrenched in his soul for all eternity? What is the price that he will pay to see how deep the melanin roots are in his skin?

Joe McClain Jr. has taken the book world by storm over the past few years. Now, as he grows to a high level in his craft, he presents to his readers P.E.E.R.S: The five step process towards achieving greatness. Joe has taken his love for motivating the masses and put it all in this easy to follow guide of steps you can take to achieve greatness here on earth. The author/poet/ motivational speaker opens up on all aspects of his life and everyone's in general, giving you the tools you need to build empires. No, this book will not tell you how to get rich overnight or become the next great singer. It can however start you off in the right direction to begin the process of elevating yourself to levels you could have never imagined. P.E.E.R.S. is a powerful book that many of this generation will be talking about for years to come.

Ricky Walters grew up in the gritty streets of San Diego California. Upon quitting his security job, he meets an ex pimp name Trust who teaches him everything about the pimp game. Ricky ends up turning out a young Asian girl name Yuki, changes his name to Jackpot, and jumps knee deep in the pimp game. Jackpot makes a conscious decision to become the biggest pimp to ever play the game and goes cross country. Here, is where Jackpot finds himself getting money, ducking the police, feuding with haters, vindictive females, snitches, and eventually doing time in the penitentiary.

Let Me Pimp Or Let Me Die 2, tells the story of a few female workers in the "Game," told through their lives as you see and find out what motivates a woman to start ho'n and sell her body. Re-visit some of your favorite characters from part 1 and see what drove them into the lifestyle that they chose. Each story different but ultimately the same.

Graphic and not for the faint of heart, the scenes take place in a realistic setting with many twist n turns you won't see coming. Find out how F.A.B Killed Sunshine and what happened in those last moments. How Green Eyes got hooked on drugs and the real reason she left Jackpot for dead in prison. Or the number one question...Will Jackpot Return To The Game?

Xavier Sands and Danielle Seville meet at the grand opening of Xavier's nightclub, and it happens to be his birthday. Not to be left out, Danielle is celebrating her birthday as well. As the two grow closer, wedges are driven between them behind the scenes, by their own mothers!

Xavier and Danielle both work for King Kole Konners, in different venues, but when the King is shot, all bets are off. The kingdom having just survived the Chase St. John mutiny in South Nubia, is rocked once again. The assassin begins picking off the King's top people, leading to Danielle being kidnapped.

Xavier vows vengeance on the person, or persons responsible for the shooting of the King. During her kidnapping ordeal, Danielle learns a horrible, life changing secret. Just as her world is rocked, Xavier learns the same shocking truth from his mother.

"Freeze mother fucker!" a cop spat, but the Skyline hardhead wasn't trying to hear it. He blindly reached on the floor for his gun as he slowly regained his eyesight. Jail wasn't an option for the young rida. He knew he had done too much to turn back. Fuck it, he was gonna hold court in the streets. As he placed his hand on the gun that laid dormant on the floor, that would be as close as he got to picking it up and letting off a shot...

Lamar Atteley III has made out a good life for himself. He has turned
Las Vegas into his own personal playground after surviving the rough
environment of Detroit, Michigan. However, with a new job offer, he
now has to prepare for a new chapter of his life that will either make or
break him. His adventure will take him to the other side of the
world......to Guam. Now, he will be tested harder than any other point in
his life. With all new surroundings, more money, women at his disposal
and a different breed of people in general, the question is can he handle it
all. When its all said and done, you will understand why we sometimes
sleep with the lights on.

Wake n Bake the natural way. Weed consumption through digestion is a lot healthier than smoking it, which is why we put together this book of tasty meals with a 420 kick to keep you happy, smiling and feeling good! From breakfast, lunch, dinner to dessert we got you covered. Enjoy some weed laced french toast for breakfast. Craving a light snack? Try some of our weed hummus. End the night with a homemade weed pizza and cheesecake for dessert. We even have a recipe for cooking oil and weed butter. Over 30 different recipes to choose from. Meals so quick and easy to make, you'll wonder why you didn't pick up this book sooner. Simple everyday recipes made easy will have you feeling like a pro in the kitchen! No more having to buy overpriced edibles from the dispensary . Now you can make all those delicious treats yourself.

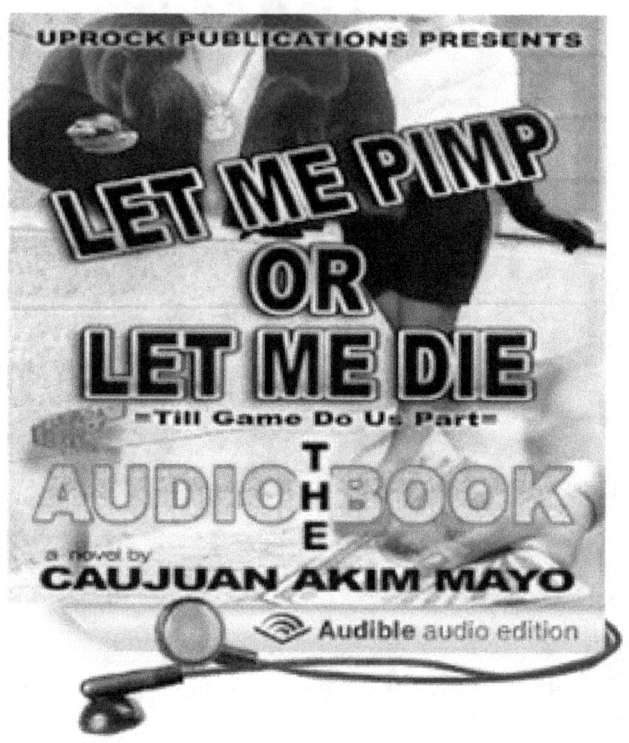

Don't have the time to read? Well, we have the solution. Pick up your audio version of "Let Me Pimp Or Let Me Die." The book by Caujuan Akim Mayo that started it all. Listen to this action pack audio book, loaded with special sound effects and cinematic music for dramatic effect, like no other audio book you've ever heard before. This is the audio book, that changed the game and set the bar.

Website: www.uprockpublications.com
Emails: uprockp@gmail.com
Facebook: uprockpublications
Twitter: uprockpub
Contact: (619) 259-0298

AUTOGRAPH

www.ingramcontent.com/pod-product-compliance
Lightning Source LLC
Chambersburg PA
CBHW071104250626
47159CB00002B/592